BOOK ONE OF THE BOSTON MOUNTAIN MAGIC SERIES

Funky Dan AND THE Pixie Dream Girl

COURTNEY LANNING

For more information contact:
Riverdale Avenue Books/Quest Imprint
5676 Riverdale Avenue
Riverdale, NY 10471

www.riverdaleavebooks.com

Design by www.formatting4U.com
Cover design by Scott Carpenter

Digital ISBN: 9781626016002
Trade ISBN: 9781626015890

First edition, June 2021

Chapter One
(Dan)

People come to downtown Fayetteville for a few different reasons. They might be students at the college, they might want to see the funky little city nestled in the Boston Mountains, or perhaps they're trying to find a unique shop to peruse.

A number of mom and pop clothing stores populate the downtown area, along with a couple of bakeries. There's even a chocolate shop. Second Street has the record store which has been open since 1942, and the old lady selling all manner of pickles has a tiny store on the historic square.

Most people will find what they're looking for at any one of those places, but some people are looking for something they can't name, something not quite written down on a list. No, this particular need is specifically ambiguous. It's necessary but unknown.

Shoppers who find themselves with this kind of particular need will be inexplicably drawn over to Block Avenue, to a store between a pizzeria called Toppings and a fortune teller shop called Odessa's Psychic Center.

Nestled between the two in a long and narrow green brick building is Funky Dan's, a store that carries a wondrous assortment of little treasures all needed by someone but not quite desired enough to be sold anywhere else.

I hardly see more than two or three customers per day in my store, and to most it's a wonder how I afford rent on such a prime piece of real estate downtown. Land by the college is worth some real coin.

Truth is, my shop is picky about clientele. I'm not picky. But my shop is. People only wander into this wondrous building when they need something no one else can sell them, something spectacular.

I moved toward a little knife that had a silver dragon wrapped

1

around the hilt. After picking it up, I plunged it into a box the mailwoman had left me.

"This thing's heavy, whatever it is," I said, taking a break wrestling with tape to scratch my bushy black beard. My long black robe with gold stitching, which most would call excessive but I'd say was needed to look the part of the particular salesperson that I am, got caught on the counter corner, so I freed it.

My shop was a fire hazard if one ever existed. The store had three narrow rows between shelves and counter space each leading back to a glass case with a cash register on top. A shaggy green carpet usually swallowed the shoes of customers that stumbled in. They always bumbled, shuffled, or tumbled into the store, while peeking their heads in cautiously. Few walked into the store with purpose.

Shelves were lined with all sorts of knickknacks and oddball items that even the most eccentric collectors scratched their heads at. But I knew each item had an eventual owner, including whatever was in this heavy box I continued to wrestle with.

A small eggshell fox with black tips on her ears walked over to my feet and stared up with annoyance.

"Do you need help with that? You're making quite a racket," the fox said.

"No thank you. I don't want you setting the place on fire, Eely," I said.

The fox scowled and hissed, "One time that happened! And the fire department didn't even get involved."

"They didn't get involved because you'd nibbled on the—you know what? No thank you. Your offer is appreciated, but I've got it under control," I said.

Eely scoffed and hopped up next to her favorite perch, a little fluffy bed next to the cash register. She nosed around until she found an ancient gold coin and bit it twice for luck.

I adjusted my black suspenders that'd caused a nasty wrinkle in my purple button down shirt and then went back to work on the box. Finally opening it, I tore through some packing peanuts.

I pulled out a bigfoot mask covered in dark brown fur.

"Yuck! What is that ugly thing!" Eely asked.

I smiled something cruel and said, "Why Eely, don't you recognize your long lost father?"

2

"That's not funny!" she yipped, standing up on her hind legs. "That thing's not even from the same continent as me."

"Oh calm down. It's payment for that old flute I sold to the gentleman last month."

"The guy with the rats who smelled of Talcum powder?" Eely asked, sitting back down.

"Yes. This is his payment. Though admittedly, I don't know what it does just looking at it," I said, flipping it over a couple times.

"Then why don't you store it outside the store? Say in the gray trash bin behind the building?"

I smirked and picked up some of the spilled packing peanuts, tossing them back in the box.

"Now, now. Tossing anything is against the rules. You know that. Everything has a purpose, and I'm bound by this shop to find each item's destiny. This one... might just take a little longer than others," I said, standing up and looking down at the first row of shelves.

Walking down a bit, I came to a purple disco ball the size of my head and shimmied it left just a bit. Sliding the mask beside it, I found it was a tight fit, but that's the best kind of fit in this store.

"It's been there for three years now."

I shrugged and said, "It's not my job to question. It's my job to unite people in need with something in this shop."

Eely snickered and said, "Well how about you pick up that polka dot phone on the wall and order a pizza to unite with my belly?"

Before I could respond, the front door opened, and a little bell jingled.

"Customer. Hush," I whispered.

"Tell you what, if they happen to see all nine of my tails, then we can worry about them hearing my voice," Eely said.

I put a hand over my face.

You never know when someone with just enough spiritual sensitivity is going to come along and see all the tails, furball, I thought.

"Hello?" a timid voice called from the front of the shop.

I squeezed behind the counter and realized my record player had been finished with its vinyl for the past half hour. Time really does fly when you can't go outside.

"I'm in the back. Feel free to take a look around and let me know if anything catches your attention."

I put the vinyl back in its casing and pulled out a sleeve in a pale color with a compass rose on the front. Carefully, I placed the album on the player and tilted the needle on the outside of the disc.

Soft guitar and keyboard began to play a familiar tune crafted in the heart of Key West.

When I turned back around, a young boy, maybe around 11 or 12 was walking in front of the register. He had some scuff marks on his face and dried blood under his nose.

"Whoa kid. Are you okay?" I asked, looking around for some tissues.

"I'm fine. Sorry, I don't have any money, but I was... running by your shop and saw some people—" he said, out of breath.

Finding some napkins unused from breakfast, I handed a clean one to the kid and said, "Relax. I'm not some kind of jerk that's going to kick you out when bullies are around. You can hang out until they're gone."

The kid wiped his face and sighed. There was both relief and recognition that he'd merely been granted a stay of execution.

He looked over at the record player and asked, "Jimmy Buffett?"

"Wow, I didn't expect a kid like you to know that name," I said.

"Are you kidding? *Changes in Latitudes, Changes in Attitudes*, 1977. It's only his most popular album," the kid said, smiling.

I cocked my head sideways. If I didn't expect the kid to know Jimmy Buffett's name, I definitely didn't expect him to know the album and year.

"How the Hell do you know that?"

"My dad's in a band. They play a couple songs from this album," the kid said.

"Sounds like a cool dad. What's your name? I don't want to be that kind of old guy who keeps calling you kid," I said, holding up a little paper basket for the boy to toss his bloody napkin into.

"It's Thomas," the boy said.

"Okay, Thomas. Do you want me to call somebody for you? Maybe your dad?"

"No, it'll be fine. I can just wait for a couple minutes and then leave when they're gone," Thomas said.

I nodded and said, "Well, okay then. Feel free to look around. I've got some pretty cool stuff in my shop."

Thomas looked around at the various items sprawled on shelves and countertops. His eyes came across a monkey with cymbals for hands, a large clock with fish swimming inside, and then a tiny silver spoon with garnets in the handle.

He continued to scan the farthest wall for even more treasures. I watched from the corner of my eye as Thomas came across a birdcage with a small fish crow inside. It didn't seem like he could tell if it was stuffed or real, which made me smirk.

Next to that item rested a glass container shaped like a lion with something inside that resembled sand. I didn't keep price tags on any items, which I could tell confused Thomas all the more.

The kid spun and glanced back at me, so I went back to scanning a magazine titled *Smoothies Monthly*.

He kept staring, so I assumed he was noticing for the first time I had two different colored eyes: one olive, one brown. Or maybe he was looking at my chrome dome.

My head is devoid of hair on top, but I often joke it all moved down my face to make this giant bushy beard.

I always felt like my age was impossible for customers to place, somewhere between early 40s and late 60s, if that were even possible. Maybe it just depended on my mood, how I stood, or how much light fell upon me.

Thomas' eyes moved down to Eely, and his mouth came open.

"Wow," he said, moving closer and then immediately taking a step back when Eely's head poked up from the bed.

"I know, I am beautiful," Eely said.

"Shut it, fox," I said, not looking up from my magazine.

Thomas looked up at me and asked if he could pet Eely.

"Yeah, she's pretty docile after living in the shop for eight gazillion years," I said, still captivated by an article on the perfect strawberry smoothie.

Thomas moved close and allowed Eely to smell his hand. Then he cautiously stroked her fur.

"I've seen people get bitten in videos online from animals they think are cute but are really wild," Thomas muttered.

"Yeah well, she's more domesticated than I am, Thomas. You're fine," I said.

"How did you get a pet fox?"

"Came with the shop, unfortunately. I can't get rid of the damn thing."

"Why would you want to? She's beautiful and seems friendly enough," Thomas said.

"Thank you! I am so beautiful and friendly," Eely said.

I rolled my eyes.

Oh brother.

"It's complicated. She's here to keep an eye on me," I said. "You'd think it was the other way around."

Thomas looked down into the glass case beneath Eely's bed and saw a number of interesting wares, like a short red blade with a claw for a handguard. Next to it was a black leather book entitled *Evisa Tortelia.*

"Why are those items in the glass case instead of out there with... well everything else?"

"Because they're dangerous. You can pick just about anything up out there and be fine, but the items in that case? They're not to be trifled with," I said.

"Whoa," Thomas said.

He continued to look down in the glass case and eventually sat on his knees, leaving Eely without any extra attention. She sighed and buried her nose in some torn newspaper that was strewn throughout her bed.

"Awesome," the boy said.

"What is it? Something catch your eye?" I asked, closing the magazine.

"That black wooden ring with all the white swirls painted on it," Thomas said, pointing to a ring in the case. It hung on a simple hook bolted to the back part of the case.

Looking down at it, I smiled. Then I recalled receiving that ring several years back from an old shaman as payment for a glass eye.

Everyone comes in here because they need something, I thought, smiling. It'd been that way for decades, but it never ceased to surprise me. Every day someone came in looking for an item they couldn't describe. Something they needed but didn't quite know they needed yet. And it would inevitably be in this shop. Thomas was no different.

"You know, I feel like I've eaten at Toppings with my dad before, but I've never noticed this store. How long have you been here?" Thomas asked.

Let's see, was it 1888 or 1889 when I got here? I thought back, never quite sure. Through the decades, I'd inevitably lost track of time.

"Do you want the long version or the short version?" I asked.

Thomas shrugged.

"Very well, since you've clearly got time to kill with those bullies outside, I'll give you the long version. More than a century ago, a young and foolish university student grew bored with his studies and wished more than anything to be incredibly wealthy. He wanted money to hire people to do everything for him, money to build the largest house in the city, and money to travel the country."

"He sounds greedy," Thomas said.

"I prefer to think of the man as... ambitious. He knew exactly what he wanted. Well, one day this foolish man met a witch who promised to grant his wish. But she warned it would not end happily as he thought it would. The student who had grown bored studying agriculture told the witch he did not think anyone with such a vast amount of wealth as he dreamed of could ever be miserable. She warned him she would return one day, and he would work for her, one day for every dollar he spent while rich."

Thomas said nothing for a moment and then went back to petting Eely.

"What happened to the student?" he asked.

"Well, he soon learned of a grandfather he'd never met before, a wealthy industrialist who recently died and left everything to his grandson in the final will. And soon the student was irrationally wealthy. He hired servants, built that funky looking old estate on Lafayette Street, and traveled the country seeing beautiful women, watching shows, drinking and eating whatever he wished. Somehow the money never ran out, and life was a never ending party," I said.

I stopped to cough for a moment, and Thomas thought quietly to himself.

"Something bad happened, didn't it?"

"Why would you say that? Doesn't it sound like the student had everything he wanted?"

"I've read enough stories to know there's not a happy ending to this story. What happened next?"

I sighed and looked down at my closed magazine.

Smart kid.

"The student lost sight of what was important. You see, while he was out traveling, the family that worked hard to send him to college never saw him. The student's father and mother continued running their orchard, hoping to see their son again. Ironically, for hiring 45 servants and building that huge house, he didn't spend much time there. And eventually, the family grew ill when a smallpox outbreak hit the town. They didn't have anybody to look after them, and while the student was away, they died, wishing to see him one last time.

That foolish student returned home to rest after long travels and learned from a neighbor of his parent's death. He was devastated. And suddenly he realized all the money in the world wouldn't buy him a second chance to say goodbye to them. It was around that time, some of the bills from his latest trips came in, and he learned the money had at last run out."

Thomas closed his jaw when he realized it had been hanging open for a second. An ambulance drove by outside with sirens on full blast. And I said not a word.

"What about the witch?" Thomas asked.

"Well without money, the student soon lost his home and found himself out on the street. His traveling friends didn't return his letters. None of his servants wanted anything more to do with him. And before long, he was at rock bottom. That's when she showed back up and asked him if he was happy. He pointed a finger at her and shouted about how she killed his parents, and he wanted another chance. The student got right in her face, but she did not flinch. He demanded a do-over. This time, he promised, he would be rich and take care of his family. It would be different, he swore."

"Did he get the second chance?" Thomas asked.

Sighing, I reached under the counter and grabbed a can of soda. I opened it and took a sip before saying, "No."

"No?" Thomas asked.

"No. She reminded him they made a deal, and she held up her end. He became wealthy beyond all imagination. It wasn't her fault he chose to spend his time and money as he had. She also told him you don't get second chances in life, not like he described. The student begged. He pleaded. He promised her anything for one more chance, but she reminded him he had nothing to offer. He was hers now, one day for every dollar he spent. So the student hung his head and accepted his fate."

8

"What did she do to him?"

Chuckling, I gestured to the store around me and said, "She put him in here. Until he'd paid off his debt to her, he was to remain put in this very shop, uniting people with items they needed to avoid making mistakes like he did."

Thomas raised an eyebrow and looked down at the floor. He stared at the carpet for a few seconds before shaking his head and going, "Nu uh. You'd have to be like... really old. It's a cool story though."

I smiled and said, "It's true."

"Prove it," Thomas said.

"You came in here because you needed something from this shop. I'm guessing you need something to help you with those bullies?"

Thomas' eyes lit up and said, "Well that would be nice. They make my life a living nightmare. But what do you have that would help me?"

The kid looked back down at the glass case and said, "Unless you want to give me that red sword so I could fight them back?"

I laughed and stopped abruptly to say, "No."

Thomas threw up his hands.

"The solution to your problem isn't standing up to the bullies. You've seen too many movies where someone being bullied gets powers and then beats up the bullies. That's not how real life works," I said.

"So what would you have me do if I can't fight back? Come here and hide every day after school?"

"Heavens no. I don't need repeat customers. The one thing about this store I like is nothing ever happens twice. Every day is fresh and interesting. No, you don't fight the bullies, and you don't run away. The smart thing to do is avoid them altogether. Then you don't have to fight or run."

Thomas crossed his arms and said, "And how do I do that? You got a Marauder's Map somewhere here in the store?"

"Jesus, I'm not Dumbledore, Thomas. Don't be ridiculous. The solution is what you were fixated on earlier," I said, reaching into the glass case and pulling out the black wooden ring.

Then I slid it across the counter to Thomas.

The kid picked it up and said, "I thought you called everything in the case dangerous."

"That's right, I did. That's a very dangerous ring, Thomas."

"What does it do?" Thomas asked.

He held it flat in the palm of his hand. Somehow, it looked like it would fit his fingers perfectly.

"You put it on, and as long as you're wearing it, the bullies will never see you again."

"Like the one ring?" Thomas asked, excitedly.

I slapped my face with a palm and groaned.

"Let me state for the record I'm not Gandalf either. Hopefully if you don't feel the bullies are a threat anymore, you can actually go outside and stop watching so many movies."

"I actually spend more time reading the books," Thomas said.

"Don't be a smartass, Thomas. Take the ring. But listen very carefully to what I'm about to tell you. Once you put that ring on, don't you dare take it off. It'll keep the bullies from noticing you for as long as necessary. But one day, you won't have bullies anymore, and it'll fall off somewhere without you noticing. If you pull off the ring yourself before that day comes, it won't just be the bullies that fail to see you. It'll be everyone, your friends, your teachers, your dad, even me. Nobody will ever see you again. Do you understand?"

Thomas nodded slowly, looking down at the ring again and swallowing nervously.

"You're just going to give this to me? I told you I don't have any money," Thomas said.

I nodded and looked over at Eely. Then I glanced at the cash register that hadn't been opened once since we set foot in this store. Its buttons were covered in dust and maybe a cobweb or two.

"You know, I don't care about money so much anymore. But you're right. I don't give stuff away for free, either. Tell you what, why don't you give me the one thing you do have in your wallet?"

Confused, Thomas reached into his back pocket and opened his Batman wallet, digging around inside. He knew there wasn't any money in there. He'd blown the last of his money on a soda from the vending machine at school, which sadly, he dropped during his scuffle and subsequent retreat from Matt and Jason Parker, as he quickly explained to me.

At last his fingers found something, and he pulled it out. It was a black guitar pick with "DATOG" inscribed in a silver font on the front.

"My dad gave this to me when I first got this wallet. I didn't have anything to put inside, so he tossed it over to me. You want this?"

"I surely do."

"Why? My dad's not exactly a famous musician, so it's not worth any money."

"I told you. I don't care about money anymore. I want that because it has value to you, and someone will wander into the shop and need it someday. The same way you needed it for your wallet" I said, holding out my hand.

Thomas looked down sadly at the pick in his fingers and then touched some of the dried blood under his nose with the other hand. He thought of never seeing Matt and Jason again and sighed before placing the pick in my outstretched hand.

I closed my palm around it and then opened it again. The pick was nowhere to be seen.

"Well Thomas, it was a pleasure meeting you. Enjoy your bully free life, and remember what I told you about that ring," I said.

Thomas closed his own hand around the ring. When he opened it again, the ring hadn't vanished like my new pick.

"Thank you. I really appreciate your help. Maybe I'll come back here someday when I've got money and actually buy something," Thomas said.

"Doubtful," Eely said.

"Goodbye, Thomas," I said.

And with that, Thomas left Funky Dan's, same bell jingling on the way out that rang when he came in.

The record player stopped playing again, and I put another album on.

Eventually I did order that pizza Eely wanted and asked the food be walked over to my front door like always.

When the cashier from next door came in, she asked why I never came over to grab my own pizzas. I simply told her I'd die if I left this store. She laughed.

"Whatever. You keep tipping well, and I'll bring over your pizza every time," she said, stopping to pet Eely.

The store remained empty for the rest of the day, and at last when the sun went down, the woman who owned the fortune teller business next door came in. She had long silky black hair and was smoking a long blue kiseru with a tiny butterfly carved into the end.

11

Her red coat covered most of her long and slender body as she let out a puff of smoke that seemed to linger around her like a thin shawl.

"Odessa, what brings you over?"

"Oh, nothing really. It's been a slow day, so I figured I'd come over and help myself to whatever wine you have stashed away for the full moon viewing party tonight," the fortune teller said.

"Uh huh. Well you don't break that out until the moon is high in the sky, you hear me?" I said.

Odessa scratched Eely's ears and said, "I bet my fox friend can help me find where you've hidden it. I did put her here to watch your every move, after all. Might as well take advantage of that."

"It's in the cabinet above the water heater under an old newspaper," Eely said.

"Traitor. I bought you pizza today," I said, scowling at Benedict Foxold.

"You know how it is, Dan. I work for her just like you do," Eely said.

Odessa smiled.

"Yes, but one of you works so much better than the other," she said.

"And it's me. The only way that oaf would work harder is if her job was to lay around all day."

"No, her job is twofold, watching you and being adorable. She does both very perfectly and works much, much harder than you at her task," Odessa said.

"Har har. Speaking of working for you. How many days do I have left? I would like to see my parents eventually, you know," I said.

Odessa frowned.

"You spent a lot of money, Daniel," she said.

"You say that every time I ask. At least give me a number so I can make carvings in the wall or something."

"A lot of money... now let's break out the wine. But not too much for you, Daniel. You do have to work tomorrow after all."

Chapter Two
(Roxie)

As I waited for band practice on a particularly dull Saturday, I looked myself over in my compact mirror for what felt like the 3,000th time. I sighed, sending a little powder flying up. Making one last glance at the green eyes staring back at me, partially hidden by chestnut bangs, I closed the compact and put it back in my purse.

Still no mustache, I thought, sighing again.

I twirled some drumsticks and started practicing that rim shot I'd yet to get the hang of in our new song "Should Have Kissed Me Yesterday."

My black nail polish became a blur as I set into a new rhythm, not really any part of the song, just something I was feeling in the moment. I continued playing, feeling my tempo picking up to match my pulse.

It wasn't long before my bombastic playing grew louder, echoing out the garage and down the nearly empty street.

Then I began to hash out some lyrics Tessa might sing. We all took turns writing songs, and I felt like I hadn't been pulling my weight lately as we worked toward our first album.

I began to mouth some words, "Ruffled hair glowing in the morning light, she lifts off the covers, starts her new day."

Another two minutes into a drum solo which, I anticipate Jenna would want trimmed, and I was done.

"I hope I can remember all that for when the girls get here," I said.

A slight *ahem* from in front of me let me know Jenna and Tessa were there.

"The girls have been here watching you play for a little while now," Jenna said, putting her purple hair into a ponytail.

I looked up and rubbed the back of my neck.

"Why didn't you say something sooner?" I asked, leaning over to take a drink from my water bottle.

13

"Because you're so adorable when you get into one of your little jam sessions," Tessa teased. "Sometimes we like to play a game of how close we can stand before you notice us. You just get into your own little world while playing."

Jenna put her guitar case down and opened it revealing her mahogany Gibson Les Paul studio. She caressed her fingers over the smooth wood and said, "I hope you're ready to practice, baby."

"Ugh, get a room already," Tessa said, pulling out her Yamaha electric bass.

She ran her bubble-gum pink nails over her red bass and stroked it mockingly.

"Oh baby. I hope you're ready to practice. Make mama proud," she said, and Jenna elbowed her.

I decided to come to Jenna's rescue and said, "Hey, that's a cute color."

"Thanks! They're-"

"You should ask your mom to pick me out a shade next time she does your nails," I said, interrupting her.

Jenna was in the middle of putting on her guitar strip when she let out a big chuckle that echoed through my mom's garage.

Tessa flipped me the bird and stuck her tongue out.

"Is that a move they teach all you cheerleaders, or...?" Jenna asked.

Tessa smirked and elbowed her friend as she got her bass ready.

Around the time we were set up and ready to practice, Mom came into the garage, walking through bays one and two.

"Hey ladies!" she called out, wiping her greasy hands on her overalls.

"Hi Ms. Rivers," Jenna and Tessa said.

"For the love of God. I'm not your homeroom teacher. Call me Melanie, or I'm taking back your rehearsal space," Melanie said.

"Sorry Melanie," Jenna said.

Mom came over and planted a big kiss on my forehead.

"Mom, I've told you you're wasting your time. You can't embarrass me like that. Tessa's mom is way worse," I said.

Melanie smirked and scratched her short black hair.

"You two ever hear about the time Roxie got the public pool shut down when we lived in Kansas?"

14

"Mom! Okay, you win. What chore do you want done? Name your price," I said, flustered and blushing something fierce.

She grabbed my chin and looked me in the eye before saying, "No chores. I just want you to remember this moment. I can embarrass you when you're 18, and I can embarrass you when you're 80."

I rolled my eyes.

Like you'll still be around when I'm 80, I thought before having a crushing realization at what I'd just said in my mind. *No wait! I love my mom. Let her still be around when I'm 80. I take it back!*

"You hear from your father today?" Melanie asked me, letting go of my chin.

I rolled my eyes even longer this time.

"Just the usual morning Bible verse addressed to Johnny. Asshole. Dear Johnny," I began to read as if he were writing the text with a quill and parchment. "I hope you'll find solace and wisdom in this morning's verse, Deuteronomy 22:5. I'm praying for you every day that you find the right path. Your father, Charles."

"Hey now. That's your father you're talking about, Roxie," Melanie said, putting her hands on her hips. "So you'll address him as Mr. Asshole," she finished, ruffling my hair and walking away.

I smiled and thought back to how supportive and great my mother was, even through the divorce, when she should have spent more time focusing on herself, she took care of me.

She didn't balk through the hormones, counseling, and during last month's surgery, she sat right at my bedside. When it came to fixing documents, mom was relentless. She got a paralegal friend of hers to help with everything.

Now her voice snapped me back to reality.

"I don't want you overdoing it, Miss Priss. I know you're excited with this being your first rehearsal back, but you've got one hour. You've got that appointment with Dr. Lyra this afternoon anyway," Melanie said. "I'll be out back working on my truck."

"You fix cars for a living during the week, and you're not going to do something else on your days off?" Jenna asked.

Before she went back outside, Melanie called back, "On the weekend I get to play with *my* vehicles."

I smiled. Ever since coming back to Fayetteville and taking over grandpa's shop, my mom had been so happy. She'd gotten to move from car repairs as a hobby, to actually supporting her family with it.

On the weekends, she let us set up and practice in bay number three.

We'd played a couple shows and even got to perform at the Washington County Fair for about 20 minutes. Best 20 minutes of my life as we rocked our top two songs "Glitter Choke" and "Glistening Steed." We even got to play our cover of Bonnie Tyler's "I Need A Hero."

But since I'd had my surgery last month down in Houston, I'd been recovering. It's amazing how painful those first three weeks were. But it was nothing compared to finally feeling euphoria, like I was finally right. Well, mostly.

The recovery had been slow. I was glad Mom had insisted we wait until summer so school wasn't an issue. But I missed playing with my friends.

Our rehearsal went well. It took a few minutes for us to find ourselves, but after that it was like we'd never separated. Jenna had warmed up her voice before walking over with Tessa, so she sounded great. We knew the band had an hour, and we didn't want to waste a moment of it.

Though I had to admit I was pretty tired by the time we finished "Full Moon Kisses." My energy still hadn't come back to its former level yet.

My doctor had said five-week recovery wasn't out of the ordinary, even for an 18-year-old. I was a little frustrated at how limited I felt. I never used to rest between tasks. Now I needed half an hour here and there to relax. Mom had reminded me she had a few bungee cords she could tie me to the couch with if I didn't rest up when I was tired. And she had that analytical mom eye. Like a freakin' cyborg, she instantly knows my energy levels, so she was completely serious about the bungee cords.

Since surgery she'd been on me like a hawk. Drink water. Go to bed on time. Eat fruits, vegetables, protein, fiber, and you'll heal faster.

As Jenna and Tessa put away their instruments, I got up and walked over to a tool chest where a wrapped gift lay. I'd used unicorn paper and a pink ribbon.

Actually, this is about the same shade as Tessa's nails, I thought, scoffing. *I mean, it's not like I hated the color.*

Walking back over with the small box, I handed it to Tessa.

"I'm sorry I missed our planned get together last weekend. I really was bedridden all day. I still feel pretty terrible," I said.

She smiled and took the gift.

"I totes understand, girl. You're still recovering. You didn't have to get me anything," she said, untying the bow gently.

"I know she didn't... but I'm still really excited to see what she got you. Roxie gifts are always the best," Jenna said.

I blushed and looked down at a nearby oil slick.

Tessa opened the paper revealing a fuzzy red ring gift box.

"Are you asking me to marry you?" Tessa asked.

"Shut up and open it," I said, rolling my eyes.

The cheerleader did as she was told and found a little necklace inside. There was a small pearl on a thin silver chain. Surrounding the pearl was a light green wire wrap in the shape of a sea turtle, so the pearl made its shell.

"Oh my God," Tessa squeaked.

"Do you like it?" I asked.

"Whoa," Jenna answered first, sticking her head in for a closer look.

Tessa wiped her left eye and sniffled a little bit.

"What is this for?" she asked.

I looked down at the oil slick again and said, "I know you've had a rough couple weeks since your aunt passed away. I just wanted to cheer you up."

She walked over and threw both arms around me.

"Thank you so much. I love it," she said, still sniffling.

"I'm so happy you like it. When Mom and I were still recovering in Houston, I suggested we drive over to Galveston for seafood. While we were there, we stayed on the beach and went hunting for oysters. The third one I found had that inside. And I knew you liked sea turtles, so I did my best to shape the wire. I threw away quite a few drafts," I said, chuckling.

Tessa finally let me go and asked Jenna to help her put it on. She obliged, and I smiled bigger. It fit her well and looked great with her red dress.

We talked for a few minutes, and then the girls left.

After they rounded the block, I noticed a younger boy from school

17

walking by. His name was Thomas, and I only knew him because our lockers were next to each other last year. He was friendly enough, but the poor kid was always getting bullied, even more than I was. And speaking of the Devil, coming down the sidewalk about 100 feet ahead of Thomas were his biggest enemies, Matt and Jason Parker.

The twins were tall and excessively cruel to me, but they usually didn't touch me, afraid they'd catch some trans disease or the gay or something. But Thomas? They loved to throw him into lockers, slap him with mud, and generally be complete asses to him.

My heart began to panic as I watched the three get closer to one another. Didn't Thomas see them? He was looking straight ahead.

I wasn't in any shape to be running out and stopping a fight, but I could threaten to call Mom out here. Or maybe she could call the police if they hurt Thomas.

My pulse quickened as they were about 10 feet away from each other now, with no visible reaction from any of the guys.

Then... it was over. Thomas walked right between the two, and they didn't even flinch. They didn't turn around, either. What was happening? Before long, all three were out of sight, and I stood there perplexed. I was ready for a beatdown on Thomas' part, but they ignored him. Had they found some better target? Did he pay them protection money for the summer?

I was glad nothing bad happened, but I was also stunned. I shrugged and shook my head. Guess the little guy found something to help.

I went inside to shower. I was all sticky thanks to that lovely Arkansas summer humidity. I sat on the couch for a little bit, and then I got up and grabbed my keys.

"Where are you going?" Melanie asked.

"I'm going to head over and walk Miss Michelle's dog," I said.

"Are you sure that's wise?"

"Mom, she just had hip surgery. She can't walk the animal. She can't even walk," I said.

Melanie cocked her head to the side in that mom/cyborg/ daughter harm calculator, and I reassured her, saying, "Mom, I'm just going to do a few laps around the block. The corgi isn't exactly a marathon runner."

"Two laps. That's it," Mom said.

"Yes ma'am."

I walked across the street and up to a little blue house with pink flowers planted beside the porch.

These downtown houses are always so beautiful, I thought.

I loved that we lived right above the garage in a little flat. It got noisy sometimes, but I loved the location. I could even walk to school.

I knocked on the door three times and announced myself loudly.

"Miss Michelle? It's Roxie. I'm coming in to walk Rufus," I said, hearing the dog scratching the door excitedly on the other side.

I walked in and found her on the couch watching a show about beach houses on HGTV.

"Hello dear," she said, looking at me.

Rufus had already fetched his leash and was jumping on my knees, pawing for his daily walk.

"Are you doing better today?" I asked.

"Much. Thanks again for taking care of the little stinker for me. You're a sweet girl," she said, smiling and adjusting her thick brown glasses.

Miss Michelle had been the high school secretary for 30 years now, and I was really close with her, had been since Mom and I moved back from Kansas after the divorce. She'd been the first person outside my family to use my new name, like it was no big deal.

Sometimes I mowed her lawn or helped her garden, but now she really just needed a dog walker. So I looked down at the little cream colored corgi, with his excited pointy ears and attached the leash.

"Ready to go, boy?"

Rufus barked and pawed at the door, eager to get on with it already.

"He seems excited, but you'll probably carry him back through that same door after half a lap," Michelle said.

"We'll see," I said, laughing.

We walked for about 20 minutes, and he stopped to sniff this flower and pee on that bush. We waited for a UPS truck to drive by, and he barked at it, but mysteriously not the FedEx truck that drove by shortly after.

Michelle was right though, because eventually the heat got to Rufus, and I carried him back inside and got him a fresh bowl of water, putting ice cubes in it.

Then I went over to hug our school secretary and said, "You've got my number if you need anything."

"I'm fine, dear. But thank you. My son will be by in a couple hours for dinner. You've done more than enough."

I smiled and then brought in her paper, opening it to the crossword section. I fetched her favorite blue pen with an ostrich ornament that dangled from the end.

"Tell Jim I said hi," I said, leaving her.

Before I was out of earshot, she hollered, "Five down? Best selling album of 1995?"

"*Cracked Rear View*," I called before closing the front door.

* * *

Half an hour later I was sitting in a waiting room outside of Dr. Tina Lyra's office. She was my therapist.

Mom had dropped me off and then went to get us some coffees.

The receptionist was a college student named Michael. He had short black hair and wore a Nirvana T-shirt. He was cute, and I sometimes thought of asking him out. He was just a college freshman, after all. Only a couple years older than me.

What's stopping you? I asked myself, already knowing the answer.

I checked my compact again, looking for that mustache shadow. It wasn't there.

He probably only dates real girls, I thought, missing Jenna and Tessa.

"Hey Roxie?" he called out.

I bolted out of my thoughts.

"Yeah?"

"So, Dr. Lyra is out this weekend. She called in sick, but Dr. Alanis is available to see you," Michael said.

I stood up and grabbed my purse. It was a big green frog with a mouth that opened to reveal the inside of the purse. The body was attached to a long green strap.

"Oh, that's okay. I don't want to-"

"Nonsense. I'm available," a woman's voice said to Michael's left. There stood a tall olive-skinned woman with long curly black hair. She was wearing a simple white blouse and black pants. She had a strange accent I couldn't even begin to place.

"No offense. I just don't-"

"Relax, I'm fully qualified in gender studies," she said, gently grabbing my wrist and leading me into Dr. Lyra's office.

I looked at Michael with a pleading look, but he was already back to watching *Seinfeld* on the computer.

Dr. Alanis' grip was benign but at the same time wouldn't let me escape.

"Why don't you have a seat, Roxie?" the counselor said, motioning for Dr. Lyra's blue couch. She sat opposite of me in a wooden chair.

My heart was racing as I softly said, "I mean no offense, but I don't know that I'm entirely comfortable with a substitute, Dr. Alanis."

"Please, just call me Selene. And I apologize for the sudden change in therapists, but tonight is the full moon, and the portal back to my world closes soon," she said.

I just shook my head at the absurdity I'd heard.

"Excuse me?"

She stood up. Before my eyes, her hair turned silver. Her eyes glowed pink.

"Is it appropriate for me to ask if I'm going crazy in a therapist's office?" I asked.

"Don't be alarmed, Roxie. I'm here to see you, and what you're seeing is real, I assure you. I apologize for the abrupt display of magic, but this should help," she said, reaching into a pocket and grabbing some blue rose petals.

She blew them in my direction with all the momentum of an evening breeze. And at once I began to calm down. I was still confused by what was happening, but my heart wasn't racing anymore.

I exhaled somehow smelling the entire season of spring in my nostrils and asked, "What exactly is happening right now?"

"It's easier for me to explain when you're calm and at peace. Are you feeling those things?" she asked.

I thought for a moment and then nodded slowly.

"Good. My name really is Selene. I'm a pixie, and I've been watching you for some time now. I need your help," she said.

"You're like... what? Tinkerbell?" I asked, still confused.

She shook her head and giggled. Two large glowing green gossamer wings came into view behind her. As they flapped, she floated a little bit.

A feather-like antenna sprouted out from the start of her hairline. "Do these look like something you get from Never Never Land?"

"Yes... yes they do look like something you'd get from Never Never Land," I said, finding it hard to form words.

She landed and said, "Oh, I suppose they are. Heh, sorry. I guess that was a foolish question."

Every full moon a portal opened, and every full moon she'd venture into the human world to help with dreams till the next full moon. Then she'd travel back to her world, the pixie world.

"That's all nice and well, but what does that have to do with me?"

She took a drink of water from a glass on the table next to her.

"Sorry, throat got dry from all the explaining. Anyway," she said, clearing her throat in between words. "When dream pixies return to their homeworld, they typically empower pure-hearted maidens, sorry, that's old timey language for you, to deliver good dreams in their place. The work doesn't stop, you know," Selene said.

I shook my head and looked at the carpet under my black sneakers.

"What's wrong?" Selene asked.

"I feel as though I deceived you, and I'm sorry," I said, my heart sinking and a tear forming in my right eye.

"How so?"

"I'm not really a—I mean, you're looking for a legitimate... and I don't. I wasn't born—" I said, failing about three or four sentences in a row.

I was crying now, no way around it, full tears.

Selene sat down on a little table by the couch and handed me a box of tissues. I blew my nose, and she said, "You didn't deceive me, Roxie. I know I've found the right girl for this job."

I stood up and shouted at her, "I'm not real!"

The sentence didn't make sense, but all my emotions were rushing to the surface, all the dysphoria I struggled with on a daily basis.

She slowly touched my left hand.

"This feels like a real hand," she said, softly. "Why don't you tell me what bothers you so deeply?"

My voice was still louder than I wanted it to be, but I was upset. This was my upset voice.

"Three years of puberty blockers, hormones, speech therapy, and it wasn't enough, Selene! Then I had that surgery because I thought that would finally make me feel real, like I wasn't some impostor. But weeks have come and gone, and even this hasn't solved my problem. I still feel like I'm just pretending to be a woman instead of actually being one like I desperately want," I said, crying and sinking to my knees.

She just listened.

"Every day I'm looking in mirrors, trying to find flaws my classmates and friends will see, revealing I'm just a fake. I'm testing my voice. I'm watching how I walk, how I react, how I—everything! Because I am terrified somebody is going to accuse me of being a fake somewhere down the line, and I just don't think I'll want to keep going after that. That's what's bothering me deep down. You came looking for a girl to help people with their dreams, and you found something like me."

Selene kneeled down and brushed the side of my face while I blubbered incoherently about my worst fears.

She waited until I grew quieter and then said, "Roxie, I didn't make a mistake. You're such a kindhearted young girl. You're always putting in overtime to make other people happy. The perfect person for this job, it's none other than you. And the fact that you're still able to make other people smile while carrying around all these emotional scars? It's even more of a reason to choose you."

I still didn't agree with the pixie as she helped me up and put me back on the couch.

"I think I can help you with this if you trust me to poke around inside your memories for a moment. Do you trust me?" she asked.

I'd never met this woman before. Heck, I didn't know pixies existed until half an hour ago. But... I did trust her. I didn't think she'd chosen the right person. But I trusted her.

I nodded, and her eyes glowed pink again. She placed a warm right hand on my head, and I was lulled into a blackness.

As things came into focus, I was in a familiar room. It was my old living room from when we lived in Garden City, Kansas. And I heard a familiar noise. It was Mom and Dad shouting in front of the fireplace.

A renewed sense of dread filled me. I'd replayed this scene so many times. I'd had nightmares about it. This was Christmas Eve, and I was nine.

Dad had just found a Christmas dress Mom had wrapped under the tree.

"You can't give our son this!" he shouted.

23

"Keep your voice down. She's going to hear you," Melanie hissed. "I can give our child whatever Christmas gift I want."

They didn't know, but a young child sat on the staircase listening to them, heat reaching from the fireplace to her already warm face covered in tears and snot.

I looked over at the stairs from the hallway I stood in, and there she was, or rather, there I was. To this day, I'd never told anyone about this fight. I couldn't bring myself to.

They continued to go back and forth, Dad's voice getting louder the longer mother argued.

"It's not right. We have a son, not a daughter. I'll be damned if I'm going to let you give this crap to him. You're just confusing him," he yelled.

"She's not stupid, Charles! She knows exactly how she feels, and everything I've read said we need to provide a loving environment for her now more than ever. She's at a critical point in her development and needs to see she's not a mistake," Melanie said.

I felt a hand on my shoulder and turned to see Selene.

"This is it, the single most painful memory you have," she said.

Mom and Dad continued their fight.

"I'm shipping the boy off to that camp we talked about first thing next week. They're going to get all this crap out of his head once and for all, really make a man out of him," Charles said.

"Are you serious? You still want to send our child to conversion therapy? You're just going to hurt her even more. Did you read any of the articles I printed off for you? Research shows—"

"I don't want to hear your biased research, Melanie! I can't believe you're actually encouraging this. Do you have any idea how much stress this has filled my heart with? That boy needs to be dealt with properly, and I'm not going to let you break him even more than he already is."

Her solid slap echoed through the house.

"Our daughter isn't broken, Charles. You are. I love her just the way she is. And I'll tell you this. She is not going to be shipped off to some camp for you to feel better about yourself. If you'd read the research, you'd see there's no 'curing' this type of thing. All you'd be doing is stifling her and increasing the odds of self harm, maybe even suicide in the future."

Charles tried to speak, but Melanie wasn't done.

"You think you're stressed? How about our daughter? She feels like she was born in the wrong body and has to wake up to it every day, imprisoned in a flesh she didn't ask for."

"How on Earth could you know how he feels? You're just projecting your desires for a daughter onto him. There's no way he actually feels like that. Nobody does," he said.

I couldn't look away as tears rolled down my face.

"You want to know how I know? Because she told me, you ass. I took time to listen to her as she cried in my arms a few nights ago. She doesn't feel like she can trust her own father after the tantrum he threw when he found that doll in her closet."

Charles said nothing for a moment and then uttered the most painful sentence that'd haunt me for years.

"For Pete's sake, Melanie. He's a boy; just look at him! You want to, what? Let him walk around in a dress? Grow his hair out? Paint his nails? He'd be the ugliest fake girl anyone's ever seen."

I sank to my knees for the second time and let out a whimper.

Selene turned my face toward her. But the first thing I saw was little me, sitting on the stairs and trying her hardest to stifle tears so she wouldn't make noise. Then I saw Selene's pink eyes.

"You weren't supposed to hear this, and it serves you no benefit. Let me erase this memory and take this burden from you. You'll still know how your father feels, but this particular shackle you've lugged around all these years? You deserve to be free from it. Please let me help," she said.

I gave the slightest nod I think I'd ever given in my life. I wasn't even sure my head moved. The last thing I saw was Melanie slapping him again, and the scene shattered into a billion pieces before my eyes, tiny shards of glass. All except for the fireplace.

The shards just floated there in the darkness until Selene pulled out a little sack, and they all flew inside with a clinking sound.

When she'd finished, the pixie tossed the sack into the fire, and my head felt numb. Then I faded into the blackness and once more found myself in the office.

"What. I don't?"

"You're fine, better than fine," Selene said, still holding her hand on my head.

When she finally moved her hand away, the pixie asked, "So, do you want to help me out?"

I remembered our previous conversation, but it felt different now. I couldn't place why I'd cried so much. She was just asking me to help people's dreams, and, to be honest, it sounded like a swell idea.

"I'd like to help," I said and stood up.

She smiled.

The pixie held up her open palm, and it flashed a bright white for a second. Then there was a small bracelet made of smooth blue beads hovering in her open hand. They glowed and had some strange symbols carved into them.

"Take these and put them on the wrist above your dominant hand," she instructed.

I touched them and yelped a little. It felt like I was touching water, but the beads were solid. Selene giggled and said, "Don't worry. You're not the first to do that."

I gingerly took the bracelet and slipped it on my left wrist.

"What now?"

"You can't use it until I exit this world, which will be tonight at exactly 1:45 a.m. local time. But after that, you'll utter the words *'Ambulate per somnia'* while looking at a mirror. The mirror will then show you the dream of somebody who needs your help. When you see the dream, say *'Immeo,'* and you'll be transported to their dream, where you'll have control of the world. Use that control to erase their unease and make them happy again. When they wake up, you'll find yourself back where you were when you first saw the dream in your mirror."

It was a lot to take, so I just nodded with a blank look on my face.

"You'll do great, Roxie. I'll be back in a month and expect a report on all the people you've helped. Then when I go away again, we can discuss your continued employment if you'd like," she said.

"One thing," I said. "If I'm helping other people in their dreams, when will I sleep?"

The pixie smiled and said, "That's the brilliant thing about this bracelet. So long as you're wearing it, your body won't grow tired. It keeps you refreshed 24/7, and you'll actually find it impossible to sleep while wearing it. So I expect you to help someone every night."

I marveled at the jewel, and she ushered me out of the office.

"I've got preparations to make, but you'll do great. See you next month," Selene said, and I walked out where Mom was waiting with coffee.

"How'd it go?" she asked.

"Really well," I said, taking my iced drink.

* * *

That night I was sitting in my bed, watching the clock on my phone. At 1:46 a.m., I pulled open my compact and said the words. Nothing happened at first, but instead of looking for a mustache, I just looked at my eyes, which had... started to glow?

And just like turning on a television, the mirror suddenly showed me a dark room, a chapel of some kind, perhaps. I heard a familiar cry coming from inside. And I didn't know how too many people sounded while crying.

Without giving it further thought, I uttered the word "*Immeo!*"

And there I was inside the chapel in my pajamas! There was a silver casket up near a podium. It was on a thick stand with black wheels on top of a thin red carpet. A wooden cross stood not too far behind the podium, and oak pews surrounded me. I'd been here once before.

I heard more crying and looked up toward the casket. There on the front row sat one of my best friends. With her head in her hands, Tessa cried, calling out her aunt's name from time to time.

This is what she's been dreaming every night since the funeral? I thought, suddenly miserable in my heart for her.

I walked over and sat down on the pew next to my friend.

"Ro-Roxie?" she stammered looking up.

"Mmmmhhmmm," I said, taking her head in my arms.

"I'm here, Tessa. I'm here for you. And I promise I won't leave you alone," I said, stroking her hair as she sobbed into my PJs.

"She loved you so much, Tessa. And she's not in pain any longer," I said once she was in a place to listen.

Then I listened as she told me just how much she missed her aunt. They'd been closer than I knew. It was Tessa's Aunt Casey that bought her the bass and taught her how to sing. They wrote songs together, spent hours discussing lyrics, and Casey came to every show we'd played so far. That's why it hurt Tessa so much.

27

When Tessa finally told me everything she'd wanted to say about her aunt, she said she didn't want to say these things to anyone else because she didn't want to seem like a baby or to bum them out.

I reminded her that I would always listen to her and would never call her names or feel bummed out. And then I said, "Let's get you out of this room."

And suddenly, I knew exactly where we needed to be. My bracelet glowed, and I waved my left arm, imagining an entirely new scene. In the blink of an eye, we weren't in the chapel, but instead under the sea. Without any need for scuba gear because, dream world. We swam through a coral reef. Brilliant colors stretched out for miles before us. I made lionfish, angelfish, clownfish and all manner of sea creatures swim through Tessa's hair and play with her. She laughed and smiled for the first time in what seemed like an eternity.

Next came her favorite part, the sea turtles. They swam by in a long row that stretched endlessly, and we swam by their side, sometimes hitching a ride on their shells. They didn't mind one bit. Tessa continued to smile, a beam that erased any sadness from my heart I'd felt for her upon first entering this dream.

We swam for what seemed like hours, until I was suddenly back in my bed with the 8:00 a.m. alarm going off.

"That's abrupt. I guess she woke up," I said and hopped out of bed to take a shower. The bracelet worked like a charm. I wasn't tired in the least.

As I waited for my frozen waffles to pop out of the toaster, my phone buzzed. I had a text from Tessa.

"I just wanted to let you know I had a dream we swam with turtles last night. It made me happy. Thanks again for the necklace. I feel great today," she said.

I smiled and responded, looking down at my bracelet.

Mom came in to grab some milk and eyed my new jewels.

"Where'd you get those?"

"A friend gave them to me," I said, smiling, knowing the next month was going to be exciting.

Chapter Three
(Dan)

Looking through my large vinyl collection, I settled on one that showed a grand theatre titled *Paradise* on the outside with lots of blues and reds. Everything was lit up and bright, and there was an entire crowd outside waiting to get in.

Satisfied, I pulled out the LP and put it on the record player.

"How long has it been since I listened to these guys?" I asked, putting the needle on the outer edge. There was a familiar soft static sound until "A.D. 1928" started playing.

Eely snored in her bed on the glass case over the cash register. The noise she made could best be described as an occasional high pitched chittering. And she'd always reveal some teeth with each noise.

I'd just opened the store for the morning. Odessa never specified the store have any specific hours, but it had to be open each and every day, regardless of whether or not any customers came. It didn't matter when I opened and closed, but the store had to be operational for at least ten hours a day. So I typically opened around 7:00 a.m. and tried to close around 5:00 p.m.

There were exceptions depending on how I was feeling, of course. I never got sick, per se. But there were nights I might have a little too much to drink, as one who had been trapped in a store for more than a century would do.

Wizard, shopkeep, whatever I was now, sometimes I felt like the Genie. I had all these amazing and powerful items within my grasp, some of which could destroy half the city if mishandled. And yet, despite all of this power near me, I was powerless to leave. Sure, I could physically walk out the front door, but not for long until I was painfully whisked back into the shop. I'll spare you the details, for now.

How many times have I tried to calculate how much money I spent 130 years back? I thought. *Too many damn times.*

The different items and customers kept things interesting, sure. I wasn't exactly losing my mind, but when this debt was repaid, I'd finally be allowed to pass on and be reunited with my parents again.

Until then, though... I'm here, I thought.

Looking back at Odessa's little white fox curled up in a mess of her nine tails, I was thankful for the little things, like Eely still being asleep. If I was lucky, I might just be able to go another hour or two with the food goblin silent and asleep. When she woke up, she'd want breakfast and would harass me until I went back upstairs to fix some French toast or poached eggs.

Eely wasn't one to be satisfied with a bowl of cereal like I was. I thought when cereal came along about 20 years after I'd gotten settled in this store, it was the greatest invention ever. Pouring milk over flavored bits of granula? It was great. No fuss or anything. I like to cook, but good grief, first thing in the morning I just want a bowl of cereal.

And it's perfect for a 2:00 a.m. snack, too. Basically, I felt like it was one of the only things here for me in the store. Eely was a selfish creature that only obeyed Odessa, and that witch was no more on my side than a tick is after burrowing into the flesh on the backside of my knee.

No, cereal was always there for me when I needed it, or at least it was when my personal shopper remembered to pick it up for me.

I flipped around the "closed" sign to "open." The closed side had a sleeping octopus on it, and the open sign had one smiling and dancing with the sun.

Walking back to the cash register, I noticed Eely's bed was empty, and I heard her little doggie door out into the back yard flipping.

"Dangit, she's awake," I muttered.

I knew there were two choices for the fox when she woke up. If she intended to go back to sleep, she just rotated around the bed a couple times. But if she was going to get up for the day, Eely would go outside to take care of business in the little fenced in backyard just behind the shop. It wasn't big, maybe about 15 x 20 feet.

Sitting down on my little red stool and leaning against the wall, I opened my latest issue of *Amazing Aquariums*. This issue was dedicated entirely to turtles. It came yesterday, and I couldn't wait to see all the exciting and creative tank setups in here. Plus, the cover advertised an in-depth article detailing how algae blooms were endangering turtles in central Florida.

I wasn't even four pages in when Eely came back in and hopped up onto the glass counter, licking one of her tails lightly.

"Good morning, Dan," she said in a chipper tone.

If anyone else could hear the fox speak, aside from Odessa or someone born with heightened magical awareness, they'd say it was the most friendly greeting the little lady could give. But I'd lived with this fox for more than 100 years. I knew every trick it had up its fuzzy little sleeve. This was just a ploy to butter me up so I'd butter her up some toast.

I know what you're up to, I thought, faking a smile.

"Morning fuzzhead," I said, going back to my magazine.

She cleaned another tail or two and then said, "You already have breakfast?"

"Yup-" I started.

"Bowl of cereal," we both finished in unison, though her tone was a little more mocking.

"Well, that cereal won't keep you full until lunch. You should have something else too, like, maybe some... French toast," Eely suggested.

There it was. The fox had revealed her hand. I knew that's what she wanted. And I was determined not to make it. But I couldn't just tell this fox no. I had to play the game, make my moves carefully, and defeat her with dialog.

"Oh, you know what? I think our milk expired a couple days ago," I said.

"Then how did you put it on your cereal this morning?" she asked, not missing a beat.

"I... ate my cereal dry," I lied.

Eely squinted. It's unnerving when a fox does that.

"You ate... dry cereal?" she asked.

"I did. Desperate times. I guess I'll have to order our groceries a day early this week," I said, moving my eyes down to the magazine but not actually reading anything.

"Dan?"

31

"Ye-yes?" I said, trying with all my strength not to look up.

"I can smell the milk you left in your bowl from here. You never rinse the thing out," Eely said with a low tone.

Dammit, I thought. *Curse my sloppy ways! Why couldn't I just learn to rinse out the dishes after I put them in the sink?*

"Okay fine! We have milk, bread, eggs, cinnamon, and everything else we need. But I can't go upstairs and make you breakfast because... the store is already open. What if a customer comes in?" I said, trying my best to mask my tone.

"Then I'll yell at you like I have for the last 140 years when you've left the room for a bathroom break or to go sit out in the back yard in that sad little kiddie pool you fill up sometimes," Eely said.

"Hey! I only do that when it gets really really hot," I snapped.

"Well it got really really hot a lot last summer, maybe 30-40 times," Eely said.

"It's Arkansas. Of course it gets hot during the summer. Anyway, it wasn't that many times," I said, feeling like I'd at least won that argument. Because it does get hot during the summer.

Eely and I stared at each other for a moment, and I began to think my laziness would win out. The fox couldn't physically force me to make her breakfast that I was aware of.

"You're out of excuses and lies, so either you go make us some French toast, or you tell me no, and I tell Odessa you're failing in your duties to take care of me," Eely said.

"Duties? Listen here, fuzzhead, I'm tasked with watching the store, managing items and helping customers. Nothing in my assigned duties from Odessa includes taking care of a picky fox," I said, scratching under my beard.

Eely continued to stare and then asked, "Do I really need to go through all the trouble of painting a summoning symbol in the dust on this case and pulling out your contract with Odessa? To unfold that long piece of centuries-old parchment down to paragraph 56 where it mentions how you are to provide a welcome home and take care of me all the days you exist until the witch releases you?"

I didn't recall much after the second paragraph, actually. But I also didn't know which would be a bigger blow to my pride, letting the fox win the argument or having the fox summon the contract, make a show, and then winning the argument. I decided the latter was more embarrassing, so I sighed, went upstairs, and fixed us some French toast.

"Thank you!" Eely called, just as sweet as when she first awoke and said good morning to me.

There was a door behind the cash register that led to a hallway. The hallway gave me access to a spiral staircase going up to my loft and some storage space. There were two rooms on the left side of the hallway, a kitchen, and a laundry room. Then on the right side was a bathroom with a tiny shower. At the end of the hallway was a back door that led out back to the little patch of grass behind the building.

That was my yard. It was surrounded by a six-foot privacy fence, which seemed silly, given how small the yard itself was. Still, it makes moonbathing naked a little easier.

I went into the kitchen and made a little French toast. And sure, I was happy to have a little extra breakfast to tide me over until lunch. And sure, I did like to cook. But the fact that a portion of this meal was going to that spoiled fox stayed with me the entire time.

We finished breakfast, and I loaded the dishwasher, mostly full after dinner last night. I started it and then went back into the store.

I finished my magazine that afternoon just in time for the mailman to come in. He dropped off a couple new magazines and said, "You're the one person in this city that still gets lots of magazines, Dan. I have people that might get a magazine or two every month, even the old ladies that get *Southern Living*. But you must have subscriptions to at least 15 or 20 magazines. Do you really read all of them?"

"Cover to back," I said.

It's the one small piece of enjoyment I get in this prison. I may not be able to leave, but at the very least I can read through these and see bits and pieces of the world, I thought. *I'm just glad the old hag pays for all of them.*

"Well, I hope enough stick around for you to keep reading to your heart's content. Most of the stuff is going online nowadays," he said and turned to leave.

"I'll have to keep the hope alive that print doesn't die entirely," I said.

As the mailman left, big afro bouncing and all, I looked through my magazines. There were three, *Pro Model Airplanes*, *Sahara Wildlife Quarterly*, and *Ultimate Cookie Guide*. Holding these and

33

anticipating which I'd read first got me over the bitterness of my forced breakfast labor earlier.

I thought back to when I first started reading them. I'd only been in the shop for a few months, and I was going stir crazy. The walls felt even more constricting than they do today, and my hatred for Odessa only grew.

I'd already tried leaving three times in three different ways, and each ended with me right back in the shop.

Odessa had put me here to collect mystical items, keep said items safe, and sometimes distribute one to a poor soul in need. But I was ready to find an item that made fire and burn the store down.

The witch came up with a solution, though. One day when I was sweeping, she walked into the shop with a little magazine called *Arkansas Thomas Cat*. It was a new publication being printed out of Hot Springs a few hours away, mostly focusing on humorous stories and political shaming. The witch set it on the counter and told me to stop my bellyaching about this feeling like a prison.

"If I wanted you to be in a dungeon, you'd be in one, Daniel. But you couldn't really help people from a dungeon, so you're not in one," Odessa told me, handing me the book.

I looked over the cover, and she said, "You've already had your vacation, Daniel. Now you work for me. And while you're not waking up each morning eating crepes in Paris, you could do a lot worse than a free home and little labor."

Putting the broom aside, I began to thumb through the magazine.

"I heard they plan to print these once a week. So if you'll stop moping and actually focus on the customers, I'll see to it you have plenty to read," Odessa said.

It was then I struck my second bargain with the witch. I may be in prison, but at least Brooks Hatlen would come by now and again with a squeaky cart offering me a book.

Time marched on slowly, but my magazine collection grew. I don't know how much money Odessa has, or if that's even a factor, but I do have all the magazines I want to read. So I don't question it, just like I don't question how the lights here stay on, despite me never having put a single penny into that register.

I was about to open the cookie guide when the front door opened, and a girl with long messy black hair walked in, looking confused about why she'd entered Funky Dan's, as all my customers do.

I should start making breakfast wagers with Eely about what people's expressions will be upon entering the store, I thought.

"Hey there! Welcome to Funky Dan's. I'm... well, Funky Dan. Feel free to look around, or if you're searching for something in particular, I'm back here by the register," I said.

I sat on my stool and reached for *Ultimate Cookie Guide*, vol. 57, issue #4. Fully expecting her to walk back and talk to me, because only about 20 percent of customers browsed, I kind of tapered my attention to the corner of the aisle closest to the door.

When she didn't come back, I shrugged and started on an article about a lifetime of eating cookie dough and no salmonella poisoning.

I was finished with that article and three others, plus a recipe for ye ole snickerdoodles when I heard, "Oh my goodness! What a cute fox!"

"Why thank you! Oh my, you're too kind. I just LOVE your little bunny necklace," Eely said, standing up and doing a little twirl where she fluffed out all nine of her tails.

"Eat it up, you little gremlin, but keep your voice down," I muttered.

"Ask her how many tails she sees. I bet it's one," Eely sassed, whipping one of her tails at my wrist.

I sighed.

"Can I take a pet of her—I'm sorry. I meant, can I pic a pet of—" the woman stopped for the second time and took a deep breath.

Then she pointed to her phone and at Eely, shortly before dropping her phone on the ground. It bounced back behind the glass case of dangerous items and over by my foot.

I picked it up and handed it gently to the woman. She looked like she was torn between fading from existence due to embarassment and crying.

"No harm done," I said. "And yes, photograph the twerp all you want. She loves attention."

Eely whipped my wrist harder with one of her tails.

Ow! I thought, trying not to give the fox the satisfaction of knowing it hurt me.

I'm a man! This little furball can't hurt me. Oh God, why does it still sting? Is my wrist on fire? Is it an invisible fire? Why does it burn so bad? I shouted in my head.

"Excuse me," I said, dashing back into the bathroom and running cold water over my wrist. After about two minutes of holding it there, the burning finally subsided.

I sighed and grabbed some paper towels, rubbing it gingerly. I didn't want to upset the wrist again. Still, the skin looked like the normal pale color it always was. When was the last time I'd seen any real sun?

Who knows? I thought.

Coming back out to the store, I found my new customer waiting patiently, patting Eely's head gently. The little fox cooed as the customer scratched behind the ears.

It was then I noticed the girl's necklace as Eely had earlier, though for a different reason. I noticed gray wisps of smoking floating off into the air around the girl.

If she knows the thing she's wearing around her neck is smoking, she's showing no sign of it, I thought.

The design was a little bunny standing up in the air, sniffing at something. In all, it was probably three inches tall and an inch wide. It certainly wasn't the fluffiest bunny I'd ever seen. But I was also having trouble placing the purple stone it was made out of.

At last it came to me, and I said, "Charoite?"

She looked up at me with a puzzled look like I'd just said something in a foreign language. I pointed at her necklace, and she gasped.

"Oh! Yes. That's what it's made of. How did you know?" she asked.

"I deal with a lot of precious stones. Actually... scratch that. Let's just leave it at, I deal with a lot," I said.

"This is a very beautiful store," the woman said, looking around at all the items arranged on the shelves.

"Thank you. I'd say I'm proud to call it my home, but that'd be a lie," I told her.

The woman wasn't very tall. I'd put her around just under five feet high. She was wearing a black T-shirt and yellow pants. I took notice, as she turned her head nervously, that her earrings were mismatched. One was a dog, and the other was a dragon. I didn't know how she could mix up the two.

There was something odd about this girl. She looked to be in her late 20s, and there was a chaotic energy about her. This poor girl wasn't just clumsy. It was almost like there were metaphorical paint cans tied to her elbows, so every time she moved, she knocked them into something.

But it was that necklace that really didn't belong here. And I had a suspicion that's why it was smoking and probably had been for more than 20 years.

"Is there something I can help you find, miss..." I trailed off waiting for her name.

"Oh, you can just call me Nurama," she said.

I nodded.

"That's an interesting name, Nurama. Did it come from family?" I asked.

She looked up and stopped petting Eely.

"I don't know. It's carved into the back of this necklace I've had since I was born. Foster family found me and named me after it, hoping it'd provide an easy way to find me if my birth parents ever wanted to look for me," she said.

I looked at the necklace again and sighed, saying, "I apologize. It wasn't my intention to snoop on your personal life or bring up any bad memories."

"Not at all," Nurama said, waving a hand.

After a moment of silence, Eely spoke up, "Boy, you really brought the awkward silence with this customer, huh?"

I was going to say something sassy, but one of her tails twitched, and I just scowled. Nurama broke the silence.

"So, what do you sell here, exactly?" she asked, starting down the second aisle and looking at a pair of shoes with little frogs painted on them.

"Uh, well, whatever people need. You see, people only come to this shop when they need something from it. And it's my job to unite them with what they need," I said.

She twirled trying to be cute and almost knocked an entire shelf over. Thankfully she caught herself, and I breathed a sigh of relief. I didn't want to clean all that up.

"Do you have any new brains laying around?" she asked, laughing.

It was a joke made at her own expense, and I could see Nurama had been struggling here all of her life. Struggling with what she

37

thought was clumsiness. But I was starting to put the pieces together. Meanwhile, that necklace of hers continued to smoke.

"What do you need a new brain for?" I asked.

"Because mine's broken," she chuckled, knocking her head a little on top, as though it were a cabinet.

"Why do you say that?"

Nurama stopped walking down the aisle and came back to the counter.

"Surely you've noticed I'm a bit of a clutz. Okay... that's downplaying it. I'm a *major* clutz. Always have been. I'm always forgetting stuff, falling over, and just generally a pretty unlucky girl."

I put the magazine away and said "Well that's not true. You're also a—" And then I stopped. I couldn't read the sign she'd been born under. I've always been able to tell what sign a person was born under simply by laying eyes on them. It'd come to be a talent I'd developed working here in the shop for more than a century.

"I'm a what?" she asked, putting her hands on her hips and displacing her little black purse which fell to the floor.

She moaned and knelt down to pick it up.

"You're also a Taurus," I said, guessing wrong on purpose.

"I don't know. My foster family said they found me in November," she said.

I rubbed my chin.

"Of course. But you weren't born under any of our signs, were you?" I muttered.

"Excuse me?"

"I said that'd make you a Scorpio," I said, smiling.

She smiled and straightened up, buckling her purse shut. Looking down at the strap, she sighed.

"To be entirely honest. I'm not really sure why I came into your store. My lunch break is over at 12:30," she said.

I grimaced as I looked over at my wall clock and saw it was 1:42 p.m.

When did she even leave for lunch? I thought, sweating a little on her behalf.

"I'm probably about to lose my job because of my forgetfulness. I'm the receptionist for a graphic design firm here in town, and I'm always forgetting appointments and times, even when I write them down on three different sticky notes. And this will be the third job I've lost this year because of my dumb brain. I think the only reason I've held onto it this long is because the owner of the firm is my landlady's husband," she said, looking down at the shaggy green carpet.

Wow, this girl is really troubled, I thought, trying to think of what I had here that would help her. Ultimately, I decided I couldn't make the decision for her. She'd have to make her purchase herself.

"I'm sorry. I don't know why I told you all that," she said, trying to laugh it off and failing to convince Eely and myself of her cheer.

"Nurama, believe it or not, you told me that because I needed to know it. It's one of this shop's quirks. People give me the information I need to help them," I said.

She looked up from the carpet and met my mismatched eyes.

"How are you going to help me?" she asked.

"Well, I'm not really going to. I'm going to offer you a choice, and you'll have to make the decision and ultimately help yourself," I said, without blinking.

She seemed mystified, but then she blinked and tilted her head.

"Are you going to like... read my tarot or cleanse my aura or something?" she asked.

While I knew a few witches in town who would definitely offer that for her, readings and cleansings weren't really my specialty. Enchanted and mystical items were more up my alley.

"Do you think either of those things would help you?" I asked.

She took a step closer to the counter.

"I don't know. Would they?"

I smiled.

"It's good to know that you're open to seemingly unique ways to fix your problem. Because it's going to take a solution that's out of this world," I said.

She was back to looking intrigued again.

"Your problem is unique, Nurama, I won't lie. You don't have a true name, and that, combined with the fact that you're not from here, is really throwing you for a loop," I said.

She raised an eyebrow.

"What do you mean my true name?" she asked.

There was no cynicism in her tone. She was genuinely curious as to what I was talking about.

39

Each person possesses two names. There's the one they're given by parents and shared with everyone. Nurama is yours. Daniel is mine. But at the age of nine, everyone also develops a true name, one unique to their soul. Most don't learn their true name, nor do they have reason to. If you know your true name, you're that much more likely to let it slip. And if someone has your true name, they have power over you. But you... you aren't from here, so you never got a true name," I said.

She popped her neck and thought hard for a moment.

"I follow you on the true name stuff. But why don't I have one? How do you get one?" she asked. "Can I buy one here? And is it on sale? I'm a bit tight on money right now."

"No," I said, trying not to smile. "It's like this. Your soul comes to reflect what's around it. Elements, people, relationships, emotions, and more. It all goes into your true name. But yours never developed, not truly. Because again... you're not from here"

Nurama nodded and said, "Well, it's true I don't know where I'm from. But do you mean I'm not from Arkansas? Is that why my true name didn't develop?"

She almost flinched after asking, as though she believed it to be a stupid question and was used to people laughing at her.

"It's a good question, Nurama. Everyone wants to know where they're from. And I honestly don't know where you're from. It's not about Arkansas. You're just quite simply not from this world. You and that stone, which has been smoking since you arrived in this world without most being able to see it, aren't from here. And since you've been in a foreign world all your life, your soul hasn't been able to really develop a true name. That's what's causing your clumsiness. But since you lack a true name, this world doesn't recognize you, and it pushes you around with all this chaos, forgetfulness, and what you perceive as clumsiness," I said.

The customer's eyes widened, and she looked down at the carpet, clearly processing.

I gave her a lot of information to absorb, so I'll just let her take as long as she needs, I thought.

We stood there in silence for a few moments. Eely scratched her ear and then turned to me, saying, "I've gotta admit. You figuring all that out in a short amount of time is actually pretty impressive."

I smiled and nodded at the eggshell fox.

When at last Nurama was done processing, she looked up at me and asked, "So... what do we do to fix this? You said you were going to sell me something that would help?"

I shook my head.

"Sell probably isn't the most accurate word for what I do, but we'll get to the price in a bit. First, you have a choice to make, like I told you earlier," I said, looking into the glass case in front of me.

"A choice? Is this like a riddle or something where I have to pick a destiny?" she asked.

"What? No. My shop isn't an enchanted fortune cookie," I said.

Eely's ears pricked.

"That's what I want for dinner. Chinese food. Dan, I want sweet and sour soup tonight, and can we get it from—"

"What are you talking about, then?" she asked, cutting Eely off.

"That's okay. We can work out dinner after you've helped this poor lady," Eely said and stretched in her bed.

I reached into the glass case and pulled out a necklace with a glass orb on the end. It was about the size of a baseball. Inside was a glowing orange butterfly with black wings. I set it gently down on the glass case and then shut the door on the back side.

"Beautiful," she said. "Will that give me good luck so I don't need a true name?"

I smiled. This girl certainly had the imagination required to run a store like this. Part of me wanted to hire her to run errands outside the store, but Odessa wouldn't approve of that. No, my only companion would remain the furball. Aside from her, this was a solitary occupation.

Walking behind Nurama and down the second aisle, I went to the end she didn't quite make it to and pulled out a narrow bamboo tube. It was about as wide as my middle finger and twice as long. The wood was ancient and cracked, so I had to be careful with it.

When I made it back behind the counter, I set it beside the necklace, even more cautiously.

Nurama started to reach her hand out, but Eely quickly placed her paw on the woman's wrist. Startled, she looked down at the fox, who was clearly quicker than my customer anticipated.

"What Eely is trying to say is, 'be careful.' These are both highly sensitive one-use items. And you need to think very carefully before you pick one," I said.

"What do they do?" Nurama said, slowly returning her hand to her side.

"Well, either will help you. But they'll do it in very different ways. The butterfly necklace you see will return you to your homeworld, to the place where you were born. All you have to do is put the necklace on, and it'll transport you there. Once in your homeworld, your soul will develop a true name for you and you'll fit right in, no more clumsiness," I said.

"Will I be able to return here?" she asked.

"I don't know. That kind of depends on how you got here the first time when you were a newborn. It might be that you return home, and you're stuck there for the rest of your life," I said.

She looked down at the butterfly taking that news in. I watched her eyes gently reflect the glow of the winged insect.

"Do you know anything about my homeworld? What if it's a futuristic wasteland devoid of nearly all life? What if I can't find my birth parents?"

I shook my head and then looked at Nurama straight on.

"I don't know where you came from, Nurama. All I know is that necklace will return you there. Could I figure out more about your homeworld or help you track down your birth parents? Sure. But I can tell you right now, the cost for that additional information is more than you will want to pay," I said.

She reached into her purse and dug around until she found her wallet. It was a little red square pocketbook with the word "glamour" on it. She reached inside and handed me a black and red credit card with her name on it.

"I don't take money here, Nurama. The price people pay for my items and services is always an equivalent trade of additional items or services," I said.

She nodded and put the card back into her wallet. Then she set down her purse and said, "I understand."

At this point, she started to reach down and take her shirt off. Eely put both her paws on Nurama's hands, and I said, "Not that kind of service. Geez, is that the kind of reputation the name 'Funky Dan' inspires in this community?"

Nurama turned her head to the side and wore a quizzical expression.

"Never mind. Forget I asked that," I said. "That's not the kind of cost I'm talking about, either. Would you want to find your birth parents if you knew it'd cost you an eye?"

Nurama looked bewildered at the thought.

"Excuse me? Why would it cost an eye?" she asked.

"What about if the cost was you could only see them for one day, and then they vanished. Would you pay it then?" I asked.

"Just one day? That makes no sense!" she said.

I cleared my throat.

"How about half of your remaining years. Would you pay that to know where your birth parents are?" I asked.

She threw up her hands, unsure of how to respond to such questions. And I stood there looking at her, waiting for it to click in her mind. At last, she seemed to understand.

"These are the kinds of costs people pay for items and services in my shop. And when I say the cost is more than you're willing to pay, you'll now understand what I mean."

Nurama nodded and sighed. Then she looked over at the bamboo tube. At one time there was writing on the outside. It had long since faded.

"What does this item do?" she asked, pointing.

"Inside that tube is a true name never before seen by human eyes. It was written by a blind seer from Nagasaki, hundreds of years ago. I came into possession of it after helping a traveling antiques dealer find his missing dog again. Where he got it, I do not know. But you open the tube, read the paper and assume the new name. Your 'bad luck' as you call it, comes to an end. This world recognizes you as one of its own because you'll have a true name originating here," I said.

"Well that sounds a lot more simple. What's the downside here?" Nurama asked.

"Downside?" I said.

"What bad things happen if I chose this option?" she asked.

"Downsides, benefits, these are all a matter of perspective. Who can say what will or won't happen if you choose this new name? If you choose it and go outside and get hit by a bus, does that mean this choice had a downside? Perhaps. On the other hand, if, while in the hospital recovering from that bus crash, you meet your soulmate, and fall in love, spending the rest of your days together, is that an upside?

Perhaps. There are always going to be risks and consequences to your choices," I said.

"Yeah, but—"

"If you're looking for divination, I'd recommend Odessa's Psychic Center next door. She's more about predicting the future than I am. Though I'd warn you to be wary of any deals she offers you," I said, rolling my eyes.

Nurama sighed and adjusted her purse, while she thought about how she wanted to word her next question.

"What are the obvious risks to selecting the true name thing instead of the necklace?" she asked.

I thought for a moment.

"Well I suppose you might not ever get another chance to return to your home dimension. I can't claim to know your future, but I can't imagine an opportunity to travel between worlds pops up very often. And there's the risk I told you earlier. If you know your true name, and you will once you read the paper in there, you're that much more likely to reveal it to someone, granting them power over you," I said.

Nurama stopped and looked at both items very carefully, as if weighing their pros and cons. She might have been trying to figure out if there was an obvious choice between the two. After a few minutes of intense staring, she gave up. This was a choice she'd have to make with her heart, not based on some miraculous sign or sneaky clue she picked up from her observation.

"So I'm basically choosing between the possibility of someone gaining power over me and putting on a blindfold and returning to a place I know nothing about?"

"Or, you're choosing between the chance to meet your birth parents and finally having a true name to protect from all the chaos you've endured in this world. See? It's about perspective," I said.

Nurama sighed and went back to observing the two items before her. She scratched her scalp and pondered for an obvious answer that once again failed to come.

"I really do love my foster family. They've been so loving to me, in spite of all my clumsiness through the years. But part of me is always going to wonder what happened to my birth parents, if they're okay, why I was separated from them. Did they give me up? It's a hard decision," she said.

"The important thing for you to know, Nurama, is there's no wrong answer here. You simply need to make the choice you think will make you the happiest or give you the future you want," I said.

Eely spoke up and said, "I don't know which I would choose, either. She's got a tough decision to make here."

I nodded at the fox again. I agreed with her. This wasn't something I envied in Nurama, a difficult decision. Though, I think I knew which I would pick. If I had the chance to wear a necklace and possibly see my parents again? Leave this shop behind once and for all? I'd take it. Odessa couldn't follow me across dimensions, could she? Could her curse follow me past this world?

"I'm going to take the necklace," Nurama said at once.

And I came out of my own thoughts to look at the item glowing on the glass case before me. Then I looked up at the girl who had a determination in her eyes that wasn't present when she first came into the shop.

"Looks like you've made up your mind then," I said.

"Yeah. I love my foster family, but the truth is I haven't found much happiness in this world. Maybe I was never meant to. Either way, having a true name and ditching all the clumsiness is no guarantee of future happiness, is it?"

I shook my head.

"Well, I guess I'm going home then," she said. "What's the price? Are you going to chop off an ear? If so, please use the left one. I'm partially deaf in it due to a blow horn mishap when I was 12," she said.

I laughed and said, "I'm not going to take your ear. No, the price is another necklace, specifically, the one you're wearing now."

She looked down at the bunny necklace.

"I've worn this since I was a baby," she said, holding it in her left hand.

"I know."

"What are you going to do with it?"

"Save it for someone else who will come into the shop needing it someday, like I do with all other items," I said.

She sighed, lowered her head, and I saw a teardrop hit the floor. But then she handed it over to me. I reached down and handed her the butterfly necklace. Then, I dug around under the glass case for a little black wooden jewelry box. It groaned but took the bunny necklace without complaint. As I shut it, the smoke finally began to dissipate.

45

After that, I put the jewelry box out on the shelf furthest from the front door next to a water gun that turned whatever got hit with its spray into a liquid for 24 hours.

Upon returning to my space behind the glass case, I saw Nurama still crying, though I sensed it wasn't about the necklace.

"I wish I could tell my foster family I love them one last time," she said.

"Nurama, I didn't say you had to use the butterfly necklace right away. You can leave the store with it and use it whenever you want," I said.

She shook her head.

"If I don't use it now, I'll lose my nerve. And besides, as long as I stay in this world, I'm still going to be a clumsy mess. I don't want to drop the necklace and break it," she said.

She's a smart lady. Clumsiness doesn't equal idiocy, I thought.

"I just wish I could say goodbye," she said.

I nodded and decided maybe there was something I could do. Looking down at my cookie magazine, I saw there was a free chocolate chip cookie postcard on page 17. I tore it out and put it on the counter, giving Nurama a pen.

"Tell you what. I don't have any use for this. Why don't I throw it in as part of our deal? You can write whatever you want and address it to your foster family. Then I'll make sure it goes out in the mail tomorrow. Eely, will you run next door and ask Odessa for a stamp please?"

"You just don't want to face her," the fox said and jumped down, walking through the doggie door in the back.

Nurama smiled and took the pen, writing out one last message to her foster family. I gave her privacy and went back to my magazine. Around the time Eely returned with a stamp from Odessa gently held in her mouth, Nurama finished.

She smiled and said, "Wow, you've trained the fox really well. How did she know to do that?"

"She's only trained when she wants to be, and she's trying to earn a nice Chinese dinner tonight after we close up," I said, side-eyeing the fox.

Nurama took the stamp and scratched Eely behind the ears.

"Aw, for that I'd go get another 50 stamps," the fox said.

I just shook my head gently.

Nurama placed the Cookie Monster stamp on the back of the postcard and slid it across the glass case with her bunny necklace.

"I guess I'm ready. And you promise that'll go out tomorrow?" she asked.

"You have my word. I must honor all transactions I commit to as the shopkeep here," I said.

Nurama took a deep breath and slowly raised the butterfly necklace. It began to glow even brighter, so I shut one eye, and Eely buried her nose in her bed.

"Thanks for all your help, Dan. I'm grateful," she said.

"Best of luck, Nurama. And if anyone from your world is heading over to this one, feel free to plug the shop," I said, giving her a thumbs up.

She nodded, placed the necklace on, and then disappeared in a puff of blue smoke that smelled like mothballs.

I waved my hands around to clear it.

"Think she'll be okay?" Eely asked.

"I have absolutely no idea. But it's nice to think so," I said with a shrug.

"As customers go, she was kind of a strange one," Eely said. "We don't often get people from other worlds popping into the shop."

"Yeah, first that pixie yesterday and now her? It's got to be a coincidence. But if Odessa heard me saying that, she'd tell me like she always does that there is no coincidence, only—"

"Dinner!" Eely said, interrupting. "There is only dinner for my belly."

I looked at the clock and saw it was about 3:02 p.m.

"You're going to have to wait another couple hours," I said.

Eely sighed.

"Is there any French toast left?"

"No. I gave you the last piece, Eely," I said, going back to my magazine.

"Yeah, that was awful nice of you. Seemed out of character. I was afraid you poisoned it," the fox said.

I sat down on my stool, leaned back against the wall and started reading an article on a new sugar substitute being tested for cookies in Amsterdam.

"I can be nice when I want to," I said with a self-satisfied smirk.

Chapter Four
(Roxie)

After a couple nights of helping people turn their nightmares into dreams, I felt like maybe I had a better handle on things. At least a little. I'd stopped looking at the words I needed to recite to get into dreams and had committed them to memory.

As I walked Rufus around the block, I was in my own head, a fairly new trait since becoming a dream girl.

Sometimes I just stopped to ponder if I knew what was really happening to me. I mean, a real pixie showed up to my therapist's office, gave me an enchanted bracelet with a few magic words, and told me I was supposed to help turn people's nightmares into dreams for the next month until she returned to our world. Easy stuff, right? Nothing your standard 18-year-old girl would have any trouble with.

My phone buzzed in my butt pocket, and I pulled it out, unlocking the screen. Oh joy, another text from the man who called himself my father. I'd ask for a DNA test to prove we aren't related, but that'd mean I'd have to actually see him and get the jerk to spit into a tube. I hadn't seen the man since Mom got full custody, and I had no plans to look on his hideous face again.

"Dear Johnny, I was out jogging this morning and saw one of my neighbors playing catch with his son in the front yard. Reminded me of how we used to play catch when you were a little boy. Praying that we can do this again one day. Your father, Charles," the text said.

"My name is Roxie, you absolute asshole!" I screamed at the phone.

Why haven't I blocked this creep yet? I thought angrily.

Rufus barked at the UPS truck that drove by, and I muttered, "Deja vu. What's with this dog and those trucks?"

As I rounded another corner, I was grateful to see Miss Michelle's little blue house. My new "bits," as I called them, were starting to hurt again, and I was ready to get home and rest.

Miss Michelle was able to walk from the couch to the kitchen a little easier now, but I imagined it'd still be awhile before I saw her out working in the garden. So I was walking Rufus every day and watering her plants when her son wasn't able to take care of the garden.

The corgi impressed me by making it all the way around the block this time. Usually Rufus just melted in the hot summer sun, despite being ready and jumping with the leash when I arrived. The dog tuckered out pretty quick.

Inside, I praised the inventor of the air conditioner.

Sweet sweet cool air. How I missed you, I thought, even though I'd been outside for a grand total of maybe 10 minutes. Arkansas summers were the worst season of the four. It wasn't just the heat you had to deal with but the humidity.

Looking down at my bracelet Selena gave me, I pondered for a moment on the possibility that I could change reality and eliminate this pesky season in one fell swoop.

Miss Michelle caught me looking at the bracelet as I hung the leash up.

"That's a pretty piece of jewelry, Roxie. Where did you get it from?" she asked.

I chuckled and told her a friend got it for me.

I use pixie magic to enter people's nightmares and turn them into dreams, I thought, as if I'd really tell her. But how much would she really hear with her attention already divided between a Hallmark movie called *The Autumn Heart* and her daily crossword from the local paper?

From where I stood, I could see she had one left, five down. She was so focused, so I decided to go for it.

"I'm a pixie," I said at normal volume.

She put the paper down and looked up at me.

"Oh my goodness. I feel bad, but is that some LGBTQ+ word I should know the meaning of, Roxie?" Miss Michelle asked with a surprising sincerity.

Now I really did burst out laughing and just said, "Nothing. It was a joke."

"I don't get it," she said.

"It's one of those meme things like from Facebook," I said, blushing a little.

How stupid can you be? Why would you even tell her that? Besides, it's not accurate. You aren't a pixie. You're using pixie magic, I thought, missing the point with my mental self speech. But that was actually pretty normal.

If I was scolding myself mentally, it'd start off solid, but then it usually derailed a little by the end. Throw in the fact that pixie magic was involved here, and I was guaranteed to mentally derail every time.

I got Rufus some more water and put ice cubes in his little silver dish. They rattled around and clicked while the dog attempted to drink twice his body weight in liquids.

"Slow down there, buddy. You'll just barf all that water back up," I said, laughing.

Then I turned toward the front door and caught one last glimpse of *The Autumn Heart*. I didn't really watch Hallmark movies, but even I understood how they functioned.

Let me guess. Big city girl travels into a small town on urgent business and intends to leave the area as quick as possible. But her car breaks down during the holiday weekend. The mechanic says it'll take a few days for a part to arrive and offers her a place to stay with his family. Reluctantly, she agrees, while secretly cursing her luck. Then she meets the mechanic's cute and single son, who shows her the down home charm of simple country life. When the part arrives, she quits her job and stays in the small town to marry her new instant love, I thought.

"Million dollars please," I muttered.

"What's that, Roxie?" Miss Michelle asked.

"I said that home renovation in the movie looks like a million dollars," I said, pointing to the television.

"I think it's close. It's like... $780,000 or something. Then they have to choose if they're going to keep the house or sell it," the school secretary said, joking.

I snorted a little and turned to leave, telling her I'd see her tomorrow and to call if she needed anything.

"Oh, Roxie!" she spoke up quickly.

"Yeah?"

"Five down is another music hint, and you always get these. It's

11 letters, starts with an 'S,' and the clue is 'band's only hit song, 1997.' What have you got, dear?"

I thought for a moment and smiled. I liked the song because it reminded me of Nirvana. But it wasn't actually by them. Charles would never let me say the song title out loud because it had a naughty word kids shouldn't use.

"Sex and Candy," I said, smirking.

Miss Michelle snickered too. After she filled it in, I went over and gave her a hug. Then I left and went home. Charles had been on my mind a lot today. And though it felt good to be changing nightmares into dreams, I felt like I needed to let some thoughts out, or my head was going to explode.

Maybe I could just go play drums for a while and hope it goes away. Then I stopped and remembered something Dr. Lyra had told me on my first visit. *Burying thoughts and feelings never works out, Roxie. They don't stay in the dirt forever, and when they come back, they're always twice as potent. If a thought or emotion sticks with you for a while, it needs to be addressed.*

"Yeah, yeah, yeah," I muttered, walking in the back door that led up to our loft. Getting to the loft from the front side where the mechanic bays are would have involved going near people, customers and Camila, a mechanic that worked with my Mom. It was almost 5:00 p.m., and Mom would be done for the night soon.

The stairs leading up to our loft were covered in a thick blue carpet. I unlocked the door with my snail key, the design featured a bunch of cute little mollusks with big goofy eyes.

Looking around the living room, I saw the place was empty. Mom was still downstairs, likely finishing things up with Camila.

I collapsed on our black leather futon and let out a huge sigh. Pulling out my phone, I saw an update from one of my favorite webcomics. It followed the story of a nonbinary rock person who had mastered several forms of martial arts. She traveled the land, always looking for a peaceful place to settle down and set up her blacksmith business. But trouble always managed to find her.

It was called *Breyla's Beginnings*, and it had this hokey 80s movie vibe I really loved. It wasn't the most popular comic on Comicverse, but it had a dedicated following and enough people to keep an active subreddit with a few hundred posts per year.

I was so absorbed in the comic I didn't even hear Mom come up through the kitchen entrance. It was the only other way into the loft, and it came up from the backside of bay two.

The episode that just came out concluded a three-week series where Breyla narrowly escaped her father's army who had been pursuing her and trying to bring her back to the Cavernous Castle by force.

"All she wants to do is find her own place to be happy. Why can't that jerk face just leave her alone?" I muttered while staring at my phone and deciding if I wanted to close the ad for Arby's that just popped up.

"Hey Priss, how's it going?"

"Sore and grumpy," I responded without even looking up.

Mom came over and looked down at me on the couch.

"Did you dilate yet? Or... you overdid it walking Rufus, didn't you?" she asked, as I could feel her analytical cyborg gaze upon me.

I buried the lower half of my face in the little fox pillow I was holding.

"No. It's just typical soreness like the doctor said to expect with moderate exercise. I didn't do any more laps with Rufus than usual," I half mumbled.

Mom looked me over and then settled her analytical cyborg gaze on my emotional state, trying to pick up whatever I was putting down. What I hoped I was putting down was, "Just leave me be," but her analysis rarely picked that up. Or if it did, she chose to ignore it.

"I'm all covered in grease and grime, so I've got to go shower, but why don't you put on some PJs, and then we can talk about it before dinner?" she said.

I shook my head, doubling down on the "leave me be," vibe. To top it off, I mumbled something into my pillow I knew she wouldn't hear.

"Is it something you'd rather talk to Jenna or Tessa about?" Mom asked.

I stayed silent this time.

"Well, if it's something we can talk about, then I can put my shower on hold," she said, sitting on the arm of the couch and pulling me close.

"Ah, gross! Ew Mommie, you're all sweaty and greasy!"

She just pulled tighter.

"Well that shouldn't matter if I love you, should it? What's a little muck between mother and daughter?" she asked.

"I'm literally going to die, Mom!"

"Oh, literally?" she asked, rubbing some smudge on my arm.

"Ew! Yes, literally going to die. Just stop. Stop it now," I screamed, trying hard to push her away but to no avail.

"Well, if you're literally going to die, then I want our last moments together to be as close as possible," she said, holding me tighter as I screamed louder.

"Okay, okay! I'll talk to you about it. Just please let go of me, and go shower! You smell like oil and brake fluid, and it's staining my favorite shirt," I said.

"That's not your favorite shirt. Your favorite is the one with the tuxedo guy and the sailor school girl whose name I can never remember," she said.

I pushed and pushed, but she wouldn't budge.

"Okay fine, you win. We'll talk, I'll spill my guts about everything. Just please, for the love of all things good and decent, go shower," I said, making one last attempt at a bargain to free me from this muck monster.

"Hmmmmmmmmm. I'll have to think about it," Mom said.

"Oh come on!" I shrieked.

At that point, she laughed, kissed me on the head, and finally let go. I picked up a nearby napkin and frantically rubbed down my arms, trying to clean them. In truth, I was overexaggerating. She really didn't get much on me. But I was still mortified and determined to put on a show.

"I'll be out in five," she said.

"More like 15," I muttered, hurling the napkin into a little living room wastebasket we kept next to the side table.

I did my make up in the living room, and Mom got tired of me leaving tape, paper towels, and cotton swabs lying around when I finished.

"You are literally 10 feet from a trash can!" she'd always yell as I ran off to school.

"That's too far," I'd reply, blow her a kiss, and shut the back door.

So, she put the little black wastepaper basket in here. I'd say 95 percent of the trash in it comes from me. No food, obviously. Just a little paper trash.

I sat there waiting for Mom for another 20 minutes before she showed up again. She came in smelling like oranges and brought me some of my PJs with little bunnies on them.

As I brushed mom's hair, she sighed.

"Okay, Miss Priss, what's got you down?"

Not ready to tell her about the pixie stuff yet, I told her about yet another text from Charles and how I was struggling with whether or not to just block him since his texts only brought misery. He'd learned years ago I wasn't going to take his calls, so he started texting every day.

I smiled and sat down on the couch next to her.

"I get so mad at him, Mom. So, so mad. Like, head is going to explode mad because of how he continues to treat me," I said.

She said nothing but kept listening.

"And every time I think about blocking him, I just think back to Tessa's aunt. They were really close, and it devastated her when her aunt died. I keep fearing that Charles is going to kick the bucket someday, and I'm going to regret not having made up with him," I said, grabbing my fox pillow again to bury the lower half of my face in it.

Neither of us said anything for a moment, and so I spoke again.

"I just want to believe that someday he's going to come around, ya know? Like, I'll just wake up one morning, and my father will be downstairs with a bouquet and 1,000 apologies for the way he treated me. But with every text he sends, and every deadname he drops, it just gets easier to hate him. And I don't want to hate him, Mom. I want to love my dad, but he just makes it impossible, and I don't know if—I don't know," I said, starting to sob.

Mom pulled me back into a hug, and we sat there for a moment while I collected myself.

"I went through the same thing before I divorced him, Roxie. I kept thinking, what if he changes? What if he gets better? But at some point, I had to make the determination that he was bad for me and even worse for you. So I signed the papers and got us the Hell out of there," Mom said.

I nodded without saying anything.

"But I can't make that decision for you, Priss. You're going to have to decide where to draw the line before cutting him out of your life for good. But here's what I can promise you," Mom said. "I won't ever let him hurt you, and I will always be here to love and support you, because you're my little girl, and nothing in this world is more important to me. If that asshole ever tries to hurt you, you can bet I'm going to bash his head in with the biggest wrench I've got down there, okay?"

I smiled as Mom pulled me tighter.

"I love you, Mom. I'm sorry you had to divorce Dad because of me," I said.

Now she turned me around.

"Honey, I didn't divorce him because of you. We never should have gotten married in the first place. We just weren't right for each other. That divorce was going to happen one way or another. But when I saw there was a choice to make between your happiness and a failing marriage, you were the easiest decision to make."

I looked down at my pillow, and Mom put her thumb under my chin and gently pushed my face up until our eyes met.

"If you want to block him, do it. If you want to hold out hope for a little longer, do it. I will support your decision one way or another," she said, softly.

Now I pulled her forward for the hug.

"You're the greatest, Mom. Thank you for always having my back," I said, closing my eyes.

"Always and forever, Miss Priss. I know I had tacos on the fridge menu for tonight, but I think we might need a little something extra to cheer you up. How about I order us a pizza from Giant Tim's?" she asked.

My eyes lit up.

"With double breadsticks?"

"With double breadsticks," she said laughing and heading toward her phone.

Meanwhile, I let out a victory cheer throughout the loft. Giant Tim's was the best pizza in Fayetteville and always worth a cheer.

A few hours later, after Mom and I had watched some terrible movie on Netflix about these kids at summer camp who have to save the world from space aliens, I was in the bathroom brushing my teeth.

I was kind of humming and swaying back and forth, in a cheery mood having just hit the "block" button on my phone's screen.

When I spit and looked up, my eyes caught my... well, eye. I wiped my mouth and leaned in closer to the mirror. My normally green eyes looked... different. When I blinked, my pupils looked a pale pink. What on earth was I looking at? This was my reflection, right?

I continued to stare, and then Mom knocked on the door.

"Hurry up! I have to pee," she said, and I heard her dancing on the wood floor outside.

"Sorry, Mom!"

When I looked back, my eyes were green again. I splashed some water on my face, dried off the marble bathroom counter, and looked again. My eyes were normal.

That was weird, I thought and opened the door.

"I'm going to bed, Mom," I said.

"Night!" she said, quickly pecking me on the cheek and slamming the bathroom door shut.

Maybe next time don't drink so many beers, Mom, I thought, smirking. *Your bladder can clearly only handle so much.*

When I got to my bedroom, I closed my door and locked it. I looked up at my Shakira poster and then plugged my phone in to charge underneath. Sitting on my Little Mermaid comforter, I sighed and fell back.

I'm not tired, but part of me does miss sleeping just a little bit, I thought.

"Oh well. Time to see who I'll be helping tonight," I said, pulling out my compact.

Looking into the mirror, I said *"Ambulate per somnia."*

It took a second, but then the mirror in my compact showed me a building. A store of some kind? I couldn't place it, but it looked like it should be familiar to me if that made any sense. There was someone sitting up on the roof, dangling his legs over the side. I couldn't really see him well in the dark.

"Some nightmare," I muttered. *"Immeo."*

There was a dizzying moment as though I was instantly being flown forward, and then I was there on the roof. I felt the warm night breeze. Suddenly, I realized where I was. I actually wasn't far from home.

"Hey, this is over by Toppings," I said, recognizing the street but not the building I was on.

At once, the man whose legs had been dangling turned around and gasped.

"Who the Hell are you?" he asked, climbing to his feet and almost dropping his wooden pipe. He had been smoking and smelled of pipe tobacco.

I looked over the tall man with an exceptionally bushy beard and stood there for a moment, unsure of what to say. The last couple nightmares I'd popped into, the dreamer was clearly in an obvious pain. But here? This guy was just sitting and smoking on an otherwise peaceful night.

"Do I need to ask in another language? Can you understand me? Who are you?" the man asked again, his long robe billowing in the wind.

Just before I could give my name, I heard a woman's voice from behind me.

"Wow, a visitor! And in your dreams, Dan. That's never happened before. What do you make of it?"

"I don't know. She hasn't told me who she is yet," Dan said.

I turned to see who was talking, and there was just an eggshell colored fox staring up at me with... way too many tails.

Counting them a few times, I said, "Nine. Never seen that before."

"Nine? Oh, you mean my tails? You can see all of them?" the fox asked.

"Nine tails, and you talk. I mean... I guess it's a dream. Anything can happen. But I didn't expect a talking fox," I said.

The fox snickered and stretched out all nine tails.

"I talk outside the realm of dreams too, you know. Name's Eely, by the way," she said.

"Ohuh? Oh, right. My name is Roxie," I said, kneeling down and extending my hand awkwardly.

Am I really shaking hands with a fox? I asked myself, realizing the awkward moment.

Eely just laughed and put a paw in my right hand.

"It's a pleasure to meet you, Roxie," Eely said, as I gently wrapped my hand around her paw and moved it up and down a couple times before letting it go.

Behind me, Dan cleared his throat.

"Hey, that's fine. You two just have your conversation and ignore my questions. I'll wait," Dan said, crossing his arms.

"Thanks for understanding!" Eely called to him. "We'd better head over and speak with him, or he's gonna get dream cranky. And it's even worse than normal cranky."

I nodded, and we walked over to the man.

"I'm sorry for not introducing myself earlier. My name is Roxie, and I... kind of travel into people's nightmares and turn them into pleasant dreams, odd as that sounds," I said.

Dan laughed.

"Trust me, Roxie. Nothing is odd in or above the store. I've seen all sorts of crazy things. But I've never seen someone enter my dream before, aside from that little fuzzball next to you. My name is Dan. And I run the store we're standing on, Funky Dan's."

I nodded, and he looked down at my arm.

"I was going to ask if you were some kind of dream seer, but I can see now that thing on your wrist is what allows you to be here. Woof. That's some potent pixie magic, all right. Don't see too many folks using it," he said.

Looking around I just saw a normal Fayetteville downtown block from a story up in the air. Wind rustled the nighttime trees and bushes nearby.

"I'm a little confused," I said.

"Yeah, I know. She's a little unnerving at first. But you learn to tune the fuzzball out after a while," Dan said, sitting down over the edge of the roof and relighting his pipe.

Eely scowled and whipped him in the back with one of her tails.

"Ow! How does that hurt in MY dream? Dreams are supposed to be painless!" he yelled.

I sat down next to the two of them and laughed.

"No, Eely is beautiful. What I'm confused by is your supposed nightmare. Everything here looks pretty calm," I said, looking up at the stars and a crescent moon.

Dan chuckled.

"Not all nightmares are thunderbolts and tornadoes, kiddo. A quiet and calm prison is still a prison. This is indeed my nightmare, and it's been the same nightmare I've had every night for more than a century," Dan said.

I looked over at the funky wizard-looking man with wide eyes. He didn't look overly young or old. But he definitely didn't appear to be more than 100 years old.

"You're more than a century old? Do you just look younger because this is a dream?"

"No, I look younger because I'm frozen in time and in this shop. That's the nightmare, Roxie. I'm cursed to run this store without being able to leave, even in my dreams. And this fuzzball next to you? She's just here to keep tabs on me. I can't get a moment of privacy, even in my dreams," Dan said.

Eely whipped his back again, and he shrieked.

"What happens if you just... walk away? Is there a barrier preventing that?" I asked.

Looking him over, it was this point I realized he had two different colored eyes.

"No barrier. But if I leave, I collapse, and worms devour me from the inside out. Then I wake up in the store again. It's a hoot, let me tell you."

"Who-"

"The witch Odessa. She runs the psychic shop next door. I made a bad deal with her back in the 1800s, and now she owns my soul," Dan said, taking a puff on his pipe.

We sat there in silence for a little bit, and I was unsure of how to solve Dan's nightmare.

I guess I could... take him somewhere? Get him away from the store? But where does he want to go? I thought.

Then Dan had a few questions of his own for me to answer. So I told him about Selene and being tasked with helping people's dreams, generating happiness. When I finished my tale, he sat there processing it all.

"I guess Odessa didn't protect my dreams from pixie magic. Very interesting indeed," Dan muttered.

As I went back through my mental notes and what he told me, trying to figure out how to help him, I remembered he said something about pixie magic.

"Hey Dan? You said you don't see lots of people using pixie magic. Why is that?"

"Well because of the cross magic species contam—" and before he could finish, a bolt of lightning struck the building. A loud clap of thunder followed. I nearly fell off the roof but managed to catch myself.

Dan looked up into the sky as it suddenly filled with storm clouds and heavy rain. And then came the wind. Hurricane force wind.

Now this is the nightmare I expected, I thought.

"Up there!" Dan yelled, to Eely or myself, I didn't know. But he was pointing at something in the storm.

I squinted but didn't see much until he gently floated down out of the lightning-lit clouds. He looked to be not much older than me and wore a black tuxedo with a thin red veil covering the bottom half of his face. He had a glowing earring in his left ear, and the wind blew his jet black hair all around it.

The earring itself looked like a golden serpent wrapped around the edge of his ear an   d glowed with a murky purple aura.

"Three of you? This is one crowded nightmare," he said with an airy and cocky tone.

"Is this a friend of yours?" Dan asked, looking at me.

"I've never seen him before in my life. Do you recognize pixie magic from him like you did me?" I asked.

The storm intensified, and the glowing earring pulseed.

"No, this is some kind of dark sorcery, but I can't place it. Who are you supposed to be? And why are so many people invading my dreams tonight?" Dan hollered.

The man shrugged and said, "No clue. I was just told to expect you. The girl and stuffed animal weren't in my plans."

"And what plans do you have?" Dan asked.

He smirked revealing a silver tooth on his bottom row.

"My name is Kairen, and the only part of my plan the three of you need to be concerned with is this first part where I dial up a personal knightmare flavor for everyone," he said, and then his earring glowed even brighter.

All at once, several chains shot out of the roof and wrapped tightly around Dan. He struggled and immediately fell onto his knees.

"Dan!" I yelled and ran over to help him, but a hand yanked my wrist and tugged me back. I turned around only to be met with Charles' face, smiling at me. Immediately I screamed

"Hey there, Johnny. Good to see you, son!"

I tried to pull free, but his grip was too strong.

"What are you doing here? How did you get into this dream? You shouldn't be here!" I screamed, feeling my heart plunge into a chest of ice. My legs started to buckle, but Charles held me frozen right in place.

Charles' brown hair seemed unaffected by the storm, and the Sunday church suit he was wearing didn't seem to be getting wet in the rain.

"Let go of me right now!" I screamed.

"Come on, son. That's no way to talk to your father," he said. "When you stopped taking my texts, I figured it was time to come take you back to Kansas and finally pull you back onto the right path, Johnny."

Tears began to build in my eyes as I struggled to pull free from his iron grip. Looking him dead in the brown eyes, I hissed, "I'm not your son, and my name is Roxie."

He shook his head and said, "The Devil really has led you pretty far astray, son. But don't worry. I'm going to get you back to Kansas, and we will return you to salvation yet. I'm never going to give up on you."

"Stop calling me your son!" I yelled.

And then he backhanded me, hard. I spit blood onto the roof and stood there visibly shaken.

"Did that knock some sense into you? Look, you're the spitting image of my son," he said.

When I slowly turned back, my neck popped. But I ignored that because I saw he was holding a mirror in his free hand. And looking back at me was the reflection of a young man about to graduate high school.

He had short chestnut hair and wore a thick goatee. I jerked my eyes from the image and looked down to see a Sunday suit covering me like the one covering Charles. Worst of all, my bracelet from Selene was gone.

"This can't be happening! What have you done to me?!" I shrieked, losing my mind.

"Returning you to the way you were born to be, Johnny. And the way you'll be for the rest of your new life back home with me. Now come on, we've got to get going," he said, starting to pull me.

This—no. I'm not. My name isn't—I don't, my mind sputtered, trying to form any coherent thought. I'd come here to help Dan with his nightmare and instead found my own Hell. And whose job was it to come into dreams and rescue me?

Charles pulled me another step forward.

"Hurry up, Johnny. If we get moving now we can be back in Kansas before sunrise," he said with a cheerful tone.

My legs, what remained that I could feel in them, were shivering harder than ever, and tears streamed down my cheeks.

"Help me! Someone please. Please!" I shrieked.

Charles turned back to face me and said, "Stop that. You're perfectly fine. Now quit—"

He was interrupted by long razor claws severing the arm holding me. I fell back, and then a stream of fire engulfed Charles. The last thing I saw was his smiling face before he dissolved to ash. I was still crying as a jaw snapped forth and ripped what remained of Charles' grip on my arm.

I slowly turned over to see a rather large fox creature bigger and fluffier than any dog I'd ever seen. It stood on long razor claws, and heat radiated from below the jaw. Thicker cream fur formed a sort of mane around the fox's neck.

"E-Eely?" I stammered, failing to collect myself.

"It's okay. It was just a nightmare. What you saw wasn't real," Eely said.

I shook my head, still sniffling. But he... he.

"You're fine. It was all an illusion. See?"

The fox picked up the mirror Charles had been holding, and I looked at it. I saw Roxie again, but I was still shaking.

"An illusion," I muttered.

Felt pretty damn real to me, I thought, as Eely helped me up.

"Where is Kairen?" I asked, looking around.

Dan was still struggling with his chains.

"He went down through the skylight into my bedroom! I think he's trying to find something in the store. Please, Roxie. You have to stop him. He can't go rifling through the store, even a dream version of it. It's just too dangerous!"

I nodded and looked at Eely.

"Go, I'll try to free Dan," she said.

I ran over to the skylight and saw a glass panel that had been lifted when Dan came out. I climbed down into a bedroom that was pretty barren. The walls were painted blue, and there were magazines scattered about on the floor. Over on the wall, a single photograph showing a man and woman standing in a field of some sort. Farmers, I guessed.

That's when I heard a crash downstairs and dashed down into the store below. Coming to a hallway, I saw another open door and ran through it. I entered into a store with three long rows of shelved merchandise, stacked with all sorts of weird items.

And Kairen was rifling through the items by the front door, tossing whatever he didn't like on the floor.

"Hey! That's enough of that!" I shouted.

Kairen looked up with genuine surprise.

"Escaped your nightmare? Didn't see that coming. Who are you, really? Because I sense that like me, you're not supposed to be here."

"I think you should be answering questions first given all the harm you've caused. What are you, and why are you in Dan's nightmare?"

He stopped rifling through the items for a moment and turned to face me.

"You're kind of cute, you know that?" He said, flashing his cocky smirk.

I scoffed, which clearly wasn't the reaction either of us expected.

"Answer my questions!" I shouted. "It's not like you're going anywhere."

"Oh, am I not?" he asked.

Now it was my turn to smile. As my bracelet began to glow, I waved my left arm. A ball and chain appeared, like something out of an episode of *Looney Tunes*. It clamped tight onto his left ankle.

He looked down and tried to lift his leg without success.

"Oh, that's cute. You can alter dreams too, huh? How do I not know about you? Seems two dream runners would have bumped into each other bouncing around sleeping Fayetteville each night, huh?" He said with a sneer. "Oh, I get it. You're new to this thing."

I stammered.

"I am not new! I've been doing this for... a really long time," I said.

"That's why you struggled with my illusions up there? If you've been altering dreams for as long as you claim you have, you shouldn't have spent more than two seconds with that creation of mine."

I looked at the ground.

He's smart, and I hate him for bringing Charles into this, I thought.

"I'll tell you what, cutie. I'll answer a question or two for ya," he said, winking.

I shivered with disgust and thought, *YACK.*

"My name really is Kairen, and I'm a phantom dream thief. I pop into people's nightmares, take advantage of the mental chaos, and steal secrets and other goodies for my boss," he said.

"But why take advantage of other people's suffering? It just seems so wrong," I said.

"I have my reasons just like I'm sure you do. And besides, it's all in their head. It's not like any of the suffering is real, so turn down the righteous judgment a few notches."

I stamped my foot and took a step forward.

"You're wrong! Dreams impact everything from a person's mental health to their health in the physical world. And what damage you cause here leaves scars on a person's heart."

"Barf. Okay goody two-shoes. I've got something important to find for the boss, so what do you say this time I just tie you up like Dan and THEN hand you over to Charles?"

Wait, what? I thought as his earring glowed purple again, and chains shot out of the ground in front of him and flew toward me.

Just before they struck me, they were smashed into the ground by a bunch of fluffy white tails.

"Don't worry, Roxie. I'm here, and I won't let anything happen to you!" Eely said, putting herself between the phantom dream thief and me.

"Eely?" I said as tears started to fall again, more flashbacks to Charles slowly fading from my head.

Kairen frowned and said, "You know, of the two people in this dream I wasn't told about, you've been the most annoying, spirit fox."

"I get told I'm annoying a lot," Eely said and then opened her mouth to let loose a long stream of fire that took up the entire aisle.

The last thing I saw on Kairen's face was a smirk, and then the fire engulfed him. When it finally cleared, he was gone. But I didn't see the same ash I'd seen from Charles earlier.

"He's slick to escape quickly like that. I think I singed him, though," Eely said, slowly shrinking back down to her normal size and plopping down on the ground. She let out a sigh, and I picked her up and hugged her tight.

"You are officially my new best friend," I said, holding the fox close.

"Aw shucks, it was nothing. But if you want to thank me, you can tell me how beautiful I looked in my full form," Eely said.

"Your fur was dazzling," I said, as one of Eely's tails wiped a tear from my left cheek.

"So dazzling!" she said.

"Oh, what about Dan!" I said, turning to run back up to the roof, but he was already coming down the stairs.

"I'm fine. The chains disappeared as soon as he did. Guess I'll have to be prepared for an attack even in my dreams now," he said. "And Eely, this guy must have been a serious threat for you to take that form."

The fox nodded.

Dan and I talked for a long while after that, filling each other in on our stories, how we came to be in our current magical predicaments, and possible motivations for the phantom thief. Dan said he had no idea what the guy was after, but we agreed to both try and track him down to prevent this kind of thing from happening again.

"I don't know how much help I can be from this shop, but if I get any leads, I'll let you know," he said.

"Do you want me to pop in once in a while to discuss updates?" I asked.

"Nah, you can't come to the store unless you need an item from it. And you can only enter once if you do come. Odessa's rules. Speaking of which, I wonder if she'd know anything about this character. Either way, if we want to meet again, it'll have to be in dreams," Dan said.

I slowly nodded.

"I don't care what it takes. Kairen needs to be stopped. It's damaging to dreamers I've promised to protect to just have him out there stirring up nightmares and making things worse for people. There's real consequences to that kind of dream interference," I said.

Dan nodded.

"And the fact that he has a boss is also troubling. It means there's a food chain of villains threatening the safety of people in this city. We need to get some research done and fast, Roxie," Dan said.

"Agreed."

I started to fade a little bit, and I knew that meant the dream was coming to an end.

"Dan, before I go, I really did want to help your nightmare. It's my job, and Eely saved me twice tonight so... I want to help you," I said.

Dan shook his head.

"Kiddo, you're fine. There's nothing you can do to—"

I interrupted him with a wave of my left hand. My bracelet glowed blue and jingled. Suddenly, we weren't in the store anymore. We were up on Mount Sequoyah overlooking the city of Fayetteville.

"I didn't know where you wanted to go, but I figured anywhere but the shop was fine. This is one of my favorite places in town. I love looking down on the city from this view," I said.

Downtown Fayetteville looked smaller from up here. He and I stood on an overhang next to a large white cross that'd been erected some time ago. Locals just called it the Mount Sequoyah Cross. An endless landscape of trees and the Boston Mountains stretched out before us.

"I gotta go, Dan. But I hope the dream will last long enough for you to hang out here for a few moments," I said.

Dan turned to look at me just before I faded away. He had tears in his mismatched eyes.

"Thank you, kiddo," he said. "See ya again sometime."

I woke up in my bed again as I had the previous two mornings. I was still a little sniffly from being haunted by Charles. It was about 6:30 a.m., and I headed out to the bathroom to splash some water on my face and try to forget the horrible things nightmare Charles had said and done to me.

Looking in the mirror I was glad to see Roxie reflected back at me, long chestnut hair and all. I decided after my nightmare I'd soon be dying my hair a vibrant color so I could forget the image I saw in the nightmare mirror.

It was then I noticed some silver roots in my hair. Gently pulling a few and giving them a closer look, I raised an eyebrow.

Isn't 18 a little young to be getting silver hair? I thought.

Splashing water on my face, I put it out of mind and decided I'd fix some breakfast for Mom and me. Then later I'd text Jenna and have her help dye my hair. I probably wouldn't do purple like hers, but this chestnut stuff had to go ASAP.

Chapter Five
(Dan)

Funky Dan's had been open for about three hours when I finished my copy of *Sahara Wildlife Quarterly*. I stood and stretched, my back popping in about three places.

Oh boy did I feel that one, I thought, realizing my ass was asleep because I'd been leaning against that back corner for so long.

But what else could I do? It was my favorite reading spot, as much as I could have a favorite spot in this stuffy prison, anyway.

Eely walked down the middle aisle of the shop and hopped up on the glass countertop.

"You all finished looking at the lions?" she asked.

"Oh yeah. Great articles in here about pride hierarchy. I mean, you wouldn't even believe how complex the lion social dynamic is," I said.

She stretched and swished a few of her tails back and forth.

"I met a lion god back in my shrine days. He was kind of a prick, really thought he was something on the Sahara, spent more time strutting than hunting," Eely said.

"Go figure," I muttered, tossing the magazine in my recycling bin and stretching some more. This time it was my neck that popped.

Oh man, if I could get out of this store, the first place I'd visit would be a chiropractor, I thought. Maybe that's where I'll ask Roxie to take me next.

Walking over to the record player, I opened the large cabinet underneath and went through my collection.

"Let's see... nah, listened to the Jackson Five yesterday, not in the mood for Journey, ah—Billy Joel sounds good," I said, standing up with a copy of *Storm Front*. Putting the needle on the spinning LP, I heard static, and then "That's Not Her Style," started playing as I hummed along.

Walking around the cabinet, I found my thoughts churning as they often did after a long reading session. My head usually felt dizzy and numb for a few minutes after I made the transition back from the reading world to the normal world. It seemed my eyes needed a moment to switch from processing words to physical objects.

I reached into the pocket of my robe and pulled out a postcard from Roxie.

She's dealing with the side effects of using pixie magic, I thought. And while I had tried to warn her about cross species magical contamination in my dream the other night, I was interrupted.

I waited for her in last night's dream to see if I'd get another chance to speak with her, but she didn't appear. Maybe she didn't have control over what dreams she appeared in yet, or perhaps she was simply too busy being the nocturnal guardian of dreams for other people in Fayetteville. With all the thousands of sleeping minds at night, there were surely quite a few nightmares for her to take care of.

Actually, something strange has been in the air over Fayetteville these last couple months. That dream thief breaking into my thoughts last night just reminded me of it, I thought.

I couldn't put my finger on it, but him showing up and ransacking the store... it just seemed like something dark was heating up in this little college town. And I needed to talk to Odessa about it. But she didn't come in yesterday. This put me in a bit of a foul mood because I couldn't walk over to Odessa's shop without dying. But she could pop in whenever she wanted.

That witch, I thought.

Eely's voice snapped me out of my thoughts, "Hey Dan?"

I turned and raised an eyebrow.

"Have you thought about lunch yet? Because I was thinking maybe you could grill the rest of those bratwurst that have the cheese in them before they go bad." Eely suggested, motioning in the direction of the kitchenette.

I did have a little charcoal grill in the backyard, but it was hot, and I didn't want to go out there and start it up. I hated grilling in the summer, and Eely knew that.

"Sleep and food. Do you think of anything else, fox?" I asked.

"Well, a girl's gotta eat. And I figured since those were about to go bad—"

I interrupted her, "You figured you'd send old Dan out into the back yard so he can stand over a hot grill and sweat for an hour to fix you lunch?"

I was a little more cross than I should have been, but Odessa not showing up when I needed her and now Eely pestering me for lunch while there were more important matters at hand, along with the fact that I'd just finished my last magazine were all brewing into something toxic..

"Okay, well it is hot out. But I figured you'd lie around in your pool while cooking them," Eely said.

"I'm not in the mood for that right now," I said, turning back to adjust something on the shelf. It was a black leather glove with red lettering sewn into the back, a foreign language long dead. It didn't need to be adjusted. I was just trying to distract myself and hope Eely would quit bothering me about food.

"If you don't want to grill, what do you want for lunch?" Eely asked, a little disappointment in her voice.

I sighed and said nothing for a moment.

Moving the glove a little to the left, I said, "I'm really not in the mood for lunch right now. I've got too much to think about."

Eely walked over to the edge of the counter.

"Well, I'm hungry, Dan. What do you expect *me* to do? Just open the broom closet and tear into a bag of dog food?" she asked.

Now I turned and scowled at the white fox. We made eye contact, and I let her have it.

"You know what? That would be pretty great, actually. If you could just feed yourself for once instead of always interrupting me and asking for food, that'd be swell. Should I have the grocery delivery person bring a bag of dog food this week so we can try out that new arrangement?"

Eely was not one to take lip from me lying down, so her nine tails poofed up, and I could tell she was angry with my tone. But I didn't care. I had more important things to worry about than feeding that damn fox like some kind of exotic zookeeper.

"That's not fair, Dan! I didn't interrupt anything. I waited patiently for you to finish your magazine because I knew you were enjoying yourself. And while we're discussing things we're tired of, I'm tired of always listening to your whining about being stuck in this shop! I listen to all your complaining about Odessa, and this prison, and how you miss your parents without once complaining myself. But when I ask for lunch once in a while, that's too much for you to deal with? You're such an asshole sometimes, Dan!"

I stormed over to the counter and just glared down at the fox, towering over the creature, which hunkered down and fluffed up all nine of her tails.

Though I would never lift a hand against Eely, it seems my yelling had caused her enough pain today. I'd never seen her agitated like this. But I was still pissed off as well. So instead of arguing any further, I stormed out into the back yard and prayed that fox didn't follow me outside.

As my feet touched grass, I sighed and tried to cool down, which wasn't going to happen since it was about 95 degrees outside. Looking over in the back corner of my yard, I saw Odessa sunbathing on a white folding chair spread nearly flat so she could lie on her stomach. Half of her was covered by spectacled shade from a witch hazel tree that she'd planted there about eight years ago. The irony was not lost on me.

"You've got to be freakin' kidding me, witch. Nearly two days I've been waiting for you to come over here so I could discuss some important things, and now I find you just out lounging in my backyard without a care in the world? How long have you been here?" I yelled.

She didn't move, but the witch did begin to talk. And though she was lying on her stomach, I could still hear her perfectly fine.

"First of all, Daniel, this is my backyard. I own this property like I own you. Second, if you had such a big emergency, why didn't you just send Eely over to fetch me?" she asked.

At the mention of Eely, two thoughts began to fiercely battle for dominance in my skull. One, that was actually a pretty simple idea, and I was stupid for not asking the fox to walk over and fetch her. Two, I was still pissed at Eely and didn't want to think about her right now.

I'm not sure which thought won, but my blood pressure was definitely the loser of that battle either way.

"Let's not talk about that stupid fox right now," I said.

Now Odessa rolled over, her long black hair moving out of the way on its own so as not to get caught in the chair. She was wearing a white tank top and loose ivory capris. She put down a book she had been reading and stretched. Even while relaxed, she sounded terse when she spoke at me.

"Oh, we are going to talk about how you've treated that poor fox, Daniel. But I know you're in a little mood right now, and any lesson I want to teach you would go in one ear and out the other because you have other things on your mind. So ask your questions, but then I'm going to teach you something about Eely and how pathetic that it's been 130 years and you're still the same arrogant, impatient, prick you were when we struck our little deal.."

I took a few steps toward the witch and started to say, "That poor fox?" but she lowered her black sunglasses and stared me down, interrupting me.

"Ask your questions, Daniel."

Her red eyes were nothing if not unnerving, so I stopped. Whatever fire I held in my belly based on Eely's actions had been smoldered.

This witch, I thought. I struggled every day to comprehend the full scope of her powers. Some days I thought she was just a parlor witch, capable of snaring my soul and maybe interpreting dreams. But other times, like with this glare, I believed she could destroy entire mountains if she wanted. Odessa was a mystery I had not even begun to unravel in more than a century's time. But now I had a more pressing matter to solve.

"Very well, witch. My dream was invaded the other night by a thief calling himself Kairen. He was searching the shop for something, and I want to know if you've heard of him. I also want to know if you have a theory about what he was looking for?" I said.

Odessa thought for a moment and adjusted her lawn chair up so it was no longer flat. Then she reached under the chair and pulled out her kiseru, lighting it with a match she pressed it to her mouth, inhaling and exhaling. As she puffed away the smoke took shape, little butterflies dancing around her head, as if they were some kind of progress bar showing she was thinking.

She let out a big puff of smoke and said at last, "But this thief wasn't the only visitor in your dream two nights ago. Who was the other person?"

I squinted and asked, "How did you know that?"

Odessa just looked at me and said, "I can tell when you hide things from me, Daniel. Who was she?"

71

I wondered if Odessa planned to curse me further for setting foot on that mountain and leaving the shop in my dream. Did she intend to hex Roxie for that?

"Don't you dare think of hurting Roxie," I said.

"I have no intention of that. Who is Roxie, and how did she come to enter your dream?"

"I thought you told me to ask the questions. And I want to know about Kairen."

Odessa smiled and said, "Daniel's not going to give an inch until he has the answers he wants. Is that it? Okay then. I don't know this Kairen you speak of. But I have had an uptick in clients coming into the shop with troubling dreams."

I raised an eyebrow.

"An uptick in nightmares?" I asked.

"That's right. Seems people all over the city are having restless nights filled with bad dreams. A few people have nightmares, and that's not news. One or two are unfortunate enough to be plagued with terrible dreams most of their lives. These are all things the pixies tend to handle. But when mothers and fathers, siblings, cousins, neighbors, children, and friends all over the city are having nightmares? That's certainly strange."

I looked down at the ground for a minute and processed this. The uptick in nightmares could be connected to Kairen. Roxie mentioned in her postcard that he takes advantage of nightmares to hop into people's dreams and steal secrets and things for his boss. That's what he told her, and what she told me.

When I told Odessa about this and Roxie, she smoked for another minute in silence.

"So this phantom dream thief is causing nightmares all over the city. I've had several clients wanting dream interpretations describe him to me. Interestingly enough, one of my clients was also a former customer of yours, a man by the name of Richard Sangus," Odessa said.

I thought for a moment and then recalled him.

"Tall muscular bald guy? He was looking for a way to hide the large scar down the side of his face he got from an accident at work. So, I sold him a new face. Guy didn't even blink when I told him his old life would disappear."

Odessa smiled and said, "You really do remember every customer, don't you? Yes, that's him. I suspect when Kairen invaded his dream, he came across powerful memories of that face and learned about the shop and its enchanted items."

I swatted a grasshopper that landed on my shoulder and moved closer to Odessa to get into the shade. This summer sun was killing me.

"So I guess the big questions now seem to be who does Kairen work for, and what was he seeking in the shop?"

Odessa smoked for another minute, more butterflies danced around the yard. I watched as they flapped their wings and then faded into the air.

"We probably need to answer the questions in the order you just asked them. Figure out who Kairen works for, and we'll probably figure out what the thief is looking for."

I nodded and thought, *Well, that does make the most sense. The witch is nothing but logical here.*

"Traveling through dreams is not an ability you or I possess on our own. Your new friend Roxie does it using pixie magic, though that'll cost her soon enough.

You only have one item in the shop that allows for traveling into dreams, and I certainly didn't give Kairen his abilities."

"So who does that leave? A rogue witch or something?" I asked, interrupting Odessa.

Odessa gave me a stare that said, "Don't interrupt me again."

Then, she said, "I know all the witches in Fayetteville, Daniel. This isn't something they have the desire, let alone the ability, to do. So... my money is on the Queen of Tears. I'd say she's finally grown powerful enough to really test the limits of her seal and try to break free."

I had been staring at the grass, but upon hearing this, I glanced back over at Odessa raising an eyebrow.

"That's funny. It sounds like you said the words 'powerful,' 'sealed,' and 'break free.' When you use those words in a sentence, then I start using words like 'scary,' 'threatening,' and 'panic.' So would you care to elaborate more on this... Queen of Tears?" I asked, sweating more from what Odessa was telling me than the summer humidity now. Well... maybe it was about even.

Odessa's eyes shifted to meet mine.

"She's an ancient evil that's sealed under Fayetteville. She predates you and she's powerful, Daniel, even more powerful than me. And it seems she's finally ready to make her move after finding a pawn."

I stood up straight and said, "You know what, witch? I don't recall you having mentioned an ancient evil beneath the city before. It seems like that's the kind of thing you would have mentioned before putting me in a shop here that contains powerful magical relics!"

"Don't be so dramatic, Daniel. It's unbecoming of you," Odessa said, rolling her eyes.

I threw up my arms and sighed.

"Fine. Let's say it's the Queen of Tears, and she is the one who gave Kairen the ability to enter dreams. What is she after?" I asked.

"I imagine she's looking for something to set her free. She and her magic are sealed behind a gate with several thick iron chains. And it's all bound together by one cursed lock. I've laid eyes on it once or twice, and it's easily one of the most powerful enchanted objects I've ever seen," Odessa said. "Crafty stuff."

"So, what? She's looking for the key to open it? Set her magic free?" I asked.

Odessa nodded.

"Seems that way. Though fortunately for us, it's a little complicated. The original key for that lock was melted down by the people who forged it and imprisoned her. So I'd imagine she's looking for another magic key to open it," Odessa said.

I thought about all the magical items in the shop and ones I'd read about through the years, powerful ancient relics I could only imagine. And then it came to me.

"The Ossa Key," I said. "Created by Portunus himself from the spine of a goat. Said to open any lock. I've only ever read about it."

The witch nodded.

"That would probably do the trick and unleash her. And it's likely what Kairen was looking for in the shop. Actually, the Queen of Tears is clever. She knows the shop is warded so only certain people can get in. But protecting dreams is a much more difficult task than protecting a physical space. So she sent Kairen in after your dream to get the key."

Shaking my head, I frowned.

"But that doesn't make any sense. I don't have the key in the shop," I said.

"Yes, but Kairen doesn't know that. And I have a suspicion that key will turn up soon anyway," Odessa said.

"What are you talking about? Why would it pop up in the shop?"

The witch smiled and half emptied her pipe beneath the chair.

"Seems it's fate, Daniel. A pixie gives this Roxie girl the ability and duty to protect dreams, and then she shows up to help you when yours is attacked by Kairen. All this happens as the seal on the Queen of Tears is weakening, and small bits of her magic are leaking through, spreading nightmares through the city. Here is my prediction, Daniel. That key is going to appear in the shop, and you're going to have to choose what to do with it. Your fate is intertwined with Roxie's, and whatever happens to the good people of Fayetteville will depend on the decisions you two make."

I rubbed my temples and tried to process everything she was telling me.

Here is my prediction, I thought. *She's never been wrong when she used those four words around me before.*

I knew Odessa wasn't going to answer any more questions about this supposed decision I was going to have to make. What did she expect me to do? Just hand over the key and unleash an ancient evil? How would that benefit me?

As I sat there thinking over all this fate stuff, Odessa stood up and stretched in the sun. She then turned to me and said, "But there's another part of your dream we haven't discussed, Daniel. Specifically, the part where Eely saved you and Roxie."

Suddenly my thoughts turned back to that furball. I wasn't agitated anymore, though I certainly had even more on my mind than before I talked to Odessa.

I didn't say anything. I expected a stern talking to from Odessa, whether I wanted one or not. But she just walked over toward the shop and lifted the tarp off my little orange charcoal grill.

"Okay already. I'll feed the furball," I said.

"I have no idea what you're talking about, Daniel. I'm going to use this grill to show you something. So come over here," she said.

I walked over as she lifted the lid off and blew charcoal dust off the surface. Then Odessa dumped the remainder of what was in her pipe over the grill and said, "*Ignis Revelare.*"

As her ash hit the surface, it shot up in a vibrant purple flame. I stepped back, not wanting to get any hotter or stickier than I already was. But then I quickly realized this fire offered no heat. And that was fine, given how hot it was outside already.

I stepped forward again as Odessa stirred the flames with her hands into a disk of some sort. The witch ran her fingers through it, creating ripples in the fire.

This was a magic I'd not seen before, so I just waited for Odessa to make her point. And she didn't take long.

"What do you see in the fire, Daniel?"

I squinted and shook my head.

"It's dark. I don't know."

"Look closer," she said.

I leaned in and focussed, my eyes trying to see through the smoke and purple flames. I looked over the grill and through the disk where at last the ripples came to a stop, and the picture grew clearer.

The image showed me some rocks, twigs, gnarled roots, dust, and then I saw it. A white fox had several cubs nestled under her thick fur.

"I see a white nine-tailed fox and several cubs, each with three or four tails," I said.

"Keep watching," Odessa said, pressing her pale thin finger to her lips.

I did as she commanded, and eventually the picture changed. The cubs were just a little bigger now, though still clinging together for warmth. Then the mother stood up and picked one up. She carried it out of the burrow. I waited for a few minutes, and then she came back, picking up the second cub. This went on with all the pups being moved except the tiniest one, the runt with only two tails.

This pup was left alone in the dark. I waited and waited, but the mother did not return. Flames danced around, and, over the popping of the fire, I heard the cub whimper and shiver as winter's chill flooded the burrow.

Now the image seemed to pick up speed as I saw day change to night, night to day, and day back to night. This went on as the cub somehow grew smaller, so small I could barely tell if it was shaking anymore.

"In case you're wondering, the mother does not come back," Odessa said.

I was about to ask something when I heard dogs barking. I looked around the yard, but we were still alone. The sound came from the fire. It was here I saw two hounds digging into the burrow and pawing at the cub. I did not know if the cub was still alive, but it certainly didn't look like it.

The cub's weak cries were drowned out by the digging dogs. But I did not observe the cub trying to move back further into the den.

At last, one dog got close enough to pull the cub out. The picture changed again, and I saw a hunter with his two children. He picked up the cub and looked it over, unimpressed. It did not open its eyes to see him.

The children motioned and cried for the cub, and I figured they were going to take it home as a pet.

"In case you haven't figured it out yet, that's Eely you're seeing, about 300 years ago. She was abandoned by her mother because she didn't think the cub would survive. So she stayed in the burrow shivering and hungry, waiting for death to claim her. Then, the hunter showed up, and he gives in to the whining of his kids, passing the cub off to them. Eely was overjoyed at the prospect of being cared for, even if it meant she would become a pet. Can you imagine how it feels to be so desperate for affection that you're glad when someone offers to take your freedom as a wild and free being and make you a pet?"

I said nothing but continued looking into the fire.

The kids returned home with their father, but their mother refused to allow the animal to stay with them. I didn't understand the language the mother used, but she pointed angrily at the fox cub, even as it whimpered, and jabbed her finger back toward the woods.

Shifting yet again, the image in the fire showed the children taking the starved and dying little fox to a nearby shrine. It was surrounded by a broken fence, and some of the stone pieces of the path were missing. I didn't think it'd been used in decades by the look of it, fallen logs and a nearly collapsed roof.

But the children still put the fox on the front steps and then ran away, believing their duty to be complete.

It was here I watched Eely, abandoned for the second time in her short life, cry out for someone, anyone to come to her aid. It was impossible for me to determine what killed her first, the cold, or hunger. But I watched the fox take her last breath and die even more alone than she started in life.

Dammit, I thought, clenching my right fist.

"Eely's spirit went on to inhabit that temple. Because it was empty when she died there, her spirit resided in that building, unable to move on. Years went by, and the occasional traveler would stop by to offer prayers, maybe even light some incense. She listened to the prayers of hundreds and thousands of people passing by over the next 150 years, but no one listened to her prayers. She blessed many, but in the end, they all left her alone, continuing on their way."

The fire died down some, but the image did not fade. I saw Odessa praying at the temple, and Eely appearing to the witch.

"Like when I found you, Daniel, Eely had a wish of her own. Do you know what it was?" Odessa asked.

I shook my head, looking down at the ground as the witch put my grill top back on, killing the fire.

"She just wanted to be in someone's life. Desperation and loneliness had eroded her standards to such depths, that all she wanted now was the presence of another person. It didn't have to be a friend, certainly not a companion, just someone so she wouldn't be alone anymore."

My heart thumped slowly as I sighed.

"I told her that I'd grant her wish, but like yours, it had a cost. The person she'd be with would be stubborn, ungrateful, obstinate, and would be unlikely to show her an ounce of affection. She told me that it didn't matter, as long as she wasn't alone. So I granted her wish. And I think you know the rest of the story, Daniel," Odessa said.

I nodded and continued to stare off into the grass, feeling like the world's biggest asshole.

"You were a selfish prick in your old life, Daniel. You didn't appreciate when your parents worked hard to send you to college. You didn't really appreciate any of that wealth that fell into your lap thanks to me. And 130 years later, you've yet to learn to appreciate the one friend I gave you in this whole world."

I did not respond. I could not, as it felt like everything from my throat and chest had sunk down into the lowest pit of my stomach. I was a bastard. Maybe I needed to be sealed up in a cave beneath the city, not the Queen of Tears.

"Eely protects you. She listens to your every pain. She keeps you company. All she asks for in return is food. And you had the nerve to complain about that," Odessa said.

"I'm sorry," I said.

Odessa put her kiseru under my chin and lifted my face to meet her own glare.

"I'm not the one you need to apologize to, Daniel. But hear me now. If you make that fox cry one more time, I will cause you such pain, that the worms eating you from the inside out will feel like a summer breeze. Are we clear?" she asked.

"Crystal," I said.

"Good. I'm leaving, but don't forget what we talked about," Odessa said.

I nodded as she walked over to the back gate and exited the yard.

Inhaling and wiping the tear on my left cheek, I put some charcoal on the grill and went back inside to fetch those cheddar bratwursts. I waited for the coals to heat as they turned from black to gray. I seasoned the bratwursts and cooked them until they were popping open and screaming, juices falling into the bottom of the grill. Then I tossed the buns on the grill for a moment. Eely liked her bread crunchy and warm.

When they were finished, I threw on some relish and onions. Then I took them into the shop. The eggshell fox was sitting on the counter facing the front door. I walked over and set the plate down behind her, clearing my throat.

She turned around and looked down at the food and then up at me.

"What changed your mind?" she asked.

"I just realized how terrible I was acting, and I wanted to apologize, Eely," I said, inching the plate toward her.

"That's awfully big of you, Dan. And did you just use my real name instead of calling me furball?"

"Yeah, well, you've put up with me for 130 years. I know I'm not the easiest person to get along with. But you are. So from now on, I promise I won't groan when you ask for meals. I'll happily cook or order whatever you ask for."

Her tails twitched.

"You don't have to do that—"

I interrupted the fox with a gentle pat of her head.

"Yes I do, Eely. You protected me in my dream the other night and even before that. You listen to me whine. You keep me company. And I just think you deserve so much more than what I've given you through the years."

Eely looked down at the food again, then up at me, narrowing her eyes.

"Are you the same Dan that stormed out earlier?"

"What are you—Yes I'm the same Dan! I'm just trying to be a better person," I snapped.

"I don't know if that sounds like something Dan would do," Eely said.

I scowled.

"You know what? Just eat your food I sweated my balls off grilling out in the sun!"

Eely took a bite and waited for me to get quiet again. Then she said, "Well if you're going to turn over a new leaf and try to treat me better, I'd like you to tell me I'm the prettiest fox in the world three times a day."

"Let's not get that crazy," I said, crossing my arms.

Eely whimpered, "But I've been abandoned all my life. I didn't have a mother to tell me I'm pretty or any family to tell me that."

"Fine! I'll tell you you're the prettiest fox in the world once a week."

"Three times a day!" Eely shouted excitedly with a big grin on her face.

Chapter Six
(Roxie)

I ducked left and then right as little goblin-looking things swung swords at me. The little boy behind me screamed as I kept backing him up against the cave wall.

The 20 or so monsters in front of me had green skin that looked like it had been stretched as leather over pointy bones. They contained patches of gray hair here and there and wore shreds of brown fabric across certain parts of their bodies I was happy not to see. The goblins snarled, swung little daggers and short swords at me.

"Wall! We're at the wall!" the boy cried, trying to wipe his nose on his pajamas for the fifth time.

The goblins in front of me snarled, and I got a whiff of breath that could best be described as a mix of rotten cave fish and bitter berries.

"Yack! If I had time, the first way I'd alter this dream would be to introduce toothbrushes. But I still have two more nightmares to hit my goal tonight. So let's finish this," I said, the aqua beads on my right wrist glowing.

It'd been 10 days since Selene had given me the ability to travel into nightmares and fight them back into pleasant dreams. I was terrified at first, but now... things we're slowly getting better. I was learning that if I could imagine it, the bracelet would almost always make it happen in the dream.

And the more time I spent in dreams with this power, the better I felt. I was happy here because it was fantastic. I was helping people on such an epic scale, fighting back their bad dreams! Who would have guessed a teen girl would be given such a responsibility. Most of us are just worried about applying for college and finding summer jobs.

Back in the real world I had a different set of problems to worry about. But here? My problems seemed easier to tackle because I had this magic bracelet. As long as I had it at my side, I felt like I could literally do anything. And here that was probably true. Every morning I came to, I found myself wishing I could use the bracelet to tackle my real-world problems.

"Didn't you hear me? We're out of room to retreat!" the boy screamed behind me.

The goblins advanced and began to chatter excitedly in their own language. I assumed they were talking about dinner.

Not tonight, I thought, my bracelet glowing bright. *Seems I'll need a weapon of my own.*

I thought back, and one came to mind based on a book I'd just finished reading.

"Give me a sword," I said, and the bracelet responded, a glowing white light appearing in my right hand.

A sword hilt wrapped in white bandages took shape with a blue pommel in the bottom. The weapon was missing a blade, and the boy behind me yelled, "I think you forgot half the weapon."

"I didn't forget anything. Just stay calm and watch this, Dillon. This girl's got a few tricks up her sleeve," I said.

The goblins did not seem impressed with my weapon as they kept on with their fighting.

Looking to the left, I looked at the stream the goblins thought had cut off our escape.

I held my empty hilt toward it, and a mass of water immediately flew to the sword as if called by some sorcery. The water glowed a light blue and then solidified into a long and narrow blade of ice.

That looked even cooler than in the panels, I thought, smirking.

Before I could think up a catchphrase, two of the front goblins decided they were done waiting for me to prepare this new weapon.

I blocked both of their daggers with my sword at the same time. They pushed me back an inch until I bumped into Dillon, who was still panicking. Then I pushed back on them, and they fell down.

I stabbed one while he was down and then slashed the other as he was trying to get up.

"There may be 20 of you, but individually you're not very strong," I said, ending another four or five of them.

Now Dillon sounded a little less panicked.

"Get 'em! Get 'em!" He screamed nervously.

The battle continued on for another minute or two, and I felt like I was in a comic book or something.

This is so cool! I thought, slashing goblins left and right.

When about half were left, they looked at each other, and I stepped back to take a breather. Dream combat was cool, but exhausting.

"Are you going to retreat now?" I yelled at them, unable to know if they even understood English.

They let out a unified screech in defiance.

Well, I guess that answers that, I thought.

I stepped back in front of Dillon and smiled, striking what I thought was a cool pose. The goblins raised their weapons and shrieked even louder.

"If you want him... come and claim him," I said, my confidence growing and feeling like a badass for maybe the first time in my life.

The goblins' eyes all glowed red in response. And they ran together in a sort of huddle.

"What are they doing?" I asked.

"Coming to claim me," Dillon said, any confidence I bestowed upon him dwindling once more.

When the light faded, I put my hand down, there stood in front of me a large goblin, whose skin looked somehow even more stretched. It was probably 15 feet tall now and held a two-handed sword of some kind.

"I guess all the daggers came together too," I muttered, looking at my sword in comparison.

The goblins let out a roar, no longer a shriek, and the warm fish breath pushed me back against the wall with Dillon at my side. He covered his ears and fell to his knees.

"I just want this to be over!" he screamed and started crying again.

"Don't count me out just yet," I said and raised my own sword, thinking about something else cool.

My bracelet glowed, and my hair turned pure silver now. With glowing pink eyes, I moved my sword toward the river as the giant goblin took another couple steps forward.

"*Nîn o Chithaeglir lasto beth daer; Rimmo nîn Bruinen dan in Ulaer!*" I recited the words from memory.

"Come on, come on," I whispered as my bracelet glowed, and the water in the stream did as well. A blasting echo of rushing water came through the cavern, and then white foaming waves rushed by in the shape of several galloping steeds.

"Yes! Take that!" I shouted, hopping up and down.

The goblin giant merely watched as the steeds galloped down the stream... about 10 feet to its right. My hope plummeted as I realized this plan would have required him to actually be in the water for that to have worked.

"Well, that was anti-climactic," I muttered.

The goblin giant now turned its attention back to me and started to charge forward again.

"Now what?" Dillon cried.

I squinted forward and held my sword tighter.

"We do this the old-fashioned way," I said, my beads glowing again as I made some protective clothing for myself, a glowing silver shirt appearing around me.

"You're going to find there's more to this girl than meets the eye," I said, charging at the giant goblin.

Our fight lasted for what seemed like several hours. His swings were wide and easy to avoid for the most part. But when he got one, I got swatted against the cave wall and had the wind knocked out of me.

With my shirt, he never got a cut in with that sword, but instead it felt more like a club when it made contact.

Eventually, after enough stabs to the abdomen, he sank to his knees, and that's when I ran up, seeing a chance to end this.

I plunged my sword straight into one of his eyes and used the last of my strength to push it in up to the hilt.

Slime and blood splattered onto my right arm, and I let go of the blade.

Major gross, I thought. But then the giant goblin collapsed face-down on the cave floor, shaking the cavern.

I took a second to kneel and catch my breath. One didn't get hurt in dreams, but nightmares? I was learning if I had to fight, I'd get hurt, and the pain was, though not as intense as it would be in the physical world, still a bit to deal with.

Thankfully, when I exited the dream, the bruises and cuts didn't follow me. And when I appeared in a different dream, I was as good as new.

Limping over to Dillon, I pulled him up.

"Let's get out of here before more show up," I said, winking.

The kid was about eight or nine, and it would make sense he'd manifest a dream like this. But I already knew exactly where those goblins came from. I'd fought them three years ago.

I waved my hand and opened a portal. Grabbing his hand, I pulled him through, and we appeared in a giant silver fountain. The water was cool, and I just decided to lie down in it. It was chilled to the touch and a few inches deep, so it didn't cover all of me, but I was still tired.

I watched Dillon regain his bearings and marvel at the fountain. It had several giant urns shooting water out, as well as grass and trees wrapping around various platforms on one side of the fountain.

The water changed between clear and silver depending on the pulse of the fountain. Neither felt different, and both were cool and refreshing on my various bruises and scrapes.

"What is this place?" Dillon asked.

"Call it a dream fountain, a more appropriate setting for one your age," I said, trying out my best "mom" voice.

"What are you talking about?" Dillon asked, his brown eyes looking over at me.

His red polo shirt was cut on the left side, and his cargo shorts were smudged with cave mud. I sighed and told him to have a seat.

"You know exactly what I'm talking about... young man," I added after clearing my throat. "I've faced those goblins before in *Dungeon Dweller 4*! That game is rated mature for a reason! It'll give you nightmares, kid."

Dillon looked down at the ground.

"All my friends play it. I just wanted to be able to talk with them. But the truth is, I can't go five minutes in the game without turning it off scared to death," Dillon said. "How old were you when you played it? Did you have nightmares?"

I rolled my eyes thinking back to a scared little girl playing *Laughing Slaughter 2: Blood Curse*.

"The point is you wait until you're older to play those games, Dillon. Otherwise, you'll have more nightmares like this. And I may not come along to rescue you next time," I said, side-stepping his questions.

Dillon nodded.

"Promise me you're done with *Dungeon Dweller 4*... at least for another few years," I said.

"I promise," he said.

"Hey, I'm up here. Look me in the eye and promise me," I said, throwing that added line in there for maximum "mom" effect.

He looked up and said, "I promise."

Nodding, I said, "Good. I'm out of here."

I slowly rose and stretched. Then, I jumped off the side of the fountain and fell into the galaxy of stars below.

Feeling that familiar falling feeling, I "landed" on my bed and gasped.

"I had no idea if that would work or not," I muttered.

Looking over at my white glowing Sailor Moon alarm clock, I saw it was about 3:12 a.m. Smiling, I exhaled and said, "Good timing on that one."

Selene hadn't really given me an instruction manual for these abilities. I was kind of left to learn everything outside of the magical words to enter dreams and the basic fact that I could manipulate them with my bracelet.

Lately I was learning that if I was efficient with my time, which somehow flowed different than real world time, I could hit two or even three nightmares in a night and help even more people. I felt like I was using the bracelet's power even more to accomplish this, but so far it hadn't given me any indication it was running out of juice.

Pulling out my compact, I looked into the glass and said "*Ambulate per somnia.*" The vision revealed to me as my reflection faded was of a forest under a stormy night sky. Pine trees were pushed nearly to a breaking point by wind, and lightning flashed out from the compact.

"This ought to be interesting. Let's hope there's no goblins this time," I said. "*Immeo.*"

I wonder if I'll run into Kairen again, was my final thought before vanishing into the nightmare.

Four hours later I reappeared on my bed and fell backward stretching.

Holding my sword steady, I took a deep breath and prepared to defend this boy, only to have my consciousness slingshotted... somewhere.

I can't say for certain because I'd never had this happen, but I figured this must be what it feels like to have a pickup truck drive by on the interstate and toss a rope around your body. One second your body is at rest. The next? You're a body in motion. Mr. Wetzel would be so proud of me. Now if I were in class I would never remember any of Newton's laws in class. My brain just thought about cookies.

What followed took place over an unspecified period of time. I was learning that's how the passage of time in dreams felt... unspecifieds.

The feeling of being yanked forward by an invisible bungee cord finally ceased, and eventually the visions started.

I found myself in a dark throne room of some old castle. Shadows crept around me, and somewhere I heard a child weeping. Whispers of tears and a dark queen rattled through my ears. Where was I?

Finally locating the source of the weeping, I saw a large cage, thick metal bars encasing a kid I'd never seen before. I took a step toward him, starting to assume this was another nightmare to fight, but that invisible rope yanked me forward again. Everything went blurry, and I dropped my sword back in the castle.

Echoes of an ice blade striking stone were the last thing I heard before leaving the dark throne room behind entirely.

My setting changed again, and when the darkness parted, I could hear a steady beeping. The smell was unmistakable, a sanitized environment with a hint of senior citizen. I was in a hospital.

Once my eyes were able to focus, I saw that I was standing next to a little boy in a bed. There were tubes hooked up to him, and he appeared to be sleeping, a coma perhaps?

I eyed his blond bangs and then happened to glance up at whoever was slumped over on the other side of the bed.

My heart jumped into my throat, and it took everything I had to keep from screaming. Sitting across the bed was none other than Kairen, the phantom thief.

He had his right arm on the bedframe, and his left was grasping the younger boy's hand.

What are you doing here? I thought. *What dream am I in right now? Am I in Kairen's dream? Is he sleeping in his own dream?*

I froze like a statue, not wanting Kairen to wake up and try to hand me over to a dream version of my father again. Lord knows I still had mental scars from the last time. But looking at Kairen, I almost felt like there was a human side to him that hadn't showed up in Dan's nightmare. It was like the boy lying across from me wasn't the same one that attacked us. At least, he certainly wasn't wearing his ridiculous outfit with the top hat. He was scowling, and some part of me suspected he had even been crying before I arrived.

Leaning over, I saw he still had the dragon earring, though. It was curled up on his ear, like it was watching me even as its wearer was asleep.

Then I looked back at the little boy under the blue scratchy blanket, the one hooked up to beeping machinery. I had no idea what was wrong with him. But he was asleep, right? Was he dreaming?

Cautiously, my hand hovered over his forehead. I looked at Kairen as he might snap awake and attack me at any moment. What was this kid to him?

Gently, I placed my fingers on his head. Then I closed my eyes. I wasn't sure if this would do anything, but I didn't have any other ideas to figure out what was going on.

With just the slightest focus on this little boy's thoughts, a pocket of electricity shot through into my brain, somewhere between a static shock and a bolt of lightning.

Simultaneously, I felt an overwhelming sense of dread grasp my heart and a giant purple moon in the sky filled my mind's eye. I couldn't look away from the moon, not with all my strength.

And just before I blinked, the lasso lurched me forward again, only this time I flopped down onto my bed, belly up.

I took in a sharp breath, looking around. My eyes went to my Shakira poster and then to the mermaids under my legs, all of King Triton's daughters. Kairen and the hospital were gone. Pinching myself, I determined I was awake, and morning had come.

Chapter Seven
(Roxie)

My back must have popped in about seven places as I stretched. I didn't know if that was good or bad. While I was busy cracking my vertebrae to Kingdom Come, my phone buzzed.

Jenna had texted me to see if we were going to have a final practice this afternoon.

I texted back, "No. If I tire myself out with rehearsal, I won't last for the full hour show tonight."

"Gotcha," Jenna texted back and added a smiley face.

I looked at my calendar app already knowing what was on it. There was an entry under 7:00 p.m. that read, "Play Bobbie Barnstun's birthday bash."

Bobbie was a classmate and ex-boyfriend of Tessa's. He also happened to be the son of Fayetteville Mayor Leo Jordan. He was a rebellious cliche as far as I was concerned, had long stringy black hair, often wore what he referred to as "guyliner," and smoked enough pot that you could smell it on him two or three times a week.

He and Tessa were on good terms, though. And he claimed to be a big fan of our music.

"Oh Bobbie," I sighed and looked over at my drumsticks on the desk next to my bed. They sat next to the postcard with a lion on it that Dan had sent me updating me on what he'd learned about the Queen of Tears. But that wasn't on my mind at the moment, the concert was. Priorities.

Part of me was nervous as heck because it was going to be a huge party up at Hilltop Country Club on the south edge of Fayetteville. It was certainly out of left field given Bobbie's persona, but he was actually a fantastic golfer. He was at the top of the school team.

How that kid hasn't been drug tested is beyond me, I thought until I remembered his dad was the mayor.

"Right," I said and came out of my room and into the bathroom. It was there that I was in for maybe my fourth or fifth shock of the month.

"Bah!" I said, looking at my hair. A couple days ago, my roots had subtly changed to silver. I made a joke about old age and moved on, trying to forget it like I did my temporarily colored eyes.

Now my whole head was covered in luminescent silver hair. It didn't quite glow like my eyes did that one time, but my heart skipped a beat nonetheless.

"How am I going to explain this to mom?" I quietly panicked.

A knock at the door further sent my pulse skyrocketing.

"Morning, Priss. Don't forget you promised to help me with grocery shopping today. So when you're done showering and getting ready, come find me so we can go," Melanie said.

I had my hands over my mouth and realized she was probably expecting an answer, so I let out a high pitched, "Yes ma'am!"

"Love you, sweetie," she said and walked away.

I slowly caught my breath and sighed.

I mean... I had asked Jenna to help dye my hair today, so maybe this isn't so bad? I thought.

Then I stood there for a moment trying to figure out if I hated the color. And the truth was, I really didn't. My hair was still the same style, shoulder-length with light bangs that partially covered my eyes. It's just... now it was this brilliant silver. The hair caught me by surprise, but when I calmed down I had one more shock waiting for me as I saw my reflected pink eyes.

"Oh no no no no no no no," I whispered, getting closer and closer to the mirror.

Pink eyes AND silver hair? People are going to think I'm cosplaying on my way to a convention or something! I thought, angrily.

"How do these changes keep happening?" I asked my reflection. She did not answer, but I suddenly recalled how Selene looked the first time she revealed her pixie form. The pixie had silver hair and glowing pink eyes like I did now.

"She did *not* mention any side effects," I thought, stomping my left foot.

Shaking my head, I saw my silver bangs dance around my forehead.

"If magical bracelet causes your hair and eyes to change after 10 days of use, please consult your physician. Common side effects of pixie magic include mild to severe constipation, and loss of sleep can be common," I mocked myself in the mirror.

At last I stopped and held my head in my hands. I had a headache, so I popped some Advil and started the shower with the hope it would wash whatever wasn't out of my hair. Turning off the lights real quick, I checked to see if my eyes glowed. Thankfully, they did not.

Yet, I thought, turning them back on and heading back over to the shower.

No amount of shampoo, conditioner, and scrubbing removed the silver from my hair. And I began to think about dying it again.

After showering and doing my makeup, I decided to blow dry my newly colored hair, praying pixie colored hair wasn't flammable. It didn't feel like it normally did. The hair felt silkier, like the girls on those shampoo commercials who made promises about your hair that'll obviously never come true.

Well, I guess this is me now, I thought.

And honestly? It could be worse. I could have wings or an antenna or shrink down to three inches tall like Tinkerbell. Two of those things didn't happen to Selene, but this was magic I was dealing with. I met a talking fox the other night and traveled through dreams. Who knew what else was possible?

Cautiously walking down into the kitchen, I saw Mom was sitting in the living room watching television. I was quiet as I headed in to fix me some toast. But as I expected, opening the squeaky bread box got her attention.

"There you are, Miss Priss. Whoa," she said, as I clenched my shoulders tighter than I ever knew they could go.

I slowly turned around as Mom walked into the kitchen to get a better look at me. Saying nothing, I just waited for her reaction.

She looked my hair over and then down at my face.

"Really liked the silver after those highlights, huh?"

"Uh... huh," I said, quietly.

"When you told me Jenna was going to help you dye your hair, I didn't know you were going to do anything more than highlights. And to be honest, I wasn't entirely sold on the silver roots. You looked like that girl... what's the one from X-Men? The skunk head?"

I coughed and said, "Rogue?"

"Yeah, her. But now that you went ahead with the full color..." she trailed off.

I waited patiently for her next words.

"I kinda like it. It's really shiny and soft," she said, running her fingers through it. "How did you get it so sleek?"

"... Jenna's a talented girl," I said. "You know she wants to go to beauty school after high school."

Mom nodded and finished playing with my hair.

"Well, maybe I should have her do mine or something. She nailed yours," Mom said.

I stepped back and turned around to put my honey wheat bread into the toaster.

"Hey, and you be careful with those color changing contact lenses, Priss. I've seen reports on the news that those can get infected easily. So be smart, okay?" Mom said.

"Ye-yes ma'am," I said, waiting for my bread to pop up.

I ate breakfast, and then we went grocery shopping. I sent some texts to Jenna, telling her not to worry about dying my hair after all. I kept nervously looking at my phone expecting a Bible verse from Charles to pop up. But he hadn't gotten through since I blocked him.

I still occasionally smiled at that, wondering if he knew he was blocked. Did his messages get kicked back to him saying, "Sorry, this number has blocked you"? I didn't know. But I shuddered at the thought of him getting mad at not being able to text me and just showing up one day for a visit. I mean, he knew where Mom and I lived.

What would I say if he showed up? I didn't want to even think about whether I'd have the guts to tell him off.

Tessa and Jenna were kicking around a finalized set list for tonight in the group text, but I wasn't really paying attention that much. I'd just go with whatever they picked out and be happy to be playing.

After grocery shopping I rested for a bit, then Mom fixed lunch. The rest of the afternoon went by quickly as butterflies continued to fill my stomach.

I went over and walked Rufus and watered Miss Michelle's garden after I found a note from her that her son wouldn't be coming until tonight. She was actually upstairs napping when I took Rufus out.

Then I went back home and rested some more. Well, half rested, half drummed onto my black practice pad sitting in my lap. When Mom shot me a glance to say she'd had enough of that, I decided to get ready for the show.

After putting my hair up in a ponytail and deciding on a gray eyeshadow, I put on a cherry red lipstick. Then I hopped into a pair of loose pink jeans and a black T-shirt with a Hellcat on the front.

Painting my nails took the longest, because I put a little star design on top of my usual black.

Heading out into the living room, Mom got a look at me and said, "You know there are other nail polish colors than black, right?"

"These are different. See? I painted little stars on them," I said, showing her.

"I stand corrected," she said, turning the television off.

I went and grabbed my favorite drumsticks, the CooperGroove Performance with easy grips. Stuffing them into my black leather purse, I slung it around my neck as I got a text from Jenna.

"They're here," I said.

"Okay. And you're sure you don't want help loading the drums?" Mom asked.

"I'm good, Mom. We got it," I said, kissing her on the cheek and opening the door that led from the kitchen down into bay two.

I opened the bay door, and outside was an impatient Tessa, full blown cheerleading squad schedule mode.

"Girl, we've been down here for— Jenna?"

"Two minutes and 57 seconds," Jenna said, checking her phone and giggling.

Then they both looked at my hair and stood there with their jaws open.

"Wow! I never would have expected you to go with silver. I figured you'd dye it blue or something," Tessa said.

Jenna stepped closer and nodded.

"It looks great, Rox. You get this out of a box?" she asked, feeling the hair.

"No, I... um, couldn't wait for you because of a nightmare I had. So I ran into a salon and got it done," I lied.

Jenna stuck out her bottom lip.

"You went to some... cheap parlor maid to have your hair styled instead of coming to a trusted friend like me? I'm so crushed, Roxie!" she fake sobbed.

Tessa rolled her eyes and was instantly back in cheerleading schedule mode.

"Come on, you two! We're going to be late for sound check. And I want to run through the final set list one more time," she said.

"Oh my God! If I hear the word setlist one more time, I'm going to scream. It's all you've talked about tonight," Jenna said, elbowing Tessa.

"Well it's an important show! Bobbie's paying us good money, and there will be lots of people there," she said.

"You sure you're not just worried about impressing your boyfriend?" Jenna leaned in close and whispered.

Tessa pushed her face away and said, "Get real, girl. That yahoo had his chance."

I laughed, and Tessa started over toward my drumset.

"Okay, let's get these loaded into the battle van," she said.

I walked over to pick up the bass drum, and Jenna crept up behind me going, "Nu uh! No heavy stuff."

I sighed and said, "Thanks for the reminder, MOM."

"Melanie would kill us if she saw us letting you pick up some of this stuff. So be a dear and grab your kickstand or stool or something," Jenna said.

I rolled my eyes and grabbed my stool. When we were all packed, we hopped into the battle van. It was actually an orange Ford Econoline E-150 from the 80s. It was a miracle the thing still ran. Mom had fixed it once or twice for Jenna. But she loved it. Inside, she had the works, shag carpet in the back, fuzzy dice under the mirror, and one of those horns that played the Bugs Bunny hat dance song. Tacky wasn't a strong enough word for this vehicle.

But it carried all of our equipment without complaint, so I said nothing. Tessa liked to tease Jenna about it often, though.

"You are never going to find a girl that wants to spend half the night together on the shag carpet, Jenna," she teased.

Jenna would just roll her eyes and rub the steering wheel saying, "Don't listen to her. You're a great vehicle, battle van."

Mom texted me and said, "Have a great show, Miss Priss <3"

I smiled as I put on my seatbelt, and Jenna turned on the radio to KASS 97.1 FM, the local alternative station. Some song by Paramore was playing, but I didn't know the title. Jenna and Tessa sang along in the front seats as we turned onto Highway 71 heading south.

The battle van handled heading up to Hilltop like a pro, and Jenna rubbed the steering wheel as we parked.

"Good job, baby," Jenna said.

Tessa made a gagging noise and hopped outside.

"You can walk your ass home," Jenna said as she opened the back doors.

The parking lot was fairly empty, but Bobbie walked over from the front doors and met us. He was wearing a My Chemical Romance t-shirt and purple skinny jeans.

"Hey ladies. You ready to rock?" he asked.

Okay, he's pretty cool, I thought, trying to avoid getting a little crush on Tessa's ex. She put her hands on her hips and smiled.

"Happy birthday, Bobbie," Tessa said, giving him a hug and kiss on the cheek.

"I was kind of hoping you'd wear your cheerleading outfit for the show," he said, smirking.

"Yeah well, even birthday wishes have limits don't they?" Tessa said, feigning disappointment.

Jenna laughed and started to unload my drums.

Bobbie walked over and then stopped.

"Can I help with your drums?" he asked, waiting for my answer before taking another step.

"Yes thanks," I said quietly.

"Cool nails," he said, and grunted as he grabbed the bass drum.

"Thanks," I said even quieter.

Tessa handed me her guitar case and said, "Why don't you grab this, and I'll carry the ride cymbal and floor tom?"

"O-okay," I said, still not used to people carrying stuff for me, best friends or otherwise.

It was at this point I realized Tessa was wearing that necklace I made her. She caught me staring at it and said, "Good luck charm for the big show tonight."

I smiled.

Bobbie led us in through the front lobby and back to a large ballroom with a red carpet. There was a raised platform at the front of the room that would act as a stage for us. Above us hung a large crystal chandelier. In the back of the room were a bunch of little round tables with folded napkins on them.

"Yeah, therey're little fancier than I wanted, but you know how my dad is," he said.

I actually did not know his dad that well. But I assume he wanted to have a fancy party, and relented when Bobbie suggested some compromises.

Black balloons and streamers hung on the ceiling with a large white banner that read, "Bobbie Badass Birthday Bash."

He caught me laughing at it and said, "Dad hasn't seen it yet. I'm taking bets on how long it'll take him to notice."

"Put me down for five minutes," I said, heading back outside with the girls.

Half an hour later we were set up and doing our first sound check playing through "Glitter Choke."

My nerves faded as I played with Jenna and Tessa. As long as they were by my side, I felt like I was on solid ground. Put us together playing? That got dialed up to nearly invincible.

Bobbie walked up when we finished and looked at all of us.

"Dope," he said. "I can't wait to hear more."

Tessa just smiled back down at him and said, "Honey, you'd best be ready to have your little party blown away."

Jenna put her hands on her hips and said, "Yeah, bro, we rock. Tell your friends."

He pulled out his phone and said, "I'll text them now and tell them to expect a dank show."

"How many people do you think he will have here?" I asked as he left.

Some nerves were starting to come back as I realized we had stopped playing and now there would be people coming in over the next hour.

"I wouldn't worry about it, Rox. His popularity never recovered after dating Tessa. Some say he doesn't actually have any friends," Jenna said.

Tessa had been fussing with her red hair, but now she was showing Jenna a nice view of her left hand with only one finger sticking up.

I took a deep breath and stretched, trying not to let my nerves get the best of me. I went and got a drink of water, and as I got back to the platform the first guests were arriving. Bobbie greeted them all.

By 7:00 p.m. it seemed like at least a third of the high school was here, along with a few adults I guessed were family. Jenna and Tessa had been brave enough to go say hi to some people, but I just sat on my stool.

I occasionally scanned the crowd forming, but I didn't see much of anything until the last sweep about 30 seconds before we were set to start playing. I saw a familiar face looking up at me from the crowd, a smirking jerk with jet black hair just long enough to cover his ears.

Jumping up, I nearly crashed a cymbal over.

The jerk was missing his top hat and tuxedo, but when I saw him lift his hair up, sitting on his left ear was a familiar golden serpent wrapped around the edge of his ear.

Did he show me that on purpose so I'd recognize him? What is he doing here? Are these people in danger? I asked myself.

Even without his tux, Kairen still looked pretty snazzy in his shiny black pants, button down white shirt and black vest.

As Tessa and Jenna slung their instruments over their shoulders I was about to run into the crowd, but Kairen just put a finger to his lips.

"You ready, Rox?" Jenna asked.

"Huh?" I looked up at them with a blank expression and then realized Bobbie was waiting to announce us. "Oh yeah, I'm good," I said sitting down again.

This time when I scanned the crowd, Kairen was gone.

He can't do anything if we're all awake, right? I thought.

Tessa winked at Bobbie, and he walked over to the microphone.

"Everyone, thanks for coming to my 18th birthday party! I know it's hot as Hell, but I hope you're ready for it to get a little hotter as these ladies rock out the room," he said.

And, to my surprise, everyone cheered.

"Please welcome to the Bobbie Badass Birthday Bash. Put your fists in the air and get ready to be rocked by Nighttime Whispers."

Right out of the gate, we wasted no time getting started with Tessa kicking off her guitar intro on "Glitter Choke." I was feeling a little sloppy as my thoughts drifted back to the thought of Kairen standing in the crowd. My heart felt like it was going to rip out of my chest like a Xenomorph would or something. Jenna seemed to notice and turned to me for a moment playing with her back to the crowd.

We made eye contact, and Jenna made a breathing motion with her lips, in and out. "Take it easy," she mouthed.

I nodded and closed my eyes, doing my best to push all thoughts away except for the drums in front of me. Half way through the song, I found my way, and Jenna smiled. She winked at me and then turned back around.

When we finished our first song, my ears seemed to stop for a moment. Was I deaf? Slowly, it came back to me, and I opened my eyes. That was... cheering? As my vision focussed, I saw a couple hundred of my classmates clapping, cheering and whistling.

Tessa turned around to me and mouthed, "You good?"

I nodded and exhaled. It seemed like I'd been holding my breath for the entire song. And now I could breathe.

Jenna moved to her microphone and said, "Thank you so much. This next one is a song I wrote about a dream I had where I rode on a horse across the sky at dawn. I don't know how to ride a horse, and I don't know what I ate before bed that night... but here's 'Glistening Steed'."

The crowd died down and listened to our power ballad. I closed my eyes again, and somehow playing the drums was a little easier. It went on this way for the next half hour as we played through "Full Moon Kisses," our cover of Heart's "Magic Man," and wrapped up the first half with "Should Have Kissed Me Yesterday."

I was tired. Half an hour had gone by, but it honestly felt like I was giving my energy to the crowd. And I was happy because they kept asking for more of it.

Bobbie came back onstage and continued clapping.

"How about another round of cheers for our very own Nighttime Whispers? They were amazing!"

Our classmates seemed to agree and cheered even louder through the ballroom. I pondered about how much more noise they'd have to make to shatter the chandelier above.

"Okay we're gonna give these ladies a little break while we cut the cake. And man, you should see this thing. It's the biggest cake ever made by Don's Bakery. Everyone will get a piece, so don't worry. Just please head to the back of the room so we can light candles and sing happy birthday to yours truly," Bobbie said, with a little bow.

People started to shuffle toward the back of the room, and I watched Jenna and Tessa take off their instruments. They came over to me, and Tessa was squealing with delight.

"Did you see that? They love us! I can't believe—Oh wow, I'm still shaking!" the cheerleader said.

"Okay girl. Just breathe. Rox, how are you doing? Do you want some water?" Jenna asked. "Do you need to go lie down for a few minutes and recuperate?"

I squinted.

"Did my mother put you on mom duty tonight?" I asked.

She shook her head.

"Melanie just asked Tessa and I to keep an extra eye on you tonight. It's your first show since the surgery, so we're just making sure you're good. I'm also picking up the slack because Tessa is too busy thinking about whether Bobbie is going to kiss her after the show."

She was posting something on her phone when she heard the last part.

"What? Hey! You listen here. I am absolutely not hoping for that. And I care just as much about Roxie. I'd murder for her. But I know she's tough, you know? There's no need to baby our friend. If she needs help, she'll say so. Won't you, Roxie?"

I looked over at her after scanning the crowd.

"Ohuh? Yeah, definitely. I'd tell you," I said, nodding.

"See? Our girl's perfectly fine," Tessa said, pointing at me.

Jenna raised an eyebrow.

"You know what? I think I'm going to get some air. Why don't you two go check out the cake?"

They exchanged glances, and Tessa pulled Jenna off the stage.

"Give her some space. Let's go see if that cake really can feed everyone."

I slowly stood up, feeling a little soreness in my bits. But for the most part, I was just tired. Still, I had to find Kairen before he could do... whatever it was he planned to do.

I cautiously stepped off the platform and looked around.

"No, he wouldn't be in the crowd. That'd be too obvious. He's lurking somewhere looking for me to find him because he wants my attention for some sick reason," I muttered.

I checked around in the lobby, a couple hallways, the bar, and he just wasn't anywhere to be found.

Could he actually be in the crowd planning something? I thought.

Heading outside, I found him rather easily. He was on the phone, facing away from me. I crept closer, trying to avoid stepping on twigs and leaves.

I didn't know what I intended to do if I caught him by surprise. It wasn't like I could spawn chains out of nowhere like in a dream. Of course he couldn't do anything, either, as far as I knew. Maybe I should just try to listen for now, and I'd think of something later.

"Okay, I understand. Thanks for updating me, doctor. Please keep me posted," he said and lowered his phone.

I held my breath as he continued to touch his phone, maybe checking social media? I couldn't tell.

"You going to say hi, cutie? Or do you just want to keep staring at my butt?"

I blushed.

"I was not—There's no way I would be looking at your butt!" I said, walking around to point my finger in his face. "And stop calling me disgusting things like 'cutie.'"

He shrugged and apologized.

"It's just, you didn't give me your name before the fox blasted me with fire. Neat trick, by the way. So if you don't tell me what to call you 'cutie,' what should I call you?" he asked.

"You can call me Roxie, and you should know that whatever your plan here is tonight, I'm going to stop you!"

He gave me that cocky sneer again, and I frowned. I hated that look! It just made me want to slap his stupid face.

"So you're going to stop me, huh?"

"That's right!"

"Do you know what my plan is?"

"N-no. But I'll stop it anyway," I said, backing up a few steps and lowering my finger.

He chuckled and looked inside.

"Believe it or not, I don't actually have any plans tonight but to eat cake and celebrate Bobbie's birthday. He's a good friend of mine," Kairen said.

"If that's true, then why haven't I ever seen you around before? At the school?"

"I'm homeschooled," he said, crossing his arms.

I looked at the ground for a moment.

"Oh." I muttered.

He laughed again and said, "How about this? You and I can't do anything to each other here in the physical world. So why don't we make a truce?"

"Excuse me?" I asked.

"Yeah, why not? You don't seem like a bad person, just a doofus. And I'm not all that evil myself. I'm just a middleman taking orders," he said. "So why not form a truce as long as we're not in the world of dreams and nightmares?"

I took a deep breath. Could I trust Kairen? Was anything he said true? It was true he'd caused me a lot of pain in the nightmare by summoning Charles, but it felt different. Rather, it didn't feel as though his actions carried malicious intent

Thinking back to my vision, I remembered seeing him in the hospital. There wasn't any evil there. Just pity.

And what choice did I really have? Reject the truce and then try to restrain him? Call 911 and tell them he's causing nightmares all over Fayetteville?

"You're just a middleman taking orders..." I said quietly.

"Yeah, that's what I said."

"But it's still wrong, Kairen! The person you're taking orders from is the Queen of Tears. She's evil, and your abilities hurt innocent people. So you can't just be aloof with that smile and pretend it's all fun and games," I blurted.

That arrogant smirk of his disappeared.

"You did your homework, huh?"

"That's right! And now that you know she's evil, you have to stop doing what you're doing!" I said.

Kairen sighed and said, "It's not that easy, Roxie."

"How could it not be that easy? You realize your boss is evil, you destroy that earring, and you live happily ever after without doing any more bad things," I said.

The sneer came back for a moment. Then it vanished again as Kairen sat down on a nearby wheel stop. He motioned to the wheel stop to his right for me to join him.

I cautiously took a few steps over and looked at the curb stop. There didn't appear to be any trap on it.

I slowly sat down and looked over at him with a raised eyebrow.

Kairen pulled up his phone and showed me his lockscreen. It was a photo of him and some boy a few years younger than him. The boy had spikey blond hair and a smile twice as wide as Kairen's. They were both holding up some catfish, and Kairen's was smaller.

"That's me and my little bro Jonas on a fishing trip last summer up in Missouri," he said.

"You both look happy," I said.

"That little guy is a big part of my world. And... I don't have him with me anymore," Kairen said.

I put a hand on Kairen's shoulder awkwardly and said, "I'm sorry for your loss."

He shook his head and said, "Jonas isn't dead. He's just... asleep. He's been in a coma up at Fayetteville General Hospital for about four months now. He went in for a simple operation, and the doctors just haven't been able to wake him up since."

"I'm sorry," I said.

Kairen shook his head.

"My dad and I run the bookstore on Dickson Street. It's all he can do to bury himself in work and try not to be sick with grief every hour of every day. That's when the Queen of Tears came to me in a dream. She told me she's the only one who can wake Jonas up. But she can't do it from where she's sealed. That's why I'm going to free her and wake up my little bro," Kairen said.

What was I supposed to say to that? Should I just tell Kairen to stop and expect his little brother to stay in a coma forever? I knew the Queen of Tears had to be lying, but I also knew I had to be careful in how I relayed that to him.

I sighed and looked down at the ground.

"It really isn't simple, is it?"

Kairen shook his head again.

I pulled my hand back and thought for a few minutes. Then I told him, "I accept your truce for as long as we're in the real world, Kairen."

He met my eyes and nodded.

"But I can't allow you to go about hurting people with nightmares," I said, softly.

A tear slid out of Kairen's left eye. It was fast and dropped to the pavement below.

"And I can't allow you to stop me from saving my brother, Roxie.

I don't care how many people I have to hurt. No cost is too great to save him. Do you understand?"

His earring glowed purple as he stood up. My bracelet glowed blue as I stood to match him.

Before I could say anything else, I heard Bobbie's voice come over the speakers.

"Would the silver-haired drummer girl please come to the stage. Your drumset is about to be towed."

"Oh crap!" I said and looked at Kairen again.

"This isn't over," I said.

"It is tonight," he replied.

It took everything I had to run back to stage as I told myself he wasn't going to hurt anyone at the party. Afterward though... no! I had to finish the gig.

"And there she is!" Bobbie said, as I came into view.

Tessa held out a hand and helped me back on the stage.

"You good?" Jenna asked.

I nodded and took my seat behind the drums again.

"Okay, please welcome back to my birthday stage, Nighttime Whispers!"

The clapping started again, and Tessa counted down as I kicked off our next song, "Dragons Paint Their Nails Too."

Every time Kairen popped up in my mind, I shoved it away as violently as I could. And I did my best not to cry while playing. I closed my eyes several times and tried to breathe.

Somehow, I finished the set over the next 30 minutes without completely screwing up any songs. Jenna turned around a couple times, mainly when Tessa had a solo. I'd always nod at her to let her know that I was okay.

Second time I've lied to her, I thought.

When we finished our last song, the crowd cheered its loudest yet. And while Tessa was busy telling everyone where they could find us on social media, I stood up and started off the stage.

"Rox?" Jenna asked.

"Bathroom," I said and left.

When I dashed into the women's room, I saw it was empty. And I was glad for that. I grabbed some tissues and wiped my eyes. I was having trouble focusing. I just kept seeing that picture of Kairen and his brother. Who was I to stop that? Didn't that make me the villain? Selene didn't mention that I'd have an antagonist. She just said to make nightmares into dreams.

But if Kairen's every day was a nightmare waiting for his brother to wake up, how did I change that for him? Was I expected to rob him of his happiness to keep this Queen of Tears sealed?

I sank to the floor and sobbed as these questions crushed me inside. I barely noticed the bathroom door open and the sound of boots coming across the floor.

"You seem to be a little lost, mister" a man's voice said.

I looked up confused and saw a face I tried to place. Wait—why was he here in this bathroom?

The man standing before me was tall and had short brown hair buzzed military style. He was wearing a blue button down shirt with a truck logo on it and jeans.

At last I recognized him. He was in some car commercials that played in between the local news segments Mom watched at night. He owned a big car lot. Parker Motors. He was the father of Matt and Jason Parker. He spoke again, louder this time. I could smell alcohol on his breath. Beer and lots of it.

"I said, you seem a little lost, mister."

"What?" I asked.

"My sons told me about you. The faggot of Fayetteville High. You dress like a girl, and I have to admit, you kind of look like one. But under all that makeup and clothing, you're a regular boy, ain't ya? Well, not regular. You're a freak, but still very much a guy."

"I don't think you should be in here," I said, softly.

"What's that? Speak up, boy!"

"Stop calling me that!"

"Ah, he does have some lungs. I came in here because I figured you might be up to no good, peeking at girls in the bathroom while pretending to be one yourself. You know, I gotta say, if I could have just claimed to be transgender in high school and snuck into the girl's locker room, I definitely would have. It's actually pretty clever."

"That's not—"

"Enough boy. I'm not going to sit here and listen to your lies about being mentally ill and really a girl inside or whatever crap you're peddling. Point is, I caught you in a women's bathroom looking to spy like a pervert. And we got rules against that here at the country club. There's standards, ya know," he said.

Then he grabbed me by the collar of my shirt and jerked me to my feet.

"You're leaving right now, pervert.. What if my daughter had been in here, you sick freak?"

I tried to speak up, but the truth was, I was terrified. I'd been spit on and laughed at. I'd had things thrown at me. But no one had ever assaulted me before. What would he do to me?

My heart sank down to my knees, and I tried to scream, but he covered my mouth.

"You shut it!" he yelled, throwing me into a stall wall.

I banged my head and sank to the floor. Reaching behind, I felt blood.

I tried to look up as he walked over and muttered, "Sick faggot."

The room was spinning, but I watched something slam him in the back of the head. There was a grunt, and then he was face down on the ground with Jenna behind him, holding her guitar case. She brought it down on the back of his head again, and there was another groan of pain before the man stopped making any noises.

"You leave her alone, you bastard!" Jenna screamed.

Tessa ran over and stopped when she saw that I was bleeding.

"Roxie! Are you okay? Oh my God! Oh my God!" Tessa said, gently touching my head.

Jenna threw her instrument case down on my attacker. He did not stir. She touched Tessa on the shoulder and said, "Go get help, now! Find a doctor and get someone to call police!"

"Right!" Tessa said and took off running, nearly slipping and falling.

Jenna took my head and cradled it in her arms.

"It's okay, Rox. I've got you. You're okay now. He won't hurt you anymore."

At that point I screamed and began to bawl. Everything that had been bottled up while he yelled at me exploded out, and my howls filled the room.

"I know. I know. I'm so sorry, Rox. We shouldn't have let you go alone. I'm so sorry," Jenna said.

She continued to hold me tight while holding some paper towels to the bleeding spot on the back of my head. And I just let it all out, sob after sob.

What the Hell had just happened to me?

Chapter Eight
(Dan)

I scribbled down what notes I was given over the phone, trying hard not to worry about wondering what they meant, and more on copying them down before I forgot them.

"Okay, thanks Vincent. I really appreciate you coming through for me on this one. Tell Gina I said hi, and good luck with that missing gnome case," I said, before hanging up the wired orange polka dot phone on his wall. I didn't use it often, primarily because I had few people to talk to.

Vincent was a paranormal investigator over in Eureka Springs about an hour east of Fayetteville. He often had his hands full with that chaotic little mountain village's supernatural activity.

"So what'd Vincent say?" Eely asked, chewing on some bacon leftovers I'd warmed up a few minutes ago.

"He was able to do a little bit of research, but there's not much out there on the Queen of Tears. She's been sealed away for quite some time, so there's not much in the way of records on her. Vincent said he'd never even heard of her before I brought it up," I said, restarting the record player with Toto IV on it.

But the investigator was thorough and followed through with his research.

"He's still using that enchanted whistle you gave him?" Eely asked.

"No, that was kind of a one-time use to drive those banshees out of one of the town's sacred springs. I'm glad he's on better terms with them now, but if there's one thing I know about Eureka, it's that you don't mess with the spring water," I said.

"So that was a one-time use, but his price to pay was endless research whenever you call? Seems fair," Eely snarked.

I shrugged.

"The shop was okay with that price, so why should I worry?" I said, picking up her empty plate and carrying it into the sink.

"So how do you know what the cost of an item is?" Eely asked.

I walked back over and scratched her head a little before sitting on my stool and leaning against my corner.

"It's hard to describe. It's not quite a feeling I get from the shop, but there's almost an inner knowledge that sort of pops up toward the end of a transaction," I said.

"Have you ever given a wrong price?" Eely asked.

"Not that I'm aware of. Shop would have told me, the way Odessa engineered it," I said.

I looked over the scribbles I'd written down on a little notepad Odessa had given me. It had the words "Marble Hotel—Your best stay in southern Idaho!" written along the bottom.

Witch sure does travel a lot, I thought, going back to my notes.

"So... who is this Queen of Tears, anyway? She sounds kind of sad," Eely said.

"Well, from what Vincent can gather, she used to be a dream seer for some trappers that lived here in the Ozarks. She was sickly, but because of her gift, people traveled from all over the midwest to hear her interpretations. It actually made her quite rich because they always brought gifts," I said.

"So where did all that go wrong?" Eely asked.

"It's difficult to say with what little we know. Vincent said her gift grew too powerful, and eventually she started using it to influence the dreams of others. I guess eventually she crossed a line, and her settlement decided to seal her away in a cave beneath what would eventually become Fayetteville," I said.

Eely scratched her ear and looked up at the ceiling.

"Well that doesn't make sense. Shouldn't she have died then? Humans don't live much past 80 or 90, right?" Eely asked.

"Vincent wasn't sure about that, either. He suspects she put her body to sleep and lives in dreams and nightmares. Kind of like... I don't know, stasis or something. Stops her from physically aging," I said.

"And now that her seal is weakening, she's ready for revenge, huh? That's a terrifying problem you've chosen to deal with," Eely said, licking one of her tails.

I stopped looking at the notes and made eye contact with the fox.

"Hey fur—Eely, I didn't choose to get involved in this. Like everything else associated with this shop, this is something that has happened to me, not with me. I don't even know what I'm supposed to do about it. Odessa said the key to free this Queen of Tears would show up in the shop, and I'd have to choose what to do with it," I said.

"Well you'd choose to hide it, right? I mean, you're not gonna set loose some ancient evil on the city, right?" Eely asked.

"How should I know what I'm going to do? Why am I the one who has to make this choice when I don't get to make any other choices for myself? If I got to choose anything, I'd choose to finally move on from this life and see my parents again. You're right most humans don't live beyond 80 or 90. We're not supposed to. And for those of us that have lived to see 110? 120? 130? It's simply too much," I said, looking back at the notes again.

Eely said nothing but looked down at the glass case. I hadn't raised my voice at her or even said anything mean, but I could tell my words still bummed her out.

"You know what, Dan? That's kind of your problem, isn't it? You keep saying you're eager to die and see your parents again, but you grew up with them and didn't once treasure any part of that experience. You begged them to send you to the new university in town, and they did. But you didn't appreciate that either, becoming bored and wishing to be rich. Odessa granted that wish, and you traveled the country doing whatever you wanted. But deep down, I don't think you treasured any of those moments, either," Eely said.

"What's your point, Eely? I know I screwed up. That's why I'm stuck here in this prison, working toward my eventual release. I want to get back to my family so I can apologize for my mistakes and hopefully have moments to treasure in the future," I said.

The fox swished her tails from left to right but kept looking me right in the eyes.

"Why do you deserve moments to treasure with them in the future if you can't learn to treasure anything you have now?" Eely asked.

I opened my mouth but slowly shut it when I realized I didn't have an answer for her. She hopped off the counter and walked down the aisle farthest from the front door. I just sighed and picked up the latest issue of *Dog Grooming Monthly*.

I kept trying to start an article on how to trim your husky during the summer without damaging their undercoat, but I had trouble focusing after what Eely had said.

What am I supposed to treasure here? I mean, the magazines are nice, sure. Should I be treasuring them? I thought.

The day went on, and we both skipped lunch for once because neither of us was feeling it. I thumbed through the magazine, forcing myself to push Eely's words aside and read a feature on this German man who had spent 45 years supposedly developing the perfect grooming brush for dogs, good for any breed, he promised.

"That sounds like a load," I muttered.

I heard the bell jingle on the front door, and in walked a new customer. She was rather tall and had the longest natural red hair I had ever seen. Wrapped around her was a form-fitting green tunic with black leggings and knee-high boots. As she walked closer to the counter, she lowered a green hood that covered half her head.

As she came closer I saw she had a couple different brown belts around her waist and one larger belt wrapped diagonally around her shoulder with an empty scabbard. Around her neck hung a bronze medallion that had an Irish wolfhound carved into it.

As she examined a pair of orange boots on the left side of the first aisle with white wings pointing out the side, I saw her hair fall forward a bit, and two pointy ears revealed themselves.

Eely ran back up to the counter and poofed her fur out, with all nine of her tails glowing red. She also lowered herself like she was going to strike.

"Dan... she reeks of blood," Eely said, growled.

The woman walked back toward me, and Eely puffed up larger.

"Oi, well if it ain't a wee kitsune?" she said with a deep Irish accent.

Eely didn't give an inch, but let out a store-rumbling growl as she got closer. The woman stopped and smiled. I saw her green eyes start to glow a bit.

"Come now, love. It wouldn't be a fair fight. I'm not armed," she said.

I stepped between the two and said, "My friend here doesn't like you because she says you reek of blood."

The woman looked at me and said, "But not human blood."

"Mythical blood," Eely hissed.

I looked back at her.

"You can't attack a customer, Eely. Odessa would have our asses mounted on her wall," I said.

"You can't serve a murderer like her. She's spilled kitsune blood before. I can smell it," Eely said.

The woman stood up and smiled.

"That's the thing about mythical blood. You spill it, and the scent never goes away. It always marks you as one who spilled it," she said.

I exhaled and looked behind me at Eely. The fox still hadn't given an inch.

"Why don't we start over? I'm Dan, and welcome to my shop, Funky Dan's," I said.

"Name's Alannah. I'm a monster hunter, and as your little fox friend will undoubtedly tell you, a nymph."

Pointing back at the fox, I said, "This is Eely. I don't need to tell you she'll roast you if provoked."

"Provoked is just a matter of opinion, love. She seems ready to let loose right now," Alannah said.

"Yes, well, she knows not to attack customers. And besides, the shop is warded. It wouldn't allow someone in that meant us harm," I said.

Alannah and Eely made no move. They said not another word.

"Right, well for my friend's nerves, why don't you tell me what you're seeking, and I'll help you find it. The sooner you have it, the sooner you're on your way," I said, motioning to the shelves.

"Right. Wee bit of history about me. As I said, I'm a monster hunter, have been for the last 200 years. I travel the world listening to the prayers of villages and towns. When they're being threatened by a monster, I kill it."

"Threatened is just a matter of opinion, love," Eely said, squinting.

Alannah smiled wider.

"Oh dearie, you're far from the first one to hate me for killing my own kind. I get it, mythic on mythic violence and all that. But some creatures threaten humans. And ye see, you humans are like wee babies in terms of species. Some of us feel bad if monsters get to chompin' on yeh. So we put a stop to it."

I nodded my head and looked back at Eely. She still hadn't taken her eyes off the nymph in front of her.

"So nymphs are benevolent toward humans like pixies?" I asked. Alannah sneered.

"Some are, love. Not all. Most nymphs won't reveal themselves unless their forest is threatened. Then you better watch out. And unlike pixies who supposedly protect dreams, those of us nymphs that help humans make an actual difference."

"I know a young lady who would disagree with you," I said.

Alannah looked around the room then behind the counter.

"Speaking of pixie... you have something in the shop that reeks of pixie."

Her green eyes continued to scan the area, though they had stopped glowing a few minutes ago. At last, the nymph seemed to find what she was looking for.

"That postcard. Got yourself a pixie pen pal, do yeh?"

I smirked.

"Partner in crime, I guess. Trying to help save the city. She's actually had a bit of a rough spot the last day. Took a real drumming," I said.

"A pixie took a drumming?" Alannah asked, raising an eyebrow.

I shook my head.

"I should clarify. She's a human girl using pixie magic."

Alannah laughed and said, "Pixies still up to their old tricks, I see."

Eely hopped on my shoulder, and I saw a few sparks slip from between her teeth.

"Her story isn't complete, Dan. She may be a monster hunter, but don't believe it's all about benevolence toward humans. Some nymphs born under the blood moon are actually exiled from their communities because they grow up as violent souls. So to satisfy their lust for violence without drawing too much scrutiny, they become monster hunters, claiming to protect human villages. But sometimes... sometimes they just want something to kill," Eely said.

Alannah sneered again and ran her fingers through her hair.

"You judge all your customers this much?"

"You're not my customer. You're Dan's. And as long as your left shoulder is coated in kitsune blood, I'll judge you all I want. Kitsune rarely ever attack humans, which leads me to suspect that it was a pleasure kill."

The nymph popped her neck.

"I guess you'll never know. I don't owe you my life story. What I will say, Dan, is I doubt that furball has told you that one in 500 kitsune succumb to fire madness and go on rampages. Tell me, Dan. Has your companion exhibited any aggressive tendencies?"

Eely's grip on my shoulder tightened, and I felt her claws dig in a little bit. It didn't hurt, but I was very aware of her tension. This might be the first time I'd ever seen her ready to kill. Even with Kairen she was a little reserved, as if she was more eager to drive him off than kill him. She certainly wasn't out for blood, and that was just a nightmare, not the physical world.

"Don't call my friend furball. Her name is Eely, and she has no aggressive tendencies. Now, Alannah, I believe you were telling me, you're a monster hunter. What chapter comes next?"

Alannah chuckled and said, "Dan the peacekeeper. I like you and pity you, shackled to a place like this. I can smell the chains all around."

I smiled but did not correct her. Because she was right. I was shackled here. Against my will even. I wondered if she had the power to challenge Odessa. What would happen to me if the witch died?

"You know my limits. Now, please tell me what comes next in your story," I said, noting Eely's nails were still in my shoulder.

She pulled open a side of her tunic, and Eely growled.

"Relax, fox. The weapon is hardly harmful anymore," she said, pulling out a hilt with half the handguard broken off. The hilt was wrapped in black leather, and the blade was gone. At the bottom of the hilt sat a ring with a metal line cutting it in half.

"This is all that remains of my blade, Caoimhe. She's traveled with me for half a century and was a fine sword. I had some truly fantastic battles with her, but last week she shattered while fighting an omukade," Alannah said.

I nodded looking at what remained of the blade. There was something about it that still wasn't completely dead, but I couldn't put my finger on it.

"Your blade still appears to have some life in it. Why not simply have it reforged?" I asked.

"Nymph tradition is never to remake a weapon. It'll only bring misfortune. When a weapon is broken, its spirit dies. To reforge it is to resurrect a monster in its place. And that is bad luck," Alannah said.

Throwing my arms in the air, I said, "Well and you certainly wouldn't want a monster hunter to have bad luck. You're on a knife's edge on a regular basis."

"Truly, and it'd be a shame if she fell off that edge," Eely said.

Alannah pointed her hilt at Eely.

"It'd be a shame if I were to come back in here when I get my new weapon and—"

"Anyway," I said interrupting the nymph. "I don't know if you'll like what I have in stock. How important are appearances to you?"

"You mean, am I a superficial and petty creature?"

"I mean, you're used to carrying a large blade on your back to let those who can see it know you're not to be trifled with. It's an obvious strength. I have but one blade in this shop, and it is not like the one you wielded previously," I said.

Alannah put her hands on her hips and then made a forwarding motion with her right hand.

"Well let me see it," she said.

I nodded and walked behind the glass case, reaching inside and pulling out a shorter blade, just a little longer than a dagger. It's gray hilt had a golden lining that ran down the middle and sharpened at the edge. The handguard had a small three-pronged claw facing the blade. A dark wood covered in jagged line work covered the sheath.

I held the blade gently with two hands, flat palms to show respect for the deadly weapon I held.

"Well that's but a knife compared to what I'm used to wielding," Alannah said, tucking her hilt back into her side.

"So appearances are important to you?" I asked.

She scoffed.

"What's the story behind this blade? I do sense something more than meets the eye about this weapon," she said, eyeing it closer and even smelling it.

I took a deep breath and tried to recall the tale as it was given to me.

"Eight hundred years ago when dragons still roamed the planet openly, there flew one who was said to breathe lightning and whose wings summoned claps of thunder with every flap. He was known as Raiken. A fierce beast, he plundered villages across northern Japan for years and years, not for hunger but for sport. Many brave souls inspired to seek justice were devoured by him," I said.

Nodding her head, the nymph said, "I like where this is going. What happened to Raiken?"

Now I locked eyes with Alannah, and she seemed to realize for the first time I had two different colored irises. She gave me a curious look.

"Desperate for protection, a village called Helgen turned toward the dark art of necromancy. They resurrected a great knight long dead. And he became their champion once more, fighting Raiken with a terrible clash that lasted for hours. Raiken grew more furious as the battle went on. No human had ever challenged him like this. Eventually, he got sloppy, which is what the knight was hoping for. And when he got his chance, he struck a fatal blow, sending the dragon crashing into a mountain," I said.

Alannah's eyes widened, clearly taken in with the tale.

I finished the story saying, "Before he returned to the grave, the knight instructed his great great great granddaughter, the town blacksmith, to take one of Raiken's fangs and forge a blade from it. He claimed it would aid the town the next time a great threat arose. She did as instructed, and the blade you see here was the result, one that came with great and terrible power."

The nymph eyed the blade again and popped her knuckles with just a simple flex of her hand. Then she raised her eyes to Dan again.

"Seems a small sword for one made from the fang of a dragon. Was the whole fang used?" Alannah asked.

"Appearances can be deceiving," I said.

The nymph smirked.

"They surely can. So how did you end up with a dragon blade, love?" Alannah asked.

Now I looked down at the blade and recalled when it came into the shop.

"Everything that comes into this shop has a purpose for someone else, and the same is true of this blade. It was given to me by a man named Jamira, a collector of swords. He witnessed four men that had tried to draw the blade and were killed by the sword's power through the years. All of them were great and strong fighters. Fearful he would one day be tempted to try, he offered the sword as payment for another item. It has been in the case since," I said.

"Surely you have great faith in my abilities to withstand this sword's strength then, or you wouldn't offer it to me," Alannah said, raising an eyebrow.

"It's just my job to offer customers what they need. To date, you're the only one who had come into my shop seeking a blade," I said as "It's a Feeling" started to play from the record player behind me.

Alannah held out her own palms, and I carefully placed the blade in them.

"I was told the blade reveals its true self to those who can endure its strength," I said.

The nymph nodded, and then grabbed the hilt with her right hand. Sparks began to fly as she touched it, and a hum was felt through the store.

"Oh my, what a treasure you've got here, Dan," Alannah said, her grin growing wider than I'd seen before.

Slowly, she pulled the blade out, and the sparks changed to bolts of lightning flying around her. I saw her hands begin to smoke, but she did not grimace or show pain.

The blade continued out of the sheath long past where it should have if the blade were an ordinary dagger or even a short sword. Still, Alannah withdrew the full weapon and wielded it with an iron grip. The electric hum continued to grow louder.

Fully revealed, the great and terrible blade resembled a katana. It glowed blue as lightning continued to dance around Alannah. When the blade was withdrawn, a mighty clap of thunder sounded overhead. Eely and I flinched, and I covered my ears.

I could feel the blade's hum in my teeth now, and my hair even.

"You were right, Dan. Appearances are deceiving. This... this is a fine blade," she said as the lightning seemed to dissipate. Finally, the blade stopped glowing, and peace returned to the store. Even the humming stopped.

"Seems the blade has accepted its new owner," I said.

"Seems so," Alannah said.

She resheathed the blade, which, once back in the scabbard, returned to its original length.

As she fastened the blade to a belt around the right side of her waist, the nymph asked, "So, what is the cost for my new blade?"

I thought, and for the first time, a price did not readily pop into my head. She raised an eyebrow as she waited, and I finally said, "Let's call it a future favor. I'll let you know when I need something."

Eely looked at me and gasped.

"Are you sure that's okay, Dan? You've never given out an item on credit before," she said, her tails twitching.

I could tell she was thinking of Odessa, but the shop wasn't exactly telling me "no."

"It'll be fine. And it's not on credit. The payment is a favor I'll call in at a later date," I said.

Alannah nodded and reached up with her left hand. She yanked the necklace and medallion off her neck. It snapped loose, and she removed the medallion from the leather necklace it was on. Then, she flipped it over to me. I caught it with my right hand.

That looked pretty cool, I thought.

The coin was much heavier than I expected, warmer too.

"When you're ready to call in that favor, flip that coin into the air, and I'll appear," she said.

Then she walked over to the counter and placed her broken hilt on top of it.

"Consider this a physical part of our barter," she said, setting it down.

And with that, she turned to go.

"Of course, if you die conveniently at the hands of a beast before he calls that favor in, the price is pointless," Eely called out.

She turned once more and said, "Don't you worry about me, wee fox. I'll be just fine."

Then, she was gone.

"You're a real charmer, Eely. You know that?" I asked.

"I just can't believe you helped that mythical bloodspiller," Eely said.

"I don't get to pick our customers, Eely. Odessa just told me to unite everyone that comes into the store with the item they need, remember?"

The fox hopped back down onto the floor and stretched.

"Being tense for so long takes a toll on you, huh?" I asked.

"Yeah. Really puts me in the mood for dinner, too," Eely said.

"What do you want?"

"Pork chops!" she shouted, excitedly. "Oh, and you haven't told me I'm pretty yet today."

I sighed and turned back toward the kitchen. It was around 4:30 p.m.

Before I'd made it out of the shop, the hilt started to rattle on the counter. It only grew more violent as I turned to watch it.

"Dan, it's—" she was interrupted by the case shattering and the hilt exploding in darkness.

A large black centipede-looking monster rose from the darkness and shrieked. It must have stood nine feet high when coiled, but I didn't want to imagine how long it'd be stretched out.

"Eely!" I yelled. "I think a piece of the omukade survived!"

"On it!" she yelled, and grew to her full size.

As she let forth a stream of fire, I ducked and watched as the monster took the blow. It shrieked, and I got the lovely scent of roasted centipede flesh.

The monster looked battle weary as it had hard chips in its armor, was missing a few eyes, and half its mandible.

"Alannah really messed you up, didn't she?" I asked.

Upon hearing the monster hunter's name, the bug turned its attention to me and let loose a screech louder than any other noise thus far.

I saw the creature's tail flicker, and then it was moving toward me at a speed I barely registered it was so quick.

I had no time to think before a white blur was upon me. I saw Eely knocking me back and being stabbed through the abdomen and letting out a yelp.

"Eely!" I screamed, as the fox landed on the ground, a growing puddle of silver blood around her.

She shrank back down to her normal size as I kneeled down to help.

"D-Dan?" she gasped.

"Why did you do that?" I asked, a fresh terror gripping my soul.

She twitched a little and said nothing. I felt her summoning her strength to speak again.

"Because you're my friend," she said. "And I treasure you."

Tears began to slide down my cheeks as her eyes slowly closed.

"Eely! Eely!" I shouted, but she did not stir.

The omukade shrieked again, clearly ready for my weeping to be done so it could slay me next.

I looked up at it with hatred in my veins.

"That's my friend," I said, quietly.

Another shriek.

"I said- that's my friend, you bastard!" I yelled.

I looked around the shop for something, anything, but my mind was in a panic. I felt the medallion in my hand. Could I call Alannah back so soon? No, customers can't enter the store twice.

I scanned the store for seconds that felt like hours, all wares passing by in a blur. Eventually, my eyes fell upon an item in the middle aisle. A black and red wand to be precise, given to me as a bonus with another payment.

Bonus, it wasn't part of the price, I thought. *I can use it then.*

Reaching out my left hand, I yelled the wand's name.

"Fieratana!"

The wand glowed and flew past the monster into my left hand. Its polished cottonwood felt warm to my grasp. It was about 14 inches long and ended in a point. The wand itself was only capable of one type of magic, making it limited to some. Actually, it was only capable of one very destructive spell. But that was all I needed right now.

Lunging at me with its one mandible, the omukade made what it pictured would be its final move.

I just pointed the wand forward and yelled, *"Disploda!"*

The omukade was greeted with a face full of boom as a fiery explosion blew off its other mandible. It flew into one of the aisles and slowly tried to get back up.

I crunched my right foot into one of its eyes.

"You can grovel and die right here, you wretch! *Disploda!"*

This time I blew the creature in half, and it howled in misery.

"Disploda!" I yelled again, killing the omukade for good. Several shelves blew over, and items went flying in every direction. My floor had a gaping hole in it now, where the omukade's head used to be.

The wand had heated to a point I could no longer hold it, so I tossed it behind me and ran back over to my friend, who was still bleeding out on the floor.

"Eely! Can you hear me? Eely!" I called.

She let out a low whimper, but her eyes didn't open.

"Good! Hold that thought and stay with me. I'm going to get help!"

Looking around I called out Odessa's name, but she did not appear.

"Odessa! Hurry up, where are you!" I yelled.

Again, there was no response.

Panic gripped me again. I was going to lose someone I loved. And it didn't matter if I was here for it this time.

"No no no no no no," I said over and over.

Scooping her up gently, I thought through my options.

"I have to get her to Odessa's shop. Surely there's some kind of medicine inside I can use or something!" I muttered.

No, I won't make it that far. That's out of my range, I thought. *I'll die before I get near the door.*

Then I heard another whimper from Eely, and I yelled, "Hold on!"

At that point, I wasn't thinking. There was no thought of whether I could make it or what it would cost me. I just bolted out the front door bolted toward Odessa's.

Three steps outside my door, I felt my legs wobble, and my strength vanish. It was not a new feeling. I sank to my knees. Odessa's shop door was 15 feet away.

"I can do this!" I shouted and forced myself to stand. "For Eely! For Eely!"

Getting another few steps in was murder, as I began to feel my joints lock up and a familiar eating senation from my stomach.

The worms are here, but I don't care, I thought.

"You hear me, Odessa?! I don't care! Fix my friend!"

Crawling now with every little ounce of strength I had left, I inched ever closer to that shop door. I wouldn't have the strength to open it, but if I could just get there. I didn't know what would happen.

The pain continued as I hollowed out. The worms were multiplying and moving into my lungs and chest now. I coughed up blood.

Still, I crawled onward... five feet left.

Coughing up more blood as the worms ate through to my legs and shoulders, I said, "Hey Eely...we match."

Two feet left, and the world began to blur. This was the furthest outside the shop I'd ever been in the real world.

"I won't let anything happen to you, Eely. Because you're my friend. This pain ain't nothing. It's nothing!" I choked, moving mere millimeters now, eyes focused on that door.

The hollowness grew up my neck now. No strength left for

talking. The worms were almost done making a meal out of me. But Eely... Eely.

"My... treasure," I wheezed, pushing the fox up against the door.

I didn't know what that would accomplish. I tried to knock on the shop door, but the moment I got my left fist, the only one still working, an inch off the ground, everything around me went black. And I felt the familiar feeling of worms eating my brain and my body dissolving into dust.

Eely, my last thought rang out.

I don't know how long it took for me to get wherever I ended up. I didn't even think I opened my eyes and was somewhere. It was more like, I simply realized I was standing somewhere and came into consciousness.

"Where?" I asked.

Looking around at the wooden table and chairs, the wind chime dangling above the kitchen window. I realized I was in my parent's house.

"Mom? Dad?" I called.

Why am I not in the shop? I thought.

I looked around and saw a familiar wood stove, along with mom's three iron skillets hanging from the wall. As I took a step forward, dust kicked off the wooden floor.

"Where is Odessa?" I asked.

The house appeared empty. Until I heard a girl's voice behind me.

"Oh, I'm sure you'll return to her soon enough. But I wanted a quick word first."

Turning around, I saw before me a young teen girl with long raven hair, parted right down the middle. She wore a few rabbit pelts sewn together around her shoulders and a simple long brown garment underneath that.

I said nothing as her purple eyes met my own.

"Dan, right?" she asked.

"Queen of Tears?" I returned.

She smiled and said, "You guessed it, wizard."

"Where am I?" I asked.

"Well, before your consciousness returns to the shop as it always does when your body reforms there, I snatched it into my dream," she said.

I nodded.

121

"Let's make this quick, for the both of us. I can't stay long because of that damn infernal lock. And you can't stay long or else that witch might know you're here" she said.

"What are you after?" I asked.

"You already know that. I've seen your dreams, your memories. You know about the Ossa Key, and I want it. Now, better yet, I know it's going to show up in your shop sometime soon. It has to," she said, smiling.

I clenched my fists.

"I don't suppose you know what happened to my friend before I died?" I asked.

She shook her head.

"I need to get back to her. Now,," I said, turning to walk toward the back door.

Opening it, I found not an exit from the dream, but just an exit from the house. Out back I could see our trees growing the somewhat bitter Arkansas black apple.

The Queen of Tears walked out from behind one holding a fruit and taking a bite.

"You won't find an exit that easily, Dan. And besides, I haven't given you my offer yet," she said.

"And that is?" I said, leaning against the doorway.

Clearly I'm not going anywhere she doesn't want me to. This is her dream I'm stuck in, I thought.

"It's very simple. I know you want to see your parents again. So my deal is easy. Give Kairen my key when it appears, and free me from my seal. Once I'm out, I'll free you from the shop. Odessa's magic is nothing compared to my own abilities."

I didn't doubt her. The witch had made it clear this Queen of Tears was more powerful than she was.

"You go free, and I'm rewarded with what? You suck me into your dream again and spawn my parents from my memories?" I asked, unimpressed.

She shrugged and took another bite of the apple.

"If you want. The rest of Fayetteville is going to end up in my shared dream, so you could too. Or I could just send you on to the afterlife after you're free, and you can meet the real thing. Imagine that, you get to make a choice for once," she said, finishing the apple.

I started to speak, but she cut me off.

"The choice is yours, Dan. Choose wisely."

And with that, I took a deep breath and woke up.

My vision was blurry, but that wasn't new. I looked around and saw I was in my room above the shop again. A picture of my parents hung on the wall.

"And he's back," a familiar voice said to my left.

Odessa was sitting on a little red stool next to my bed. But I didn't even really look at her. What caught my sight was a little eggshell fox curled up on my stomach. She had bandages wrapped around her abdomen, and she was clearly still asleep.

"Oh Eely!" I whimpered and started to cry, biting my fist.

"Is she...?" My voice trailed off.

"Going to be fine? Yes. It was quite a sight, returning to my shop right as your body disintegrated and left a bloody fox on my doorstep. Not quite the sight I wanted to see after lunch"

I let out a long sigh of relief.

"That must have been quite a refresher in dying. You haven't left the shop like that in 100 years. Did you miss the feeling of worms eating you alive?"

I shook my head.

"Then you were that desperate to save the friend you treasure?"

I nodded, gently rubbing the top of Eely's head. She did not stir much.

When I looked up, I could have sworn I saw a brief smile on Odessa's face. Then it was gone, assuming it was ever there in the first place.

"I leave for one afternoon, and you let an okumade into my shop, destroy half the store with a wand and nearly get your friend killed. Is that about right?"

I nodded.

"Go ahead and punish me however you will. I don't care as long as Eely is alive," I said.

The witch said nothing for a moment.

"You already died once today, Daniel. I think you've paid enough. And it seems you've learned something on top of that. You rest up. I've returned the shop to normal, so I expect it up and running first thing tomorrow morning," she said standing up.

I nodded and put my head back down on the pillow, feeling Eely breathing gently on my stomach.

"Anything else I need to know, Daniel?" Odessa asked, eyeing me with a quizzical nature that seemed to come easily to her.

I just slowly shook my head.

"Okay then. Pleasant dreams, Daniel."

She left, and I stroked Eely's fur softly. She cooed quietly in her sleep.

"You are never sleeping down in the shop again. I promise. Your spot is right there every night," I said and leaned back again.

As my mind drifted off into slumber, I thought about the queen's offer. I honestly had no clue what I'd do.

The last thing I muttered before falling asleep was, "You're the prettiest fox in the world."

Chapter Nine
(Roxie)

Standing there with one one finger on the light switch and another on the smooth bathroom counter, I sighed with my eyes closed. I'd just turned the lights off, so I don't know why my eyes were closed. Darkness is darkness.

Except I did know why my eyes were closed. I didn't want to look at my reflection and confirm another change. Another change to my appearance I seemingly had no control over after an already chaotic couple days.

Taking a deep breath, I figured, maybe I hadn't seen it. Maybe it was just in my imagination. The silver hair and pink eyes were real, but the glow-in-the-dark part? That was just a quick illusion of the light or something.

Ironic how much time I've spent in this bathroom seeing as I was attacked in one a couple days ago, I thought.

I'd cycled between crying more pitiful tears and screaming into my pillow wishing I could hurt him like he hurt me. No, I wanted to hurt him much worse. I'd watched Jenna slam his head twice with her instrument case, but it wasn't enough. His bleeding was probably worse than mine, but it wasn't enough.

He'd robbed me of more than blood. It was security. I'd never been assaulted before, let alone in the bathroom. That was supposed to be a safe place. Now he'd shattered that illusion.

That ass, I kept thinking.

I'd hardly left my room or even the loft in the past two days, only to pop over quick and walk Rufus. But even then I just took him on a walk for half a block. Any more in this heat, and the back of my head would throb.

Mom had done her best to simultaneously give me space and let me know over and over she was available anytime I wanted to talk. Somehow I wanted to take her up on both offers at once.

A knock on the door brought me back to the present.

"You okay, priss?"

I didn't say anything. Mom and I hadn't spoken much since the officer took our follow-up statement. I hoped she didn't take it personally. I hadn't even spoken to Jenna and Tessa since they rescued me. They'd texted to check in on me several times each day, and I just responded with little emojis. Symbols were easier than words at this point.

With my back against the door, I just leaned there, continuing not to say anything.

"Okay, Priss. Can you just knock twice to let me know you're okay in there?" she asked.

That was fair.

I softly knocked twice, and she said, "Well if you need me, I'm going to be in the kitchen getting dinner together. I'm making pork chops tonight with mashed potatoes."

God, she's fantastic, I thought. She'd been making all of my favorite meals lately to help me feel better, and it'd really helped.

"I'd give it 30 minutes until they're done," Mom said and left.

Tonight I definitely need to eat with her instead of in my room, I thought. *Okay, let's do this.*

I opened my eyes and saw maybe the outline of the toilet and a little light coming in from under the crack of the door. Slowly, I raised my eyes up to the mirror.

There looking back at me was a set of glowing pink eyes.

"Aw come on! I can't just explain this one away. Mom's not going to believe I found glowing contact lenses... or would she?" I muttered.

Either way, I was done. I was done with everything, lying to Mom, trying to chase down Kairen, letting thoughts about this creep consume me, all of it, done. For someone who wasn't supposed to be tired with this bracelet on, I was exhausted emotionally and mentally.

Guess Selene only promised it would stop physical exhaustion, I thought.

Sighing, I turned the doorknob and prayed I could just stay in the light for the rest of my life so nobody saw my glowing eyes. Though eventually Mom was going to ask how many pink contact lenses I had left, and I had no idea what I'd say.

When she texted me and said dinner was ready, I took a deep breath and left the sanctity of my room.

I walked over to the kitchen table, pulled one of the wicker chairs out and sat down. Mom had made me a plate with a pork chop and a couple spoons of mashed potatoes with peas mixed in.

"Hey Priss," she said. "You feeling any better?"

"I don't know," I said, eating some of my veggies.

We sat there in silence for a few moments, eating. Mom was patient. She knew I needed to get this crud out of me, but she also knew I needed to do it when it felt right.

Mom updated me with the latest news of what was going on down in the garage. Business was great after Gary's Garage shut down around the corner.

Gary and Mom had a friendly rivalry. But he was battling arthritis at the age of 72 and decided to retire. Before he shut his shop down, he referred all his loyal customers over to Mom, including a local used car salesman named John. He'd buy cars on the cheap and bring them all in for an honest assessment on if they were worth fixing up to sell or just scrapping.

That kind of repeat business was good for Mom.

"I'm happy for you," I said, forcing myself to smile.

Mom returned that smile, and I finished my dinner. Part of me wanted to immediately return to my room, but there was another part of me that felt sick, not from the food though.

We continued to sit there for a hot second. I looked up, and Mom smiled at me. I looked back down, unable to return it this time. Sensing what was about to happen, she got up and came over to me.

She stood behind my chair and gently wrapped her arms around me as I slammed both my fists down on the table with a wail. There was no quiet sob to work up to it. I just wailed.

"It's not fair!" I screamed, as Mom pushed my plate away so I wouldn't accidentally hit it if I pounded the table again.

"What's not fair, sweetheart?" Mom asked softly.

"I didn't do anything to them. I *never* do anything to them. And they attack me just the same. What gives them the right to do that?" I yelled.

Mom didn't answer.

"They've thrown yogurt into my hair at lunch, they've screamed, laughed, and ran out of the bathroom when I enter, and they throw me into bathroom stalls. But I've never once hurt any of them. I've never provoked them, but they... they keep," I stopped, and pounded the table again, tears sliding down both cheeks.

"When's it going to be enough, Mom? How many times do I have to get hurt before they finally see I'm not a threat to them?" I said, whipping around and standing up in the kitchen.

Mom had done nothing but taken care of me since the attack. I loved her with all my heart, but here I needed to get this toxicity out of me, and she was ready to take it all.

"Do I have to let them kill me, Mom? Is that what it's going to take for people like Mr. Parker to realize we're not a bunch of perverts out to hurt their families?"

Mom shook her head.

"Then what? What do I have to do to get them to stop and let me live my life as a woman?"

Again Mom just shook her head.

"I don't know, Priss," she said.

"I just wish—" I stopped, not sure of what I wished.

I stood there, breathing harder and harder, the room blurry from all the tears in my eyes. Then I yelled, "I wish I could hurt them all! I wish I could just take a baseball bat and beat them while they cried for help."

"Priss..." Mom said, softly.

"I wish for just one second they could feel the absolute terror of knowing there are people there that want to kill you for no other reason than the fact that you exist. I wish they could feel the unending shame of having people point and laugh at them. I wish they could cry and pray that the floor swallow them up when they realize nobody is coming to help," I said, my knees buckling.

At this point, I wasn't really seeing the room or Mom. I wiped my eyes with my left arm, but it didn't seem to help much.

"I wish... I wish," I trailed off, sinking to the floor and sobbing uncontrollably.

Now Mom came forward. God, how did she always have the perfect timing for this sort of thing?

She sat down on the floor next to me and held me while I cried and tried to finish that last sentence. I never did.

After a few minutes when I stopped, she stood up and went into the bathroom. I heard her walk back, and she handed me a wet washrag.

I wiped my face, which I knew was a disgusting mess after two days of tears and snot.

We sat in silence for another moment or two before Mom finally spoke softly, "I know you're upset. You have every right to be, Priss. I don't have good answers to any of your questions other than there are just hateful and ignorant people out there. The only two ways I know to deal with them are to try and show them they're wrong or wait for them to die out."

I laughed a little at the last bit.

"How much longer do you think Mr. Parker has?" I snickered.

Mom smiled.

"With his diet? You never know. Heart disease is a solid bet given recent statistics. Want me to make him some bacon sandwiches and drop them off at the jail?" she asked.

I was laughing now for the first time in what felt like centuries. It was probably just two days ago I was laughing, but that's my high school teen perspective going full steam ahead. Forever can be five minutes if I'm waiting on my pizza bagels to cool. Two days can be forever if I'm cooped up in my room full of bitterness.

"Bacon sandwich is one thing, but I want to tell you something. It's natural to want to hurt the people that have hurt you, Priss. I get it. I've been there. I got to hurt somebody that hurt me once, and I can promise you, the idea of revenge always feels great. But once you actually get it? It's a terribly cold and lonely place. And there's no joy or happiness in that place, you hear me?"

I looked her in the eyes, able to see clearly for the first time since I started to cry.

"Who did you hurt, Mom?" I asked.

She sighed and clearly wanted to look down at the floor. But my Mom is strong, and she fought that urge. She just kept her eyes on me.

"When I was 15, I was running around with a young man named Billy Bespin. He had this really sweet blue Chevy Bel Air. And when I rode around with him in it, I felt like I was on top of the world. What I didn't know about was the price to ride in that car. Billy would let girls ride in the front seat. Hell, he'd even buy them dinner. But eventually, he was going to want to move them into the back seat."

My eyes widened.

"Mom... did he—"

"He tried. But I got away and ran all the way home. All the no's and screaming in the world didn't seem to make a difference. Billy was a determined bastard. As you can see, my bad choices in men started early," Mom said.

I expected her to be crying. I certainly would be in her case. But Mom just continued to look at me with a face of silent regret.

"What did you do?" I asked.

She sighed and said, "I waited until the next weekend when I knew his dad would be out of town. I took my dad's rifle over to Billy's house. He took away any sense of security I had in that high school. He took away my blissful ignorance about boys and what they sometimes do to young girls. And all I could think about was making him feel hurt, feel scared, feel alone and desperate, crying for help. Sound familiar?"

I nodded.

"I found Billy in the backyard chopping wood. I got into position in the bushes about 20 feet away. And I shot his knee out."

"Jesus, Mom," I said.

Now she nodded.

"And where I expected to feel triumph and emerge from the woods laughing at his pain, I instead found a potent mixture of horror and revulsion. He fell to the ground, and God was there a lot of blood. I could see it from where I was. He screamed and cried for help, exactly like I wanted. But instead of going over to laugh at him, I just wanted to cry. I'd done that, Priss. I hurt him, and I felt like a monster, despite what he did to me," Mom said.

Now I wanted to look down at the kitchen floor. I wanted to very badly, but I couldn't turn away from Mom's gaze.

"What happened to Billy?" I asked.

"He cried loud enough a neighbor came over. He got to a hospital, and they did the best they could. But ultimately I cost him his basketball career. To this day I think he still walks with a limp," Mom said.

I took a deep breath.

"Mom, I know this sounds bad, but I think he got what he deserved," I said.

Mom nodded. She understood why I would feel that way given recent events.

"Maybe he did, Priss. But I didn't get what I deserved. Peace. The guilt and panic ate me alive for years, robbed me of almost as much inner peace as Billy did in his car. In the end, kiddo, it's not about what they deserve. It's about what you deserve. You deserve to feel happy and secure," Mom said.

"Did you ever get caught?"

Mom shook her head.

"I thought about confessing because some nights the guilt was too terrible. But in the end, the fear of going to jail won out. That was an exhausting couple of years. And some nights, it still haunts me. So while Mr. Parker may deserve to be beaten with a baseball bat and cry for help. You do not deserve to feel like I did after shooting Billy. And I promise you, you would."

I slowly nodded.

"My daughter has a strong and pure heart. You don't have to forgive that man, but you do need to eventually find a way to put him out of your thoughts. Let the prosecutor handle him. You just worry about healing up, okay?"

Smiling, I told Mom I'd do that.

"Hey, I recorded *Air Force One* while it was on TNT earlier this afternoon. Why don't we go in and watch it?"

"That is one of my favorite movies," I said.

Mom scrunched up her face and scowled. She deepened her voice and growled, "Get off my plane!"

I laughed and pushed her a little.

"Okay, okay. You go load the movie up. I'm gonna start some popcorn."

A couple hours later as Harrison Ford had successfully been rescued, I was feeling better than ever. Mom had done it again.

"Hey Mom?" I asked.

"What's up, Priss?"

"Thank you," I said, and hugged her.

She returned the hug as I dug my head into her shoulder.

"You will always be my Roxie, and I will always be here for you anytime you want to talk about anything," she said.

I lifted my head, and at this point, my pixie secret was burning a hole in my chest. I wanted so badly to tell her. But how could she possibly believe me?

This wasn't like a superhero situation where if she found out my true identity she'd be in danger. I'd just be in danger of not being taken seriously. She thought my hair and eyes were just some sort of teen phase. How did I prove everything to her without showing up in her dream? All the things I could do to prove it could only happen in dreams.

I'd been looking at her for a few seconds now, so she asked, "Something wrong, Priss?"

I shook my head and hugged her tight again.

As I closed my eyes, I began to feel my head numbing.

What is that? I thought.

After another second, noises began coming to me. I could hear an engine revving. Was it outside? No, it was in my head. Then there was a flash, and I could see cars racing around a track. Cheering fans, hot dogs, exhaust fumes, and heated concrete.

What the hell is happening? I thought again.

Then I was right up against the fence, like the camera angle changed. And as the cars came around, I looked up, seeing Mom driving one of them. She had a huge smile. She was laughing even, looking in the rearview mirror at all the losers eating her dust.

"Mom," I muttered.

Then she turned to look at me. Well, not me, but the me that was standing next to the fence and cheering her on. She flashed a thumbs up, and then she was gone.

"What is it?" she asked.

And I let her go and looked up at her confused face.

Then it hit me. I was seeing her dream from last night. My bracelet had decided to make another change on its own. It'd been doing that since I first got it, and I was getting tired of having no warning when the thing decided to make a change in my life.

Am I going to see the dreams of everyone I touch from now on? I thought. *Because that could get super weird in no time.*

I shook my head and gave Mom a smile.

"You're my hero," I said, hugging her one last time and heading to brush my teeth for the night.

* * *

As I got into bed, I took a deep breath. The last couple nights I hadn't been able to travel into dreams. I didn't have the emotional or mental strength to help others. Selene might have frowned on that, but she wasn't here right now. She was in the world of pixies or whatever it was called. All I could do was explain it as best I could when she made her way back.

Taking another deep breath, I pulled out my compact.

"Maybe helping someone else will help me clear my mind a little more," I muttered.

Opening the compact, I looked in the mirror. Glancing down at my lip for a second and deciding the lack of mustache was still my reality, I looked at my eyes glowing in the darkness of my bedroom.

"I don't know if I'll ever get used to that," I said. *"Ambulate per somnia."*

The mirror didn't waste any time going through a few shades of darkness while it honed in on someone's nightmare. There was immediate fire. Everything was burning. Tables, chairs, walls, ceilings, an entire home.

"You know I don't have any firefighting training, right, bracelet?" I asked. "Oh well. Hope I can breathe through all the smoke. *Immeo.*"

And into the nightmare I went.

Looking around, I felt the heat of this burning home, but breathing seemingly wasn't an issue for me.

"Dream physics continue to puzzle me. And I doubt that's a section we'll cover in AP physics next fall," I muttered.

I stood in a hallway connecting a living room to a dining room. I couldn't really see much in the way of colors or decorations because all of it was burning. There was just a bright yellow and orange everywhere I turned. I shielded my eyes more than once.

"Who am I even supposed to be helping here?" I muttered before hearing a shout from upstairs.

I turned and walked up the stairs, avoiding the handrail that was burning.

When I got to the top, I saw three doors, and one was on fire.

"Hang on, Randy! Daddy's gonna get you out!" yelled a familiar voice.

"There's no way," I said, turning to see a young Mr. Parker. He couldn't have been more than drinking age.

At once, fear and revulsion shot through me like lightning. Why had the bracelet sent me into the nightmare of the one who had caused my own nightmares these last two nights? The man who attacked me, who humiliated me, who took away any sense of security I had.

"You!" I seethed.

He turned to face me with fear and tears in his eyes.

"What are you doing here?" he asked.

"I'll tell you what I'm not doing here is helping your pathetic ass," I yelled.

I turned to leave when he called out.

"Wait! Please help me. My son is in there. Can't you hear him crying?"

I stopped. His son? Which one did he mean? Matt? Jason? No, Who cares? He was garbage as far as I was concerned. His sons were too. His whole family had made my life miserable at some point, and I refused to help any of them, even if it was my job. Why was I still here? Surely there was someone else who needed my help tonight.

"Hang on, Randy! Hang on!" Mr. Parker yelled, resuming his efforts to beat down the stuck door.

Randy? I thought. *He doesn't have a son named Randy. He has twin boys. Did one of them change their name?*

I almost turned to leave again, but there was something that caught my eye in the fire behind this desperate father. A person? No wait. There was something there.

Squinting, I saw Kairen step out of the newly-parted flames, his familiar tuxedo and hat not singed in the least. His earring was glowing with a murky purple aura once more.

"Ka-Kairen?" I shouted.

"Heya cu- I mean, Roxie. I guess my boss knew what she was talking about when she said you'd show up tonight," Kairen said.

Mr. Parker turned to look at this new stranger and seemed like he wanted to ask who he was. Then he took a second to look over Kairen, with a thin red veil covering part of his face.

"Are you supposed to be some kind of wizard or something?" Mr. Parker asked.

Kairen smiled and said, "Something like that. I prefer phantom thief myself. That young lady down there, whom you hurt if I read right in the paper, prefers dream priestess."

I blinked and then snapped at him, "I do not prefer that, you dork."
He shrugged.

"I thought it sounded cool. If we're going to keep meeting up in nightmares like this, you should probably think up a really cool title, you know? Roxie is fine in the real world, but you travel into dreams. That ability deserves a person with a cool name to go with it."

I slapped my face with my hand.

"What are you doing here?" I asked.

But Mr. Parker took the conversation over.

"Can one of you two please help me?! My son is in there scared and crying! My house is on fire for Christ's sake. And you're talking about cool names? What's wrong with you two?"

Kairen frowned.

"I think you've done enough these last couple days to be making any demands of us, especially my fine friend down there."

I blinked again.

Did he just call me his fine friend? I am not his friend! I thought, angrily.

Somehow this had become my nightmare. I'm here with the phantom doofus and my attacker. But was someone coming to save me from this nightmare? Probably not.

I was brought back to reality, well... dream reality, by Kairen's earring glowing again.

Before I could ask what he was up to, four serpents made of fire rose from the burning wall behind him. I braced for some kind of attack, but he put his hand up.

"Not for you, Roxie. You've suffered enough recently. Which is why I'm going to give you a gift," he said.

Mr. Parker took a step back, and the serpents lunged at him, sinking their fangs into his wrists and ankles. The car salesman screamed out in pain and flew back into the wall across from his son's door. What wallpaper hadn't melted yet now peeled back and crumpled as the fire serpents reformed into fiery chains, suspending my attacker about a foot above the floor.

He continued to scream, and I gasped.

"What are you doing, Kairen?" I asked.

"This piece of garbage hurt you, Roxie. And now I'm going to give you the opportunity to take some revenge. Those chains aren't going anywhere. You feel free to hurt him as bad as you want. Or, you can just watch the hope fade in his eyes as he realizes he can't save his kid and the house collapses around him," Kairen said, punching mr. Parker in the gut.

Mr. Parker winced, trying to lean forward. The chains kept him tight against the wall.

"Did you come here just to hurt Mr. Parker?" I asked.

"Of course not. I'm looking for something in his memories. And I knew you'd get in my way. So, my boss told me to offer you a shot at revenge. And I think it's a great idea, personally. You can hurt him as much as you want in here, and it's not like any of that damage will transfer back into the real world," Kairen said.

"Please! My son. I'm begging you—" Mr. Parker was cut off by Kairen punching him in the gut again.

"And there's an added bonus here. The deeper into his memories I go, the more pain I cause his subconscious. So why you're hurting him up here, I'll be hurting him down there. It's a win/win," Kairen said.

With that, he turned to walk back through the parted flames.

"Have fun, Roxie. And I hope you're doing okay," Kairen said.

Then he was gone, and I was left with my attacker pinned to a wall.

Part of my brain was asking why I'd let Kairen go. The other part was looking at a suspended Mr. Parker, crying for his son. And... it just wasn't enough. One of the blue beads on my bracelet began to change into a shade of purple as I took a step toward him.

Why shouldn't I rough him up a bit? I thought.

Sure, this would cause some mental scars, but it wasn't like he was actually going to wake up tomorrow covered in burns. His wrists and ankles were practically black now. Still, he begged me for help. But I toned that out as I thought of what I'd do to the man who hurt me. The man who made me feel like dirt.

As a few more beads changed color, I began to think, *Yeah... why not? He can hurt a little more. He owes me that much.*

I stood inches from him now. He was in a sea of turmoil both physically and emotionally, and I was happy to see it.

A small girl's voice lifted itself into my ears.

"Remember how he hurt you?" it asked.

I felt it again, for about the 1000th time, cold bathroom tile on my knees, anger giving way to fear as I was insulted and then picked up by my shirt. Terror upon realizing I was alone in a bathroom with someone who wanted to harm me. Shame at being unable to truly fight back. And pain as I was slammed into a wall for no reason other than my existence.

I still felt the blood dripping down the back of my skull, how rattled my brain was by the sudden violence.

He wasn't going to get away with this. It wasn't enough that he was facing second-degree battery and assault charges. It wasn't enough that he felt justified in his actions because of who I am.

"It's not enough!" I screamed and hit the wall next to him, causing the flames around us to pulse and grow. He screamed even louder. But as much pain as he was in, he still pleaded for his kid.

He wasn't apologizing for what he did. He was asking for my help.

What a self-absorbed ass, I thought.

None of it was enough. But I was here, and I had the power to tip the scales and make it enough.

My bracelet was half covered in purple light now, and I felt right. I felt an intoxication growing inside my chest. His screams, his tears, his agony, it was everything I wanted.

"We can do more," I said, my bracelet glowing.

The fire engulfed every inch of the hallway. Just when I thought his eyes couldn't grow any wider, they found another size.

"Do you remember me, Parker?" I shouted.

He nodded.

"And do you remember what you did to me?"

He nodded again.

At last, he lowered his head, unable to plead for his victim to help anymore.

There it is. Recognition. You know what you did, I thought.

"I'm sorry," he muttered.

"Too late," I yelled, slapping him with everything I had.

"Keep going. He deserves worse, and you have the power to give it to him," the voice whispered in my ear again.

I slapped him again.

"What's the matter? Done pleading for help? Or did you finally realize you don't deserve it? That Matt and Jason probably don't deserve it either?"

His head shot up.

"But Randy didn't do anything wrong!" he yelled.

"Shut up!" I said, this time punching him and splitting his lip.

That intoxication grew with each strike. I was hurting him, but it still wasn't enough. We weren't anywhere close to even.

"Kill me if you want, but please, I'm begging you. Just open the door and let my son go," he said.

I shook my head.

"No, I don't think so. That's too easy. If you're willing to sacrifice yourself, that tells me you don't value yourself. And if you don't value yourself, what good are you to me?" I asked.

Two things weren't burning upstairs, myself and the door to his son's room. That was the key.

I turned to the door and raised my bracelet. Only two beads were still blue at this point. The whole item glowed with a purple hue as fire engulfed the door.

"No! Don't please! Take me! Take me, take me, take me!" he yelled, pulling against the fiery bonds that held him. He pulled so hard, I expected his limbs to snap, but they didn't.

He continued to scream, louder and louder.

"There! That's what I wanted from you. Do you feel that hopelessness? That absolute pit you've sunk into, realizing someone else holds all the power? I've spent the last two days screaming and crying because of what you did to me, you monster," I screamed, jabbing a finger at him. He had no defense.

I looked deep into his eyes, his bloodshot hazel eyes revealed by the very fire that held him. And it was here I watched the last specs of hope draining away like sand in an hourglass.

The intoxication in my chest reached a fever pitch, and I suddenly remembered my words from earlier. That voice slithering in my ear brought it back.

"I wish I could just take a baseball bat and beat them while they cried for help!"

A smile crept over my lips.

That's what I'm missing, some good old fashioned pain, I thought. My bracelet glowed again. A metal baseball bat with a yellow "slugger' sticker on it appeared before me. I grabbed the brand new leather grip and smiled.

"You go ahead and watch what's left of your son's door burn, and I'm just going to start pummeling you, beating out any last shreds of hope still in there, okay?" I asked.

Maybe half a bead was still blue on my bracelet as I took a step toward my attacker. I raised the bat, tensing my muscles, ready to put everything I had in this swing. Would I hit his head? Maybe a hand.

Let's just swing and see what I strike, I thought.

Just before I let it fly, I paused.

"Give that monster what he deserves," the voice hissed.

I wanted to. I pictured it all over again on repeat: shove, slam, shove, slam, shove, slam. The blurry vision, the cry for help, my body being trashed against the bathroom tiles, it mixed with the intoxication in my chest until I could barely breathe.

Then a different voice came to me, and it said, "And where I expected to feel triumph and emerge from the woods laughing at his pain, I instead found a potent mixture of horror and revulsion."

"What?" I asked in front of an eternally flinching Mr. Parker.

"He screamed and cried for help, exactly like I wanted. But instead of going over to laugh at him, I just wanted to cry. I'd done that, Priss. I hurt him, and I felt like a monster, despite what he did to me," the voice said.

I blinked, frozen as the fire raged around me, smoke drifting over the bat.

In Mr. Parker's eyes, the last spec of hope was about to drift out of the hourglass. And just before it did, one more voice popped up in my head.

Roxie, I didn't make a mistake. You're such a kindhearted young girl. You're always putting in overtime to make other people happy. The perfect person for this job, it's none other than you. And the fact that you're still able to make other people smile while carrying around all this negativity and emotional scarring? It's just more proof.

Mom... Selene, I thought.

Looking away from my attacker, I saw a bathroom at the end of the upstairs, with a large mirror positioned over the sink. And I saw a monster in the hallway. It stood there, holding a baseball bat, ready to inflict pain on a father who had already lost more than I'd realized earlier.

It all clicked now. Randy wasn't Matt or Jason with a name change. He was Mr. Parker's first son. The younger Mr. Parker, the

139

house, the fire, this nightmare was based on a memory. And I guessed it was one he relived often, making it perfect fruit for the Queen of Tears to tempt me with.

My attacker was an asshole, but it all originated from this very moment. My bracelet glowed, and I saw the memory in Mr. Parker's psyche. The fire was caused by a candle he forgot to blow out before bed. The dog knocked it over, it spread, and he wasn't strong enough to get Randy out of the house before collapsing from smoke inhalation.

I watched a frantic dad listening to his son crying on the other side of that door. His son was three. He pounded, but somehow the door had gotten locked, and he didn't have the strength to break it down.

Just before the house collapsed, fire crews pulled him out. And when he woke up in a hospital bed a few hours later, I got to watch my attacker find the worst news imaginable, that he had been inches away from his son and unable to save him.

Naturally, he blamed himself, thought he was too weak. So when he had the twins, he did everything he could to make them strong. Never again, he kept telling himself. He would not lose another child to weakness, his own or theirs.

And I was using that pain against him.

"You called me some names and threw me into a bathroom stall. And in return, I somehow found a way to make your son's death even more painful than it already was," I muttered, dropping the bat. It hit the floor with a thud.

My bracelet slowly returned to a blue glow as I summoned forth hundreds of gallons of water to flood the house. It washed over me as I fell to my knees. The water took away the bat and doused the flames. It also freed Mr. Parker.

I waved my arm, and my fully-blue bracelet drained the water and unlocked the door behind me. A three-year-old boy ran out over to his father screaming. I lowered my gaze to the carpet, revulsion and horror taking me.

"Is this what you felt after shooting that man, Mom?" I whispered, as tears came to my eyes. "Is this why you picked me, Selene?"

Mr. Parker and his son cried together and drowned out my noise, but make no mistake. I was still sobbing.

At some point, I climbed to my feet, and Mr. Parker picked up his son, doing the same.

"Thank you, Roxie. Thank you," he said, clinging to the boy.

I shook my head, still crying.

"Don't you thank me, not after what I did here tonight. I'm a monster," I said.

He said nothing for a moment and then set Randy down.

"Go find momma," he said and watched Randy slowly climb down the stairs. When the boy was out of sight, Mr. Parker looked me in the eyes.

"I hurt you in the bathroom at the country club. Now you hurt me. I get it. You did what I would have done, Roxie," he said.

I snapped at him, "Don't you see?! That's the problem! You lost your son in a fire. And you thought weakness was to blame. So you spent the next several years trying to become as strong as you possibly could. And when you had Matt and Jason, you tried to make them as strong as possible. You beat strength into them so they would never be weak, never die like Randy did."

He nodded.

"That's exactly right. "

"The problem is you screwed up! It wasn't your weakness that cost Randy his life. It was a freak accident. And in your quest to show your boys true strength, you raised them to be assholes, just like you'd become. Strength isn't about how hard you can hit someone or how much of life you can toughen out. Real strength comes from character, being good to others. Your sons are bullies, and they learned that from you."

Mr. Parker said nothing.

"Matt and Jason are monsters that pick on people weaker than them because that's what they think strength is, to permanently place yourself at the top of the food chain and screw over anyone below them. And tonight, I sunk even lower than they did. Real strength, Mr. Parker, is learning to work through your weaknesses and using that knowledge to help others climb up with you. There's no strength in knocking down those weaker than yourself."

He still had nothing to say, and I sighed, leaning against the charred wall behind me.

"My sons are bullies at school, huh?" he asked.

I just nodded, wiping my eyes.

"I never intended to teach that to them. What you've said tonight makes a lot of sense. Roxie, I promise I'll try to teach them better. I'm... I'm sorry for everything my family has done to you," he said.

Looking at the melted remains of carpet, I shook my head.

"I'm sorry for hurting you tonight," I said.

We didn't say anything to each other for another moment. Some of the wood in the house was still crackling.

"If it helps, I forgive you for hurting me tonight. And I hope someday you can forgive me for how I behaved the other night at the party. You didn't deserve that," he said.

Meeting his gaze, I sighed again.

"Thank you. I know this is terrible to say, but I don't know if I'm ready to forgive you yet. I'm not strong enough," I said.

Mr. Parker just nodded and raised his hands.

"That's fair. You take your time. I'd like to begin to make amends by offering to reimburse your family for the ambulance and hospital bill after I... threw you into that stall," he said.

I nodded.

And for a moment, I began to see a little bit of a path where maybe I did forgive him someday in the future. What I didn't see was a path where I'd ever forgive myself for what I did in retaliation.

Collapsing to his knees, Mr. Parker began to scream. He held his head.

"What's wrong?" I asked, taking a step toward him.

"My head... it feels like a thousand drills," he managed to choke out.

I looked around, and at once it clicked.

"Kairen," I said. "Hold on! I'm going to go stop this!"

I ran downstairs and out the front door.

How do I find him? Where is he?

Standing in the driveway surrounded by dirt roads and flat nothing, I remembered what the phantom thief said he was after.

"A memory," I muttered, raising my arm and imagining a door into Mr. Parker's subconscious.

I hope this works, I thought as a basic white wooden door appeared.

I grabbed the brass knob and opened it, greeted by a long black and white hallway filled with other doors of all different wood types and colors.

Running down the hallway, I felt everything begin to shake. And

I suddenly became very aware of the stress having two dream influencers inside Mr. Parker's head was causing.

"I have to hurry," I said.

Running down the hallway, I went past door after door.

"How do I know which one?" I asked.

Then I saw it. Up ahead on the left was a red metal door that had purple smoke leaking out from under it.

"That's gotta be it," I said, and threw the door open.

Inside was a simple storage room with only a few boxes. And about 15 feet in front of me stood Kairen.

"Kairen!" I shouted.

He turned to face me while holding a small metal box with a broken lock on it.

"Hey, Roxie. You get bored of torturing the old man?" Kairen asked.

"No, that was a mistake. I should have been the bigger person," I said, hearing Mr. Parker's scream in my head again.

Kairen looked taken back.

"You're joking right? After everything he did, you just let him off the hook?" Kairen asked.

"No, Kairen. I hurt him... a lot," I said, looking down at the dusty wooden floor of this storage shed memory room.

"Oh good. I bet that felt great," Kairen said, chuckling.

"It felt great for a few minutes. And now it'll feel terrible for the rest of my life," I said, my voice thick with regret.

"Oh come on, he'll be fine. It's not like you were physically tormenting the bastard. It's a dream. He'll be fine," Kairen said.

I shook my head.

"That's wrong. What I did tonight will leave emotional and psychological scars on him and myself for the rest of our lives. Worse yet, I let the Queen of Tears manipulate me, just like she's doing to you, Kairen. What is she after here?"

He scoffed and held up the box.

"I don't know about all that emotional scar crap, but this box contains a memory she's after. It was tucked away and was a pain in the ass to find, but it should help free her," Kairen said.

I shook my head.

"How would a memory free her?" I asked.

Kairen looked at the box and then back up at me.

"This man's ancestor made this key thing. And my boss is hoping his memory of seeing that key will reveal where it is currently. It puts me one step closer to freeing her and getting my brother woken up," the thief said, preparing to open the box.

I raised my hand and took a step toward him yelling, "Don't!"

Kairen looked confused.

"I know we said our truce only stood in reality. But do you really want to get into a fight here? This is the only way I'll get my brother back," he said.

"She's evil, Kairen! She's just using you. I wouldn't be surprised if she was the reason your brother fell into a coma in the first place. The Queen of Tears is just manipulating you to get free."

"I don't care!" Kairen shouted, and I flinched.

He'd never yelled at me before.

"I want him back. You're an only child, Roxie, so you don't understand this. But he's my brother, and I have to do whatever it takes to get him back. Every day without him... it's like there's this hole in my heart. I can't mourn him because he's still breathing. But I can't talk to him because he's not awake. We share secrets, we fight, we play games, we help look out for dad, we take on the world together, Roxie. I want him back. I've waited long enough!" Kairen said, tears running down his cheeks and disappearing behind the red face cloth.

I took a deep breath. I had to try to reach him. Kairen wasn't evil. He had pain like I did. And the Queen of Tears was exploiting that to get free. I couldn't let that happen.

I don't want to fight you, I thought. *Please don't make me fight you. My heart can't take any more tonight.*

Kairen reached for the box again, and I rushed forward, putting my hand on top of his, pushing the lid back down.

"Roxie! Don't get in my way!" he said.

He tried to move my hand, but I just put my other hand on top of his, doubling down on my strength.

Showing teeth and growing, I could see him growing more frustrated. And his earring glowed for a moment.

"Will you hurt your friend, Kairen?" I asked.

His face fell, and the earring fell dark. He said nothing, but I could tell he was resolute not to hurt me.

At last, I knew how to reach him. Though I didn't know if the plan was the right one to take.

"Kairen, you're only working for the Queen of Tears so she'll wake up your brother, right?"

"You know that, Roxie. I don't care about all this dream crap. I want him back, and this is the only way to make that happen," he said.

I looked down at the beat up metal box and our hands.

"I'll do it. I'll wake your brother up. If you just promise me you'll put the box back on the shelf and leave, I'll do it. Then you won't need to work for the Queen of Tears anymore."

He gasped and looked over at me, finally stopping his struggle to overpower my hands.

"Can you really do that? Would you?" he asked.

Can I? I have no idea. Will I if I can? Absolutely, I thought.

I couldn't hesitate. If he sensed any doubt or loss of confidence on my part, he wouldn't go through with this.

"Of course I can. But you have to put this box up right now," I said.

He looked down at our hands again and thought through it all. I could see his mind crunching all the facts and what he knew about me. A bead of sweat ran down his cheek.

"Kairen... please trust me," I said. "Please."

Time seemed to stand still in the memory storage room.

Finally, I felt his hands slack a little. I moved my grip away, and he slowly put the box back on the shelf.

"I trust you," he said, and then he vanished.

I let out a deep sigh and collapsed to my knees. Everything went dark, and when I came to, my Sailor Moon alarm clock showed it was 8:34 a.m.

I was covered in sweat, and I sighed.

Honestly, I didn't know if I wanted to cry, sleep, slap myself or a mix of the three. But I was determined to help Kairen's brother and free him from the Queen of Tears. I felt like I owed the universe that much good and more after the terrible things I'd done through the night.

"Selene. I'm so sorry," I said, hearing Mom's words in my head again.

"The guilt and panic ate me alive for years, robbed me of almost as much inner peace as Billy did in his car. In the end, kiddo, it's not about what they deserve. It's about what you deserve. You deserve to feel happy and secure."

I began to cry into my pillow.

I don't deserve either of those things right now, I thought.

Chapter Ten
(Dan)

I sat on the roof smoking and looking up at the stars with Eely at my side. She was stretching all nine of her tails, and I chuckled.

"I already told you you're the prettiest fox in the world today. Your stretching isn't going to earn you another one," I said, scratching my brown beard.

One of these days I should consider shaving this thing, I thought.

"Did it ever occur to you that I might just be stretching for once?" Eely asked.

I shrugged and resumed watching the best stars my dream could generate.

"I wonder if Roxie could make some better stars when she gets here," I muttered.

"She's coming tonight?"

Nodding, I stood up and stretched.

"Hey, and I wanted to ask you a favor if you would, Eely," I said.

"You know how favors work, Dan. First you need to offer me something," the fox said, snickering.

"That's not how best friends do things," I said, smiling.

The grin on the fox's face vanished, and she muttered, "What do you want, Dan?"

I smiled.

"It's not really a favor for me. It's for Roxie. What do you think of her?"

"She seems really nice. I don't know if she fully understands what the pixie magic is doing to her, but I like her a lot. She's got this pure heart and has been really kind to me the last couple times she's popped into your dreams. Why?"

Looking down at the fox, I squatted and said, "I want you to give her your fox medallion so she can summon you if need be. I really wish I could help her more as we try to solve this Queen of Tears stuff, but I can't leave the shop. You can. If she needs to summon you, I'd like her to be able to."

Eely said nothing for a moment and then looked over the side of the building.

"Dan, I don't—Listen, when mythical creatures give their medallions out, it's an act of their deepest trust. We're saying, 'I trust you're worthy of summoning me and won't misuse this ability.' Roxie is nice and all, but I don't know that I really trust her on quite that level yet, you know?"

I nodded. Then I popped my neck and sighed.

"I hear you. And I wouldn't be asking this if I didn't think it was important. It's just, the Queen of Tears can show up at any time. And if we lose Roxie, any efforts we make to save this city can be thrown out the window. Plus, she's still a kid. She probably needs backup more than we know and can't admit it," I said.

Eely looked back over at me. She sighed.

"I get all that, Dan. But to give a medallion away? It's just too much to ask right now. I'm not there with Roxie yet. I'd give you one if you asked, but that's about it," she said.

I sat back down with my feet dangling over the edge of the shop and looked at the street below.

"You're right. And it's your medallion. I respect your right to say when to surrender it."

"Good," Eely said, hopping into my lap.

As I scratched her lightly on the neck, a cruel smile spread across my face.

"Would you give your fox medallion to Odessa?" I asked.

Eely jumped with a start and looked up at me.

"Tha-that's not a fair question, Dan! And besides, she doesn't need a medallion to summon me. She has other magic at her disposal!" the fox barked.

My smirk grew wider.

"That's not really answering my question, Eely..."

We were interrupted by a light appearing below on the street. Out from the light, Roxie appeared.

"Saved by the pixie," I said, laughing and standing up.

I waved down to Roxie and called her up to the store roof about two stories above where she currently stood.

A few minutes later, she was on top, her silver hair blowing in the night breeze. She had on a black Paramore T-shirt and a white skirt.

These new band names just keep getting stranger and stranger, I thought. *What even is a Paramore?*

"Good to see you, Roxie," I said, but she did not return the greeting as friendly.

The girl muttered "hi" or "hey" under her breath and turned to look at my back yard. She didn't really make eye contact.

"Something wrong, kiddo?" I asked.

She shook her head but didn't really give an answer.

Eely walked over and looked up at Roxie, but the girl still didn't want to make eye contact with either of us.

"Your postcard didn't really mention what you needed me for, Dan. So what's up?" Roxie asked quietly.

"That can wait. First, I think we need to figure out what's eating you alive and attend to that problem," I said.

I honestly expected her to sidestep or refuse flat out to answer me, but instead she just locked eyes with me and nodded with an expression of tearful frustration on her face.

"You want to know what's eating me alive, Dan? Fine!" she yelled. "I can't tell my mom or best friends why I cry at random points throughout the day because they can't know I'm using pixie magic to fight nightmares! I hate lying to them, and that's just the start of my issues."

She went on for the next five minutes with a discordant scream highlighting what she'd done to her attacker in his dream, how she used her abilities to torment him, and what the Queen of Tears had convinced her to do. The girl wrapped up by revealing she'd promised to free Kairen's brother from the Queen of Tears... somehow, and all of this was just crushing her.

"I don't even think I want to be a dream girl, anymore! I just want to take this bracelet and chuck it into the middle of Lake Fayetteville," she finally finished and tried to catch her breath.

Eely and I exchanged glances as she let out a scream of frustration and picked up a rock from the top of the roof, hurling it down the street. It made a loud THUNG as it struck someone's truck.

Good thing that's a dream truck, I thought. *Matthew wouldn't have been happy with a huge dent in his Bronco.*

I walked over and stood a few feet from Roxie, putting my hands up by my chest.

"Okay," I said, "Let's just take a deep breath and figure all of this out. Can you just breathe for a moment?"

Roxie scowled at me but did as I requested.

When it finally seemed her notch had been turned down from 11 to 10, I sighed and started again.

"Roxie, you screwed up," I said.

She looked at me with venom in her eyes, seemingly ready to strike. If I could have been smacked upside the head with a glance, she would have done it.

"You don't think I know that? Were you even listening to me?" she screamed.

I could tell she'd been carrying around all this frustration since the nightmare a couple evenings ago, and it'd only built up. She couldn't talk to her mom about this, so I was getting the brunt of it.

Not even bothering to tell her to breathe again, I just tried to speak as calmly as I could.

"Roxie, you screwed up, BUT that's normal. Humans make mistakes, especially ones who are manipulated by supernatural inducers of nightmares like the Queen of Tears. It sounds like you realize what you did was bad, and you know not to do it again."

"You don't understand!" she yelled, pointing a finger at me. "I don't get to make mistakes. Not me!"

I crossed my arms.

"And why is that?"

"Because Selene chose me to be her dream girl for a month. She chose me, Dan! She entrusted me with pixie magic because she said I had a pure heart. And then I go all psycho. The Queen of Tears being involved doesn't excuse my behavior."

"Okay, it's pressure enough for a teen girl like yourself to protect a city from nightmares. But come on! Listen to yourself. You don't get to make mistakes because you've been entrusted with too much authority?"

"That's exactly right. I've been trusted with too much to make a mistake like I did. What I did makes me no better than the Queen of

Tears. It makes me a monster, and when Selene gets back, I'm sure she'll tell me as much to my face."

I rubbed my temples.

Eely turned her head sideways, apparently unsure of what to think about all this.

Even if I hadn't been imprisoned in this shop, I don't know that I would have wanted any kind of parenting on my plate, I thought.

"Roxie, let's get some perspective here, okay? You're a teenage human. You're going to make mistakes. Adults are going to make mistakes. It's the human condition. You gave into temptation from the Queen of Tears and tortured a man. That's terrible. But you don't stop helping others because of that!" I said.

She jumped back, shocked by my tone.

"You're under pressure without adding an extra 1,000 pounds from your own self-imposed rules of perfection. Take that crap and shove it somewhere else. You want to know what separates you from the Queen of Tears?" I asked.

Roxie just stood there with her mouth open and slowly nodded.

"You hurt someone, and then you stopped. You apologized, you ate yourself alive, and then you were brave enough to confess all this to me. The Queen of Tears is just going to go on hurting people without remorse. You aren't, because you feel guilty for what you've done. You recognize it's wrong and are trying to do better. The difference between being a human and being a monster is what happens after you hurt people. Good and pure souls like yourself, who are still very capable of screwing up, will seek to become better people. Monsters, like the Queen of Tears, won't give pain a second thought."

The dream girl looked down at my roof and then back up at me. She thought about what she wanted to say for a few minutes and then said, "It sounds like you're just dismissing my actions."

Now Eely looked down at the roof and then decided to lie down for a moment, her head on her paws.

She certainly seems to be meditating on Roxie's confession, I thought.

"I am not. You misused your power, Roxie. But then you apologized and decided to keep doing good by swearing to free Kairen's brother. After that, you ate yourself alive for 48 hours straight. You have a conscience, and it's clearly working. This is the kind of stuff that's supposed to happen after something that's not supposed to happen, if that makes any sense," I said.

A tear slid down Roxie's cheek, and she took a deep breath.

"I still don't think anyone's ever going to trust me again, let alone Selene. I don't even trust myself," she said, crouching and holding her knees.

I walked over and sat on the roof next to Roxie, danging my legs off the front of the store. For a minute, I paused to gather my words.

"I trust you for a big mission tonight. And I'm sure Selene will trust you, too. I don't know everything about pixies, but it seems to me she gave you that bracelet without any kind of owner's manual. Typically, in a case like that, it's because she trusts you'll figure out how best to help others. And there's room built in for errors like the one you made. It's called a learning curve. Now you know what the Queen of Tears is capable of, and you won't make that mistake again," I said.

She smiled for what I guessed was the first time in a couple days and wiped the tear from her cheek. Shortly afterward, Eely came over to her left side with something in her mouth.

"Hold out your hand," she said, muffled.

Roxie held her hand flat on the ground, and Eely dropped a pure white medallion about the size of a half dollar. On both sides were a fox head staring at the holder of the coin.

"This coin is warm. What is it?" Roxie asked.

"It's my fox medallion. I want you to know I trust you to have it, Roxie. You hold it tight in your grasp and say my name. Then I'll come to you instantly, wherever you are. You use it anytime you want, except for when I'm eating. You shouldn't have to ever face temptations like you did alone ever again. So next time you feel yourself slipping away, or you're in any kind of danger, summon me," Eely said.

Roxie began to cry again and snatched Eely up in a hot second, holding her really tight and burying her face in the fox's fur.

"That medallion is a huge sign of trust, Roxie. Eely hasn't even given one to her oldest friend Odessa yet."

"Thank you so much," Roxie said with a high pitched cry.

Eely just glared at me.

After Roxie had some time to calm down and was breathing normally again, I noticed she looked more relaxed. That was when I decided to broach her with my idea for her next mission. Maybe that made it sound too military-like. Tonight's... quest? No, this wasn't some fantasy adventure in a comic book. I'd think of a better word later.

"Roxie, I called you here tonight because I have a plan that should help us."

She looked over at me and set Eely down. Then she stood up and scratched her silver hair a bit, pushing some out of her face.

"What do you need?" she asked.

"I need your magic to open a door," I said.

Roxie shook her head.

"I don't understand," she said. "What door?"

I reached into the pocket of my gray robe and pulled out an iron cube, no bigger than a Rubik's Cube.

"This door," I said. "It leads to a mystical place where all kinds of knowledge is stored. We can use it to learn everything there is to know about the Queen of Tears, and, hopefully, how to stop her."

Roxie held out her hand, and I put the cube in it. She looked it over, but in many ways it just appeared to be a hunk of rough metal. Its sides weren't even, though there were little runes carved into random spots.

"What am I supposed to do with this?" she asked.

"You simply command the door to open, and it will. Literally say the word 'open.'"

"O—" she stopped. "Oooooo—"

When she tried again, the cube was lightly glowing red, but it would turn back off every time she stopped speaking.

"This is going to sound strange, but I can't say the word. It's like, every time I try, there's a thousand pounds holding a door in my throat shut. What gives?" she asked.

"Gaining access to the Library of Seshat is no easy feat. In reality, it requires a massive amount of magical energy to open the door. But in a dream? I figure the amount to open the door is considerably less in a world where you can alter reality to a certain degree."

Roxie tried to say 'open' a few more times, but the closest she got to was "op—"

She leaned over and put her hands on her knees while she caught her breath.

"This thing is a piece of work. Where did you get it, anyway?"

"I bought it from the shop," I said.

"You... bought it? You have to buy things from your own shop?" Roxie asked.

"Well... yes. Odessa actually owns the shop. And the rules she established when she created this place are ironclad. Rules about me leaving and everything in the shop that's not a free gift being purchased before it can be used. I am no exception," I said.

Roxie raised an eyebrow.

"Did you mention you might need this item to save the city?"

I nodded.

"And she didn't budge?"

I shook my head.

"Wow. Well, wait a second. She literally owns your soul, right? And she's not exactly paying you. What did you pay her?" Roxie asked.

Thinking back to earlier in the day, I could still hear Odessa's voice say, "You're already working for me one day for every dollar you spent while on vacation. Do you want to add more time in the shop as a future debt to pay off?"

"Yes, if that's what has to be done," I said.

Odessa nodded and said, "Then take the doorway. Use it as you see fit, Daniel."

Looking at Roxie, I just said, "More time."

Roxie tried fruitlessly to open the door, and Eely cheered her on.

"You can do it! Really put your might into it, girl! You're doing this to save your friends, family, and the city!" she shouted.

The dream girl hung her head in defeat.

"I can't do it. I don't have enough magic, Dan."

I walked over and knelt down in front of Roxie.

"It's not the magic that's the problem, kiddo. You haven't even touched your magic. My guess is you're still holding back after that last nightmare. You have more magic than you know, a pixie nuclear warhead there on your wrist," I said, pointing to the blue beads that made up her bracelet.

Roxie looked at the beads and nodded.

"You're not going to hurt us, Roxie. Trust yourself, forgive yourself, and let's go learn how to kick the Queen of Tears' ass."

The dream girl nodded and said, "You know... pixie nuclear warhead doesn't sound all that safe. But here goes."

154

You have no idea, I thought.

Roxie slammed the metal cube with both of her palms as her bracelet began to light up.

Girl's got it, I thought.

"Ooopppeeeeee—" she yelled, her bracelet lighting up even brighter.

The roof began to shake. Actually, the entire building began to shake, and cracks formed under Roxie the louder she screamed.

I stepped back a few feet with Eely.

"Damn you. I said ooopeeeeeennnnnn!" she screamed, her bracelet now so bright I couldn't even look at it.

The metal cube began to crack as the runes on it lit up solid red, mixing with Roxie's blue light.

She hurled the cube across the roof, and it shattered upon contact with a rail. A red mess of sparks began to fly about, and then a heavy looking iron door formed with a grinding metal sound. It was covered in rust and had a crank to open it on the center.

"Good job, kiddo. Now let's go get some knowledge," I said.

"Careful, Dan. You're venturing into after school special territory," Roxie said, grabbing the round crank and turning it to the left.

The door looked like a two-dimensional doorway from the side. Looking from the rear, one would have just seen an open door. But from the front, I saw a long stairwell descending into darkness. When at last it fully opened, Roxie led Dan and Eely inside.

Eely hopped up on my shoulder as Roxie and I continued on downward via stone steps. The occasional floating paper lantern lit the way for us.

After what felt like hours, we came to a large yet equally dim stone room with a grand golden door ahead of us. The room must have been about 200 feet wide and tall, and the golden door was covered in thousands of symbols all arranged in neat rows and columns.

In front of the door stood a woman with floor-length raven hair. She had a dress of caracal fur, and she wore green earrings with spirals. Her eyes were covered with charcoal-colored eye shadow that looked burned into her skin. The woman's eyes themselves were actually red. She had been sitting at a desk covered in scrolls writing.

As the three of us approached the stone desk, she looked over at us. She locked eyes with me, and I felt my mind instantly viewed through what felt like 1,000 different eyes. There was a burden of knowledge to this woman even I couldn't comprehend.

I caught myself and bowed, motioning for Roxie to do the same. She bowed as well, and I said, "Oh great Seshat, we would like to request access to your library please."

She crossed her arms and responded with a voice that, though soft, commanded our immediate attention. We would not speak until she was finished.

"I reveal my library to anyone who can open the door. It contains centuries of knowledge I've meticulously recorded and stored away," she said.

"That is most generous, my goddess," I said, still bowing.

"However. I have one rule before you enter. All who pass through these doors must take an oath before me. And if it's broken, you will be imprisoned here for the rest of time," Seshat said.

Roxie spoke up timidly.

"An oath?"

"Yes, daughter who seeks knowledge. You three must swear that you won't use any of the information obtained from my library to alter fate. My knowledge is open to any who can find it. But it is only for personal betterment and study. It is not used to wage war, to gain wealth, or to change the course of history. Do you understand?"

We all nodded.

"Then repeat after me: I, who enter the Library of Seshat, shall not abuse any knowledge I obtain here. Knowledge obtained in this place is only for my personal study and nothing else," Seshat said.

Roxie, Eely and I took the oath, and then the golden doors before us opened to reveal a seemingly infinite hallway, with thousands of other hallways branching off from it full of books and scrolls. The air was thick with the smell of old pages and inks of varying origin. The smell wasn't terrible, but it was almost overwhelming.

Torches of blue light clung to the sides of many bookshelves.

I guess that blue fire doesn't burn paper, I thought.

"How are we supposed to find what we're looking for in this place?" Roxie asked quietly to me.

Turning to Seshat, who appeared about ready to sit down and resume work, I asked, "Pardon me, goddess. We seek knowledge on the one known in our time as the Queen of Tears. If it's not too much trouble, could we ask for a hint as to where we might find it?"

She turned to me with a gaze that didn't show annoyance but instead was one of businesses. The goddess had no time for idle chit chat. There was always knowledge to copy, record, or store.

"Hallway 543,978, column 43,876, row 73, a blue book with a red quilt pattern on the outside. Page 531. You place your hand on the page, and it'll reveal the knowledge it contains."

With that, she sat back down in a limestone chair and returned to work writing quickly on a piece of parchment that appeared freshly made.

We walked into the endless hall of hallways and continued on past many shelves. The numbers of the hallways were marked in cuneiform, and I struggled to recall how to read that. Through the years I'd mastered a number of languages, but ancient Egyptian was always a pain. I hated it almost as much as I hated Sumarian.

You know, for the goddess who created writing, she could have included a few more numbered markings on these hallways from different cultures, I thought.

The smooth black marble floor beneath somehow had decent traction. I figured it'd be more slick based on the appearance, but my boots didn't slide once.

We walked onward until we got to the right hallway. It was on our left side, and I pointed it out to Roxie and Eely.

"About time. I was getting tired," Eely said.

"Oh, I'm sorry. Is riding on my shoulder getting too tiring?" I snapped at the fox.

She shrugged and said, "Okay, maybe tired isn't the right world. Bored is more like it."

Roxie giggled and said, "Eely, are you telling me that the idea we're surrounded by literally all the knowledge of everything is too boring for you?"

"I'm a simple fox, Roxie. I like to be told I'm pretty and eat food. These books accomplish neither of those things," Eely said.

We came to the right column and looked up toward the top of the stack. The bookshelf, which was made from a dark and ancient wood of some kind, stretched up for hundreds of shelves.

"Roxie? Can you make an elevator or something?" I asked.

"Can I do that here?"

"I don't see why not. We're visiting this place, but it's still inside my dream so..." I trailed off.

She shrugged and closed her eyes. The girl's bracelet lit up its usual shade of blue, and the ground below us moved upward at a slow pace. I looked down and saw a column beneath us provided the ride upward.

When we got to the 73rd row, I saw books of all different colors, some appearing older than others.

"How do you think she organizes this stuff? Like... one day she writes about toasters and the next she writes about ancient agriculture?" Roxie asked.

I shrugged and said, "The workings of this goddess are probably too complicated for our minds to wrap around."

When I finally found the blue book with the red quilt pattern on the outside, it was actually smaller than I figured it would be. It appeared to only contain about 700 pages.

Opening the book, I heard the crisp pop of a spine that hadn't been touched in decades, if not centuries. The pages contained no words, just numbers in the bottom left corner.

"How are we supposed to read a book with no words?" Roxie asked.

"I think the book pushes the knowledge directly in our minds," I said, turning to page 531.

The page was yellow just like the others.

"Well? I guess everyone who wants to know about the Queen of Tears should place a hand... or paw... on this page. And buckle up for a mental journey," I said, hovering my left hand over the book.

Eely and Roxie did the same.

"Do we all do it at the same time? Should we count to three or something?" Roxie asked.

"Oh for Kurama's sake," Eely said and put her paw on the page.

She stopped talking at once, and her eyes went solid white.

Part of me wanted to remove her paw to see if she went back to normal. But we were holding a magic book here, and I didn't want to take any risks that might hurt her.

"I guess we just do it," I said, putting my hand flat on the top half of the page next to Eely's paw. At once, my vision went to pure white.

Oh wow, dizzying, I thought. *So do I wait for words to appear or...?*

I didn't have to wait long as scenes began to play before me as though I were an invisible ghost spectating. I watched the birth of a young baby girl, born to proud parents in a small community of fur trappers somewhere in what would become Northwest Arkansas.

The girl already had some hair on her head. Her father was a heavy-set man, and he held her high as the baby cried. Scenes flashed before me at high speed, but I gained their knowledge all the same.

What a trip, I thought, noting that I could not see Eely and Roxie. *I guess they have their own visions.*

The girl was named Hiawatha. And as the child was held by the little community's solitary midwife, she predicted the child would grow to be extremely powerful, strong willed and ambitious, though fragile and small.

Rumor has it that the midwife was the only person who had arrived in the settlement after the little village had been established. Nobody knew where she came from, but there were whispers among the fur traders she wasn't entirely human. They claimed she was touched by the fey, perhaps a descendant, and that there was magic in her blood that allowed her to see small visions of the future.

Because the midwife used her abilities for the betterment of the fur trappers, they gave her a place in the settlement and listened to her words on rare occasions when she'd speak. Nobody dared hassle her for fear she would curse their future.

The memories sped up before me, until I saw a little girl.

She was different from her friends. I watched three boys and two girls jump into a pond to swim in the heat of summer, and while they easily made it across, Hiawatha struggled until water overtook her. She had to be fished out. I wondered what the problem was until I saw her legs, slim and slender. I didn't know what was wrong with them, but they looked fragile, like they'd shatter if someone looked at them with a fierce enough glare.

This girl had the spirit and will to keep up with her friends, but not the health. As she got older, I saw her weakness pull her further behind. A group of children from her settlement ran through the woods, racing home after foraging, and the girl collapsed a quarter way there, having to be helped by her sister the remainder of the journey.

As she got older, her anemic legs did not improve. And that weakness spread through other parts of her body, like her lungs and shoulders.

The inability to do much of anything seemed to bring much shame to her family until she turned 12. I watched her screaming in the middle of the night as many from her community ran to her family's house to see what the commotion was. She'd had some kind of terrible nightmare, and she was screaming about a friend of hers being attacked by a bear.

Her father backhanded her and ordered her back to bed.

The next day when she sat outside her family's home, some of her friends ran into the village screaming. A few of the adults gathered around to find out what happened, and they learned a bear had killed a child from the settlement.

The midwife that helped deliver Hiawatha proclaimed her powers had awoken and instructed anyone in the settlement who had troubling dreams to visit Hiawatha, pay her family tribute, and get her interpretation of their dream. In this way, good fortune would befall more members of the village and dangers could be avoided.

So she could see pieces of the future in addition to interpreting dreams, I thought.

Over the next several months, I watched as she became more confident in her abilities. She couldn't help prepare food or harvests. And it's true she spent most of her time sitting around the village, but she interpreted dreams well, telling people what they should plant, who they should marry, solving nagging worries, and many other things.

It wasn't long before travelers from other settlements came to her for dream interpretation. She grew to be something of a local legend. I watched the joy on her face with every person that she helped. Hiawatha had a true talent for what she was doing, and it made her proud to help provide for her family and her community in a nontraditional way.

I thought of Roxie and how much the Queen of Tears and her had much in common.

Both were granted an immense power at a young age without any real oversight or training. Our pixie dream girl seemed to have already suffered from that. But I had yet to see that same suffering for the Queen of Tears, even though I knew it had to have happened given the way she turned out.

How did you go from a happy girl to the Queen of Tears hellbent on trapping this entire city in a nightmare? I thought.

The book seemed to sense my question, and life again flashed forward to a 14-year-old Hiawatha.

* * *

(Hiawatha)

I sat with Tala as she put yellow flowers in my hair. They were a gift from an expecting mother who had traveled far from the west.

"Do you want me to use some of the red ones, too?" Tala asked, her shorter brown hair blowing in a breeze that also rattled our family's makeshift wind chime. Tiny pieces of tin held together by multicolored string on a wooden square hung just outside the main entrance to our home.

"No, I think I'll save them as a gift for mother," I said, smiling. "Thanks for helping me."

Tala smiled and laid her head on my shoulder.

"Do you think father will be back from the hunting trip today?"

"How would I know that?" I asked.

"Well, wouldn't you see it in a dream?" Tala asked.

I shook my head, loosening a couple flowers.

"I don't see everything that's going to happen. Only bits and pieces."

Tala nodded and put the red flowers aside.

"But to be entirely honest, I don't need dreams to know when he'll be back," I said.

"Oh? How will you know?" Tala asked, her face close to mine.

I looked in her curious brown eyes and whispered, "Simple. I just need to smell the wind. When he returns from a hunting trip, he often smells like deer carcass."

She snorted and laughed, falling fully on my shoulder. I giggled too.

"Hiawatha?" Tala asked.

"What is it?"

"Do you think we'll always be together like this? I like this. It's nice, just the two of us, you know?"

161

I smiled. Tala was a couple years older than me, and I knew she would marry a proud hunter from our settlement named James. I'd already seen their marriage and two children, both strong handsome boys. But she didn't need to know all that just yet. If she was happy together with me here and now, I didn't want to spoil that by pushing her into thoughts of the future.

I wish it could always just be the two of us, I thought. *I truly do.*

We got along wonderfully, and sure we had our quarrels as sisters often do, but at the end of the day I enjoyed making her laugh more than anyone else in the village. And she never looked down on me for my inability to really do much around the village. She never complained about helping me stand or move about. She always helped me, not for my dream interpretations, but because she loved me.

"I hope so," I said.

That night, I had trouble sleeping. But that wasn't unusual. Dreams often make you feel as if you're awake all night, walking about until sunrise. What was unusual as I tossed and turned on my deerskin bed was the clarity of the sequence of events I was witnessing.

Our family had grown quite wealthy because of my gift. People from all over brought payment, and my father was perhaps a little too proud of our wealth. I knew some in the village resented him for discussing what was given to our family because of my services.

But in my dream tonight, I sensed great resentment from Robert, the leader of our group of trappers. When I looked at him, I saw a deep shadow lurking. His shadow took the shape of a giant snake with massive wings like that of a dragonfly. It coiled deeply around him and poisoned his heart against my family, me specifically and my gift.

I saw him kill two of our group's best trackers, Edward and George. He planned to blame their deaths on me and turn everyone against me. Then he would use the distrust of our people to become the brave leader he always wished to be.

You fool. You'd really let your jealousy of my family's wealth drive you so mad? I thought.

Robert had much to be proud of. His son was the best archer in the village, and he'd helped defend us from attack three times already. He was an honorable man in every right. And yet... it wasn't enough. Our leader saw all the food and weapons a poor sickly girl had earned her own family, and he wanted that.

I awoke from my dream just a little before sunrise. By now Edward and George were likely already dead. I didn't have much time to prepare so as not to fall into Robert's trap. I had to gather the village in the center before God and tell them all what happened.

Thinking up all I intended to say, I realized I had to choose my words carefully. Though I had performed a great service for my village for two years now, I sensed they were still quick to stop listening to the words of a young sickly girl if she wasn't directly interpreting a dream for them.

It frustrated me a bit and actually seemed a little selfish, I realized. The folks in this village were eager for me to speak of their own good fortunes, but should I start to grow ominous and reveal the misfortunes of others, I saw their interest vanish like the last bit of ice in a warming pond as if I were somehow responsible for their misfortune.

After breakfast, I asked Tala to get word to everyone I had an important announcement to make in the center of our settlement. It took a couple hours, but a little before the sun was highest in the sky, everyone had gathered at the center of town. I was seated before a large fire on my dream log where I would always make predictions for the town. It was old and carved with symbols from different dreams I'd interpreted. Tala had helped me decorate it, and that thought made me feel safe. People seemed to pay more attention to me when I sat on it.

Everyone was whispering. What did the dream seer have to say to everyone? Was it a deathly warning? Was the harvest to be especially strong this year? They wondered as I scanned the crowd of men, women and children.

I found the leader sitting not too far from me, actually. He was to my left. The absence of Edward and George confirmed to me they were dead.

"Thank you for coming to hear me, my friends. You know I see many great and terrible things in my dreams. Last night I witnessed a traitor in this group killing two of our best trappers!" I yelled.

People began to murmur among themselves now, looking around. Robert's blank expression did not change.

You will not win, I thought.

"Can anyone tell me where Edward and George are?" I asked.

A wail came from the back of the crowd. The mothers of these two trappers pushed through to my feet.

"Please tell us where our sons are!" they screamed in unison.

I winced. I wasn't particularly close with these women, but I had to now tell them that their sons were murdered by our well respected leader who had protected our settlement for many years. My throat seized, and I had to force it open. I took a deep breath and said in one quick breath, "I'm so sorry, but they're dead. They were murdered."

They wailed all the louder. Siblings of Edward and George came forward to help carry their mothers away from the crowd. They tried their best to hide their emotions, but I knew they were heartbroken.

"My friends, I know this is a terrible truth to process. But there is worse news to come. For the person responsible for their murders..." I stopped, trailing off.

Once I launched this arrow, there was no putting it back into the quiver. Still, I was confident they'd listen to me.

They know me. They trust me, I thought.

Glancing through the crowd, I watched their individual faces. There was Anna, who had worried about her child all through pregnancy, until I predicted she'd birth a beautiful and healthy baby boy.

Next to her was William, our village's herbalist who struggled just last year to find the right medicine for everyone in the midst of a pandemic. Following my specific instructions, he'd found the proper herbs and mixed exactly what everyone needed.

Looking left, I saw Samuel, who I'd warned to avoid participating in a hunt with other men from a nearby settlement. I dreamed they'd be killed by bandits. He grumpily heeded my warning, and a few days later word reached us a group of men from that neighboring settlement hadn't returned from their hunt.

Behind him was Emma who had misplaced her entire family's life savings. It took me a couple weeks to see it in a dream, but I eventually did find it.

Through so many calamities I'd saved their lives and instilled hope. That had to mean more to them than Robert's jealousy or any evil he was willing to commit.

I pointed at Robert. "You murdered them! You stabbed them in the dark last night with the very blade you now sit over. Do you deny it?"

Gasps echoed out from the crowd, even a scream or two. Robert had never been accused of any wrongdoing. But two of our own were dead now by his hand. I had to show the others it was him.

He stood up at once, his long curly black hair swaying away from his face. He wore a red scarf over a brown shirt and trousers.

"I confess I killed these two men myself!" he yelled.

The grieving mothers shrieked and wailed even louder now. They thrashed their arms and kicked to the point their sons could do nothing else but let go. I gasped, surprised by Robert's honesty. I did not expect him to confess so openly.

There was much shouting until he raised his hands and called for silence. Eventually the townsfolk settled down. I knew they would not have done the same for me. A deep pit formed in my throat along with a sinking feeling of dread.

"I killed these men myself, but I am not guilty of any crime. The guilty one is Hiawatha," he yelled, pointing right back at me.

The crowd gasped.

Would they truly suspect me? A sickly girl?, I thought.

"Hiawatha has become too dangerous for us to tolerate any longer! Last night she came to me in my dream and took control of my body. She said Edward and George had refused to marry her and must be killed. When I refused, she possessed my body and forced me to commit murder. I had no control as I killed them. The only thing I could do was shed my tears as I watched my own two hands end the lives of two very precious boys," he said.

He's insane! Nobody will believe this! I thought.

An expression of shock and horror fell over the faces of most of the villagers as they looked at me.

"It's not true! I can't do that. He's lying!" I screamed.

"Because of Hiawatha, mothers now weep unending tears. The blood she forced me to spill will forever haunt this village's memory. It sentenced us all to eternal grieving. She is truly a Queen of Tears."

"He's making all of this up!"

As I screamed and cried, I saw that it was no use. I could see in the eyes of the villagers they believed Robert over me.

"My brothers and sisters, as much as we all love dear Hiawatha, she's too dangerous. She clearly can't control her powers and must be sealed away. Please, join with me this day to save any more from dying by her hand!"

The villagers were upon me instantly, no matter how much I screamed. I looked for my father, but I didn't see him. As they carried me out of the village toward a fate unknown, I saw Tala on the outskirts of the village.

"Help me! Tell them I didn't do this!" I yelled. "Please, sister!"

But she just looked down at the ground and wept.

They carried my body into the woods, and I had no strength to fight them off. I screamed for them to drop me, but they just smacked me and chanted, "Queen of Tears... Queen of Tears... Queen of Tears."

"You can't do this to me!" I screamed, my voice finally going hoarse. The midwife that delivered me walked behind the crowd with her head down in shame, perhaps believing that she should have never told me of my gift. And in that moment too I wished she had kept my powers a secret, leaving me as a frail little girl with a quiet existence.

After some time we came to a cave in the base of a mountain I did not recognize.

What are they going to do to me? I shrieked in my mind.

They carried my weak and fragile body down into the darkness far from the sunlight. I reached for the fading light, but it was no use. I could not grasp it any longer, and I'd never see it again in the physical world. At long last we came to a dead end in the cavern, and they laid my body down on a flat and narrow slab of stone, with two men holding me down, as if I had any strength left to fight them.

The remaining villagers spent the rest of the day carrying in metal and wood and constructing a crude gate that went from the floor to the ceiling. The noise was loud, but at last they finished late at night. Or I assumed it was night. There was no sunlight down here. They'd been working by torch light.

After the gate was finished, they brought forth an iron lock, something I recognized as being built by a smith in a neighboring settlement. It was the same story for the chains they wrapped around the gate. The men who were holding me down left just before the door slammed shut.

With the chains wrapped around the door, they placed the giant lock through several links. Then the smith who forged the device prayed over my lock, chanting different things.

When I had finally regained my energy to walk, I approached the gate and pressed my hands to its cold metal touch. When my skin met iron, my hand singed. They'd sealed me in here just like Robert said he would.

Not long after I touched the gate for the first time, Robert came forward. His face was covered with a sickening grin. He had gotten what he wanted. But later at night in his dreams, when he thought he was safe, I really would try to possess him and free myself.

I almost asked him why he did this until I remembered what I had seen in my dream.

Greed. I thought, feeling my stomach turn.

"You won't get away with this. As soon as I sleep, I will be free," I said.

He shook his head.

"No you won't, Queen of Tears."

"Stop calling me that!"

"These gates don't just seal you in here physically, they seal your magic, too. Even in your wildest dreams you'll remain in this cavern, alone, trapped in the dark. So you might as well just go lie down and wait for hunger to take you, child."

"You're a monster, and if what you say is true, then I promise this: I will survive this. I will live long enough to grow in strength and get out of here. And even if you are long gone and dead, I will ensnare your descendants and the descendants of everyone in this village in a terrible nightmare from which there is no escape," I said, glaring at him.

"Your threats are as empty as your stomach will soon be, child," he said and left.

I heard his footsteps fade out, and then I heard nothing, save for a little dripping water in the distance.

Curling up on the slab, I cried.

Queen of Tears, I thought.

Over the next couple of days, my hunger grew rampant, as did my thirst. They really meant for me to die here, didn't they? Trapped in the dark and dying of hunger like some kind of wounded animal is what they wanted for me. But that would not be my fate.

No, I will keep my promise of vengeance, I thought, furious.

My heart twitched with fury, each beat stronger than the last.

"If I stay here, I'll die. So I'll sleep. I'll sleep until I have my vengeance. No... my sleep will become my vengeance," I muttered.

Focussing all my remaining strength, I laid straight as a board on the smooth slab I'd been abandoned on.

"My death is not here, Robert. One day I'll be free, and then I'll haunt the dreams of your descendents, changinging them into nightmares that will engulf their every waking thought. Your children's children will not know joy, only tears as they cry for their nightmares to end."

My body glowed a deep purple as a hazy fog crawled through the cavern. I slammed my eyes shut like the gates that had been closed on me, and at once my body froze. I did not draw breath. I put my body asleep and became fully alive in spirit. I stretched the dream to fill the cavern, but that infernal gate kept it from physically spreading any further.

Still, in my dream I could create light. I could create an open field under a warm sun. I could visit anywhere, eat anything, drink my fill. In this dream, I was my own leader, and no one could take that from me.

Over the decades, I grew stronger in my dream, and I found that seal weakening, bit by bit, year by year.

It wasn't long before I could reach outside the cave with my influence, even if only for a few minutes. Eventually, I would be free. I would find a key to open that lock and unleash my nightmare on everyone who lived above me, descendants of those who imprisoned me or simply people who fraternized with them.

I didn't care how long it would take, decades, centuries, I had all the time I wanted in this dream. They would be ensnared… someday.

* * *

(Dan)

My eyes left the darkness of that cave and returned from their faded white state to the Library of Seshat.

"Oh lord, what a trip," I said, holding my head.

Roxie and Eely were back at the exact same time I was. But our reactions were different. Eely was silently looking at the other books around. Roxie was crying. And I was more determined than ever to find a way to kill this evil.

"Well, that was something, huh? Can I assume you all saw what I did?"

Roxie nodded and said, "The tragedy of Hiawatha, yes."

"We've got to stop the Queen of Tears at all costs. Hopefully we can use something we learned here to do just that," I said, putting the book back on the shelf.

Roxie lowered us back to the ground, and the elevator faded back into the smooth floor, as if it'd never been raised.

"If you saw what I did, then surely you sympathize with her, yes?" Roxie said.

"Of course, kid. I get that. She was dealt a terrible hand. But the rest of us don't suffer for that. We don't look at the tragic childhoods of serial killers and go, 'Oh, they had a bad past. We'd better let them go.' We use what we learned today to find a weakness and then save the city," I said.

Seshat's voice spoke up behind us.

"So, you always intended to break your oath? That's disappointing," she said.

I turned to see her standing there.

"Aw hell. Listen, Seshat, we meant no offense, but we have a city to save."

"You swore an oath! I allowed you into my sanctuary of knowledge, and you betrayed me!" she yelled.

Her words carried such a weight to them they rattled my very being.

"I know! And I'm sorry. But surely there are exceptions if we're going to stop a monster, right? Surely you understand the need for good to triumph over evil?"

Her red eyes narrowed, and so did the valves in my heart as I felt my chest tighten with fear. We'd pissed off an ancient goddess.

"I have written much on what you call good and evil, foolish man. I merely record history and knowledge. I gave you access to that knowledge freely, and you broke my one rule. Surely you know what happens next. You will not be allowed to leave," she said.

As she spoke, stone figures began to rise out of the floor all around us. They were shaped like humans but larger. They carried clubs, spears, and other basic weapons with them. The lack of a face on these creatures creeped me out.

"Oh great. The goddess of knowledge has an army of golems," I muttered. "Listen! If we don't get out of here, a lot of people are going to suffer, trapped in a terrible nightmare. You have to understand."

Seshat shook her head, and her green earrings rattled.

"I understand that you broke your oath. Now you will remain here for the rest of time," she said.

Great, I've swapped one prison for another. I wonder if they get magazines here, I thought.

"Wait! Order your golems to stand down! Surely with all your knowledge you know what a kitsune is," I said.

"I know everything about them. What is your point?" she asked with a cool tone.

"Well then you must know Eely here can breathe fire. We'll burn every book in this library if you don't let us go," I said, taking a gamble. "All that knowledge lost forever. How do you like that?"

Seshat glared somehow even more fiercely, and I swear my heart stopped for a moment. Having a goddess scowl at me was terrifying, and my subconscious wanted to slither off somewhere out of sight.

"You foolish man, do you think that knowledge leaves my brain forever when I put it on paper? If you burn these books, I will simply rewrite them. Your threat is empty," she said.

I cursed my luck and took a step back against the bookshelf.

"Well, no use trying any other gambles. Roxie, Eely, seeing as I'm not much of a fighter, you'll have to fight our way out of here for me," I said.

Eely took her full-sized form and let loose a stream of golden fire upon Seshat and her golems. Roxie's bracelet glowed, and she yelled, "Hang on!"

We rose up again, but this time the elevator bent forward and got us over the burning golems and goddess. Once we were back on the ground, we bolted. Running as hard as we could, we got back to the hallway of halls.

"Which way?" I shouted, unable to see the entrance since we'd come so far.

"You had one job, Dan! Keep track of where we were!" Eely yelled.

More golems began to rise around us, and Seshat's voice boomed from the air above.

"You will not escape."

Roxie put her arm in front of me and said, "Step back!"

Her bracelet glowed a bright blue, and it started to rain all around

170

us. Somehow, even though we were underground in a library, rain fell from the darkness above.

"You going to turn the golems into mud?" I asked as they grew closer.

They were not fast, but I sensed they were strong, and I didn't want to get into a fist fight with them.

Eely covered my mouth with one of her tails.

"Ignore him, dear. You keep going!"

Roxie began to grimace as she grabbed her bracelet with her free hand. Then the water began to circle around us. It took the form of a tube, and then the tube changed again. It grew legs, hair, eyes, fangs, and before long a 40-foot aquatic dragon stood over us.

"Wow," my muffled voice said under Eely's tail.

"Get on!" Roxie yelled.

When I looked over, I saw she had a new addition to her form by the way of glowing silver antenna coming out of her bangs. They twitched with a certain sensitivity as Roxie closed her eyes.

"That way!" she pointed with her glowing bracelet, and the dragon took off just as I sat on it with Eely wrapping several of her tails around the body. Our dream girl sat just behind the head, and I was behind the dragon's claws with Eely behind me.

The dragon slithered through the sky or... open air in the room. We raced forward with great speed flying over the golems, and that worked pretty good until we got back to the large golden doors finding them sealed shut.

On the floor was a pissed Seshat, ready for her prisoners to stop these shenanigans.

"Cover your ears!" Eely yelled.

We did as we were told, and she began to shake. A large golden ball of fire began to spin in her jaws. I'd never seen her do this before.

Oh crap, I thought, torn between wanting to hang onto the water dragon and keeping my ears covered.

At last Eely shot the fireball forward, and it smashed into the door with a deafening boom. The shockwave knocked me off the dragon and shattered the nearby bookshelves. Bookshelves a little further away were burning.

Roxie had the dragon catch me with its claws, and I thanked her.

When the smoke cleared, the golden doors had been blown

outward into the large room. Roxie had our water dragon fly through and toward the stairwell leading back up into my normal dream.

We landed as the dragon was too big to make it up the stairwell, and Seshat now appeared behind us at least 75-feet tall.

"Enough! Surrender immediately, oathbreakers!" she yelled.

"Group vote? Stay or leave?" I asked.

"Leave," Roxie and Eely said in unison.

"Then it's unanimous, we haul ass up those stairs," I said.

Roxie ordered her water dragon to turn into ice and coil around the stair entrance after we'd taken off.

We heard Seshat banging on it as we ran up the stairs, but we didn't stop. Onward and upward we dashed. My knees and lungs told me to stop and take a break, but the fear of being imprisoned in Seshat's dungeon spurred me forward. At last, we could see the rusty door that let us in here.

The goddess finally broke through and scaled the stairs almost instantly behind us. Her elongated form stretched up at us, and I made the mistake of turning around to see.

"Stop at once!" she yelled, filling the entire stairwell with her booming voice.

Roxie was through the door first, followed by Eely and myself. We turned to close the door and saw Seshat growing closer and closer. We pushed the door shut with everything we had, and the last thing we saw was an angry knowledge goddess three steps from the top when it finally slammed shut.

We fell backwards from the force she hit the door with. She banged on the door, and it rattled, seemingly ready to open at any second.

"How do we make the door go away?" Roxie yelled.

The banging only grew louder, and dents were starting to appear now.

"You have to end the dream, Roxie. Wake me up! Wake me up!" I yelled.

"Later!" she said as her bracelet glowed.

I bolted awake at once, overheated and covered in sweat, looking around my barren room for some sign of Seshat.

Eely was instantly awake too as I stood up and ran to the bathroom to splash cold water on my face.

"Oh my Kurama," she muttered, hopping onto the floor.

I wandered downstairs into the bathroom, turning the knob for cold water. I let it pool in my hands and then splashed it on my face. When I closed my eyes, I could still see Seshat's elongated face just before we slammed the door shut.

I went on splashing water over my face for what felt like an hour or two. Finally, Eely called down the stairs, and I shut the water off, grabbing a nearby red towel.

Holding it on my face for a few seconds, I let out a muffled, "Coming."

I tossed the towel in the hamper and went back upstairs.

"Well, that was a terrifying adventure," I said.

"Yeah, let's never visit that library again, overdue fees be damned," Eely said.

We sat on the bed in silence as my eyes floated over to my parents picture on the wall. I remembered how the Queen of Tears promised to reunite me with them.

If just trying to find a way to beat her was this tough, how difficult would it be to stop her? I felt like I'd aged another 130 years in this dream alone. I didn't want to do that again.

Sighing, I put my head in my hands. I didn't actually intend to hand the key over to her. That was just crazy thinking on my tired mind's part. Still... I didn't even want to start going back over what we'd learned in that book to try and find a weakness. Not yet. I needed a break, a break from my sleep. That's how insane this night was. Usually sleep *was* the break.

"What time is it, Eely?"

"It's 2:15 a.m."

"What time does that midnite cookie store stop delivering?"

"I think 3:00 a.m." the fox said.

"Want me to put an order in? I'm not eager to head back into dreamland just yet. I want to give that door plenty of time to dissolve if it didn't instantly disappear," I said.

"Yeah, cookies sound good to me," Eely said, sounding equally exhausted.

I headed down the stairs and picked up the polka dot phone on the wall. Stopping the Queen of Tears was going to be a pain in the ass.

But for now... cookies were all I had to worry about.

Chapter Eleven
(Roxie)

I was a little tired after walking Rufus who, surprisingly, wanted to do two full laps around the block today. Though that may only have been because we saw two different UPS trucks he wanted to bark at and chase.

My cyborg mother honed in on my exhaustion as soon as I came into the kitchen. She had been fixing herself some crackers with mayo, bacon and lettuce on them.

"Couch, Priss. I want you resting up until Tessa and Jenna get here," she said, pointing.

"I'm fine, Mom. Besides, I wanted to warm up a little before practice," I said.

She crossed her arms.

"I can do that too, see?" I asked, crossing my arms and smirking.

Mom took a step toward me. That was her warning shot. She did not fire it twice. But I was determined to warm up. Plus, I wanted to finish some lyrics.

I took a step toward Mom, and my smirk grew.

I'm 18 now. She wouldn't dare, I thought.

She must have been feeling extra merciful today, because her widening eyes gave me one more chance to back down. I chose not to and was already trying to finish the last verse of a new song called "Fishnets."

Without warning, Mom bolted forward, and I only had time to gasp.

"You wouldn't dare!" I screamed as she swept my legs and caught me in her arms. "I am 18! You can't do this anymore. I'm too big!"

As Mom carried me over to the couch she said, "You can be 18 or 88. And if I want to carry you to the couch and put you in timeout, I will."

Then she tossed me onto the couch like a sack of potatoes. I bounced around, flummoxed, trying to figure out if that really just happened. Mom hadn't picked me up and carried me anywhere in such a dramatic fashion since I was 16.

"Now you park it there until practice, Priss," Mom said, putting a finger in my face.

I crossed my arms and looked off to the left. Although I was planning on pouting for a few minutes longer, I saw Mom had left out her charcoal nail polish on the coffee table.

Two can play at this game, I thought, smiling.

I was two nails in when Mom came over and turned on the television. She saw what I was doing and said, "Oh come on, Priss. That's my favorite color."

I stuck my tongue out at her.

"That's what you get for treating me like a ragdoll," I said. "Can I have a cracker?"

Mom shot me a faux glare.

"You steal my nail polish, and now you want to steal my food?" she asked, moving her black bangs out of her face.

"Yeah!" I said with a big grin.

"And all that came after you disobeyed me, requiring me to put your ass on the couch?"

"Yeah!" I said with a bigger grin.

She rolled her eyes and held her plate over to me. It was an old plate I had begged her for years ago because I was in a horse phase. It only took one set of riding lessons for me to get over that ignorant phase. The plate actually featured the mustang from the movie *Spirit* standing in an open field and looking off into the sky.

Mom claimed this wasn't her favorite plate, but I saw her using it every time it was clean, and she only washed it by hand.

"You check the mail today?" Mom asked.

"Yeah," I said, still painting my nails.

"Anything in there? I didn't see it sitting on the counter."

"Just another postcard," I said, finishing the cracker with my free hand.

Mom snickered.

"You're really dedicated to that pen pal, aren't you? What's his nickname? Psychedelic Pete?"

I laughed at Mom, and I knew I would have to tell Dan about that name when I saw him next. Or I could just put it in tomorrow's postcard, whichever came first.

"He's Funky Dan, Mom," I said, still laughing.

"Oh, right. He's just got such a funny name. How did you two meet again?" she asked.

I twitched a little. How did I tell Mom I was sending postcards back and forth with an old man without it sounding creepy?

"He runs a shop here in town I stumbled upon one day. He's not really able to leave the shop due to his... advanced age. So I write him, and he writes me," I said.

Mom looked over at me and smiled.

"That's really sweet of you, Priss. You've got a good heart in your chest, you know that?"

I looked down at the floor.

Except for when I'm torturing fathers who have lost a kid, I thought.

And then Dan's words came back to me, "You have a conscience, and it's clearly working just fine. This is the kind of stuff that's supposed to happen after something that's not supposed to happen, if that makes any sense."

I need to remember not to let my mistakes define me, I thought. *I screwed up, I owned it, and now I'm moving on, trying to do good.*

I just smiled back at Mom and then glanced down at my phone.

"Looks like they'll be here in about 10 minutes," I said. "This polish is the quick dry kind, right?"

Mom scowled at me.

"What, you don't read the labels of things you steal?" she said, a little smirk forming in the corner of her mouth.

"Hey, if you don't want me using it, keep it put somewhere else. Anything out here is fair game," I said.

Mom thought for a moment and then flashed me a devilish grin.

"Anything out here, huh?" she said.

Suddenly, I was regretting my words as she slowly sauntered into the kitchen and opened the silverware drawer. She pulled out a black cloth bag that was instantly familiar to me.

"No!" I yelled. "Not those. You can't use them. They're my special ones Jenna brought back from Kyoto!"

Mom ignored me and opened the bag. She pulled out two Hello Kitty chopsticks.

"Oh come on! You can't eat crackers with those. You're just doing this to spite me," I said, crossing my arms.

She walked back over to the couch with her plate and sat back down. Amazingly, she was able to grab a cracker and keep the toppings on while moving it toward her mouth slowly to taunt me.

"Okay, okay! You made your point. I'm sorry I used your nail polish without asking. It won't happen again," I said, raising my hands toward her.

"Ahhhhhhhhh," she said, her mouth wide.

"I said I'm sorry! Please, those are my favorite, and you're going to get your cooties on them!"

Now, Mom closed her mouth and cocked her head to the side.

"My what?"

Crap, I thought.

She put down the cracker and then just began to threaten to lick the chopsticks.

"You want to see mom cooties? I can show you mom cooties," she said.

"Mom no!" I yelled, snatching them from her grasp. Though, to be honest, I'm pretty sure she let me take them to prevent my blood pressure from rising any higher.

"Don't touch this polish again, you hear me, Priss?" Mom said.

"Yes ma'am," I said, cradling my chopsticks before I went to put them back in the kitchen drawer.

I sat back down on the couch and let out an exasperated sigh at Mom. She had given her attention over to the television, a "Cops" rerun.

Tessa and Jenna showed up a few minutes after they said they would, and I went down into bay three to set up with them.

They both gave me a big hug, and as usual, without any control, I was able to see what they'd dreamed of last night. Jenna had dreamed she was skiing down a mountain of mint chocolate ice cream, which was pretty typical for her. Tessa, though, had dreamed about being a finalist on *The Bachelor* and being chosen by Bobbie.

Oh honey... I thought, trying not to laugh.

"How are you holding up, Rox?" Jenna asked.

I nodded and said, "Best as I can figure? I'm doing better."

"You know if you're not up for practicing yet, we can always go upstairs and watch a movie or something, right?" Jenna said.

"Jenna, we talked about this on the way over. Our girl is fine. If she didn't want to play, she wouldn't be playing, right Roxie?" Tessa said.

I nodded.

"I really do appreciate your concern, Jenna. But I really... really just need an afternoon of playing music with the people I love," I said, looking at the van.

Tessa coughed and said, "Gay."

Jenna and I scowled at her and then started laughing while we finished setting up for rehearsal.

We warmed up separately and then played our cover of Pat Benatar's "Love Is A Battlefield." It felt good to be back in the saddle with my friends. I looked over at both of them as we finished. Jenna smiled and Tessa shook her head.

"I don't think we ended that song like we normally do," Tessa said.

"I thought it sounded fine," Jenna said.

"Yeah, well your ears are bad. You play in a band with loud instruments all the time. My ears can pick things up better," Tessa said.

"What?! That makes no— Tessa, you're in this band too!" Jenna yelled.

I laughed at the two of them. Truth was, I loved it when Tessa said illogical things just to get a rise out of Jenna. The two of them were hysterical.

We played through "Should Have Kissed Me Yesterday" and "Glitter Choke." Then I convinced them to try a new song I'd written called "Breathless."

"Okay, so for the intro guitar, I was thinking you take it at a pretty good pace, Jenna. Kind of like... the intro to 'Long Way Down,'" I said.

Jenna just stared at me for a moment.

"Long Way Down?" she asked.

"Yeah, you know, Goo Goo Dolls?"

Jenna sighed and then chuckled.

"What is it with you and 90s music? It's all terrible. You should just skip that decade, the next one, and pick back up with rock music in 2010," she said.

"Oh come on, Jenna. It's not all bad," Tessa said.

Jenna crossed her arms and said, "Oh yeah? Name one good song from the 90s."

Tessa thought for a moment, and then a smile grew on her face. She started shaking her hips and sang, "When I dance they call me Macarena..."

I immediately started laughing, and Jenna set her guitar down.

"I can't deal with you two right now," she said. "I'm going upstairs to get some water from Melanie. Rox, while I'm up there, I'm deleting your whole iTunes library."

Tessa and I scoffed for a second. Then the cheerleader put her curly scarlet hair into a ponytail. We briefly exchanged glances, and I felt my pulse quicken.

Jumping up from my stool, I ran for the door behind bay two that led up to the kitchen.

"Jenna, don't you dare!" I yelled halfway up.

After we came back downstairs, I found Tessa admiring a red 2006 Mustang in bay one. It was sitting there while Mom waited on a part to come in for it. The owner had decided to leave it here over the weekend.

"Any chance we can convince Melanie to loan us the keys to this one for the afternoon? I mean... I'd happily take this home over a ride in Jenna's battle van," Tessa said, leaning on the car.

Her purple sundress got caught on the side view mirror as she walked by, and Jenna freed her.

"Hey genius, if it's sitting at the mechanic's shop over the weekend, that's probably because it's broken. But you're still welcome to walk home, or you can hop on the bus. Roxie, isn't there a stop three blocks down?" Jenna asked.

"I think it's five, actually. But who's counting when you're lugging a bass guitar case in the hot summer sun?" I asked, putting my hands on my hips.

Tessa rolled her eyes and said, "Whatever. Let's just get back to Roxie's new song."

We tried our hand at it for the next 45 minutes, but it just wasn't coming together like I wanted.

"Man, that's a rough second verse," Tessa said.

"Don't worry. We'll get it. I can really feel this song. We're gonna rock it. It's our Ka," I said, clenching my fist.

Tessa and Jenna exchanged glances.

"Ka?" Tessa asked.

"Yeah, you know. Like... didn't you both read *The Dark Tower* series?" I asked.

Tessa snort-laughed a little, and Jenna just shook her head.

I sighed and said, "Just forget about it."

That's when I felt my phone vibrate in my butt pocket and reached behind me to pull it out. Unlocking the device, I saw a text from Kairen. It was a pain in the ass to get his number. I had to have Tessa reach out to Bobbie, who had it. Then I endured 15 straight minutes of questions about whether I had a crush on Kairen, how I knew him, and why I suddenly wanted his number.

Dan may not have had a cell phone, and I wasn't allowed into his shop until I truly needed something, so the postcards made sense for us since they had next-day delivery in town.

But there was no excuse for Kairen and I not to have each other's phone numbers, particularly given our dream/nightmare relationship.

"Roxie, need your help fast. It's bad. Grandma talked Dad into pulling the plug on Jonas. He's going to do it tonight after he closes the book shop. Please help. I need you to free him like you promised," his text read.

My heart sank. When I made that promise, I was just trying to get Kairen out of the nightmare. I didn't actually know if I could wake his brother up.

I guess my bluff is being called, I thought, unsure if I used those terms right.

Typing as fast my fingers would let me, I responded. Then I told the girls and Mom I had to rush to the hospital to see a friend. They were reluctant but let me go when they saw urgency in my eyes. My heart was pounding, and it was no time to choke. I gave Kairen my word.

* * *

Twenty minutes later I walked into the general entrance of the hospital. My blue sneakers squeaked on the black and white tile floor. A wooden wrap-around desk with three nurses behind it sat to my right, and above me was a long row of fluorescent lighting.

It was chilly inside the waiting room, and I heard about two or three people coughing and sitting in some rather uncomfortable looking red chairs. One older woman sat alone on a bench looking at her phone.

"Roxie," I heard a voice call, and I looked over to see Kairen standing down a hallway to my right.

He was wearing a red t-shirt and jeans, standing by an elevator.

I walked over and could immediately tell he'd been crying. His eyes were red and puffy. Kairen took a step forward like he wanted to hug me and then quickly stopped and rubbed his right arm.

"Thanks for coming," he said, looking down at the ground.

Without really thinking about it, I pushed forward and hugged him, with my arms wrapped around his chest. He smelled like old books, and I assumed he'd previously been at the bookstore with his father.

"It'll be okay," I said, as he very lightly put his left arm around me to awkwardly return the hug.

"Kairen, if a girl hugs you first, you can return the hug," I said, and I felt his right arm wrap around me now.

I could feel Kairen shaking, and not from the cold lobby.

"I'm terrified, Roxie. What if I lose my little bro?" he asked.

I pulled away and looked him in the eyes.

"Jonas is going to be just fine," I said. I wasn't sure if I was saying that to convince him or myself.

Heck, who was I kidding? There was no way I'd break my promise to Kairen. If I did, that would ruin whatever friendship we were developing and drive him even further into the arms of Hiawatha.

I watched Kairen force a smile, then push the elevator button. I looked at my reflection in the metal doors as we waited and caught an older couple to our left staring at me.

When I looked back at them, they didn't stop staring, which got me heated. It's one thing to be rude and stare. I'd been stared at a lot in my life, especially before I started to pass. But when someone catches you staring, you're supposed to be polite enough to at least look away. These people did not. I was about to turn around and say something like, "Can I help you?" But the elevator dinged, the doors slid open and Kairen gently tapped my shoulder to push me forward.

When we got in, I immediately smelled weed.

"Whoever stood in here before us reeked," I complained, coughing on the strong odor.

Kairen didn't seem to mind, but he looked me over and said, "How do you... bring your dream appearance into real life? I mean... I don't exactly walk around with a top hat during daytime hours."

I sighed and said, "It's not really something I have control over. Dan mentioned something about pixie magical contamination or something before. I keep meaning to ask him about it, but it always slips my mind."

"So... you didn't choose to have silver hair and glowing pink eyes?"

I shook my head and looked down at the white floor of the elevator.

"This is actually how pixies look, or at least the one who gave me my abilities. In my last dream, I actually had a little antenna. The only thing I'm missing so far are the butterfly wings. And since I'm trying to keep my nighttime activities a secret, I'm really hoping they don't show up one day."

Kairen snickered and said, "Butterfly wings. You're really prepared to go full Tinkerbell, huh?"

I put my hands on my hips and said, "For your information— you know what? Forget it. Let's just focus on waking Jonas up."

The doors opened on the fourth floor, and Kairen led me down a few different hallways. There were quite a few senior citizens on this floor. We passed a few walking by with canes and their IVs. One strangely smelled of chocolate pudding.

Jonas' room had one of those flat door handles you had to lift up on to open the door. Going inside, I felt nervous again. I was confident that I was going to do this, but it was still sending shivers down my spine.

Over on a bed with wheels and side rails down was Jonas, lying motionless and covered by a scratchy green hospital blanket. He had a long plastic tube covering his mouth, and a beeping machine was helping him breathe. The kid's eyes were closed, and his blond bangs partially covered his left eye.

I'd seen Jonas in this bed!

A small television was mounted to the wall behind us up near the ceiling. Over by the window were a couple of small blue chairs and a round table with flowers on it. A few deflated balloons sat under the table.

"The bookstore closes at 5:00 tonight. We don't have much time," Kairen said, walking over and putting his hand on Jonas', gripping it tight.

"Why is your father doing this?" I asked.

"My grandma... she's kind of the religious one in the family. And by kind of, I mean, very religious. She convinced my grief-stricken dad that Jonas being kept alive with this machine is keeping him from going to Heaven."

I shook my head and frowned.

"And he's just going along with what she says? Why won't he listen to you?" I asked.

Kairen looked down at Jonas and grabbed his brother's shoulder.

"It's all icing on the shit cake at this point. I'd heard Dad say we were running out of money to cover hospital expenses, and we don't have health insurance. I think my grandma's words are just a final push toward pulling the plug," Kairen said.

I didn't know how to respond to that. There were times I had desperately run out of gas in my life, but my mom and friends had always picked me back up. I guess Kairen and his father were a little more isolated.

"But don't you worry, Jonas. Roxie is going to get you back," Kairen said, and squeezed his brother's shoulder a little more.

I felt my chest tighten and looked over at the little side table next to Jonas' bed. There was a picture of Kairen and his brother on it, along with a plastic cup of water. It said "Fayetteville General Hospital" written on the outside, along with the motto, "Where patients come first."

"Are you ready?" Kairen asked.

I slightly nodded and walked over to the opposite side of Jonas.

"Have you ever tried to enter his dreams?" I asked.

Kairen looked down at Jonas and said, "Yeah, several times. But my earring just won't let me in. It's very strange. It's like... I can visit any other nightmare I want. But his is off limits."

I frowned.

That certainly sounds like this is Hiawatha's doing, I thought.

Placing my hand on Jonas' forehead, I felt he was actually kind of cold. Closing my eyes, I could feel his nightmare... but it was difficult to pull in anything else. It was like a TV with a bad antenna or something.

It was at this point a memory shot into my head like lightning. I'd been here before, in this room. I took a deep breath and sighed.

That earlier vision was just like this with Jonas and Kairen, I thought.

A moment of silence passed.

"He is dreaming," I said.

"Great. Can you wake him up?" Kairen asked.

I shook my head and said, "It's not that simple. I've never done this before. I can't just pull him back to being awake. I'll have to go inside the nightmare he's trapped in and free him there, I suspect."

Kairen nodded and said, "Then please take me with you."

Great. Add on another thing I don't know if I can do, I thought.

"I'll do my best. Give me your hand," I said.

Kairen gave me his, also cold, hand, and I kept my other on Jonas' forehead. Why were they both so cold?

I closed my eyes. Though I could see Jonas' nightmare just a little clearer, I could not enter. I kept waiting for that usual *whooshing* feeling that came when I entered someone's sleeping vision.

"Is there a problem?" Kairen finally asked after a minute or two.

"Just trying to concentrate. Like I said, I've never done this before," I said.

Finally opening my eyes, I took a deep breath and exhaled.

Maybe it's just impossible for me to enter the dream of somebody through physical contact alone, I thought.

Then I saw a little table mirror with puppies painted on it next to the water cup. Looking into the reflection and seeing my glowing pink eyes, I said, "*Ambulate per somnia.*"

At once, the mirror's surface darkened until I could no longer see my reflection.

Kairen looked at the mirror, confused, but it didn't seem like he was looking at the same thing I was. I assumed only I could see what came next.

There was that castle again. I could see it clearly now. Lightning flashed and rain poured down from black, puffy clouds. I was watching the fortress from the bottom of a mountain, like staring up at the top of a tree.

"I see his nightmare. Hold on, Kairen."

He tightened his grip on my hand, but not too much. There was a hesitance to him, like he was trying to keep from shattering me.

"Your demure behavior is appreciated, Kairen, but if you want to go with me into this nightmare, you need to hold tight when I tell you to," I said, squeezing his hand harder.

"*Immeo*," I said, and darkness rushed around me. Only this time, there was a weight on my arm, and I knew it was Kairen. It felt like I was pulling him through the air, like a balloon with something attached to it.

Then at once we were inside. I looked around and saw shelves and shelves of books. It smelled like these were even older than anything at Kairen's bookstore.

The books looked primitive, too. It was like they weren't made with a modern printing press but were instead from medieval times when copying a book was done by hand.

A long wooden table stood behind us with red chairs to sit on. The room was dark, save for a few candles hanging on stone columns in the middle and the occasional lightning flash that would come through a large oval window to my right.

"Where are we?" I asked, looking around.

Aside from my voice, the only sound in the stone room was the crackling of large candles.

Above one bookshelf was a mountain boar's head. And this pig was huge, with tusks large enough to rip through all of me.

"Kairen?" I asked, turning around.

He looked mystified as well. But his confusion was different than mine because he knew where we were. I could tell that much. But his furrowed brow told me he didn't believe where we were.

"I don't... wow. This is uncanny," he said.

"What is it? You recognize this place," I said.

He slowly nodded.

"This is Castle Tormund."

"Castle what?"

"It's a... popular setting for my little brother's *Dungeons & Dragons* games. He has a bunch of friends that come over about once a month, and they play at the back of the bookstore. Then he tells me every detail of their adventures afterward. It's kind of cute in a dorky way, but I love how passionate he is. I keep telling him he needs to become a writer," Kairen said.

"We're in your brother's *Dungeons & Dragons* game? That's his nightmare?" I asked, raising an eyebrow.

Kairen threw up his arms.

"It's not like we're in the game itself. I think this is just a common setting for him. He was always describing it to me, the layout, showing me sketches, reading me passages he'd written about this place. It's where the vampire king lives in his game. I guess on some level, he put so much of himself into this place trying to make it scary, that it became scary for him."

It was at this point I realized Karien was wearing the same clothes as he was in the hospital.

"Hey Kairen? Why aren't you dressed up in your phantom thief costume?" I asked.

"It's not a costume. It's a... mystical uniform," he said. "And... I don't know. I can't make it appear, no matter how hard I try."

Why can't he use his abilities here? I thought, my mind wandering back to our location.

"Anyway, how do we get to... wherever we need to?" I asked.

Kairen rubbed his chin for a minute and closed his eyes.

"Hang on. I'm trying to remember. This is the royal library. It's on the first floor. I think there's a secret staircase to the throne room behind the bookshelf under the pig's head," he said.

I smiled.

"Don't you mean the razor—" he interrupted me.

"Don't start that," he said.

I threw my arms up in the air and walked over to the large bookcase under the boar's head. It was made of a thick oak and polished to a smooth surface.

How would you get something so polished back in the middle ages? I thought.

I tried pulling on some different books, hoping for a switch. But not a single book led to an opening. There were about 34 books in total in front of me, and none of them helped.

"Okay, Mr. Dungeon Master. How do we open this thing?"

Kairen looked around the room and then pointed to a fireplace.

"We need to light this, and then it'll open, I think."

He raised his hand toward the fireplace, but nothing happened. I kept waiting for his dragon-shaped earring to glow purple, but it never did.

I could hear him making grunting noises and shaking his arm, but nothing was happening to the fireplace.

"It's not working. My powers aren't working," he said.

I raised an eyebrow and then focussed on the fireplace with my own bracelet. It glowed blue, and then there was a small fire in the pit.

186

"There you go," I said, smiling.

It took a few seconds of grinding gears, but the bookshelf finally opened a crack. It took both of us pulling it for several minutes to make a gap wide enough to get through.

"Next time your brother makes a castle, have him include some WD-40 lying around in random areas, okay?"

"I'll tell him that," Kairen said, going up the tight spiral staircase. There was no railing, and the stairs were only wide enough for one person to go up at a time.

Kairen got to the top, and it was dark, so I made my bracelet glow and held it up for him. In front of us was a stone wall.

"What now?"

As we waited, I nearly screamed as a rat ran over my foot.

Before Kairen could figure out how to open it, my bracelet glowed bright blue, and the wall exploded outward away from us.

He frowned at me, but we walked through the dust of my explosion.

It truly was something. Statues of vampires lords and hellhounds lined each side of the room. It was probably 300 feet long and twice as wide. The ceiling above had several multicolored chandeliers, all lit. And precious stones were mixed into the floor we walked on.

A long red carpet stretched from giant wooden doors that I guessed served as the entrance up to the metal throne itself. The throne looked familiar, and as the dust cleared, I saw it looked like a bunch of swords melted together.

Really? You can make an entire castle, but you have to steal the most popular throne of all time? I thought, unimpressed.

Upon further study of the room, I realized I'd been here before, too. That wild night I'd bounced around multiple dreams and saw Kairen's little brother in the hospital.

This is the dream I entered briefly back then, I thought.

"Kairen? Is that you?" a boy's voice called out.

I looked, and in the center of the room about halfway between the entrance and throne was a large metal cage, 30 feet wide and tall. Inside, was Jonas, calling out for Kairen.

Kairen smiled and ran forward calling for his brother.

I ran after them, and as Kairen got close to the metal box, his brother told him, "Stay back! Don't touch the bars, or you'll burn. They're cursed."

Kairen looked at his brother and started to tear up.

"Is this where you've been all this time?" he asked.

Jonas nodded, also tearing up.

"I've been so lonely here. And I don't know how I got here, either. I remember falling asleep for the surgery, and then I woke up in this cage. There's a woman who comes to visit every now and then, but other than that, I'm all alone in here," he said, weeping.

"Well it's over now, bud. You're trapped in a nightmare, but we're going to get you out, I promise," Kairen said. "Just hold on."

Jonas wiped his nose and looked over at me.

"Are you my brother's girlfriend?" he asked.

I twitched and scowled immediately.

"He wishes! I'm just here to keep a promise, Jonas. We really are going to get you out of here," I said.

And then I felt a weird pulse enter the room, as if the air pressure changed. The hairs on the back of my neck stood straight up.

She's here, I thought and looked instinctively at the throne.

There she sat, Hiawatha in the same garb I'd seen in her past.

"Well ,well. My phantom thief. What are you doing here?" her voice called out.

Kairen turned to her and scowled, his face full of hatred.

"So it was you! You imprisoned my brother here and lied to me!" he yelled.

She did not look impressed with his deduction. Instead, she looked annoyed that he was even here in the first place, like he lacked property authorization or something.

"So what if I did imprison him? I didn't lie to you. I said I was the only one who could wake him, and that was true," she said.

"We'll see about that!" Kairen yelled and turned back toward the cage.

He ran over to the bars and tried to pull them apart, only to be shocked by purple lightning.

I watched it course through him as he screamed and glowed. At last, he fell backwards onto the castle floor.

"Kairen!" Jonas screamed.

I ran over to him and saw his hands still smoking.

"Why can't I... free my brother?" he asked.

I helped him stand back up, but he looked pretty sapped. I could smell burning coming from his whole body.

"I gave you that enchanted item, remember? It's my power that allows you to enter nightmares. Why would I allow you to use my power in a way that goes against my plan?"

"And what exactly is your plan for these two?" I called out.

"Roxie... that explains how Kairen got in here. I should have smelled your pixie magic stink in this place. I'm surprised you're here helping Kairen after the torment he's put you through. Aren't you his mortal enemy?" Hiawatha asked.

I frowned and looked back at Jonas.

"No. He's my friend. We've put that behind us, and I promised to free his brother today," I said.

Hiawatha leaned her head back and laughed.

"You're going to free him from my grasp? That's a humorous notion, pixie girl. You've been dream walking for weeks, but I've been doing it for centuries! What hope have you of getting Kairen out of here, let alone his brother? That cage is impenetrable."

I set Kairen down, and he looked back at Jonas.

"It'll be okay, I promise," he said. "Just hang in there."

Hiawatha stood from the throne now, running out of patience to deal with what she considered unwanted pests.

"I'm tired of you meddling. Listen up, phantom thief. I will grant you the power to use your abilities here if you kill the pixie girl. Just do it quick," she said.

Kairen slowly stood as his earring began to glow purple again. He took his usual form with the tuxedo and top hat appearing in a puff of smoke over him. The red cloth that hid the bottom of his face materialized next.

"If I do this, will you finally free Jonas?" he asked, as I looked back with shock.

"Not a chance. I need that boy to keep you in line. I will, however, forgive you delaying the search for the Ossa Key and working with this girl behind my back," Hiawatha said.

Kairen frowned, and I saw him reach up toward his ear.

What is he doing? I thought.

With a scream, he ripped the earring off his ear, taking a chunk of flesh with it. His clothing returned to normal, though he was now bleeding and shaking. Hiawatha looked bewildered by the turn of events.

"Go to Hell, Queen of Tears. I vowed to serve you to free my brother, but now I find you're the reason he's unconscious in the physical world. Roxie didn't make any demands of me. She just promised to help Jonas because she's a real friend. I'm done being your servant. I quit!" he yelled, and threw the earring at her.

It stopped short and dashed off to the left like it had been thrown by some unforeseeable force, then disappeared in a puff of smoke.

"So that's how you're going to play it. The only way to leave my service is death, Kairen. You want to die? So be it," she said, and snapped her fingers.

The 20-foot statues of vampire lords and hellhounds began to rattle and shake.

What the hell did she just do? I thought. The statues clenched their fists and jaws. Then the vampires drew swords, and the hellhounds began to growl as they all advanced toward Kieran, Jonas and I.

"Goodbye, pixie girl. When I get free and plunge this city into a nightmare, I'll be sure to have a special torment for your little friends, Melanie, Tessa, and Jenna," Hiawatha said with a laugh.

I gritted my teeth and took a step toward the throne. My bracelet began to glow.

"You know what, Hiawatha? It's true. I've only had these abilities for a couple weeks now. And that's nothing compared to your experience. But I have learned a few things. Like the stronger will dominates in dreams and nightmares," I said, my bracelet beginning to shake.

"Oh? What else have you learned, pixie girl?"

A bright blue light encased my entire left wrist and fist now, and the stone under me started to vibrate.

"I've learned that I'm done letting you threaten the people I love! Dammit, I just wanted to help people's nightmares become peaceful dreams. But you... you've forced me to fight for the very survival of my loved ones. If that's the fight you want, it's the one you got!" I yelled, the ground under me quaking now.

I didn't intend to kill her, but maybe to reach her, I just had to knock her down a peg inside a nightmare of her own creation.

A blinding light filled the room, and everyone but me shielded their eyes. I stood there entirely glowing blue, with my antenna perked up over my forehead. The new addition to my body was half a set of highlighted gossamer wings. I felt the dream around me in a new depth now. I could see a purple aura emanating from Hiawatha, with her roots spread throughout the entire room.

These energy roots were wrapped around each statue now approaching us.

I raised my left arm with the bracelet still shining blue.

"Arise my knight!" I shouted. A blue circle filled with magical runes and alchemical shapes appeared on the stone floor in front of me. It expanded... five feet... 10 feet... 20 feet... 40 feet. And then the room began to shake.

The vampire and hellhound statues froze in their tracks upon seeing this unfold before them.

Out of the circle rose a giant suit of steel armor. It wielded a large broadsword with a silver hilt with both hands. The armor's visor was down. Behind it fluttered a massive black cape.

"Holy crap!" Kairen yelled.

Hiawatha did not look pleased with this recent development.

Once the knight had risen entirely from the ground, it kneeled before me.

"My knight, I command you to protect your princess," I yelled.

At once, the knight stood up and turned its back to me. It was a little shorter than the vampire and hellhound statues, but what it lacked in height, it made up for in strength. The armor was thick, but that didn't stop my new protector from moving swiftly and steadily to defend me.

The statues started forward again after Hiawatha yelled, "There's still just one of that thing. Kill them all now!"

"Do not fail me now, my knight," I yelled.

It parried the first vampire's strike and then disarmed it easily. My knight then pierced it through where its heart would be, and the statue crumbled. A hellhound leapt at us, causing Jonas to scream.

My knight ran forward and kicked the hellhound into a side wall with a resounding CRASH. Two vampire statues raised their blades and swung them down at us, but I didn't even blink. My knight blocked both blades with its own sword.

The vampires pushed it back a few inches, but then I yelled, "Drive them back, and finish them!"

My knight's visor eyeholes glowed blue, and a herculean grunt came from the armor. It drove both back, and while they stumbled, my knight cut them each in two.

As my knight defended us, I walked over to the cage bars and stood inches away as I examined them for some form of weakness.

I raised my left arm to the side, and Jonas and Kairen both yelled in unison, "Don't!"

A large silver gauntlet appeared over my left hand, complete with spikes on the knuckles and everything. It felt heavy, but I lifted it with all I had and forced it between the bars. When it made contact, the entire gauntlet began to burn with purple lightning. I could feel it heating up, but the lightning did not travel down my arm to the rest of my body.

I slowly wrapped my fingers around one of the thick iron bars. The lightning grew even more spectacular, shooting off into wild directions.

"Let go of it, Roxie!" Kairen shouted, moving toward me. But I held up my right hand and ordered him to stop.

Slowly, I pulled the bar I grasped back. It didn't budge for about 30 seconds, but then it began to groan and bend.

After I got it back a couple inches, it snapped in two like a piece of bamboo. I repeated this process with about three more bars, my left hand burning like it was in an oven the entire time. But I pushed through, gritting my teeth through all of it.

When I finished, there was a gap large enough for Jonas to exit through.

I held up my right hand, and he took it, stepping out of that cage for the first time in four months.

Then he hugged me, and I smiled.

"You're safe now," I said, the room still rattling with my knight smashing statues all around us.

Dust and rock pieces flew everywhere. I handed Jonas off to Kairen just in time to see my knight lose an arm due to a vampire's keen swordsmanship. He shattered it by tackling the statue into a wall, though.

Rising slowly, my one-armed knight returned to me and knelt once more, awaiting orders.

I set my eyes on a rather pissed Hiawatha. Her eyes glowed purple, and her long black hair flew up and around her.

"I'm done playing around with you three," she hissed.

Jonas held Kairen close, like Jonas was scared he'd vanish if he let go. Jonas was crying softly, saying, "I missed you so much."

His older brother smiled and slowly stood, pulling them both up.

"You're almost done with all of this crap. I promise. Now go with Roxie here and exit the nightmare. I'll finish this," Kairen said, standing in front of me.

I turned to him.

"Excuse me?" I asked.

"Roxie, I can't thank you enough for freeing Jonas. I'd like to ask one more favor. Please get him out of here while I finish off the Queen of Tears," Kairen said.

"Absolutely not! You don't have your powers anymore. Why do you think—"

"Please, Roxie," he said, interrupting me. "This bitch took my brother and tormented him. I need to finish this. Leave your giant knight here and give me a sword or something. I'll be fine. But it has to be me that kills her. It just has to."

I smiled and decided to let him think that sword just happened to be here instead of me crafting it in a previous dream.

Then I locked eyes with Kairen and saw no hesitation. Jonas looked frightened at his brother's request.

"No! You come with us!" he yelled, holding Kairen tighter.

Kairen smiled at him and said, "I need to finish this Queen of Tears now so she never hurts us again. You be a good kid and go with Roxie, okay? Keep her safe for me?"

When we're out of here, I need to have a talk with this guy about his protection expectations, I thought.

The throne behind Hiawatha was engulfed in purple fire now, and the steps down onto the red carpet started to burn as well.

"Please take him," Kairen begged.

I sighed and took Jonas' hand.

"Hey, can you get me out of here?" I asked.

Jonas looked from Kairen back to me. And then he slowly nodded, fresh tears coming out of his eyes.

He started to lead me toward the not-so-secret staircase passage I'd blown out of the wall, and I turned, raising my left hand.

"Don't make me come back here and save your ass," I said.

"You won't have to worry about that," he said.

Before we were out of the room, I heard Hiawatha yell, "There will be no escape!"

She raised her hand and hurled a large ball of purple fire at us. It raced across the castle floor, and my knight arrived just in time to split it in half with its sword.

Smoke rose from its singed armor as it stood up again.

I called up to my knight and pointed at Kairen.

"She's your new princess, now. You protect the princess."

The knight bowed and then walked back over to stand in front of Kairen. He hollered back, "Why can't the knight protect its prince, huh? I am not a princess!"

I winked and said "I think princess is a state of mind, and you'd make a great one. See you at the ball."

With that, Jonas snickered for probably the first time in months and pulled me into the staircase.

"My brother would make a funny princess," he said. "With a big poofy dress."

I smiled, knowing that plot point would likely make it into a D&D game in the future with Jonas' friends.

Jonas led me by the hand back down the staircase and into the royal library. We ran down the entire length of the library to the doors. The room shook several times above as I assumed Kairen and Hiawatha were locked in a fierce duel.

When we got to the library doors, there was a large explosion that rattled the room and threw us to the sides.

Part of the ceiling collapsed and made a ramp up into the throne room. It was here I saw my knight in pieces, and Kairen kneeling with a broken sword in front of all those pieces. He was covered in soot and blood.

He looked like he barely had the strength to keep his body upright on his knees. Hiawatha threw another purple ball of fire at him, and he tried to block with what was left of his sword. The explosion knocked him back into a piece of my former knight, and Kairen lost his sword arm.

"Kairen!" I screamed.

Jonas started to stand up, but I kicked open the library doors and pushed him out of them.

"You know the way out, right? Head straight for the main castle exit. When you walk through those doors, you'll wake up back in the hospital, and this will all be over. Can you make it?" I asked.

Jonas started to look up at his brother, but I stood in his line of sight.

"Can you make it?!"

He stopped trying to look around me and nodded.

"Then go! Hurry. The sooner you make it out the castle gate, the sooner this ends," I said.

He took off running into what looked like a castle dining hall of some kind. Several tables and large wooden chairs were set up and covered in silver dishes and wooden bowls.

I ran toward the makeshift ramp and did my best to climb back up into the throne room. I saw Hiawatha standing before Kairen, maybe five feet away, holding a large ball of purple fire in her right hand.

Kairen was panting and looking up at her with his one good eye.

"Like I told you, phantom thief, you only leave my service through death," she said.

"Then get on with it already!" Kairen yelled with the last of his strength.

"You could have been my knight in the grand nightmare to come. Nevertheless, I will be strong enough to make my own servants soon enough," she said. "Now die."

She hurled the fireball down upon Kairen, and I saw him close his eyes.

There was an explosion of purple fire that shook the entire throne room, blowing out the windows behind the throne. As it cleared, I saw Hiawatha's cruel smile change into a snarling glare.

I was standing over Kairen's body with a knight's shield on my left arm. He was unharmed.

"I thought I told you I was done letting you hurt the people I love." I told her, scowling up at Hiawatha.

She scoffed.

Behind me, Kairen coughed, and I asked, "You still with me back there?"

"Barely," he wheezed.

"I thought I told you not to make me come back and save your ass."

"You should have left me two knights. She blew that one to pieces right after you left," Kairen said. "Where is Jonas?"

"He's fleeing for the exit. Once he gets out of the castle gate, he wakes up, and this dream disappears," I said.

Hiawatha glowered down at us, and I saw her right hand crackle as purple sparks flew from it.

"Hear me, Hiawatha!" I yelled.

"Don't call me that! I'm the Queen of Tears, you pixie garbage," she yelled back.

I ignored her and stood up to my full height.

"This is the last time you threaten my loved ones, you hear me?"

The room around us started to fade to black, and I knew at once Jonas had made it to the castle gate and was waking up back in the physical world.

"Next time I see you, we're going to end this," I said. "I don't fear you."

Hiawatha squinted at me as we stood in a void of darkness now.

"You may not fear me, Roxie, but I do know what you fear. And I'll send it your way very soon."

I said nothing as we faded into the darkness, along with Hiawatha.

Slowly, light came back to my world as we stood in the hospital. I heard sobs and looked over to see Jonas crying and hugging his brother.

At some point, the oxygen mask that had been sticking out of Jonas was removed and hanging on the side of the bed.

Dream magic is weird, I thought.

"Is it really over?" he asked.

"It's really over, bro," Kairen said, crying himself.

I walked over and ruffled Jonas' hair.

"You did so good getting out of that castle," I told him.

He looked up at me and then hugged me, too.

"Thank you so much. I'm just so happy you came to help," he said.

I smiled and almost cried myself. This felt pretty dang good.

"I'm happy too," I said.

The door opened, and in walked a woman with black hair and a white doctor's jacket. She had a little mole on her chin and looked flabbergasted to see her patient awake. She was holding a clipboard. Just behind her was a balding man with remnants of gray hair I assumed was Kairen's father.

They both said not a word, but Jonas called out, "Dad!"

Sensing it was time to leave, I smiled at Jonas and walked out of the room, saying "Excuse me," as I passed the doctor and Jonas' father.

"My boy!" I heard the dad yell before the door closed behind me.

Before I got to the elevator, Kairen caught up with me. He was still sniffling a little and said, "Roxie... how can I— I just don't know what to— Thank you."

I put my hand on his shoulder and said, "That's just what friends do for each other."

Kairen gave a little cocky smile and asked, "So... we're friends now?"

I poked his nose and with as serious an expression as I could summon, said, "And that's all we're going to be. So don't get any ideas. And if your brother asks if I'm your girlfriend again, I'm going to lock you in a nightmare room full of clowns."

"I'm not actually scared of clowns," he said, smiling wider.

"Well then... whatever you're scared of! I'll find it and lock you in a room with it if I hear that question again from him, you got that, buster?"

He threw his hands up and said, "Whoa, I'm gonna have to go if you're using such strong language. Buster? I'm not prepared for that."

I slugged him in the shoulder and pushed the elevator button.

"Don't be a jerk," I muttered.

"That's what you love about me," he said, that cheesy grin growing even wider.

The elevator doors opened behind me, and I said, "I don't love anything about you. I like that you're an adoring big brother. And I like that you're not a total jerk, just a little one."

I walked backwards into the elevator, and before the doors closed, he said, "Thank you, Roxie. You're a great friend."

I winked right as the doors shut.

We got a win, and I wasn't going to let Hiawatha's last threat about knowing my fear ruin that. I'd tackle that at a later date. For now, we had a victory.

Chapter Twelve
(Dan)

I took a piece of an orange I'd peeled from the little saucer sitting on the glass case beside me. Eely was asleep, and I wasn't concerned about sharing this particular piece of fruit with her.

Red and pink hues dotted the sky outside as the sun began to set. I was sitting on my stool, back curled up against my favorite corner reading through Roxie's latest postcard. She'd sent one with a bunch of petunias on it. It still smelled like Dollar Tree, not that I was complaining. The card was pretty.

The girl is impressive with how much magic she's been able to draw from that bracelet, I thought. But then I shuddered a little, and a shiver went down my spine when I got to the part about her latest pixie dream form.

"Looks like she's about half a set of wings away," I muttered. "I hope she knows what she's getting into."

Part of me wanted to write her a card back warning her about how close she was getting to a certain threshold, but after our last big disagreement over how to handle the Queen of Tears, I wasn't sure she was willing to take any warnings from me. I figured it was best to play it cool and trust she knew what she was doing. Last thing I wanted to do was make her cry again.

I shrugged and put down the postcard, wondering where we were on that whole "saving the city" thing.

Roxie had mentioned a bit in her postcard about the Queen of Tears soon making her own servants after losing Kairen as her phantom thief. She had no idea what that meant, and while I lacked specifics, I did not lack apprehension about her growing abilities.

Sighing, I reached over for another orange slice and popped it into my mouth. I tossed Roxie's latest postcard in a little shoebox under my stool with the rest of them.

A little bit ago I'd flipped over Yes' album *Fragile* onto its backside and started it on my record player. I hummed along now as "Mood for a Day" started playing.

Picking up my half-read issue of *American Fishing Lures Quarterly*, I began to imagine what it'd be like to get out of this shop and out onto the Buffalo River for some fishing. I daydreamed about spending an entire morning hooking smallmouth bass. No, dream bigger. Spending an entire day hooking smallmouth bass.

It'd just be me sitting in a fold-up chair on the rocky shore, probably over east of Ponca, I thought, smiling. Wind would blow through the pines around me, and I'd sit back and adjust my shades. I guess Eely would be asleep next to my feet or something.

Taking another orange slice, I spilled some of the juice down my beard and wiped it with the sleeve of my brown robe.

I picked back up where I'd left off in an article on hooking the perfect rainbow trout.

"Maybe I should try fly fishing if I ever get out of this store," I muttered.

The next couple articles were shorter advertorials on the most lifelike lures. Advertorials were becoming more frequent in this magazine the last couple quarters. I anticipated it wouldn't be around a few quarters from now.

Bummer. This is the only fishing magazine I get, I thought, frowning.

Reaching over to take another orange slice, I found my little saucer baren of any fruit. Looking up, I saw little juice droplets on the glass case leading back to Eely's bed. She was still pretending to sleep, but she was in a different position now.

"Hey! I was eating that!" I said, putting the magazine down.

Eely did not respond. She actually started snoring.

"Foxes don't snore!" I yelled.

"We do too," she said, then went back to snoring.

"Well, they definitely don't argue in their sleep," I muttered.

"Yes we doooooo," she said in a sleepy tone.

I stood up and popped my back, knees, and shoulders.

"Listen here, Eely. I wanted those orange slices to tide me over until dinner," I said.

She rolled over and stretched, lying on her back.

"Oh... hey Dan. Why'd you wake me up? Did you need something?"

I snapped and pointed my finger at her.

"You weren't sleeping. And you stole my fruit!"

The eggshell fox yawned and stretched some more, fluffing out her tails and getting comfortable.

"There's no need to yell. Now what's this about fruit?"

I reached forward with a sudden grip on the fox, and she yelped a little bit. Eely was fully awake now.

Under her in the bed were three orange peels. Pointing down at the leftovers of my orange, I said "Hmmmmmm?"

She looked over at the wall and said, "I've been framed. Anybody could have slipped those there while I was sleeping."

"You know what I think? You need to be more efficient with your theft. Next time eat all the evidence," I said, setting her down on the bed.

She looked up at me and said, "But the peel is so nasty! I don't like it."

I got in her face and smiled, saying, "So you DO confess."

She nudged her nose forward to mine and said, "I was speaking hypothetically. If I did eat an orange, and I haven't, I wouldn't eat the peel because it's nasty and tough to chew."

I leaned up and shook my fists at the ceiling.

Eely hopped up on my shoulder and said, "Now now, there's no need to get upset over orange pieces that someone ate and then framed me for. Look on the bright side."

"Which is?" I muttered.

"Now that you have nothing to tide you over until dinner, you can start dinner! I personally think you should whip up your spiced orange salad. I haven't had an orange in forever," she said, smiling to reveal her canines.

"You just had oranges. My oranges, Eely!"

"Oh Dan. You're so cruel to accuse poor little me with such an unprovable claim. As your best friend, I am hurt, truly hurt," she said. "And if foxes could cry..."

I shook my head, and she hopped back down onto the glass case that held up her bed. We continued to bicker over dinner and theft of fruit until the last bit of sun vanished from the dusk sky outside.

"Why don't you close up for the night?" Eely asked.

"Because I slept in so late this morning. You know Odessa's rule about how many hours the shop needs to be open."

"Oh... well you can still start dinner while I keep a watch on the shop," she said, her ears perking up.

I finally relented and started to head back toward the kitchen when the door opened, and in walked a man in a black T-shirt and jeans. He had long brown hair pulled back into a low ponytail. I realized at once his eyes were a frosty silver. His skin was pale and smooth, not a blemish on it. And yet, despite its youthful appearance, there was an aged wisdom to this flesh. It'd been many places through the centuries, rained on by sky water from different continents and periods throughout history.

Eely hopped back on my shoulder and whispered in my ear.

"He reeks of blood, Dan."

"Like Alannah?"

"No... it's not mythical blood I smell on him. It's human," she said.

I did my best to put on the smile of a friendly shopkeep, but I was starting to feel a little like how I imagined Eely did when Alannah came into the shop.

"Welcome to Funky Dan's," I said, still wearing that smile.

"Thanks for the welcome," the man said, walking forward.

I saw now his black T-shirt had some sort of pattern on it with multicolored squares. And his jeans were studded up near the pockets.

He looked briefly at some different items on the shelf to his left, his attention drawn the most to a small wire necklace with several teeth on the end.

"You've quite a selection here. It's like nothing I've ever seen before," he said, before looking back at Eely and I.

"And I'd wager you've seen... a lot," I said.

For a second, there was a smirk on the edge of his mouth. It was held just long enough for him to let me know I'd guessed right. Then his smirk faded, and he was once again a curious customer.

Eely's paws clutched a little tighter on my shoulder.

When the man was about 15 feet away from Eely and I, he stopped.

"Something I can help you find?" I asked.

I tried to lift my left foot and pivot over to offer the customer a handshake, but my legs stayed right where they were. Whether it was fear or Eely squeezing some pressure points paralyzing me, I couldn't say.

One of the man's trimmed eyebrows raised, and he asked, "Are you this tense with all of your customers?"

"I seem tense to you?" I asked, keeping up that shopkeep smile.

"You look like your left fist could squeeze a piece of coal into a diamond," he said.

I glanced over at Eely for a moment, but she didn't say a word. I could tell she wasn't afraid of this man for herself, but rather for me.

"Apologies. It's been a long day. I guess I'm just a little high strung," I said.

The man slowly shook his head.

"You shouldn't lie like that, Dan. Your heartbeat makes it too obvious when you do," he said and crossed his arms.

Although he didn't exactly look shredded, the man before me was deceptive in his appearance, both in age and strength, I could tell.

"That seems wrong on some level, eavesdropping on my heartbeat like that. Though, as you say, perhaps some fault is with me for lying. I apologize for that," I said.

The man waved it off and said, "You two are either this distrustful of all your customers, or you behave this way because you know what I am… and I'm guessing it's the latter."

Eely and I exchanged glances.

"You know, as common as they are in books and movies, I've never actually had a vampire in my shop. And seeing as you aren't exactly feeding on pigs, deer, or other wildlife, you'll have to excuse my apprehension," I said.

That smirk came back for good now.

"You don't have to worry, Dan. You two are very perceptive, but your logic is lacking. I can feel the great magic in this shop, the same magic that only let me in because I needed something. This magic wouldn't have let me in if I intended to do you harm," the vampire said. "Besides, your furry friend here clearly knows how weak my kind is to fire, or she wouldn't be perched on your shoulder like that. She could incinerate me pretty quick if I was a threat, I'm sure."

Now Eely spoke up, all nine of her tails twitching.

"So long as you understand what I'm capable of doing to you, then

I think we'll be okay," she said, still not releasing my shoulder from her grip.

Ever since that attack from the omukade, she's been all kinds of protective, I thought, feeling her nails lightly dig into my shoulder.

Locking eyes with the vampire felt like my blood was turning to ice. It felt harder to breathe the longer I maintained eye contact, like some kind of cold wire was wrapped around my lungs. I also felt my thoughts growing sluggish, slipping into melancholy. And yet, despite this harmful grasp, I couldn't break eye contact.

Now I coughed a little as my lungs struggled to take in air against their newfound binding. Eely looked down at me and wrapped three of her tails around my neck.

"Hang on," she said and started to glow with a shade of gold.

I felt my blood begin to warm again. Whatever it was slowly slid away from my lungs and out of my chest. And I broke eye contact with the customer, taking deep breaths of air.

"Okay, I'll make that salad for dinner," I said, patting Eely on the back.

As my thoughts caught up to full speed, I recalled reading humans were not supposed to lock eyes with vampires. Now I knew why. They had a natural dominating effect that left most humans feeling weak and overcome.

"Apologies, Dan. I can't really turn that off. Here, let me see if this helps," he said, pulling a pair of dark sunglasses from his pocket and slipping them over his eyes. His glasses were round in shape and had no arms. They simply clipped onto the top of his nose.

I could still feel his silver eyes behind the glasses even if I couldn't look directly into his pupils anymore.

"I think a proper warning would have been in order," Eely said, glaring at the customer.

"I assumed since Dan could spot a vampire, he knew the proper precautions, specifically, not to make direct eye contact with them. But I suppose that was my mistake, and again, I apologize."

Eely did not let her glare up, and it took me a few seconds to regain my composure. Taking one last deep breath, I stood up straight again and looked at the vampire. This time I tried to keep my gaze down away from his sunglasses covered eyes.

"Perhaps we got off on the wrong foot. Forgive me, as though I have spent many centuries on this planet, I haven't spent much time in the modern American south. I may be awkward and oblivious to your customs. Can we start over?"

"Let's," I said.

"My name is Salvatore, and I am from Bari," he said, extending his hand.

I looked over at Eely, and she nodded gently. Then I took Salvatore's icebox hand and gave it as hard a squeeze as I could. He was amused, if anything.

"Italy?" I asked.

"Sì," he said.

I nodded. An Italian vampire. That was certainly not what I expected in my shop. I always figured I'd meet a vampire someday, but I had no idea they would be from the Adriatic region.

"Well, Salvatore," I said, clearing my throat. "Why don't you tell me what you came all the way to Fayetteville for?"

"Happily. What I seek is... well, it's complicated. Perhaps I should start at the beginning of my tale."

I motioned for him to do so and side-eyed my stool in the corner, wondering if I should be seated for this.

"I was born in the year 1450."

"I'm sorry... is that BC or AD?"

That smirk returned to his face, and Salvatore said, "AD. Although I think they've changed it to CE now."

I brushed that off with a gesture and said, "Yeah, but I didn't want it changed, so I don't acknowledge that. Thanks for clearing that up. Continue."

Salvatore nodded and cracked his knuckles.

"I was apprenticed to a locksmith by the age of 12 after my father became too sick to fish anymore. I quickly learned the inner workings of tumblers and latches. By the age of 15, my teacher turned me loose upon the world. I opened a locksmithing business of my own and moved my family to Naples. Once people saw my craft, how advanced my locks were compared to men three and four times my age, they hired me for all sorts of projects, mainly protecting valuables."

Eely glanced over at me, and I let her know I was fine. She could move back to the counter if she wanted as I wasn't quite as uncomfortable. Perhaps that was a weakness of mine. When someone began an interesting story, I became enthralled fast. Could have been because of his vampiric charisma. Afterall, they do make good predators.

Either way, my fox made it clear she wasn't leaving my shoulder until this vampire had left the store.

The vampire continued his story. "I didn't meet the man who turned me until I was 22. He showed up in Naples one day, a diplomat from the royal court of Vlad Dracula."

"Wait... THE Dracula? That's who you're talking about, right?"

Salvatore nodded and said, "Sì. The first vampire. He had only recently figured out he could turn others into a creature of the night like him. And the man who came to Naples was the fifth person Vlad Dracula turned. His name is Anghel."

"What happened when he showed up in town?" I asked.

Salvatore looked down at the shaggy green carpet of my store for a moment, as if he were reliving the memories he was about to reveal to me.

"He drank. He killed. He drank. He killed. For months, he terrorized the city. Nobody knew who he was because he left no survivors," Salvatore said.

I shook my head.

"Surely there'd be a trail, right? You go around creating that many vampires, one of them is bound to lead-"

"That's not how it works, Dan," Salvatore said, interrupting me.

I raised an eyebrow. And I prepared for my eventual magical biology lesson. Because I had to admit, while I had read up on lots of mythical creatures and beings through the decades from Athena to xenarthrans, vampires were a chunk I'd skipped. I dunno, I guess I'd read too many bad novels about them for that kind of research to really interest me.

"A vampire doesn't turn a human simply by biting them or killing them. To turn a human, a vampire needs to bring its victim to the brink of death. And just before the human draws their last breath, the vampire has to feed them its blood. Even then, there's only a one-in-three chance the human survives the biological change into a vampire. Most die of system shock as their bodies change," Salvatore said.

"Well I guess I learned something new today," I said. "How did you meet Anghel?"

"Blind luck, I suppose. He broke into my family's home one night and killed my parents. Then, just before he could kill me, I begged for my life, telling him I had dreams of one day crafting such a great lock that it could even hold a god. I was stupid back then, had unrealistic goals."

I cleared my throat and asked if Salvatore cared if I got my stool. I also offered him a seat, but he declined.

So I grabbed my stool and dragged it over to the edge of the glass case, motioning for the vampire to continue. Unlike him, my joints were not regenerative and supernaturally strong.

"Anghel was amused with my groveling and ridiculous dream. So he said he was going to drink my blood one way or another, but he would give me a chance to continue on afterward. He was fast upon me before I could give consent. His fangs found their mark on the left side of my neck and tore in," Salvatore said.

He stopped his tale, slid his T-shirt down a little and tilted his head to the right. I saw two large scars about two inches apart. And these were no slender fangs. Anghel had been merciless in his feasting, it seemed.

When he was satisfied we'd had time to observe his only wound that would never heal, Salvatore continued his story.

"He drained most of me, Dan. And as if by some sick instinct, he knew exactly where that threshold was before I died. I began to feel numb, beyond light-headed. The room had been spinning for a minute by that point. And at last, all was beginning to fade to black. That's when he fed me his blood.

"At some point, I began to convulse. Every muscle felt like it was contracting and spasming uncontrollably. Organs were twitching, my blood became ice, and my very soul itself felt as if it were shivering. There was no thinking it through or preparing myself for the change. I screamed until I was hoarse as my body burned with a hellish kind of cold few had ever witnessed. I regretted every second asking that vampire to let me live. I cursed myself over and over, just praying that it would all stop, and I'd die."

Eely and I exchanged glances. I felt a slight kinship form with this man before me, in that, we'd both died horrible deaths throughout history. I'm sure his conversion wasn't the first time he had to be brought back to life.

"There's no hiding anywhere in your mind from the frostbite of inner death. And that is what it means to become a vampire, dying quite literally on the inside. Sure, your body still moves, even better than other bodies. But your heart doesn't beat. You don't breathe. Your blood doesn't move. You just... are, somehow. A dark and ancient sorcery brought into this world by Vlad Dracula sustains you.

"After chronology lost its meaning, and I became immune to the flow of time, I eventually opened my eyes. It was morning, and I'd survived the vile transformation into what you see before you. If I hadn't gone through all that pain, I might have told you I'd been spared. But for all the abuse I endured that night with the transformation, I knew better. I'd been given a living death sentence, and all because I had to beg.

I learned that night that when death comes for you, you must take it, or else fate might punish you with something far worse," Salvatore said.

When death comes for you, I thought as his words repeated in my head. I thought back on all the times I'd wished to die and rejoin with my parents again. Then I thought back of all the times I'd died from those worms eating me from the inside out, and I awoke on my bed. I thought of how the feeling made you feel hollow inside, like how nothing you would ever do would correct the wrongs you made in the past.

Salvatore's words brought me back to the present.

"It took me a while to realize every single thing Anghel had taken from me that night, my family, the sunlight upon my skin, a good night's sleep, warmth of any kind, and so much more. I wanted to end my life. How many mornings did I almost just walk outside into the sun and let it take me? But I couldn't do it. I eventually decided I wanted to take something from him the same way he took my old life away from me."

"You mean to kill him?" I asked.

"Worse. I mean to lock him up and let him rot for the rest of eternity. Take away his freedom to live, to experience the world, the same way he did to me. Over the last few centuries, I've been honing my locksmithing skills and incorporating powerful magic. I believe I've perfected the design on a lock powerful enough to lock him away forever."

Eely and I exchanged glances as I stood up and popped my lower back. Pushing the stool away and sensing storytime was over, I asked, "That's a great story, but... what do you want from me? The means to find Anghel?"

Salvatore shook his head. His long brown hair swished back and forth.

"I believe I know where he is. What I need from you, what I pray you have somewhere in this shop, is a component I need to finish the lock."

Nothing was coming to my mind. I didn't exactly have bars of iron or a smelter in my shop to offer him. I had a few keys that would open gateways to other realms, but somehow I doubted that's what he was after.

"What component, exactly? For the first time in my life, I'm not sure this shop has what the customer is looking for. Wait until Odessa hears about this," I muttered, with a grin.

"I need something not of this world to forge the lock with. That's what the magic I'm using calls for. It'll help ensure nothing can set Anghel free once I locked him away with it."

My brain had begun to finally picture an item when the vampire continued talking.

"I've seen and learned much in my travels through this world's history. Every time I think I've seen it all, something bigger reveals itself to me and shatters my expectations. Can you imagine my surprise when I learned there were other worlds out there? Ones so very different from our own?"

I nodded. He was correct. There were numerous worlds out there, so many you'd have to be a god to count them all. And even then, you might not be able to.

"You're looking for a stone from another world to forge into your lock?" I asked.

He nodded.

"In that case, I have something for you after all," I said, motioning that I needed to move past the vampire.

He backed up and gave me space as I walked quickly by him. Eely turned and kept her eyes on him the entire time. Salvatore did not move an inch.

Walking over to the shelf farthest from the front door, I picked up a black jewelry box just a little bigger than my hand. There was no design on it. It was simply a polished wooden box to most.

I made my way back over to Salvatore and told him, "This is what you're looking for."

With that, I opened the box. It gave out a groan as it opened, and a couple weeks worth of smoke eked out.

Salvatore raised an eyebrow but patiently waited for me to explain. I reached inside and pulled out a simple necklace. On the end of the necklace sat a little carved bunny, poised as if it were sniffing the air.

"What is that?" Salvatore asked, gently leaning in for a closer look. He quickly found his boundary of how close Eely would allow him to get to me when she growled.

"This is a bunny necklace carved out of a rare stone called charoite, though not from this world. It's from another world, as you desire," I said.

The vampire's eyes widened, and I figured this was the first time he'd been genuinely impressed in quite some time. Longevity had a way of robbing you of that awe-inspired feeling. You eventually come to believe you'd seen it all. And this guy was much older than me, so I could imagine how he felt

"How did you— Have you traveled to other worlds?" he asked.

"Only in my dreams... once. Anyway, this was given to the shop by a girl born not of this world. She paid it as a price to return to her homeworld," I said, thinking back to Nurama.

This may be the fastest turnaround for an item coming into my store and then being needed, I thought.

When I felt that Salvatore was satisfied with my presentation of the stone, I put it back in the box and shut it, once more clearing smoke from the store.

"Why does it smoke?" he asked.

"It's simply the stone's reaction to this world," I said.

Salvatore nodded and said, "Well that settles it. I need that stone, and I think I have something worth trading for it."

"Do tell," I said, holding the jewelry box in both hands.

"My locksmith master was a devout Pagan. Even as Christianity was the dominant religion of western Europe, he refused to sacrifice his beliefs. Every year he would make a pilgrimage to Rome to the Forum Boarium so he could pray."

"Interesting," I said. "And what you're offering to trade came from the man you apprenticed under?"

Salvatore nodded.

"Yes. It's something he left to me after he died. You see, my master was a devout follower of Portunus, claimed the god inspired him to locksmithing in the first place."

At the mention of that name, my heart skipped a beat. And I felt my stomach begin to descend. I suddenly knew where he was going with this, and I did not expect it tonight of all nights.

Eely sensed my tension, and she looked over at my face, which fell immediately pale.

"Because of his devout worship, even as other worshippers for Portunus converted, the god gave my master a special key forged from the spine of a goat," Salvatore said, reaching into his back pocket and pulling out a piece of folded ancient leather.

As he opened it, my breathing stopped.

"The Ossa Key," I muttered and swallowed hard.

"You know of it?"

It took me a few seconds to find my voice again. I cleared my throat.

"It's the original skeleton key, opens any lock," I said.

"Yeah, I figure if I give it to you, the odds of it being used to free Anghel once I imprison him drop drastically. No one will be able to steal it from me. You must have a deep appreciation for this particular enchanted item. You're almost as pale as me, Dan. And you're sweating like... are you okay?"

I took a deep breath and remembered there was no use lying to this vampire.

"I've just been dreading this day is all," I said.

And while I wished more than anything that I could decline his payment, say it was too much or not enough, I felt the store in my soul telling me this was the only acceptable deal. Any attempt to alter the deal would not be allowed.

My arms felt like rusty metal as I slowly lifted them to give him the jewelry box.

"You have a deal," I whispered.

He refolded the leather and placed it into my right hand. Once it met my flesh, it was almost as if lightning had struck my open palm. I did not want this destiny-setting object in my grasp. I didn't want it in this store. I didn't want it in this city or even this state. Because I knew who would be coming for it one day.

The lightning in my hand seemed to strike my heart after a second, and my pulse picked up quite a bit. And finally the sweat hit my hands.

"Well, I would enjoy staying and learning what has you so tight, but I need to get back home and start on my new lock. It was a pleasure doing business with you, Dan," Salvatore said and headed out the front door.

I wish I could say the same, I thought, regretting a customer for the first time ever in my life.

Then a stupid idea hit me. This is the only thing that can set the Queen of Tears free. If I broke it here and now, she'd be stuck in the cage forever. Problem solved.

"Eely, hop down onto the glass case, please. My shoulder needs a break from your claws," I said, lying.

She did as she was told and then looked nervously up at me.

"Dan... what are you thinking about?" she asked.

"Something stupid," I said, unfolding the cloth and taking half the key in both hands.

As if the store sensed my motives, I felt a bolt of fear shock right through me. Rules of the store forbade me from using any items without paying a price first, like any other customer. And destroying any items or tossing them was an even bigger no-no.

"I don't care!" I yelled and immediately threw all my strength into snapping this ancient key in two.

The lights began to flicker, and the store groaned with disapproval.

"Stop, Dan! You know that's against the rules!" Eely yelled.

"This is the only way!" I yelled. The whole building began to shake. The key groaned, but it didn't yield. It simply wouldn't bend.

"Come on! You're centuries old. If you were in a museum they'd keep you in an airtight case to protect your fragility," I said.

I threw everything I had into snapping the key. My hands began to burn, and then I realized a green fire had engulfed them. The lights continued to flicker, and Eely pleaded with me to stop. But I couldn't. This was the only way to ensure the Queen of Tears never got free.

"I can do this. I have to do this!" I yelled, as the shaking had spread to the entire city block. I heard screams from customers next door in the pizzeria.

The key groaned louder, and that fire burned more intense than ever. Still, I persisted. If I did this, the fight would be over. It was... it was. My thoughts began to fade as I felt a familiar empty pit in my stomach. Then there was an intense hollowness. Eely saw it in my eyes. The worms were back, even if I hadn't stepped foot outside the store.

I felt them eating away at my intestines and screamed, falling over on my side and hitting my head on a shelf.

"Dan!" Eely yelled.

"I'm... okay," I said, cursing Odessa for having a lack of originality in her punishments. What? Breaking every rule led to worms?

With the last of my consciousness, I screamed again, feeling the worms enter my chest. And then everything went to black, and Eely watched my body dissolve into dust.

"You know the rules, Daniel," Odessa's voice said over and over again in my head.

I awoke sometime later that night on my bed, with Eely curled up on my stomach. Groaning and trying to sit up, I felt the fox stir.

"You idiot! You had me worried!" she yelled, and smacked me with one of her tails. I felt heat on my cheek where it hit.

"Ow," I moaned.

Then I noticed Odessa sitting next to my bed on a stool, smoking her kiseru.

"More than 130 years in this shop, Daniel. And you still break my rules," she said.

"At least this time I did it for a good reason," I said.

She smiled.

"Good and bad are merely perspectives, Daniel. I taught you this."

Looking down at my hands, I saw they were covered in burns. They still hurt quite a bit, but they felt better when Eely licked them.

"That was never going to work, Daniel," Odessa said.

"I had to try," I said. "There was too much at stake with the Queen of Tears."

The witch shook her head and blew smoke in my face.

"Breaking that key wouldn't have solved your problems, Daniel. It would have ensured she stayed locked up for only a bit longer. But her power still grows, day by day. Eventually, she would have grown strong enough to break her seal. Keeping her locked up doesn't solve the problem," Odessa said.

I nodded and sighed. She was right, as usual. What I'd done was impulsive and foolish. The goal might have been heroism, but what I got was more of the same pain.

Odessa handed me the folded leather.

"Shouldn't we at least lock this up somewhere?"

"No. As I told you before, you need to have this. Because ultimately you must choose what to do with it," Odessa said.

I thought back to the Queen of Tears' offer if I just handed the key over to her. Kairen wasn't around anymore, but I'm sure if I was crafty enough, I could get it to her if that's what I really wanted.

"Why give me a choice of what to do with it unless you expect me to hand it over? If we want to keep this city from being sucked into a living nightmare, then there is no choice. We protect the key, end of story. Why even pretend there's a choice unless you expect me to give it away?" I asked.

I hadn't told the witch about the offer. Could she have known? Either way, why did I feel so furious at the idea she didn't trust me? I've never thought of myself as one who cared what Odessa thought of me. But... the thought of thinking I was going to betray everyone really pissed me off.

Odessa smiled again and said, "We rarely see the entire truth about choices until we arrive at the moment they need to be made. Goodnight, Daniel. Get some rest."

With that, she stood up and walked out of the room.

I wanted to follow her and argue, but Eely seemed determined to keep me in this bed so I could follow the witch's instructions.

Looking down at the key, I sighed. What did she mean by that entire truth of choices crap?

Putting the key under my pillow like it was part of some bizarre tooth ritual, I stretched.

"I'm really sorry about worrying you today, Eely. How about from now on, I run all stupid ideas by you for critique?" I asked, scratching her head.

The fox scowled at me.

"Why don't you just stop thinking stupid ideas?"

I sighed and said, "I'd really love it if I could do both."

It didn't take long for sleep to take us after the events of today. I'd have to update Roxie on the key with a postcard tomorrow. And I'd have to write it early in the morning so it could be ready to go out when the mailman arrived.

But that's tomorrow's problem, I thought, just before everything faded to black for the second time today.

Chapter Thirteen
(Roxie)

Walking Rufus around the block and dodging cracked, slanted sidewalks had become fairly routine over the past few weeks. And I was happy to do it. The corgi had such a cute fluffy butt, I got some exercise that didn't entirely kill my surgery recovery. Plus, it helped my neighbor who just had a hip replacement. That always made me feel good.

I was grateful for all the trees planted throughout downtown Fayetteville. It was hilly as all get out, but the city made sure there were plenty of London plane trees along sidewalks to provide some resemblance of relief through the Hell that was Arkansas summer.

Cicadas rattled in the trees, so they were a bit of a double-edged sword. Right under the heat, cicadas were something I hated about summer.

I got a kick out of reading people who weren't from the south romanticizing it in their novels, as if there was something magical about a bunch of insects rattling loud enough you had to go indoors to hear people talk.

"The forests were thick with Spanish ivy, and a thin blanket of moisture floated through the air," I mocked.

Rufus paid me no mind.

There's ticks and chiggers in the woods, that Spanish ivy is actually poison ivy, and nothing about summer humidity was a thin blanket. It's a wet quilt that smothers you to death.

Thinking about college, which was something I hadn't done much of since becoming a pixie dream girl, always left me torn. I wanted to go to school someplace cold and get away from here. But I didn't want to leave Mom behind, no matter how childish that made me seem. I needed her desperately.

Throw in the thought of leaving behind Jenna and Tessa with it, and I usually didn't spend much more time thinking about where I wanted to go to school. To the shock and dismay of my history, math, and science teachers, I still hadn't sent out any applications or even taken the ACT.

Someday, I thought, losing focus and watching ants march around my faded red sneakers.

Spacing out, I really didn't register the screeching tires behind me, nor the heavy footsteps running up behind me.

Rufus barking alerted me to something, but by that time, handcuffs were thrown on my wrists, and my world went dark.

I didn't even have time to scream before I was hoisted off my feet and tossed into a vehicle.

"What the Hell are you doing?" I finally managed to choke out as I slammed onto a bare metal floor in the back of some long vehicle.

I didn't get a response.

Then the tires screeched again as the vehicle lurched forward, and Rufus' barks were the last thing I heard before a panic attack set in.

My pulse quickened, chest tightened, and the worst thoughts imaginable filled my head. Was I being abducted for the sex trade? Was some psycho going to murder me in his tool shed? Would anyone ever hear from me again?

Breathing became rapid as the dark mesh hood over my head let in zero light. With each tight turn I was flung to the left or right of the vehicle.

I must be in the back of some crazy person's van, my mind concluded, but that was the only logic getting through at the moment. Tears began to work themselves down my cheeks as I realized how little having magical dream powers benefitted me in reality.

I pictured myself being slowly gutted by some creepy guy in his basement for kicks. I'd be the missing girl people talked about. Down south in Alma there was a young girl who went missing from the ballpark named Mariah Nix. That was 20-something years ago, and people still talk about her.

My heart continued to tear in two as I pictured Mom crying for me night after night, and Jenna and Tessa putting our band on indefinite hiatus following my kidnapping.

How efficient were police at tracking missing people, anyway? In reality, the odds were probably better than my crackling mind was willing to grant them at this very moment.

The hood on my head smelled musty, and the back of the van smelled like someone had spilled some gasoline. In truth, I was getting a headache, but I wasn't sure if it was the fumes or my panicking causing it.

I completely lost track of where we were traveling because of all the twists and turns. And without any light, and my head starting to pound, I felt like clothes in a dryer on spin cycle. It was a wonder I didn't puke.

We traveled in one direction for maybe 20-25 minutes. At one point I felt us turn onto a gravel road, and my mind went into overdrive again, imagining the rusty shed waiting for me.

The van bounced, and I flew around the back more than before. My back slammed into something I assumed was a toolbox, and I cried out. There was no response from my captor.

Will it be like the movies? Will he just kill me, or will he torture me first? My mind circled around the horrid thoughts for the 15th time.

I thought of Dan, Eely, Selene, Kairen and even Hiawatha. Being abducted sort of put all their problems into a separate category. Dreams and nightmares were one thing, but here I was being taken in reality, proving it to be the most terrifying place of all. Little did I know how false that would turn out to be. My own nightmare hadn't even begun.

When at last we got to a stopping place up some driveway in the middle of godforsaken nowhere, Arkansas, I found enough courage to steel myself. I didn't know what I could do, but maybe if I did it fast enough, I could free myself.

I have... 12 percent of a plan, I thought, trying to slow my pulse even a little to... I dunno, get an advantage of the situation or something.

The sliding door opened, and I tensed my legs to jump or pounce, or run, whatever came first. But as the hood came off, I felt all that energy and planning fade away when my eyes adjusted to the sunlight. My captor was immediately known to me, and a whole new level of terror rose from the lowest pit of my guts. My stomach wasn't doing flips anymore, it was lying dead in a pile of mud, where I'd rather be right now.

"Hello, Johnny," my father said, looking down at me with a smile that rattled me to my very core.

216

A look of horror sank onto my face, and he looked indifferent to the expression. Without thinking any further, I let out a wild scream for help till my throat burned. I waited, looking around, hoping someone would hear me. But as I stared at the empty grass field with coiled hay bails inside for acres and acres before fading into a dense treeline, my hope faded. I was completely alone with my sicko father.

"Nearest neighbor is a mile-and-a-half up the road, Son. Nobody is here to take you away from me this time, not some misguided judge, not your mother, not any onlookers. It's just the two of us out here," he said, hoisting me to my feet.

I tried to body slam him, but the effort was laughable. He barely recoiled from the blow. Instead, he wrapped his arms around me and said, "It's good to see you again, Son."

I writhed as though I were being bathed in venom.

This man I've spent years of my life hating thinks he gets to lay a finger on me? I thought, feeling a little fight come back to me.

"Get off me, you bastard! I don't want anything to do with you," I shrieked.

He let go of me and then struck me with the back of his hand. My left cheek burned from the impact, and I fell to the gravel crying.

I looked up at the man staring down at me, his neat brown hair and three-piece suit looking out of place from whatever patch of abandoned farmland he'd dragged me to. His brown eyes stared at me, calculating just how long I needed to stay on the ground for my crimes.

He kneeled down, and I heard joints popping in both knees as he did so.

"Now Son. Why did I strike you?"

"Stop calling me your son!" I yelled.

He raised his hand again, and I flinched.

"I struck you because you cursed. Not only did you curse, you cursed at your father, whom you've been instructed to honor.

"Does your Good Book tell you it's okay to abduct and strike your child?" I growled.

"He that spares his rod hates his son: but he that loves him chastens him early. I tried to chasten you early, but your mother played some sob story before a judge and took you away from me. I'm not going to let that stop me anymore," he said.

He stood up and yanked me to my feet again. The handcuffs were digging into my wrists now, and I figured they were not far from drawing blood if I took another spill.

"Walk," he said.

"Where?" I sassed.

He pointed ahead of the van to a large red and brown barn. I wasn't sure how I missed the two-story structure yet. There weren't any animals around. It was mostly used to store grass for the winter, probably for another piece of land where horses and cows are actually kept.

There were three small windows on the left side of the barn, and the left door was leaning forward a little bit. The paint was faded and chipped in many areas from years of standing under a beating sun and the occasional hailstorms that passed through the area.

"Get movin'" he said.

"Kiss my ass. I'm leaving," I said.

He backhanded me again, but this time I fell backward against the van, hitting my head. My left cheek was bruised and throbbing now.

"We've got lots of work to do. Now my spirit and flesh are both willing. We can do it the hard way or the easy way. I can beat you like a beast of burden, or you can avoid further pain by doing as you're told, boy."

I spit onto the ground, aiming for his shoes. But I missed. He ignored that slight and grabbed my shoulder, shoving me forward.

As we got into the barn, I smelled plenty of dried grass and damp wood. It must have rained this morning. A rusted ladder on poles to my left led up to the second story where some brown sacks of grain were stored.

The floor was dirt topped with sawdust, and it kicked up a little as my father pushed me forward.

About three stalls stood to my right, all empty. Sunlight filtered down through cracks in the roof and caught on a web where a black and yellow garden spider sat hoping for a snack to fly in. Off in the corner I saw what looked like the nest of a barn owl. Nobody was home.

"Okay, genius. Now what? You want to talk about our feelings, or are those forbidden in your barn of doom?" I asked.

Father led me over to a wooden chair he'd bolted to the ground. It looked like something he'd picked up at a thrift store and spent a few hours turning into a prop from one of those gore movies.

Shoving me down into the seat, he spun me around and undid my handcuffs, only to loop them through the seat back behind me and tighten them further.

"I've finally figured it out, Johnny, what the problem is here between us," he said.

"You mean aside from the child abuse and violation of several state and federal laws?" I asked.

"What you call abuse, I call necessary discipline to get you back onto the narrow path. It's necessary for the preservation of your soul. And as for these state and federal laws, what challenge do they pose when faced with the laws of God almighty, Johnny?"

I clenched my jaw. Most of my terror had been replaced by loathing right now. I absolutely hated the man in front of me. He was everything about my past I longed to ditch. But here he was, forcing himself into my life again. If only there was a reality block button.

"I'm 18 now, Dad. If I say you don't get to be in my life anymore, you don't. It's as simple as that," I said. "And my name is Roxie."

Dad shook his head.

"With your mental disease you're more like a child than an able-minded adult. But that's okay, because I finally know what's wrong with you and how to fix you, Johnny."

The way he kept saying that bothered me more than hearing my deadname did. I ticked every time I heard the wrong name used for me. I double ticked when he said "son" with his condescending voice he often mistook for love.

What does he plan to do? I asked myself, trying to imagine what would happen to me if I didn't get free some way or another.

And yet, how would I escape? This chair was solid oak, not likely breaking anytime soon. The handcuffs were about to tear my wrists open, and there was nobody likely to come for help anytime soon. How long would it take for Mom to realize I was missing? Would Rufus run back to his owner's house and bark to let Miss Michelle know something was wrong? Was he smart enough to do that?

I sighed and resumed glaring at my father, waiting for whatever crackpot idea he was about to reveal.

"I was actually in town last night for a minister's retreat up on Mount Sequoyah. I wanted to stop by because the little icon on my phone showed you weren't viewing my texts anymore. I assumed that meant you blocked me."

"Great detective work," I muttered.

"Anyway, I stayed the night at the retreat center, and in my dreams an angel of the Lord came to me. He told me exactly what was wrong with my son and how to fix him. You're possessed by a demon, Johnny. That's why you've gone astray and poisoned your body, letting doctors cut it up. It's disgraceful, but not unfixable. I'm going to fix you," he said, with a calm assurance that did more to unnerve me than anything else I'd seen so far.

A thought occurred to me. He was in Fayetteville, and he had a dream where someone told him to do this to me. My eyes widened as Hiawatha's words from our last encounter came back to me, "You may not fear me, Roxie, but I do know what you fear. And I'll send it your way very soon."

Hiawatha had visited my father in his dream, and the idiot fell for it. She knew exactly what I was most afraid of in the world and had indeed sent it my way.

"Listen to me. You weren't visited by an angel. It was actually—" I was cut off by him backhanded me again.

I flew to the right with my cheek feeling like the bone might have finally broken. The chair and handcuffs kept me from flying too far. It groaned as I leaned over, spitting out blood on the sawdust-covered floor.

"You don't get to tell me about the 'truth' when you lie about who you are every day, Son. But not to worry. Like I said, I can fix you," he said.

My teeth were starting to hurt now, so I was reluctant to ask if he had hired Father Karras to come perform an exorcism. I decided against it.

Slowly, I leaned back up and glared at him again.

"The angel told me to bring you to him. So that's what I'm going to do," he said.

"The angel is in a cave under Fayetteville locked behind bars. Nobody is getting to her," I said.

Father shook his head again.

"I'm not going to physically drag you anywhere else. I'm going to send you into a dream, and the angel will deal with you there. He'll cast out the demon wrapped tightly around your soul, and heal your body back to the way it once was," he said.

A dream? Does Hiawatha want a one-on-one showdown or something? I thought, puzzled.

Now my father reached into his back pocket and pulled out a long beaded necklace with an iron cross on the end. It glowed with a familiar shade of purple. With his right hand, he ripped my bracelet off and tossed it out the barn door behind him.

My hair and eyes returned to normal at once, and I shouted, "No! Give it back!"

I watched the ends of my hair start to revert back to their original chestnut, and my eyes watered all the more as they felt increasingly dry. I imagined their pink glow was fading as well. My body was reverting back from my pixie form, and inside my chest I felt an emotional crack forming. I sobbed.

"By the grace of God. You're one step closer to looking like my son again. No more of this dyed hair and colored eye nonsense. When I get you back, Johnny, we're going back to Kansas. And I will never let your mother poison you again," he said.

I was still trying to break free and reach for my bracelet. It was everything I needed to be a pixie dream girl. Without it, I was just... normal again, somehow less, I felt. The skin on my wrists had definitely broken now, sending a new searing pain up my arms.

"Father, listen to me. Whatever you think you're doing, it won't work. You're helping an ancient evil claim this city as her own. You need to give me that back now!"

My voice had grown shrill, and now tears were beginning to fall down my cheeks.

"You go ahead and tell all the lies you want, demon. I'll rejoice in seeing my son free of your grasp. I can't wait to take you home and introduce you to the elders as a reformed sinner. This is going to fix everything that's gone wrong in my life for the past several years," he said.

As he raised the necklace that glowed even brighter, I shrieked, "Don't you see that color? The necklace is evil!"

"Sssshhhhhhh. It'll all be better soon," he said.

Everything went black as he tugged the sack back over my head. But instead of going over my entire head, this time it felt like the sack had gone over my brain.

"Mom..." I whimpered.

Suddenly I was on my bed again. It felt like I was waking from a nightmare, but a quick glance at my room showed the nightmare had just begun. There was a desk in the corner with a black leather Bible and concordance on top. On my walls hung posters of LeBron James and a map of the world.

My comforter was just a simple brown color with no real patterns, like my sheets and pillowcases. Over my window hung a medium-sized crucifix, with a Jesus screaming in agony, looking down at me.

His expression matched how I felt on the inside.

"Finally," a familiar voice said, as I turned to look at the door.

There stood Hiawatha, in all her brown garb and glowing purple aura.

I leapt to my feet and raised my left hand toward her, imagining chains forming around the vile nemesis. And yet, nothing happened.

"Not today, Johnny," she said with a sly smile. She took a few steps toward me, maintaining her wicked grin. "I've had your father rid you of that filthy pixie magic. You're powerless here."

Looking at my wrist, I saw my blue bracelet was indeed gone. Not only that, but my nail polish was gone too.

I looked down and saw the cross necklace my father had placed on me still clasped around my neck. But the wife beater I'd been awoken in revealed fresh horrors to me. My chest was flat and hairy. My arms were also covered in hair, and my hands were bigger than I'd ever seen them.

As I whimpered I looked down at my boxer shorts that had a bunch of cartoon dogs wearing sunglasses on them. Something I spent years hating had made a comeback, and that was enough to make me scream in pain as my head grasped this cruel new reality.

Renewed feelings of dysphoria flooded my mind, and it felt like my brain was made of splintering glass. My mother and best friends helped me combat dysphoria each and every day. And with their help, I'd gotten it down to a manageable level. I was... dare I say it... happy, at least some days. But now every feeling of not being feminine enough to be considered a real girl came crashing down on me like a dam had instantly vanished and the waters rushed in around me.

A confused grimace escaped my throat, and it was much lower than any voice I'd heard in the last few years.

Vocal cord surgery undone too? I started to wail with a voice I was completely unfamiliar with.

"What did you do to me?" I yelled in a voice I did not dare claim as my own. It clung to the inside of my neck like a thick syrup slathered on all sides of my throat. And it filled me with a vicious loathing.

"Well Johnny, let me tell you how this goes. You've become extremely powerful in a short time, a real threat to me, I'm forced to admit. In the few weeks you've had these powers you've freed more than a dozen people in town from my nightmares. You turned my faithful servant against me. And you released his brother from deep within my grasp. So I'm removing you from the field, so to say."

"You don't have to do this, Hiawatha," I said, each word nails on a chalkboard to my ears. By God I hated this voice.

"I do, actually. Step one, let's look at the new and permanent you," she said, snapping her fingers. A full-body mirror appeared to my right, and I saw a somewhat greasy faced teenage boy with a trimmed goatee staring back at me. My brown eyes and crew cut hair burned holes in my pupils.

I started to cry again.

"Here's how this works, Johnny. You're going to live your new life in this nightmare until it breaks you, and you finally accept who you used to be. Once that's done, no matter how long it takes, I'll release you. Your father can take you back to Kansas, and I don't ever have to worry about the pixie dream girl ever again."

"My name is Roxie!" I screamed. I felt my body convulsing at once, a purple electricity shocking everything. My body burned with an agony I'd not witnessed before, and I screamed anew. It felt like the very liquid in my eyeballs was sizzling.

I fell to the floor, smoking and still twitching in misery. I whimpered in pain and didn't move until I finally regained control of my body.

"There's really only one rule in this nightmare. You live your new life as Johnny. No mentioning Roxie or being a woman. No mention of your old life, no Roxie. If you do, you will be shocked the very same way you just were. No exceptions. Your time as the pixie dream girl, let alone any girl of any kind, is over. You're a good Christian boy now, just like you were meant to be."

I kept quiet, hot tears running down my cheeks.

"Now get up and head out there. You're going to be late for Johnny's first day of school," Hiawatha said with a big smile.

I rolled over, not wanting to be Luke Skywalkered again. When I looked up, Hiawatha was gone. Getting up, I went out into the bathroom. Overall, the loft looked mostly the same. A few decorations were changed, and there were crosses hanging in each room. But the shape and furniture arrangement carried little difference to my home in reality.

Getting into the bathroom, I saw that I had no makeup or hair dryer. I saw one that might have been Mom's. It took all my strength to get in the shower and not puke from the stress of seeing my full nude body.

The renewed war between my body and mind left me feeling nauseous and sick. After I got out of the shower, I couldn't hold it back any longer. I vomitted in the toilet.

I brushed my teeth and went back into my room to look at my clothing. My entire closet was filled with khakis and polo shirts. There was a sweat jacket in the back I assumed was for cooler seasons. It was green and had the words "Center Rock Second Baptist Church" on the back.

Sighing, I put on clothes belonging to a gender I hadn't recognized in more than a decade.

My self esteem was in the toilet where I'd lost whatever meal I ate last night. I didn't even bother to comb what little hair Hiawatha had allowed me in this nightmare.

Walking out of my room to the kitchen table, I saw father reading a worn leather Bible with a folded newspaper next to his plate of bacon.

"Morning, son," he said, and I resisted the urge to vomit again.

Mom was standing over by the toaster putting a couple of pieces in, I assumed, for me. She looked like no mother I'd seen before, though. Her hair was grown out all the way to her back, and she wore a purple ribbon tying it back. She was wearing an orange sundress and slippers.

I ignored father and walked over to her.

"Hey... Mom?" I asked, with a shaky voice.

She turned to look at me, and I asked, "Do I look... different to you today?"

Quickly looking me up and down without any cybernetic scan whatsoever, she shrugged and said, "No, why?"

And in those two words, I recognized at once what I'd lost in this world. Every single late night we stayed up making popcorn and watching action movies, every dysphoric breakdown she held me through as I cried, every playful moment she'd tossed her stubborn daughter on the couch, and every loving moment of brushing her daughter's hair before bed, it was all gone.

It was replaced by a cruel indifference from a woman who worked to be what I assumed was a satisfactory stay-at-home-mom. She didn't hate me. She just viewed me as another chore to keep fed and cleaned.

I excused myself as the toaster popped and went back to the bathroom, where I cried for a solid 10 minutes.

My brain made one pitiful attempt to remind me that wasn't my real mother. It was a cruel image created by Hiawatha to shatter me. But it was just too overwhelming a feeling to witness a woman who looked and sounded exactly like Mom be so indifferent to me.

Two words from her was all it took for me to see this new Mom and everything that meant for me.

Father started pounding on the door, telling me I was going to be late and to get out here. I opened the door and asked, "Can I stay home today? I don't feel good."

"Were you in there puking?" he asked.

I nodded.

"Well then don't you feel better?" he asked, laughing.

It was a stupid worn 'joke' he used to play on me when I asked to stay home from school as a young boy. If I didn't puke, he'd claim I wasn't sick. If I did, he'd say I must feel better because everyone feels better once they get it out of their system.

The joke was just a reinforced cruelty now in this nightmare.

Mom came over with my toast wrapped in a paper towel.

"You've got that history exam today, Johnny. You can't stay home and miss it. It's a quarter of your grade," she said and went back into the kitchen as I half heartedly took my breakfast.

"Your mother's right, Son. Get to school. You don't want to miss the bus. Remember. Proverbs 1:7 teaches that only a fool despises wisdom and instruction. Go ace that test!" he said and slapped my butt.

I wanted to slap him straight across the face, but I knew that would bring about more lightning, so I grabbed my black backpack with a white cross emblem on the back and headed outside.

I tossed my breakfast onto the sidewalk, not hungry at all. Then I looked up to see we still lived above a garage, but it was somehow Gary's Garage, even though his building was supposed to be elsewhere.

How long do I have to stay in this nightmare? Maybe Kairen will come save me, I thought, taking a few steps toward school.

Then I remembered he no longer had his dreamwalker ability. I fought the urge to cry again. Who else could I turn to for help?

After a few seconds, an idea came to me. I could ask Dan and Eely for help! I turned the opposite direction and practically ran all the way to where Funky Dan's shop was. When I arrived, I found a familiar pizzeria called Toppings.

Where Funky Dan's was supposed to be sat an empty lot instead. It was filled with weeds, trash, and even an old tire.

Dammit. Hiawatha really did think of everything. She's recreated all the worst parts of my city and took out any hope I had of escaping, I thought, fresh tears coming from my eyes.

Squeaking tires behind me and a big HISS made me turn. There was a school bus, with the driver motioning for me to hurry up.

There shouldn't have been a stop anywhere near this place, but Hiawatha's nightmare was ensuring I didn't try to escape whatever fresh Hell awaited me at school.

I did my best to rub my eyes, swallow sadness, and get on the bus. I'd have to think of something else to escape.

Sitting down on a torn gray leather bench alone, I stared mindlessly out the window, trying to keep even more fractures from creeping across my fragile brain. The bitter reality I faced in this nightmare was weighing on my very soul, and it felt like at any second I was going to drown in it.

All I could do was breathe. But even then what little I managed were shallow breaths.

It didn't take long to get from downtown to the high school. We pulled up to a familiar large building with a dark roof and big glass windows at the top. Under them sat giant letters "FHS."

A purple doberman, our school's mascot, was painted along a brick wall to the side.

I sighed and entered the main hall, not caring where my first class was. One last ray of hope entered me as I saw Jenna and Tessa leaning against some mauve lockers. They were holding a history textbook and chatting about something. Well, Tessa was talking excitedly, and Jenna was just nodding her head and listening in her usual way. That's how most conversations between them went.

Running over, I startled them a bit. And I said, "I am so happy to see you two!"

Just then, I knew I was going to get it all back. Things would be fine as long as I had my friends beside me. I'd weather any nightmare, no matter how desperate I was to cling to hope these two were still my BFFs.

Jenna looked up at Tessa and scratched her purple hair.

The cheerleader raised an eyebrow and said with an annoyed tone, "Can we help you?"

I refused to acknowledge my heart sinking. These were my best friends. They always had my back. There was no evil magic Hiawatha could cook up strong enough to take them from me. They knew me. They remembered me. I was sure of it. Because I didn't know what I would do if they turned out to be just like nightmare-mom.

"It's me, R— your best friend," I said, praying, maybe for the first time in my life, that some look of realization would pop into their eyes.

I'm Roxie!" I screamed in my head. *Your drummer and best friend!*

Looking down, I noticed Tessa wasn't wearing the turtle necklace I'd made her.

"Whatever, guy. I'm not sure what you're on about, but you should probably get to class," the cheerleader said.

My heart was springing several leaks as my inner self groaned. But I cast one last line of hope. If I just held out a little longer, they'd remember me. They'd come through. How could they not? We loved each other.

"But... it's me," I said, tossing that line with all the strength I had left.

"Okay... you. We're going to get to class now. Bye bye, and don't talk to us again," Jenna said, closing her locker and walking away with Tessa.

Don't talk to us again, echoed in my mind over and over again as I felt my heart detonate inside my chest.

I hit my lowest point of the nightmare, and the purple and white tiles under me started to spin. Everything was spinning. The office behind me, the lockers in front of me, class doors all around me, it was all some merciless merry go round spinning at the speed of light, and I wasn't allowed off for any reason.

My brain finally did shatter, full glass sprinkling down into the void of my mind. And I couldn't take this reality for one more second.

Looking somewhere for something, anything, I saw a janitor's closet open about 20 feet away. I ran inside, frantic, as though it were a secret passage back to reality.

Behind me, I heard Vice Principal Warren shout at me.

"Hey! Get out of there!"

I slammed the heavy wooden door behind me with a resounding BOOM and flipped the two locks.

Warren proceeded to bang on the door shouting, "Johnny! You open this door right now, young man!"

I tried to ignore him and backed up, slipping on a can of glass cleaner. I fell onto my rump, and a couple mops topped onto me.

Good. Bury me now, because I'm dead. I'm done and ready to go. I can't— I just can't— I thought, unable to finish coherent sentences in my mind.

I bawled like I never had before, covering my ears.

Outside, I heard more teachers and students banging on the door now.

"Johnny! Johnny! Johnny!" they yelled in varied cries.

I pressed my hands against my ears and cried louder, hoping for anything to drown out their voices. But it wasn't enough. And then I heard Tessa and Jenna start calling out my deadname as well.

"Johnny! Johnny! Johnny!"

The banging grew more intense.

"Johnny! Johnny! Johnny!"

Madness and terror took me. I wasn't sure where I was or who I was anymore. Was I falling down into a pit of eternal darkness or chained to a wall being hit with a baseball bat? Who knew? Both? Neither?

"Johnny! Johnny! Johnny!" the voices grew louder and louder as I screamed myself hoarse.

"Make it stop! For the love of God, make it stop!" I cried, curling my knees up to my face. I sobbed into my khakis and began to rock back and forth, just wanting to die, to fade, to do anything to stop the pain.

And at last, I knew how.

"If I just admit I'm Johnny. This'll stop," I muttered. "My name is... it's... it's."

I was hung up on that last word. And just before I gave in and started the "J" sound, a blinding light appeared in the closet.

I didn't bother to shield my eyes because any pain caused by the light was nothing compared to the cacophony of voices chanting outside.

"Your name is Roxie," a familiar voice said.

As I slowly looked up, I saw a woman wearing a long white dress that seemed to float and billow around her. Her hair moved slowly in waves with the gown.

All other noise drowned out, and as I laid eyes on this new visitor with long silver hair and glowing pink eyes, a sliver of light found its way into my heart. Behind the woman was a set of sizable, luminous green gossamer wings. My tears started to float around me as the woman leaned over and offered me a hand.

Feeling like I had little to nothing left inside, I mindlessly took her hand and was helped to my feet, mops falling to the left.

I didn't hear anything around me anymore except her voice.

"Your name is Roxie. And you're the pixie dream girl," the woman said with a voice I now recognized but thought I'd never hear again.

Slowly coming back into itself, my shattered mind put two and two together. I continued to gaze at the woman before me with my mouth agape. Tears continued to float around me, but I'd stopped sobbing for the most part.

"Who... you're... me," I whispered. "How is that possible?"

The woman wiped what remained of tears on my face and smiled, tilting her head to the side.

"Dreams are so much more powerful than you realize, Roxie. Space, time, magic, it all folds together in a space of endless possibilities. I'm you from half a century into the future," she said.

I just blinked at her. By the looks of this woman, I'd grown up fine. And I didn't look half bad for 50.

"I really don't look 50. I mean, you don't look 50," I said, gently scratching my head.

"Pixies don't really age much," Future Me said.

"I... have so many questions," I said, feeling like crying again, upon realizing I might never look like the woman before me if this reality persisted.

As if she was reading my mind— or... our mind, future me gently placed her hands on my head.

"Hold on, dear," she said, and I began to glow silver.

The outside of me shattered like glass and fell to the floor around me. Then, the remnants of my form dissolved into nothingness. Future Me's hands moved down to my arms and said, "You're restored. Nothing Hiawatha can do to you is permanent."

I slowly looked down at a body and clothing I was much happier and familiar with. My silver hair and pink eyes had returned as well. I was just missing the antenna and wings my future self had.

I started to cry again as more tears joined the air in a space around me.

"Thank you," I sobbed, with a voice that was also familiar to me.

"It's okay. It'll all be okay, Roxie," future me said, pulling me into a warm embrace.

"How do I even begin to fight this?" I asked, pulling back after a few minutes and looking at her.

"Listen, Roxie, I don't have much energy left. The most important thing for you to know is that you aren't alone. You'll never truly be alone. That's how you'll win."

She began to slowly fade, and I reached for her desperately, not done yet. I needed answers.

"Wait! I need you to guide me! How do I beat Hiawatha and save the city?" I called out.

"Go to the pixie world, and learn the truth from Selene. It'll be a hard truth to hear, but you can bear it, Roxie. You're strong. And with your friends, you're steadfast," Future Me said, sparkles and glitter falling around her fading form.

She was just about gone when I reached for her, and my hands went through future me's image.

"Go to the pixie world? How do I even begin to get out of this nightmare?" I blurted.

As Future Me vanished, she uttered one last question, "What has it got in its pocketses?"

And then Future Me was gone.

What has it got..., I repeated in my head.

It was a riddle I was intimately familiar with, and one I wouldn't need three guesses for. The door began to rattle once more as I reached into my right pocket and found nothing. Then, with my left hand, I found something warm in my left pocket.

Pulling out a white medallion with a fox head on each side, I nearly stopped breathing. Did Hiawatha forget to remove this? Or had Future Me placed it there?

Either way, the door was starting to violently rumble now as outside occupants banged it with some heavy object.

I remembered Eely's words, "You hold it tight in your grasp and say my name. Then I'll come to wherever you are instantly."

I grasped it, feeling a deep heat in my left hand, wrapped tightly around the medallion.

"Eely," I said, loud as my voice would allow.

For a second, my heart was about to plunge back into the abyss it had before future me showed up. She didn't appear. Then I heard a voice behind me say, "Roxie! Thank goodness!"

I turned to see a friendly white fox perched on a box of industrial floor cleaner. I squealed and ran over to hug her.

As I threw my arms around Eely, I began to sob again. If it was possible to dehydrate myself in this nightmare world from tears, I was set to do it.

"I am so so so so so glad to see you, my friend," I said in between sobs.

The door rattled something violent behind me.

"Where have you been? It's been two days, and everyone is worried sick about you," Eely said.

"Two days? Never mind. I don't have the minutes to calculate dream time versus reality. My father kidnapped me and slipped this necklace from Hiawatha around my neck in a barn somewhere outside Fayetteville. I've been trapped in this nightmare since then," I said.

A crack now formed in the door now as the angry mob bashed their way through.

"I need you to get me out of this dream, Eely. Father took my bracelet, so I have no control here."

The fox nodded and said, "I can sense the Queen of Tears' dark nightmare magic from your necklace. You can't remove it, can you?"

I shook my head, not wanting to think about being zapped again.

"Lean forward as far as you can and dangle it off your neck. I'm going to melt it, and we'll wake up in reality, okay?"

I did as I was told just as the door was battered inward. I flinched, but Eely let golden fire fly from her mouth, and it melted the necklace in seconds.

I felt a normal feeling return as I exited the dream and woke up in reality, still chained to the chair.

This time, I wasn't alone. Eely sat at my feet. I didn't see Charles, but the barn was dark. It was nighttime outside.

"Hold on," Eely said, running behind me.

"Your wrists are bloody, Roxie. But the cuffs are still there. Can you hold your hands apart so I can melt the chain?"

I did as I was told, but it sent waves of pain up my arms again. I grimaced, and Eely said, "Hang on."

My hands and wrists felt warm as the fox gently melted the chain on those cuffs. When my hands were free, they fell to my sides, and I sighed with relief.

Pulling them around front, I gasped when I saw the dried blood caked around the scars on my wrists. It was at this point I saw what remained of the melted necklace on the ground. I was happy to see that if it was destroyed in the nightmare it was also destroyed here.

"Forty-eight hours indeed," I winced.

I stood up and popped my back and legs. Then I popped my neck. Eely hopped up on my shoulder.

We started to walk toward the doors when Father came in.

"Johnny! How did you get free?" he asked.

"Get out of my way, Father. We're leaving," I said.

He blocked the path and said, "You get back into the chair right now. We're going to find another way to get that demon out of you."

Eely let forth a stream of golden fire, and father barely had time to dodge to the right.

"What did you just do? Did you call one of your demon friends to free you?" he asked.

"Want me to roast him for you and end his life?" Eely asked, opening her mouth. A small fireball took form in between her teeth.

I looked at Father's face, one full of confusion and hate. He seemed devastated that I'd gotten free and that I had yet to return to being his son. Part of me wanted Eely to just go ahead and kill him for the Hell he left me to languish in. I clenched my fists and thought of a world without this man. This hateful man who spent years denying my existence as a woman.

And then I recognized this emotion coursing through me. It was the same as back in that burning house. Part of me called for a fiery execution.

I looked at Father's face again, and the hatred and confusion shifted to bitterness and confusion.

"I don't understand," he said, a small tear forming in his left eye. "Why can't I have my son back? What do I have to do?"

Putting a gentle hand on Eely's head, I walked over to Father and kneeled in front of him. His bitterness was even more pathetic up close.

"You never had a son. You've only had a daughter, whom you've spent years denying. Here's what you're going to do, Father. You're going to put the van keys in my right hand," I said, holding my palm flat. "Then I'm going to consider not having my friend melt your face off. If the goodness in my heart prevails, you're going to leave Fayetteville and go back to Kansas. You will never communicate with Mom or I again. I never want to see you again. And that means forever. For the rest of my life, you will not be present. We're done, period. Am I clear?"

He looked like he wanted to say something, perhaps even a Bible verse. But when he saw Eely's glare, he nodded and reached into his jacket pocket. I heard jingling, and then he placed the keys in my hand.

The keychain had a pineapple on it, and there was just one long silver key for the dusty red van outside. On the windows it had a message written in soap, "For sale. Cold air and new tires."

Standing up, my back popped again, and I lamented being strapped to a chair for 48 hours.

"I'm going to leave this van at a pizzeria downtown called Toppings. You can walk or hitchhike there and get it. Goodbye, Father," I said.

Then, Eely and I went outside and headed toward the van.

We walked by where my bracelet had landed, and I picked it up again, feeling the watery beads in my hands.

I am so glad to have you back, I thought, about to slip it back onto my wrist where it belonged.

"Don't do that yet, Roxie. Dan told me he wanted to talk to you before you wore the bracelet again," Eely said.

I stopped and nodded. As long as I had it with me, I felt better. Though I couldn't help but wonder what heavy truth I needed to hear from Selene or what Dan wanted to tell me. I guess I'd find out when I got there.

The driver's side door handle sat over a large silver button. I pushed it, and the door squeaked something fierce as I opened it.

Well, I guess it worked okay as a kidnapping vehicle, I thought.

I sat in a patched seat and smelled gasoline again.

Starting the vehicle, I heard its engine rattle. But when I turned on the AC, it did, in fact, blow cold air.

"At least that wasn't false advertisement," I muttered, eyeing a little tiki bobblehead mounted to the dashboard.

I didn't have my license, but I wasn't prepared to let that stop me from reaching my destination of "away from here."

"I don't know where we are, Eely. Can you navigate or something with your mystic fox senses?"

"Remind me to teach you what spirit foxes do and don't do in the future, Roxie. I can at least sense where Odessa's shop is from anywhere. Hopefully that'll be enough. Head down to the gravel road and make a right," the fox said.

I did my best not to lurch the van forward too much with its sensitive gas pedal. The thing had a surprising amount of "get up and go."

After the Hell I'd just been through, there was really only one thing I was sure of, and that was I needed to visit with Selene. It was time for me to become a customer of Funky Dan's.

Chapter Fourteen
(Dan)

Wind chimes blew in the summer breeze filling the kitchen with pleasant noise as I sat at the beech table with matching chairs beside my parents. They were both waiting for me to finish my piece of cider cake.

I had about three bites left, and Mom smiled at me when I looked up at her. Her short red curly hair was messy, given that she'd spent hours in the kitchen this morning getting my favorite lunch and cake together. I'd had two bowls of beef stew with carrots, beans, and cucumbers in it before the cake.

Her brown apron still had flour spots on it from the dessert, and I giggled.

"What's got my 10-year-old boy so giddy? Surely he's not laughing at his dear mother who worked so hard to make this meal?"

I smirked, couldn't help it really.

"You still have flour on your apron, Mom," I said, giggling again.

She looked down at her apron and then reached behind her to untie it. Slowly she stood up and took it off.

"Are you sure this is flour? Maybe you should take a closer look!" she said, quickly throwing it over my head and rubbing it tightly.

"No! Mom! You're going to get me all cook dirty!" I protested, thrashing my arms and trying not to laugh. I was annoyed, not having a good time!

My lips betrayed me, though, and more laughter escaped.

When I finally got the apron off, Mom was seated once more, only now she was wearing her checkered dress, sans apron.

I scowled at her, trying to make the smirk go away. She pretended to look out the window, as if there was something interesting out in the orchard. When her brown eyes returned to mine, she feigned surprise.

"Daniel! You've got flour in your hair. How did that happen?" she asked, with a large gasp for extra effect.

"You know how! You got up and covered me with your dirty apron," I said, tossing it on the floor.

"Me? Never!" she said, dramatically putting a hand on her chest.

"You're guilty! Dad saw you too," I said, looking over at my bearded father. He had specs of gray in his thick facial hair. They'd shown up not long after I was born, Mom would always say. He was reading a copy of *Hans Brinker, or The Silver Skates* when I pleaded for him to be my witness against Mom's mischief.

Slowly, he closed the book, putting in a flat piece of grass to make his page.

"What now?" he asked, scratching his salt and pepper hair and flicking a cricket off his striped trousers.

"You saw Mom smother me with the apron, didn't you?" I asked.

He looked over at the woman he'd married 12 years ago, and slowly a smile creeped over his face, as it always did when they locked eyes. I just gagged, knowing it was over.

"I'm sorry, son. I was busy reading my book," he said.

"You always take her side. You have to take my side on my birthday!" I said, standing up.

Mom winked at him and then threw her arms up in the air.

"No witnesses, no charges. Case dismissed," she said, laughing.

I crossed my arms.

"That's not fair. I want a lawyer," I said.

Dad snickered and said, "Well, actually, since you were seeking to bring charges against her, she's the one who needs a lawyer. You want a prosecutor to take up the case."

I always forgot my Dad had completed a year of law school before dropping out to marry Mom and take over her family's orchard.

Sitting back down in my chair, I took another bite of my cider cake.

"What's your book about, Dad?" I asked, taking another bite.

He looked down at the black cover and said, "It's about a country across the ocean called the Netherlands. And a pair of siblings who long to take part in an ice-skating race to win some silver skates."

I finished my last bite of cake, losing interest in my Dad's description of the book. Countries across the ocean didn't really appeal to me. That was just like more of the boring stuff Mrs. Thomas was trying to teach us in school.

After I finished my last piece of cake, I thanked Mom, and she took my plate and fork. As I took a drink of water, Dad said, "I've got one more surprise for you, son. Sit tight."

"You do?" Mom asked, in a disapproving tone.

"I do," he said, avoiding her equally disapproving glare.

He disappeared into their bedroom for a moment and came back with something wrapped crudely in a thin brown paper and string.

"What is it?" I asked, my heart racing.

My smile only grew wider as he placed it in front of me on the table. I pulled the string and unfolded the paper to reveal a gift I'd been wanting for the better part of a year now. A red and gold box faced me with three flowers on the left side of the box. In bold print on the right were the words, "The Checkered Game of Life."

"Yes! You got it after all!" I practically screamed.

I thought back to seeing Dillon play Life one day after school. We stayed late so we could play a game. Mrs. Thomas didn't seem to mind. She watched us with intrigue.

Ever since then, I'd wanted my own copy.

Mom and Dad had both told me I was unlikely to get it this year because we weren't "doing well."

My mother seemed to remember this as I ran over to hug Dad and thank him 1,000 times for the gift.

He just chuckled as I ran over to Mom. He put a wooden pipe in his mouth, lit the end and inhaled quickly to get it going. Smoke started to rise and float around his brown eyes. It never seemed to bother him.

After I hugged Mom, she put her hands on her hips and glared at my father. She motioned for him to join her over across the kitchen by her three cast iron skillets hanging from the wall.

I opened the box gingerly, though with enough caution not to damage anything. It was the perfect blend of excitement and gentleness.

Inside I found the folded board. It made a slight cracking noise as I unfolded it and put the board on the table. My eyes glossed over the red and gray checkered squares covered in words like "industry" and "cupid."

Mom looked over to make sure I wasn't paying attention before letting Dad have it. They thought I couldn't hear them, but I could. It was a fact I never let them know because it allowed me to eavesdrop on great information once in a while, like yesterday when Mom told Dad she was going to make me a cider cake.

"I thought we agreed not to buy that for him this year because we're just about out of loan money," Mom said, putting her hands on her hips.

Dad inhaled his pipe and looked over at me.

"Look how happy he is, Tonya. Isn't that part of our jobs as parents, to make sure he has a better life than we did at his age?"

Her scowl intensified.

"And how good of a life is he going to have when we can't afford food next month? How happy is he going to look when you have to take that back to sell it and pay a bill, Ted?"

He threw his hands up slowly and said, "We're going to be fine. I'll do a little extra work for Mr. Davis shoeing his horses next week, and the Farmer's Almanac showed me we're in for a great harvest come October. We'll be fine."

Mom sighed and put her hands on her forehead.

"Why am I the only one who has to be realistic around here? Your little book can't predict how our harvest will turn out. We already lost a quarter of our trees in the fire. And yet, you went out and spent the last of our loan money on a game," Mom said, shaking her head.

Ted gently took her wrists and pushed them down to her sides. Then he wrapped his arms around his wife and pulled her in tight.

"We'll be okay. I always make sure of that," he said. "I just... I know we can't give our son the world. I just want to make sure I provide him with as big a piece of it as I can. He's going to have a hard life inheriting this apple farm one day. Let's favor him just a little bit longer while he can still be a kid, before he has to worry about agriculture loans from the bank or harvest yields."

Tonya sighed and eventually gave up.

"Maybe I can ask Mrs. Fowler for a shift or two at the market in town next week. I just hope Daniel grows up to inherit my good sense, not your frivolousness," she said, and that was the last she spoke of their money woes for the afternoon.

I walked across the squeaky wooden floor and placed a hand on each of their shoulders.

"Can we play a game now? Please?"

I held up the teetotum and said, "But I get to go first because it's my birthday."

Mom looked down at me and nodded. But then she caught herself with a sudden thought.

"Did you finish raking the brush this morning?"

"Awwww. No chores on my birthday," I said, pleading and looking over at Dad.

He just went back to his book. After the argument he'd just had with his bride, there was no way he was coming to rescue me.

Mom said nothing but just stared at me, tilting her head slowly to the side. Her lips said nothing, but her body language said, "What did you just say to me, boy?"

I sighed, put the teetotum back on the board and went outside.

Half an hour later we were gathered around the table, and I spun the teetotum, getting a three. I landed on the "Happiness" space.

Mom groaned, and Dad laughed.

"Beginner's luck!" she said, snatching the teetotum from me.

I smirked and then looked down at the table. There was a patch of white fur there. Mom spun the piece, but I wasn't paying attention.

Although I didn't recognize where this fur came from, it still looked familiar.

We don't have a dog or a cat, I thought, picking up the fluff in my hands.

I held it up close as Dad took the teetotum. Still, I wasn't paying attention. Mom said something and patted my shoulder, but I ignored her.

"Eely!" I finally gasped.

Looking around, I saw the fox was nowhere to be found. When I looked up, Mom and Dad were also gone, but the game was still sitting out on the table.

I glanced back down and saw I was my right age again, wearing a red robe and black pants.

Scratching my beard, I sighed and said, "Come on out, Queen of Tears. I know this is your doing."

The girl who looked no older than 14 appeared in the doorway to Mom and Dad's bedroom. She smirked.

"That was such a pleasant memory, don't you think? One of the last times you were truly happy, before you became a rotten ungrateful soul."

"Enough. I'm well aware of my past mistakes. And I won't let you use them against me," I said. "Where is Eely?"

She shrugged.

"No telling. Just before I snatched you from tonight's dream, she vanished. I'm not sure where your pet ended up."

I did my best to keep a blank expression.

If Eely vanished from my dream, it was probably because she'd been summoned elsewhere. Odessa was unlikely to summon her, but Roxie might have done it with the fox coin Eely gave her. If that was the case, the missing pixie girl shouldn't be missing for much longer.

"So I'm in your dream. Eely is gone. And where does that leave Roxie?"

The Queen of Tears let a smile slowly sneak onto her lips.

"The pixie problem is being taken care of. That's all I'm going to say," she said.

"You were behind Roxie's disappearance?"

"I just created a solution for one of my bigger problems, wizard. Now there's the question for you."

"Oh yeah?"

The Queen of Tears crossed her arms, and her eyes gleamed. Her long black hair began to glow.

"Are you going to be a solution for me and provide the Ossa Key's location, or are you going to be a hindrance to me and try to hide it?" she asked. "I can reunite you with your parents again, and it can be just like this. Nothing but good times. Isn't that all you've wanted for more than a century?"

What awaited me outside of this dream? A shop, Odessa's orders, and my friend Eely. I wanted a second chance with my parents more than anything... that is... until Eely almost died protecting me. I still wanted to leave the shop and see my parents again, but now I just wanted my friend to be happy. And she always seemed happiest at my side.

"No dice," was all I said.

The Queen of Tears frowned.

"Maybe you need a reminder of just how bad you messed up with your parents," she said.

I shook my head.

"That regret is constantly with me. Like I said. I won't allow you to use it against me."

She scowled and slowly wandered over toward me, her eyes glowing with a lighter purple. The Queen of Tears believed she had successfully eliminated one obstacle in the last day. What was one more?

"Wizard, you underestimate exactly what I can use against you in this space. There's nothing for you to 'allow.' Anything in that little head of yours is mine to use whichever way I please." Then her pupils disappeared into a solid sea of purple within her eyes.

The table and chairs flew against the wall as I backed up toward the sink.

Looking down at the floor, I saw my parents again, covered in sweat, dust, red pustules.

My heart sank, and the dread I'd been ignoring since I realized the Queen of Tears was behind this washed over any inner levees I'd thrown up in haste.

"You recognize them in this state, don't you?" she said, kneeling over the corpses.

"This was how they found them, you know? They died in misery on this very kitchen floor, holding each other in their arms."

I clenched my jaw and fought back tears.

I can't let her see that this is getting to me, or she'll just have more fuel against me, I thought.

Although I felt like the Queen of Tears couldn't read my mind, she could read my expressions and emotions.

"Oh wizard, there's no point in trying to hide it. I know that this guilt is rising inside of you like a storm. You try to forget it, occasionally, but it always comes back. That conversation in the orchard where you convinced your father that paying for your tuition at the Arkansas Industrial University would ultimately benefit the family when you returned."

I recalled the conversation she was referencing as clear as anything else burned into my memory. I lied to my father, something I was doing increasingly between the ages of 16 and 18. And I hated myself for it now.

"You'd seen how your friend Dillon grew up in a wealthy family, and greed ate away at your soul once you were old enough to understand what it meant to be poor. You coveted everything Dillon had and grew more bitter to your own family every single day for not being able to provide you with a world like his."

"Enough! I already know all this!" I screamed, tears evading my defenses and sliding down my cheeks.

"You knew it'd bankrupt your father to send you to college, and yet you went anyway. You lied to your mother and said you had every intention of using what you learned in school to come back and help the family. But did you?"

I was shaking now, nearly convulsing with self-loathing and bitterness.

"You broke them, wizard. You blame Odessa for your problems, but the lust for riches was already long established in your heart by the time she showed up offering you that deal," the Queen of Tears said. "I've seen men like you throughout the years. You take and you take, but you never give. Like children, hoarding your toys. Then the world takes something back and suddenly the world's not fair. You men don't know what loss feels like, but *I* do. But I gave a lot to the world. I gave them everything. So, I'm just taking back what's mine. An equal transaction. I think you'll understand, given your position at the shop."

She looked up at me and smiled as my knees buckled. Falling to them, I was brought even closer to the bodies of my parents.

There isn't a single memory in my head she lacks access to, I realized.

"Face it, wizard. You need a second chance with them. Take my deal, and reveal the Ossa Key's location to me. I'll give you what Odessa never could... another opportunity to be happy with your parents and you won't ever hurt anyone here ever again   "

I closed my eyes and tried to force my brain to think. She needed me to give her the key because Kairen was no longer under her control. And because she was still sealed, the Queen of Tears didn't have any other way of reaching into the physical world.

Apparently I wasn't paying enough attention to the Queen of Tears because she started talking again, "You know, in their last moments when they were burning with fever, and their bodies were so dehydrated they were shriveling up like dried sponges, they thought of you."

I tried to tune her out.

Then mom's corpse twitched, and, with a raspy voice as dry as crisp autumn leaves, said "Daniel... where are you."

I wailed, apologizing to my mother.

"I believe on the day they died you were in London. Tell me, what were you doing that day?"

Still shaking, I managed to get out, "Spending time with a girl named Ava."

"Perfect. While they died alone, wanting to see you just one more time, you were shacking up with a woman named Ava, not even thinking about them. That has to feel great," she said.

It didn't. When I got back home and discovered they were dead, I felt as though I'd truly lost everything, even though I'd spent the last few years buying anything. I sat there on the dusty floor of my parents' kitchen, sobbing. The Queen of Tears knew she'd broken me.

I just kept playing out that conversation with Odessa in my head over and over. I was covered in mud, huddled up against an old shack just trying to get under some semblance of an awning and out of the rain.

She walked by in her long black jacket holding a black umbrella and smoking her kiseru.

"Are you happy, Daniel?" she asked.

"What?" I muttered, looking up and trying to focus through all the rain.

"Are you happy, Daniel?" she repeated.

Once I realized it was her, I spent the next several minutes accusing her of swindling me, trying to bully her into a second chance. I wasn't ready to accept the blame for my parents' deaths. If I'd been here, I could have nursed them back to health through the outbreak. But I wasn't here. I was out galivanting across the world, spending money I'd pay back in days at the shop.

No matter how much I bullied Odessa, her red eyes never wavered. She was truly unshakable.

At last she told me, "You don't get second chances in life, Daniel. Not like you described, anyway. I offered you a bargain, and you accepted. Now it's time to pay me back."

Odessa was not the villain in my story. I was.

"Odessa," I muttered, some sort of silent prayer for her to hear me and rescue me from this nightmare. Right now, I'd rather be in the shop, not facing my past failures and greed. I longed for the shop, for Eely, for customers, for anything other than this.

"Odessa, please," I muttered again, one last tear traveling down my left cheek.

"Of course... you can't give me the key," the Queen of Tears said.

I looked up at her through tear-soaked eyes.

What did she say? I thought.

"You can't give me the key because you don't have it. The witch would never trust you with the item necessary for my release. It's preposterous!"

"What are you... talking about?" I asked, squinting.

"You can't lie to me, wizard. I know you gave the key to your witch master. If you don't have the key, I have no deal to strike with you. But don't worry. I'll be by shortly to collect the key from the witch," the Queen of Tears said. "I have no idea what happens to your soul when she dies, but who knows? You may still get what you want out of this."

I stood up and tried to explain.

"Wait! She doesn't have—"

"Goodbye, wizard. See you soon," she said, cutting me off. With a snap of her fingers, everything went black.

I woke up screaming, "Odessa!"

Looking around, I saw my barren bedroom, complete with a single red footstool and framed photograph of my parents.

I was covered in sweat and still out of breath. My heart felt like it'd been shaved over a cheese grater for several hours.

Outside, it was still dark, with the moon high in the sky. Downstairs I heard screeching brakes from some sort of large vehicle. Throwing on my red robe and black pajama bottoms, I ran downstairs and turned on the shop lights.

Unlocking and opening the front door, I saw Roxie and Eely getting out of a large red van.

"Roxie! Eely!" I shouted, and they ran to my arms.

Between the nightmare and being reunited with these two, my heart had been on a roller coaster for the past few hours.

"You smell like a barn," I said, looking at Roxie.

"Nice to see you too, Dan. If that's your midnight breath, your morning breath must be enough to kill a rhino," Roxie said, laughing.

I laughed with her until Eely said, "It almost makes me want to sleep downstairs again."

Shaking my noggin, I scratched her head and asked, "Where have you two been?"

They just looked at each other, and shook their heads. Roxie spoke up and said, "Trapped in a nightmare of epic proportions."

"Me too. Seems the Queen of Tears is putting the final phase of her plan into motion. All she needs now is the Ossa Key, which I have in the store," I said.

Roxie walked into the store and marveled at the shelved items.

Wait... if she's here in the store, that means she needs to purchase something, I realized.

Eely walked in and stretched before going back to the glass counter and hopping on top of it.

"I really love these ladybug earrings. How much are they?" Roxie asked, pointing to some small red earrings with black spots on them.

"The price for those is one black cat," I said, chuckling.

"You... don't take debit?"

I shook my head, and Roxie shrugged.

We caught up on our nightmares, and honestly, I couldn't tell whose was worse. The Queen of Tears knew exactly where to hit us and how. Roxie only escaped because her future self and Eely came to the rescue. And I was let go. Jeebus, we were in trouble.

"So... what was it like meeting yourself?" I asked.

Roxie looked down at the shaggy carpet and then smiled.

"It felt... reassuring. The strange thing is... my future self looked like a full-bodied pixie. But I didn't see my bracelet on her... my arm."

The light bulb in my head went off again, and I realized I finally needed to deliver this warning to Roxie while we had a chance.

"Roxie, listen to me. I should have warned you about this a long time ago, but it just never seemed like I had the right chance. Something always came up," I said. Her pink glowing eyes turned toward me.

"Eely mentioned you wanted to talk to me about my bracelet. She told me not to put it on again?"

I nodded.

"Pixie magic is very potent, and there's always a high percentage of cross magic species contamination. It slowly changes the people who use it into full-blown pixies, and once you've changed, there's no going back to being a normal human. That's why the only people who typically use pixie magic are... well, pixies," I said.

Roxie nodded slowly and looked down at the floor.

"I'm not an expert on pixie magic, but I can recognize that just one month of using this stuff has changed you in some pretty big ways. Your hair and eyes, for one. I imagine in your dreams you've also taken on wings and an antenna?" I asked.

Roxie nodded again and raised her eyes to mine. There wasn't necessarily a fear there, but there was a deep confusion, a need for answers I couldn't completely supply.

"The woman who gave me this bracelet... she made it sound like I was just filling in for her. She said I was just supposed to turn nightmares into dreams for a month in her place while she went back to the pixie world. Then she'd be back, and we could talk about where I wanted to go from there," Roxie said. "And... I don't understand. She had a human form, Dan."

I shook my head and sighed.

"She presented the illusion of a human form with her magic. Once mastered, I'm guessing all pixie magic isn't limited to just the dream world. But make no mistake, Roxie. If you put that bracelet on one more time and use it like you've been using it, it'll change you permanently. I won't be able to change you back. Heck, I don't even know if I could change you back into a full human right now. Odessa might be able to... wait...Odessa!" the Queen of Tears, she was coming.

Roxie raised an eyebrow and looked over at Eely.

The fox asked, "What's wrong with Odessa, Dan?"

"Nothing yet. But the Queen of Tears told me she was coming for Odessa because she's convinced I gave her the Ossa Key," I said.

"Why would she think that?" Eely asked.

"Because in my nightmare, I called out for Odessa to save me. The Queen of Tears thought I was calling for Odessa to give her the key," I said.

Walking back and forth across the carpet, Roxie looked to be deep in thought. Maybe she was calculating odds or something.

"Dan, this just doesn't make any sense. I freed Kairen from her grasp. She shouldn't have any way to get at Odessa, right? I mean... your boss is a powerful witch, isn't she?"

I nodded but added, "Odessa has made it clear to me that the Queen of Tears is stronger than she is. But the witch hardly ever sleeps, so normally, you'd be right about the Queen of Tears having no solid option to get to her."

"What do you mean normally?" Roxie asked.

Scratching my beard, I sighed and sat down on my favorite stool propped in the corner.

"It was something she said before ending the nightmare. The Queen of Tears told me she'd be by shortly to collect the key, as if there was some impact she could have on the physical world. Maybe the gate has weakened so much that she can manifest her power up here now.".

Walking into the kitchen, I poured myself a bowl of cereal after offering both Roxie and Eely some. They declined.

Standing at the glass counter crunching, I thought about how much the queen's power could have grown through the decades. She may look like an innocent 14 year old, but she was clearly older than me and much more bitter than I was.

I looked around the shop and thought back on what I'd come to revisit in my nightmare. Odessa wasn't the villain. I was. And I was trapped in a... prison.

Damn it. The Queen of Tears is just me without anybody to help her, I thought, scratching my head.

I thought back to my last argument with Roxie about reaching her. The pixie dream girl said she also saw some of herself in our adversary. I'm guessing from their last nightmare, Roxie didn't exactly reach her. I wanted to ask if she still felt like reaching the Queen of Tears now, but after all that's happened, I just decided to stay silent. One thing hadn't changed my mind. She still had to be stopped, one way or another.

"Dan, I need an item from you while we're thinking," Roxie said.

I looked up and wiped some milk from my beard.

"Sure, kiddo. What did you have in mind?" I asked.

"I need something to transport me to the pixie world. I'm not going to find the answers I need anywhere else." Roxie said.

Sighing, I racked my brain. What she said made sense. I just didn't think I had any items that were specifically designed to transport people to the pixie world. I had a pair of glasses that would let one see into the pixie world for about 60 seconds per day, but nothing to take someone there specifically.

Eely spoke up and said, "Dan, she can use the Moon Mirror."

I looked over at the eggshell fox and nodded.

"Good idea, Eely. She has the bracelet for the mirror to focus on. We just need to get it outside under the moonlight and pour water on the surface," I said.

I looked over at a clock on the wall.

"It's 3:34 a.m. We need to get a move on," I said.

Then I stopped. The store rattled, and I knew I was getting ahead of myself, nervous about the upcoming clash with the Queen of Tears.

I Crossed my arms. "Roxie, there's a price you have to pay for using the Moon Mirror. No matter how bad the situation, I can't give away anything in this store for free."

Eely stared at me but kept silent. We both knew this was the way things had to be.

"I understand, Dan. Name your price. I'm prepared to pay it," Roxie said, matching my gaze with her own.

I rubbed my foot over a piece of shaggy carpet and said, "Leaving this world to enter another isn't easy, and it's never cheap. Leaving this world with a round trip ticket? That's even more expensive. For two uses of this mirror, the price will be two friendships, the things you treasure most in this world."

Roxie gasped and looked at me as if I'd just asked her to jump off a cliff. And for all I knew, maybe I had done just that.

"You must be joking. Two friendships, what does that even mean?" Roxie asked, angrily.

I could tell I touched a nerve. She loved her friends more than anything else in this world, and that's exactly why the shop demanded such a high price.

"You name two friendships, and those people will lose all memory and affection for you. I'm sorry, Roxie. But interdimensional travel... it comes at a high cost. And most of the high costs in this shop mean something your heart values deeply."

Roxie started to cry again, and I heard her mutter, "Jenna... Tessa. There's just no way."

I looked down at the green carpet and ran my foot over it again.

Maybe I can convince Odessa to change the rules just this once, I thought. *Yeah right. How many times have I thought that in front of a crying customer?*

Then, Roxie looked up and wiped her eyes. An idea seemed to have come to her mind.

"What's the price for one trip through the mirror?" she asked.

I hadn't considered that, but I also didn't think it'd help her much. She seemed to really love whoever Jenna and Tessa were. Having to pick just one of them somehow seemed even more cruel.

Closing my eyes, I felt for an answer from the store. Logic would seem to just cut the price in half, but that wasn't always the case with magic transactions. The price for one trip might just be a kidney or Roxie's ability to say words starting with the letter 'C' for all I knew.

When I had an answer, I looked at Roxie and said, "One friendship, a rare display of math and logic from this store."

Roxie took a deep breath and let it out slowly.

She's made her choice, I thought. *Dang this girl has grown strong in the weeks since she first popped up in my dreams. The resolve it takes to pick a friendship and end it for some sort of greater good? Mindblowing,*

"Kairen!" she shouted, followed by, "I'm sorry," And a quick shrug

And just like that, the store rattled for a few moments and then returned to normal.

"It seems your price has been paid," I said.

"But I don't feel any different. And I remember all my adventures with Kairen over the last month."

Taking one last bite of cereal, I wiped my mouth with my robe and said, "It doesn't affect you, Roxie. It's Kairen who will lose his memory and any affection he had for you. Ironic, seeing as he's the one who called the shop to warn me you'd gone missing in the first place."

Roxie frowned and sighed again. She ran a few fingers nervously through her long silver hair and closed her eyes.

When she opened them again, she asked, "But... our lives have been so entangled in all this dream mess. How will the price affect his memory of events over the last few weeks?"

I shrugged and took my bowl into the sink, dumping the milk and rinsing it out for once.

"I can't say, kiddo. His memories with the Queen of Tears will definitely still be there. He'll remember being the phantom thief. But as for your involvement, it might just be a gray blob. Or they'll just be holes in his memory, and he'll definitely sense that. Kairen is a smart guy."

Roxie put on her calculating face again and gathered up all her hair into a ponytail before letting it fall behind her.

"What about his brother? He'll still remember me rescuing him, right?"

"Your price doesn't impact anyone but Kairen, kiddo."

"Then couldn't his brother fill him in on everything that happened?"

"Well sure. But it's one thing to be told something happened. And another to still have the feelings and mental images associated with a certain event. If I told you I ate a plate of sushi, you could picture it in your head. But it's nowhere near as powerful as actually eating a plate of sushi to your senses. I know you're looking for a loophole, but it's called a price for a reason, Roxie."

The dream girl sighed and then asked, "But Kairen could come in here and pay a price of his own to get those memories and affections back, right?"

I shrugged again and took a few steps toward the mirror, remembering time was growing less every second.

"I suppose he could, but I won't have any idea of what that price would be until he gets here. And he may not want to use his one time in this store to get those memories back. He may have another need," I said, not knowing how true that would be.

"I don't understand, Roxie said, walking around me and getting to the mirror first.

It was a full-body mirror connected to two stands that were ornate carved oak, decorated with carvings of vines and flowers. The wood that held the mirror itself had the phases of the moon carved above it.

And yet, the object was surprisingly light, given what it could do and the materials it was made from.

We lifted the mirror and carried it carefully between the second and third aisles of my shop. Eely ran ahead and hopped up onto each doorknob, opening them for us to walk out into the back yard.

"It's like this, Roxie. Each person that comes into this shop can only do so physically once. Customers are only allowed in when they need something. They pay a price. Then they leave, never to return again. Nobody gets two visits to this store. Those are the rules," I said, stepping down into the grass with my bare feet.

There wasn't a cloud in the night sky above us, but the evening air was humid, typical Arkansas summer night with deafening cicadas and everything.

We set the mirror down not too far from my fence, and I walked over to the back corner of my little yard. Waving my left hand over what appeared to be nothing, I muttered, "Ostenda."

A small well appeared, made of cobblestone. It had an aged wood crank with a little metal bucket attached to a rope. A little roof with chipped shingles covered the well, which was about five feet wide.

"That's a neat trick," Roxie said, looking at the mirror and then the well.

"Odessa showed it to me. It stays cloaked back here for use in certain rituals that require water from deep in the earth. I guess I've never appropriately credited Odessa for just how much she's taught me about magic and the mystical world," I said.

"And you've never thanked her for introducing you to me, making your life 200 percent better," Eely said, prancing out into the yard.

I chuckled and said, "You're the most gorgeous fox in the world."

"Aw shucks. Thanks, Dan," she said, using her paws to position the mirror at an angle where it reflected as much of the moon's rays as it could.

I lowered the bucket deep into the well, probably 200 feet or more. When I felt the rope slack, I pulled the bucket back up. Crystal clear water greeted me as I asked Eely to fetch me a ladle from the kitchen. She did so and brought it back to me.

Taking the ladle, I scooped as much water from the well as possible and let Eely drink the rest.

"Hold out your bracelet on the mirror's surface, Roxie," I said.

She did as she was told and pressed it against the smooth reflective glass, which showed the night sky above.

"Ater," I said, slowly pouring water in beads that raced down the mirror's face.

In the moonlight, the phases above the glass began to glow blue, and the glass appeared to wave and move around, as if it were a pond on a stormy night.

"Roxie, you can remove your bracelet now," I said.

The image stabilized after she did so and revealed a lush garden at twilight. It was full of bushes carrying fruits we couldn't identify and some kind of spotted honeybees that were about twice the size of earth's own insect.

Shades of azure and mauve created patches in the sky above this garden. It looked breathtaking, but this journey wasn't mine to take.

"Roxie, you're free to enter, but you've only paid for one trip. I don't know how you plan on getting back. I suppose you'll be at the mercy of the pixies. Maybe they'll use their magic to connect to this mirror and send you back through," I warned.

She nodded and gave me one last hug. Then she did the same for Eely.

"I'll be back soon," she said. "I promise. Just hold the city for me while I'm gone."

Then she took a deep breath and stepped through the mirror, the surface appearing to wash over her and distort the pixie girl.

When she'd finally crossed over, the mirror fell dark and returned to normal, reflecting the night sky.

Chapter Fifteen
(Roxie)

My first thought upon setting foot in the pixie world was that the air smelled like an extremely earthy cinnamon. It was like the best parts of 50 different candles, and it honestly overwhelmed me for a solid 30 seconds.

Then it was time for my eyes to be overwhelmed from looking at the sky. The absolute range of hues from ultramarine to indigo brought such peace to the very core of my eye sockets. It was as though my mind was getting drunk on color, and it was all my being wanted.

I stood there with my neck turned upward, and it surprised me that I didn't drool for the five literal minutes I was frozen staring at the sky.

The only thing to pull my gaze back down was one of those large bumble bees landing on my shoulder and... I dunno, smelling or tasting my hair or something? I just kind of giggled and looked at the insect, which buzzed off to a different part of the garden.

My eyes followed it until they came upon some kind of orange gourd-like fruit that looked like a cross between a bell pepper and a squash. As I got closer, the smell drew me in until my nose was practically on the piece of produce.

Three or five or seven different variations on an orange/cherry combination floated up into my nostrils. I was suddenly ravenous, not for any food, but for this one piece of fruit I was smelling.

Reaching forward, I grabbed and pulled it off the thick vine wrapped around the top. In fact, the top of this fruit that was the size of my hand popped off and stayed attached to the vine. The smells only grew stronger, and I looked inside to find at least three or four ounces of juice.

Without pausing to think about whether pixie fruit would be poisonous to humans, I tipped up the fruit and took a swig. My pupils dilated, and then I downed the rest of the juice, a sweet array rushing over my taste buds unlike anything I'd ever tasted before. When the juice was all gone, I immediately sank my teeth into the fruit. More juice dripped from my chin, but I didn't care.

I took a second bite, then a third and rolled over onto my back like some kind of stupefied sea otter, holding my fruit over my chest.

I've never been this happy, I thought and took another bite. My eyes found the sky again, and all the magic of these fresh highs maxed out my attention span, essentially breaking my consciousness.

So, for the next several minutes I just stayed there on my back, giggling, drooling, munching, crunching, and melting my brain in a sea of pleasure. It was unlike anything I'd ever felt before. It was also probably the reason humans weren't allowed into the pixie world.

A shadow fell over me, taking the sky away, but it took my brain a few seconds to process someone was looming over me. In the end, I decided I didn't care because I was working on my third piece of fruit from whatever bush this was.

"Roxie?" the voice said.

"What's that?" my mouth finally formed words.

"Oh, my sweet child. What are you doing here? And how are you still a human?"

"Pudding!" I yelled and then giggled some more.

A pixie, which was beginning to become familiar to me, giggled a bit herself before leaning down to help me up.

"You see? This is why we don't allow humans in the pixie world. There are just too many sensations that overwhelm you. You end up a drooling mess. And although you're probably having the time of your life, I've lost three pieces of fruit from my favorite bush," Selene said, putting her hands on her hips.

It was no use. I was only comprehending about every third word I heard her say.

The pixie rolled her pink glowing eyes and said, "Hold on, child. I'll help you."

She reached into a pouch attached to the right side of her hips by a narrow black belt. In her hand were blue rose petals I'd seen once before. The pixie blew them straight into my face but without any force.

It felt like a tiny rope was being given to each of my five senses, and they were being tugged back to my center of attention. The pedals had no odor, but they worked all the same as they did in Dr. Lyra's office when I first met Selene.

I took a deep breath and wiped the fruit juice from my chin, blushing something fierce. My mind was no longer a frying egg in a skillet or whatever it was supposed to look like on drugs.

"Do you have a wet rag or something?" I squeaked out.

Selene smiled and nodded. Then she held out a flat palm, and with a little poof of golden smoke a soft pink cloth appeared folded in her hand. It was damp, exactly as I asked.

I sheepishly took it and muttered thank you. Wiping any sticky parts off my face and hands, I took another deep breath and then awkwardly held onto the cloth, unsure of what to do with it. There wasn't exactly a clothes hamper in the garden.

"Just toss it over your shoulder, Roxie," Selene said.

"Oh no. I wouldn't think of littering in such a beautiful—"

"Just trust me," Selene said, interrupting me.

I nodded and lightly tossed the cloth over my left shoulder. It vanished in the same puff of golden smoke it appeared in.

"Whoa," I said.

Selene smiled and helped me to my feet. When I finally got a look at her with my unclouded mind, I saw she was wearing a loose-fitting garnet garment that covered her from shoulders to knees. It all appeared to be one piece of clothing, except for her narrow brown belt tied around her stomach.

When the wind blew, her clothing floated around her just like that of my future self. Her hair did the same thing. Whether this was magic, pixie biology, or something else, I wasn't sure. Selene's gossamer wings stuck out behind her outfit, and I wasn't sure if there were holes for them or not. The way her outfit seemed to float, I couldn't tell how her wings got through.

"I felt some sort of disturbance in my garden. Imagine my surprise when I come out here and discover you sitting under a bush eating my fruit. Those take 12 human years to bloom, you know?"

I grabbed my cheeks and moaned.

"I'm so sorry, Selene. I'll plant you some more, I promise," I said.

For a moment, her expression changed, and she said, "It doesn't matter. Today's it, anyway."

When I looked up at her, the gloomy expression evaporated, but it looked like it took quite a bit of effort on her part to make it happen.

"Tell me, Roxie. What are you doing here? And why are you still in a somewhat human form?"

"In dreams I have a mostly pixie form, if that helps," I said.

"Give me a moment, then," Selene said. "May I place a hand on your shoulder?"

I nodded, appreciative that she asked permission before touching me in any way. Too many in the human world don't do that. They just go in for a hug or a slap on the back. I absolutely hated that. The only people who had 24/7 infallible permission to lay even a finger on me were Mom, Tessa, and Jenna.

As she placed a hand on my left shoulder, I felt as though my body was humming on some sort of magical frequency.

"Oh my. You have certainly progressed, haven't you?" Selene asked.

"Progressed?" I asked.

"You're practically a pixie already with the amount of magic you've used. You really have been busy in my absence, haven't you?"

I just nodded, thinking about Hiawatha and all I'd been through in the month since Selene had departed. It had been the best and worst summer vacation of my life. The joys and the trauma had each peaked.

"I'm going to bring out your full form so far, okay?"

I nodded, unsure of what that meant. Dan said I wouldn't fully transform into a pixie until I put the bracelet back on. And I wasn't even sure if that was something I wanted. I felt like that decision would have major consequences, but I needed to hear what they were from Selene.

The humming throughout my body increased as Selene changed it. My usual antenna formed on my head, and my single set of gossamer wings sprouted behind me. And then there I was, one wing short of becoming a full pixie.

As if Selene was reading my thoughts, she said, "You're so close, child. Why don't you put your bracelet on and complete the transformation?"

I winced. Was she trying to trick me into this? Her urgency was slight, but it was there, a detectable tone under her words.

Working up the courage, I said, "A lot has happened since you left Selene. And I need some important questions answered."

The pixie flashed a brief sad expression toward me again. Her lips seemed to quiver, and her eyes actually stopped glowing momentarily. But she nodded all the same and said, "Okay, let's go inside, and we can discuss this."

* * *

(Dan)

"Aw crap. Now I have no one to help me get this back inside," I muttered.

"You can do it, Dan. You're stronk!" Eely said.

As I struggled with the awkward size of the mirror I asked, "Stronk? Where did you hear that word? What does it even mean?"

Eely laughed and said, "It's a thing. I promise."

When I finally got the mirror back inside, I set it down and sighed.

The clock said 4:02 a.m., and my body told me it wanted to go back to sleep... or maybe another bowl of cereal. Signals are hard to read when one is up so early.

I started toward the kitchen when I heard a massive crash outside the shop. I darted toward the front door and peeked outside to see what made the noise. Before me, a dark figure stood about 10 feet from the store, out in the middle of the road.

As it arose from a kneeling position, I saw a dark suit of armor about nine feet high. It wore a massive bastard sword on its back, and it was glowing purple.

"Uh... Dan? I'm guessing that's not one of our friends," Eely said, jumping on my shoulder.

I didn't answer because my eyes were glued to the street where Odessa calmly walked over to the suit of armor.

What is she doing? I shrieked in my mind.

The dark suit of armor looked down at the woman in black with red eyes and huffed black smoke through its closed helmet visor.

Odessa looked up at the knight and shook her head, unimpressed. "It's a bit much for a simple item retrieval mission, wouldn't you agree, Queen of Tears?" Odessa asked.

Eely called out for Odessa, and I did the same. She paid no mind to us.

The dark suit of armor took a concrete-shattering step toward the witch.

"The... key," it hissed through its visor, its eyes glowing solid violet.

"No," Odessa said calmly.

The suit of armor reached forward with a blinding speed and grabbed Odessa by the throat. The witch gasped and then started to kick as he lifted her from the ground with ease.

"Eely! Go!" I yelled, and the fox raced out the door, transforming into her full-size form in an instant. But before she could open her mouth and let fire rain down upon the suit of armor, it raised its left foot and kicked Roxie's van toward the shop with a violent speed.

Dust rattled off the van as its tires squealed across the pavement and slammed into Eely.

It continued forward and slammed my fox into the wall of Odessa's Physic Center, pinning Eely. I heard her yelp and clawing against the metal as she tried to free herself.

Running just outside my shop, I thought about starting the van and driving it out of the way. Then I realized Roxie took the keys with her.

"Eely! Are you okay?" I shouted, looking at the pinned fox.

"I'm fine! Save Odessa!" I heard her yell. But she wasn't fine. I could see blood dripping from her glistening fur down her front left leg.

Around the van, I could hear Odessa gasping for air.

"The key, witch," the armor hissed, louder than before.

Odessa shook her head and then clapped her hands and threw them on the armor's vambrace. I saw her growl, calling power forward. This was the first time I'd seen the witch being anything but calm.

The armor rattled, and the concrete around both of them further cracked and sunk. It seemed like she was applying some type of intense pressure on the amor. Upping gravity, maybe?

This went on for about half a minute, until finally Odessa's arms fell and hung limp at her sides. Her face was sweating. And the armor was unphased. There wasn't even a slight dent on its armor on it.

"Your sorcery is nothing compared to that of my master," the armor hissed.

It squeezed Odessa's neck tighter, and I heard her raspy voice say, "Then I simply need to up the price."

Odessa began to shimmer in a bright red as her black hair shot up straight into the air from magical force. Then it arced around her.

I could sense from the way her energy gathered around her like a magical, ticking bomb that she intended to blow herself up to take out this knight armor and protect Eely and myself.

"Don't do it, Odessa! I can figure this out," I yelled, lying, unable to even leave the sidewalk without being eaten alive by worms.

Her head turned toward me as her red aura grew in size.

"Daniel... you're not the same selfish jerk that I placed in the store. You've grown so much, and... I'm proud of you. When I take this monster with me, you free Eely and take good care of her. I'm sorry I can't do more to stop the Queen of Tears, but I can buy time for you two to escape," she said. "After I die, your binding spell will be broken, and you can leave the shop."

I shook my head as the Queen of Tears' words echoed through it, "You may still get what you want out of this."

"That's not what I want!" I yelled back at her. "It's not just Eely that I need. I need you too, Odessa!"

For the first time, that witch let me see her real smile. This witch who gave people readings and granted wishes was powerless to stop the Queen of Tears. That fact kept rattling around in my head.

For all the times I grew furious at Odessa or complained about her, I realized she was busy working to make me a better person. It only took 130 years, but I liked to think that recent influence from Eely and Roxie had helped me change.

She wasn't holding me prisoner here. She was just keeping me from relapsing into old tendencies and throwing my life away, I thought.

"The key, witch. This is your last chance," the armor said, squeezing as tight as it could.

Odessa gagged and kicked her feet, but the red aura did not fade.

"And... . yours," she said, smiling and looking deep into the visor in front of her without a single ounce of fear.

This witch had walked the earth for centuries, fully knowing death is a door that everyone passes through, no matter how long it takes. Eventually, it comes for us all, even her.

My heart raced, and a tear slid down my right cheek as I watched it all unfold before me. Eely cried out, "Dan! Save her!"

And I wanted to, but the cost... the cost would be astronomical. Just before I saw Odessa's soul leave her body, I made up my mind.

Reaching into my robe pocket, I found the Ossa Key and hurled it at the suit of armor.

Without even looking at me, the armor caught the key with its free hand. Then it looked down to see the key resting in its gauntlet.

"There's your damn key, monster! Take it and leave my master alone!"

The armor surprisingly let Odessa fall to the street. As Odessa lie there gasping for air, the suit of armor turned and simply walked away.

I cried for a minute, watching Odessa struggle to get up, knowing I'd just doomed this city. But I couldn't face a future without her. I just couldn't. I'd already lost the two most important people in my life. And I wasn't prepared to lose the other two. So I sank to my knees and placed my face into my hands.

Unsure of how much time had passed, I heard Eely melt her way through the side of the van, then limp over to Odessa. She'd recovered some by then, but her face was still a brush of purple.

Together they walked over to me. Eely put a paw on my left shoulder, and Odessa put a hand on my right shoulder.

I looked up with tears in my eyes and met Odessa's thoughtful gaze.

"I'm sorry," I said.

"For what?" she asked, in a blameless tone.

"For being weak."

"Do you consider saving your loved ones to be a weakness, Daniel?"

Her question had a quizzical nature to it, also devoid of any criticism. She helped me up as   Eely jumped up on my shoulder.

"I've doomed 100,000 students and residents that call this city home," I said, still sniffling.

Odessa gave me her deepest gaze yet and said, "To save a loved one. And we don't know that the city is doomed. Not yet at least."

"But that key will free her magic! She'll plunge the city into a giant nightmare!" I yelled.

Odessa just nodded.

"You made your choice, Daniel, exactly like I said you would when I prophesied the key's journey into this store. Now, all we can do is wait to see what the Queen of Tears does next and do our best to hold the city until your pixie friend's return," Odessa said. "Come on, let's go have a drink."

Odessa led me inside, and I saw Eely walk back into the kitchen. She returned with a bottle of Kokuryu Daiginjo sake in her jaws. She placed it on the glass counter, then went to get three glasses. When she finished fetching it all, she shrank back down to her normal size and jumped back up to the glass counter.

My master unscrewed the metal lid, and I suddenly felt like I hadn't slept in five weeks.

As she poured us each a glass, Odessa raised her own and said, "Here's to no more deaths tonight."

"Here, here," Eely said.

I just stood there in a trance. Did neither of them realize a great evil would soon be unleashed upon the residents of this city? We were perhaps minutes away from the Queen of Tears' freedom, and Odessa wanted to stand here and drink now of all times?

"Daniel... take a drink and breathe. Panicking won't solve what's to come," she said.

I did as she said, taking a drink and scowling. This wasn't my favorite beverage.

"And what is to come?" I asked quietly.

"A gift," Odessa said gently.

I cocked my head to the side.

"Excuse me?"

"You're excused," Eely said.

Odessa reached into a pocket on the side of her kimono and pulled out a present wrapped in thin brown paper and bound with a simple black string.

I took it and stupidly asked, "For me?"

She nodded and let me see another rare smile.

"It took me a while to track down, but I finally managed to find something I think you'll love to read," she said.

I slowly pulled the string and lifted the crinkly paper to reveal an old black tattered book. The pages were yellowed, and it took everything I had to keep from crying again as I read the title out loud, "*Hans Brinker, or The Silver Skates.*"

Sniffling, I asked, "Is this... the same-"

My voice faded, and I couldn't finish the question, so Odessa nodded, continuing her smile for a new record.

I held the book close to my heart and Eely asked what it was. I ignored her question and rushed forward to hug Odessa. She wrapped her unnaturally slender arms around me and said, "It's okay, Daniel. It's okay."

In the middle of our hug, a sonic boom trembled the shop. When the sound faded, a low rumbling picked up where it left off.

Odessa, Eely, and I ran to the front door and looked up to see a large jagged moon in the sky above Fayetteville, complete with an immense glaring face looking down at the city. The behemoth couldn't have been more than a few hundred feet above Fayetteville, and its eyes glowered purple as waves of similar colors began to smother the night sky around us, blotting out the normal night moon, stars and sky.

The moon's face sneered down at us, complete with a pointed nose and several carved rocks in the mouth to look like teeth ready to devour this city if the moon smashed into it.

When purple lights rippled across the land, completely blanketing the night skycolors ranging from plum to eggplant finished blotting out our normal night sky, I began to hear screams from across the city. The ground began to shake. I saw dozens of those black armored knights falling from the sky, landing on houses, trees, sidewalks without any regard for anyone nearby and more. They were ready to terrorize, maim, and otherwise kill as ordered by their master.

"Well, I'm guessing she's free and succeeded in plunging the entire city into her nightmare," Eely said.

Odessa nodded, and I sighed. I had no clue how we were going to beat her and return the city to normal. Did we kill her? Could we? What would happen if she decided to crash that giant moon into the city? How far was she prepared to go in revenge for her imprisonment? I had an eerie feeling that I had no answers to these questions.

"Dan! Hey Dan!" I heard a familiar voice yell. And as I turned to look down the road, there was Kairen running up to the shop. He was wearing jeans and a blue shirt with the words, "Got Game?" displayed across the front. He took a moment to catch his breath.

"Kairen? What are you doing here?" I asked.

"Daniel, why does anyone come here? He's a customer, of course. See to his needs," Odessa said, some usual criticism returning to her voice.

"Now?" I emphasized just how crazy that sounded.

"Yes now! Get going," Odessa said as another suit of armor crashed into the van next to the shop. "And quickly, please."

"Yeah, Roxie's dad better hope the ladybugs restore that," Eely said.

"What?" I asked.

"Nothing," the fox said and resumed her large form, roasting the armor with a blast of white fire and then body slamming it backward.

"I got this! Take care of Kairen!" Eely yelled, and continued blasting the armor with a fireball and sending it flying in reverse about five or six more feet.

"I'm here to help however I can. My mind feels fried, but I remember this was my former master's plan, plunging the city into a nightmare. I want to protect my father and brother however I can," Kairen said.

"What about Roxie?" I asked.

"Who?" he returned.

"Nothing," I said, seeing the effects of the price our pixie girl paid for her trip.

Odessa pulled us both inside the store and said, "I'll get to work on a barrier spell. We need to protect that mirror so your pixie friend has a way back. Daniel, get Kairen suited up. There's one item in this store that should allow him to dreamwalk and protect his loved ones."

At once, I knew what she was talking about. I pulled Kairen onto the second row and came to a model head standing on the top shelf. Around it was a black eyepatch with ancient Greek writing covering the inside of the patch and the back of the band. The lettering was done in liquid silver and looked ast fresh as the day it was written on the item.

I pulled down the head, being careful not to knock off the glass tank with an icy snake off the shelf under it.

"Don't want her getting loose," I muttered, removing the patch from the model head and replacing it on the shelf.

Holding the eyepatch in my left hand, the entire object became highlighted in silver, with the letters appearing to darken a little bit.

"What's this?" Kairen asked, pointing at it.

"This is an enchanted item crafted by the god Morpheus himself. It allows the wearer to dreamwalk and incrementally shape nightmares around them, similar to how your old item created by the Queen of Tears functioned.

Kairen slowly reached for it, and my hand withdrew. He looked up at me, waiting for an explanation.

"Kairen, there's a price paid for every item in this store. And it's always hefty, depending on how valuable the item you're taking is," I said.

He looked down at the green plush carpet and then nodded.

"I did a lot of terrible things in the service of the Queen of Tears. It only makes sense I pay a price trying to redeem those mistakes," he said with a look of determination in his eyes.

"Very well. The price you'll pay for taking this item is your sleep. To be able to dreamwalk with this, you'll never sleep again. You won't grow physically exhausted, but your spirit will feel it after a while. And it'll grow as an itch you can't scratch, even if you take off the eyepatch or stop using it altogether. Do you understand, Kairen?"

He closed his eyes for a minute, pretended to snore, and then reopened them.

"I wanted to get one last cat nap in before it goes away," he said, smirking.

I snorted and handed him the eyepatch.

His whole body immediately glowed in a silver aura. I reached over on the counter behind me and pulled out a small nondescript glass jar, holding it up to Kairen's head.

It slowly began to fill with some kind of blue gas being pulled from the boy's skull. When the jar was full, I tightly screwed a lid on it and put it inside the glass case.

"What was that?"

"Your ability to sleep," I said.

"I figured it'd hurt more than that," he said.

"Some pain takes longer to form, but rest assured, Kairen. Yours will form," I warned.

His smirk faded and he nodded.

As he started to slide the eyepatch over his head, he asked, "So how does this work?"

"The eye you leave uncovered becomes your reality eye. You use it to see normally in the real world. The eye you cover first becomes your dream eye. When you want to enter someone's dream and manipulate it, you'll stare at them with your reality eye and then cover it, revealing your dream eye. At that point, you'll be transported into the target's dream and be able to manipulate it to some extent," I explained.

Kairen slid the patch over his left eye and gasped as his right eye started to smoke a little bit.

"Is this normal?" he grimaced, in some pain.

"Steel yourself. The enchanted item is attuning to your body," I said.

He hissed and walked over to the full body mirror Roxie had stepped into. There was an explosion outside I assumed was caused by Eely, and I hoped she was keeping things under control. I needed to be out there joining her soon.

As Kairen looked in the mirror, he gasped.

"My right eye is a solid silver now."

"Your left eye should be as well. The item is finished adjusting to your body," I said, walking over.

"You should have put that on the warning label. I rather liked my previous eyes, and most of the ladies did too," he said, that smirk returning.

Roxie is going to miss this goofball, I thought, realizing that even this was a hard price for her to pay, regardless of who Tessa and Jenna were.

"Great. Now the entire city has been swallowed into a nightmare, so switch eyes, and you'll be able to control bits and pieces of it," I instructed.

Kairen did so, and his body was once more highlighted in silver. In a bright flash, his clothing changed, and I covered my eyes from the light.

When I lowered my hands, I saw he was wearing a white tuxedo and top hat, with a white cloth covering the bottom half of his face.

"Why the ridiculous outfit?" I asked, sighing.

He turned to me and said, "I think it looks dramatic and cool."

I just shook my head. It looked exactly like his phantom thief gettup, only now he had an eyepatch. And somehow, he'd changed it to white as well.

Didn't know he could do that, I thought.

He held up his right hand, and a gleaming narrow light filled it. It took form into a slender blade with a black leather grip under the handguard.

As he stood there, I told him to turn toward me.

"Listen to me, Kairen. You started out in the service of evil, bent on destroying the lives of those in this city. You were her phantom thief. Now I charge you as a new protector of the people in this city... guard their lives from your former master. Be the light that cuts through darkness thrust upon us by the Queen of Tears. Go!"

Kairen nodded and leapt up through my ceiling, disappearing into the night sky.

After another fiery blast outside, I raised my right hand high above my head and called for my wand. It flew into my grip, and I rushed outside with Eely, blasting any dark armor that revealed itself.

"Disploda!" I yelled, and a dark armor flew backward into a green pickup truck, detonating it.

"Can those ladybugs you talked about fix that?" I asked, Eely.

She shrugged and body slammed another suit of armor.

We have to protect that mirror and hold on until Roxie returns, I thought. *I know she'll be the key to saving this city.*

No matter how many dark armors Eely and I blasted, more kept appearing. We were in the thick of it now, and there was no choice but to endure. The people in this city depended on it.

* * *

(Roxie)

Selene led me through the garden, and we stopped here and there to allow the giant spotted bumble bees to cross the path and get to all manner of fruits and flowers I knew weren't native to earth. I started to feel my mind become tempted to slide back upon all the different food and flowers, but I stopped and forced myself to focus. My friends needed me. And I needed answers.

Selene led me along a stone path to a little white wooden fence. Hanging on it was a small sign that said, "Selene's Garden." And a little sketch of a bee buzzed around the sign.

Whoa... so cool, I thought.

Outside the gate, Selene led me around to her home. It was a round dome house, single story, with windows placed in random areas along the enormous roof that came all the way to the ground. The whole home was probably 50 feet wide. In front of the home, there was no lawn, per se. There was just wild grass of many different shades of green growing wherever it pleased. Large thick trunks of trees that looked like a cross between oak and birch stood to shield the house with their branches.

From lower branches, Selene had hung two or three wooden

266

chimes in different shapes. One was in the shape of a deer grazing and made a twinkling sound when the wind blew. Another was shaped like a mother goose leading her babies in a row. They all blew and chimed together with an even higher pitch.

The final chime was a long bamboo-looking tube with three holes carved in it.

"That one makes different sounds depending on which direction the wind is blowing from," Selene said.

The wind seemed to be coming from the north, if that direction existed in the pixie world, so it made a low whooooooooo sound without any breaks. The notes were smooth as they entered my ears, making them a little numb.

Selene led me up to the front door of her home, which had a dozen large yellow flowers with short pointy petals growing in different spots on it. One of the flower stems made the door handle she lightly pulled on to open it and head inside.

Inside, I was greeted with the smell of honey and a smooth wooden floor. We walked into a living room with a long bench decorated with blue cushions, each depicting a different kitten rolling and playing with yarn. Two fountains stood behind the bench, one with a larger pixie woman standing with her palms out. She was wearing a crown, and the water flowed from her palms down into an urn below.

To the right of it was a fountain that had three tigers, each the same size, on a cliff. The water flowed from their open mouths and down into a little valley.

Each fountain probably came up to my shoulders.

I looked up and saw various woven crafts in each skylight window, combinations of sticks and brilliantly colored yarn glowing in the sunlight and projecting its color down onto the floor.

Each woven craft was a circle of sticks with the yarn making different symbols and line shapes inside the boundaries.

Against the wall by the front door stood a large stone bookcase that had five shelves. It was taller than I was and filled with at least 50 books of different sizes. I saw titles like, *The Swan and the Dragon* and *Nurturing the Dream*. A part of me wanted to read each one because there was so much to learn about pixies and their world, their history.

What questions did I ask? Mythology? Would I be rude to call it that because mythology implies a false story ancient people once considered real, and these pixies are very clearly real. What about biology, relationships, social order?

I didn't see any other houses nearby, but outside I heard other pixies talking, as if they were just on the other side of the trees. Did pixie cities exist? Technology?

No, Roxie, you have to focus. You're here to find out why Selene chose you, what that means, and what, if anything, she knows about Hiawatha.

Selene re-entered the room holding a wooden tray with two blue teacups placed on top, each set on a white saucer.

She set the tray down on a little stone table in front of her bench and motioned for me to sit with her.

I walked over and sat down, crossing my legs while she offered me a cup with some kind of warm red drink inside. A little steam rose from it.

"We call this drink 'tuana.' It's nectar from the silk flower heated and mixed with honey and local herbs native to our world," Selene said.

It certainly smelled like honey, but the beverage seemed creamier than I expected. I took a drink, and my tongue might have moaned in ecstasy. There was so much flavor, both sweet and rich. My mind threatened to melt solely for this beverage, and it took everything I had to keep it focused.

Setting the cup down on the tray, I turned to face Selene.

"Thank you for your hospitality," I said. "But I do have some questions."

"Can I ask just one first so I can get a better picture of what's going on?" Selene asked.

I motioned for her to continue.

"Roxie, how did you get here in your human form? And why aren't you wearing your bracelet? Sorry, I guess that's two questions."

I sighed. Selene kept focusing on the bracelet and my human form, which led me to believe she really did have some plan she wasn't telling me about.

"Both are because of a friend of mine named Dan," I said.

Selene's eyes widened.

"The shop wizard."

"Yes! You know him?" I asked.

She nodded and said, "I stopped into his shop after I ran into you,

268

Roxie. And... I never would have imagined you would have also wound up meeting him. It all makes sense now. He told you to take the bracelet off and provided you a way into our world."

I reached into my pocket and felt the bracelet. Everything came back to this item. Looking up at the skylight to my left, I saw a black and yellow bird fly overhead. It was the size of a sparrow.

"Selene, my friends and city are in danger. A woman named Hiawatha is about to swallow up the city in a nightmare. My Mom and friends will be caught up in that. And I need some answers about... everything."

"Ask your questions, child," Selene said, taking a drink of her beverage. She did not appear to be enjoying it as much as I had.

"When I was trapped in a nightmare that Hiawatha created just for me, I was rescued by my future self. She had a full pixie form. So I can only assume I choose to become a pixie in the future and leave my human form behind. Before I ask about that, though, I want to know what you aren't telling me about the day you chose me and set me down this path of dreamwalking and magic."

Selene looked down at her beverage. I felt like our roles were reversed from the first day we met in Dr. Lyra's office. I could barely make eye contact with her, and she was eager to see me. Here, the opposite seemed true.

"My future self said you had a hard truth to share. She said I needed to hear it. So, what is it?" I asked.

The pixie who introduced me to this world took a deep breath and spilled a drop of her tuana. It raced down the teacup and onto her left index finger.

At last she looked up at me, and I saw a terrible burden in her eyes. My heart quivered a little. What exactly did this woman have to share with me that had eaten her so?

"Your future self, meeting her would only have been possible in the world of dreams. Who would have thought you'd meet both Dan and future you? But I'm glad you did, child. Someone had to help you through all of this. I know your path hasn't been easy, and what I'm about to share won't be either. Roxie, it wouldn't be accurate to say I've kept some truth from you. I flat out lied to you the day we met. And I've been using you, hoping you'd clean up my biggest mess."

I gasped and tried to keep my heart rate from shooting off too fast.

269

She's been using me? This woman who took away my most painful childhood memory, who I was so grateful to for choosing me, affirming me, was using me? It wasn't making any sense.

"What are you talking about?"

"Oh, by the gods how I've messed up. And I'm about to pay the price. I'd been searching for years to find a human to replace me. Roxie, pixies don't reproduce like humans do. We aren't born. We're transformed. When humans use pixie magic, they slowly become pixies themselves. And when I found you, saw just how pure your heart was, and how powerful your transformation would be, I knew you had to be the one to take my place. So I lied to you about the bracelet, what it would do to you, what I wanted from you, and left. I hoped... hoped that you would keep using pixie magic, and that bracelet would transform you so there wouldn't be any turning back. Then you could..." she trailed off.

"I could take your place," I finished for her.

She nodded and closed her eyes, calming her breathing.

Meanwhile, I felt so very naive and foolish. I felt like some overeager child. A strange magical woman had shown up one day and just given me an enchanted item. "Go turn nightmares into dreams," she commanded. And I just went along with it, not giving a second thought to the consequences of doing it.

I felt angry, ashamed, and embarrassed. Because I should have had just a little bit of common sense! I should have been honest with Mom or Tessa and Jenna about what I was doing. Mom would have smashed the bracelet with a monkey wrench. Jenna and Tessa would have lit it on fire and run it over with the battle van. None of them would have let me fall into this trap where my humanity was slipping away with each dream I stepped into.

And I still had no idea what that actually meant!

Slowing my breathing, I knew that getting upset with Selene would just hinder the answers I wanted. So I bit my tongue and asked another question.

"Well that's pretty messed up, Selene. So tell me. What was the mess you wanted me to clean up? And what did you lie to me about?" I said, scowling.

She twitched a little at the mention of her mess.

"The Queen of Tears is what I wanted you to clean up, Roxie."

My mind started racing again.

"What... what do you mean? I saw how Hiawatha became the Queen of Tears. Your name didn't exactly pop up in the story."

"You saw it from her perspective. She doesn't know what I did. Roxie when I saw her power as a young girl... her raw ability to interpret dreams, I knew she would grow to be so much more powerful, and it terrified me to my core. Because she was able to achieve so much without pixie magic," Selene said.

"What... what did you do?" I asked the pixie beside me, my eyes burning into her own.

"I felt that she would eventually become a threat, so I— I'm the one who possessed the village's leader and forced him to kill those two men. Then I convinced him it was Hiawatha so they'd finish her off. I didn't have the guts to face her myself," Selene said, starting to whimper.

I shot off the couch and raised my voice. I couldn't believe what I was hearing.

"My God, Selene. Do you know what you put that poor girl through? How betrayed and angry she felt? She's been rotting in a cave, alone and trapped in darkness for centuries, Selene. Centuries!"

"I didn't think they'd do that to her! I honestly thought they'd execute her. And even if they did imprison her, I figured she'd starve to death. How could I have known her fury would power her ability to put her body to sleep and live entirely in dreams?" she asked.

I walked across the living room, feeling like I needed to kick something. All the pain I witnessed in Hiawatha's village betraying her. Her anger toward the wrong people. It was... it was infuriating. And now the entire city was at risk because of it. Selene's actions had single handedly doomed my city.

Clenching my fists, I closed my eyes, trying to get a lid on things. But I couldn't. Enough of me was still human, still righteously indignant over the evil things this pixie had done.

I spun and jabbed a finger at her, yelling, "You're the reason for all of this, Selene! Your cowardice has put an innocent woman through centuries of hell, a city at risk, and my own heart through a blender. You had no proof she would eventually turn evil. You didn't even talk to her to see what she was like. Instead, you saw what she could do, and you let your mind run rampant. So you slunk to the lowest depths possible and got other people to do your dirty work for you. And then to top it off over the centuries, you didn't learn anything! You tried to do it again with me!"

She was crying now and dropped her teacup to the floor. It didn't shatter on the wood but still sent her drink flying everywhere.

"I know! I know! I'm a terrible creature, and believe me, I'm paying the price, Roxie."

"What price? You're sitting here in a gorgeous pixie world, growing a damn garden. Yeah, it looks like a real torment hiding here, Selene. Hiawatha doesn't deserve to be locked up in that cave. You do!"

We both cried together after that. I meant what I said, but it still hurt me to actually speak such hateful words. I'd never felt such a level of betrayal like this before. Even with my father, I hated him for what he did. But I expected his behavior. He never pretended to be my friend before launching into one of his tirades.

But Selene had shown up in my life when I was at a low point and seemingly blessed me with a magical ability. Now I was learning that she had caused all the problems I'd spent the last month trying to fix. And she... had the nerve to suggest she was paying some sort of price.

Wait... she said replace her in some kind of court, I thought, recalling Selene's words.

I turned back to her and said, "Once you'd tricked me into becoming a full-blown pixie, what did you intend to happen? You kept saying I was supposed to replace you. But that would imply you were going somewhere. Are you planning a vacation, Selene? With a beautiful home like this, where would a pixie even go on vacation?"

She continued sobbing, face in her hands muffling the sound some. Then she wiped her nose with another magically summoned rag and looked up at me with puffy eyes. I knew instantly that confession time wasn't over yet. This pixie had more pain to share. I took a deep breath and steeled myself for what was to come, some sort of cowardly plan.

"The bracelet I gave you is called a soul kite. It begins the dreamwalker trials to determine if you can handle pixie magic and alter dreamspaces. You obviously can, and you've proved that over the past month through your encounters with the Queen of Tears. After a month of heavy use, the magic was supposed to transform you into a pixie, and I intended for you to take my place in what's called the Dream Court, serving our pixie queen and being charged with helping humans face their nightmares.

I figured if I found someone to take my place in the Dream Court, then maybe Queen Andrama would just overlook my unannounced retirement.

Part of your charge, I figured, would be to eliminate the Queen of Tears, finally ending this 200 plus year-old mess once and for all."

I had more questions about this court and what it was all about, but I needed one more clarification first. Taking a step toward Selene, I said, "But that still doesn't explain what you meant by *I* would take your place. Where are you going?"

Selene whimpered again and looked down at the floor. One of her tears fell and splashed onto the wood panels beneath us.

"To put it simply, I'm dying, Roxie."

I felt all of my rage and anger toward her just... fizzle out, and a sudden sadness replaced it all. She'd done terrible things, but the finality of death... I certainly never had the guts to deliver that punishment to someone. Lock her up in a cave, sure. But taking this pixie's life? I don't know.

"What are you talking about, Selene? You look fine. Do pixies get sick?"

She shook her head.

"We don't. And normally, we live to be 1,000 years old. But when you break one of the three sacred pixie laws, the punishment is death. One of those laws is never to lie to mortals. Our magic is powerful, but the three laws are woven into it. They flow through our bodies. And when we break a law, the punishment cannot be escaped."

Out of the mess of emotions in my head came the thought... she's dying because she lied to me. She's not going to die because she possessed someone and used their body to kill two innocent souls. She's not going to die because of the dark path she damned Hiawatha to or the danger she put Fayetteville in. She's going to die for lying to me, and that reignited at least some anger in my heart.

"When I found you, I was coming up on the end of my month in the human world. So, I acted rashly, trying to trick you into starting the dreamwalker trials so you could hopefully deal with the Queen of Tears for me. But it seems I'm not as cunning as I thought, and in my attempt to tiptoe around the truth and motivate you, I told an outright lie, triggering my own death sentence."

I sighed and looked down at my drink. Any urge I had to finish it was gone now. My heart was sinking, and I was buried in my own thoughts and feelings, even knowing full well Fayetteville was at risk while I stood here wallowing in my pain. But I couldn't help myself. This was a pit I didn't have the strength to climb out of, not with all these daggers in my back.

"I told you I needed to travel back to the pixie world for a month. That much was true. What got me in trouble was adding that I would return in a month to check on you. I had no intention of returning to you, Roxie. I don't know if I was planning to run and hide or stay here forever or what. But I had no intention of seeing you again. I just wanted you to deal with the Queen of Tears and then... I don't know, keep helping people, I guess," she said. "And now I have these."

She stood up and pulled apart her red garment, showing me her right ribcage. Her skin was smooth and pale, but there were five jagged black lines that looked like some kind of ink, wiggling and crawling about her skin.

"These appeared when I lied. I noticed them when I got back here, Roxie. They've caused me a lot of pain this past month, not that you're a stranger to that feeling. I don't tell you this expecting any sympathy. I'm just answering your question. In pixies, the heart moves to the right side of your chest. And these curse marks have been inching toward my heart every day. And any minute now, they'll pierce it and kill me," she said, closing her shirt, wincing as she did so.

I started to breathe heavily and rubbed my temples. She was going to die, and I was supposed to take her place, clean her mess. I was angry with her, but there was also sympathy for her fate. I couldn't help it. So I started crying again.

I looked at her, and she just sighed again, lowering her mouth.

"You found me on a day I was already emotional. You led me into a space I previously felt safe. You knew Dr. Lyra regularly got me to open up, so you used that location to gain access to my emotions and vulnerabilities. You took away a painful memory to gain my trust and inspire gratitude, lowering any guards I had left. And then when I was fully in your grasp, you tricked me into starting some kind of trial, knowing it would come with new pain, greater than what you took away and that I would forever be changed. You're despicable, Selene."

"I know. And my biggest regret now is that you got here a day early. I intended to use my last moments to write you a letter, confessing all this so I wouldn't have to face you," she said, tears streaming down her cheeks. "But here you are, confronting me like the past mistakes I've never been able to truly escape."

My fists were shaking. My eyes were watering. And I hated Selene for the coward she revealed herself to be.

Don't meet your heroes, I thought, glumly.

"Well I'm sorry to have ruined your getaway. But I'm on the clock. My friends need me, and my city is in danger. So what now?" I asked, unsure if she could reveal anything else to lower my opinion of her even further.

"Now... I pay for my crimes," she said and coughed up an orange blood. Selene fell to her knees and screamed. I heard what sounded like the crunching of bones and glass breaking inside of her.

Seeing her in this pain, my sympathy returned, and I kneeled down to grab her, pull her back up, do something, I don't know.

I managed to lift her up onto the couch. She'd stopped convulsing and screaming but now she had this little twitch and with each one the black cracks crept across her body.

Her breathing became ragged, and I cried, "I know you've done terrible things, but you're taking the easy way out. You need to stay and fix everything!"

She smiled and lifted a hand to my head slowly, moving a piece of hair from my forehead to my side.

With what little breath she had left, Selene said, "I meant... what I said about your pure heart. Even after all the pain I've caused you, you're sitting here mourning for me. I don't deserve that, Roxie."

"Maybe not, but I'm still here, Selene. And I'm willing to do whatever it takes to save you. You can make this right," I said, tears hitting the wood floor beneath me.

"You know... when humans think about mythical creatures like unicorns and fairies, they seem to assign a layer of perfection to them, as if we're somehow incapable of making mistakes. Maybe that gives them some comfort. I don't know—" she coughed up more orange blood, and it splattered on the table in front of the bench. "But I hope if I taught you one thing, it's that mythical creatures make just as many mistakes. We're not perfect by any stretch."

She closed her eyes for a moment, and I grabbed her hands.

"Stay with me! I mean it, Selene, I'll save you if you'll just tell me how," I screamed.

Her eyes fluttered, and she looked over at me, seemingly taking a few extra seconds to see me, even though I was inches from her face.

"Roxie, I won't ask you to forgive me because I know I don't deserve it. But I do want you to know I'm sorry for everything I did to you."

"I forgive you! Just help me fix this," I pleaded, my voice squeaking.

Selene slowly smiled and said, "Life... doesn't give you second chances... not like you're describing."

Then she closed her eyes one final time, and the black cracks covered every inch of her body. With one final splintering noise, her body disintegrated into a silver dust that faded away in the air around me like powdered snow cast up by the wind.

And I just sat there on the couch weeping. I cried for what she did, what she intended to do, and what she could have done to fix it all if time had allowed.

However long I sat there crying, it wasn't enough. But there was a rush of wind that flew through Selene's home, and it came over me before I could react, sending my hair flying in every direction. For a split second, I felt weightless, and then I was kneeling on a cold surface.

Opening my eyes, I saw that I was kneeling on a stone floor with many precious gems mixed into the ground.

"Stand," a woman's voice commanded, and I thoughtlessly did so.

Looking around, I saw I was now in some kind of giant throne room, with high arching windows and stained glass depicting what I assumed were various scenes and nightmare battles throughout pixie history.

Before me stood a pixie only a couple inches taller than me. She was stout, and instead of long silver hair like all the other pixies in the room, counting myself, she had bobbed golden hair that glowed under a bronze crown with a rainbow of jewels embedded into it.

Her eyes glowed pink, though a darker and bolder shade. The wings behind her looked thicker than Selene's or my own single set.

I immediately recognized her from the fountain in Selene's room. *This must be the pixie queen she spoke of,* I thought, having to quickly put away my mourning.

"Human, what is your name?" she demanded to know with a gruff voice.

I just stared at her. She was wearing a long silver gown with an indigo collar piece that resembled some kind of scarf in the shape of a diamond. The queen wore red earring studs and what looked like gold cuffs on each wrist. Long red boots extended up toward her knees.

She stood with a powerful presence that almost left me too squeamish to answer. Selene's presence had been nothing like this. But the queen demanded subservience.

"My... my name is Roxie," I sputtered.

Two guards holding silver halberds stood on either side of the queen's throne, which was richly decorated with a rose-carved pattern and more precious stones.

"Roxie, you stand before Queen Andrama of the pixie realm. She is the ruler of all pixies, and you must now answer questions before the Dream Court you've been summoned to," the pixie on the queen's left said.

I nodded. I looked to my side and behind me. Pixies in different kinds of royal garb stood around me, mulling about, waiting to see what Selene's supposed replacement would look like and do.

"I will do my best," I said.

"The best is what I expect from every pixie I rule over. I give my best when I sit on this throne and each day lead an entire species into a never-ending battle with nightmares across the human world," the queen said.

She seemed more like a military commander than a queen, and maybe here those positions could be one and the same. Either way, I was now in the Dream Court Selene had spoken of.

"My dream knight Selene is no more, correct? She has perished?"

I nodded and said, "Yes, your grace," trying to recall how you answered royalty and praying what I'd seen on "Game of Thrones" would suffice.

"And you appear to be at the end of your dreamwalker trials, one step away from successfully completing them, yes?"

"That's correct, your grace."

The queen looked at each of her guards and then walked over to me.

"Then I suppose there's just one more question you need to

277

answer. Will you take Selene's spot in my court as she seems to have intended for you to do?"

I looked into the queen's eyes and realized I still didn't have enough information to make that decision. Selene had died before I could ask her about the consequences of becoming a pixie.

"May I inquire as to what all service in the court entails, your grace?"

"You may. You finish your trials, become a full pixie, and swear an oath to serve your queen for as long as you live. Selene served me for 465 years. You will spend one month doing battle with nightmares as I command and one month in this world attending to the business of the court. Your human life ends the moment you agree to serve me, Roxie. That's the choice you have to make," she explained.

I gulped. No more high school? Would I get to see Tessa, Jenna, and Mom during the month I spent in the human world? Would I go to college? Would I really live to be 1,000 like Selene had said? All these questions just created more questions, but the queen wasn't having any hesitation. She wanted an answer, and her gruff expression said she wanted it now.

My expression must not have been satisfactory to the queen because she asked, "What's the holdup, Roxie? What prevents you from making this decision?"

Oh, I don't know, the possibility of not seeing my loved ones again! I thought, but didn't dare say.

"I don't know if I can trust you, your grace. Selene did some horribly rotten things to people that have put my loved ones in jeopardy. She did terrible things to me. How can I know this court won't do the same? How can anyone ask me to serve a court and give up my loved ones if I don't know who I can trust?" I asked.

The guards looked nervously at each other, and I heard hushed voices in the peanut gallery behind me. Clearly one did not question the queen like this. I expected a harsh rebuke based on their reactions, but the queen did not offer one. She kept her same blunt tone with her answer.

"Selene broke a law. She paid the price for that action, and she is no more. Transaction completed. End of story. I don't give any further thought to the people she hurt because it won't accomplish anything. She'll still be dead. As for who you can trust, let me show you something."

She led me over behind the throne and past the guards to a large and shallow golden cauldron, perhaps 30 feet wide. It was filled with water even clearer than the stuff from Dan's well.

The queen ran her right index finger over the water creating ripples on the surface. When they smoothed, I saw a scene before me. My mother, Jenna, and Tessa were all at the body shop, covered in cuts and motor oil.

I gasped as some suit of dark armor approached Jenna and Tessa. But my mother ran forward with her favorite monkey wrench and smashed the tar out of its helmet. She continued to fight it off somehow, but I didn't know how long that would last.

Then the scene changed, and I saw Kairen in a white suit fighting three dark armors at once. He appeared to be in the food court at the mall, trying to defend customers as they fled from the area. He hurled a table at one dark armor, but another charged him and slammed him into a piano with its shoulder. Kairen wiped some blood from his lips and stood slowly, picking up his sword. He smirked and said something, but I couldn't hear what it was.

When the scene changed for the last time, I saw Dan and Eely outside the shop, blasting suits of dark armor with fire from every angle. More and more kept coming, and they kept fighting. But Eely and Dan looked exhausted.

Everyone was in danger, and I knew they were waiting on me to return and help them. My pulse quickened, and I clenched my jaw.

Hiawatha had to be stopped. She'd already plunged the city into her nightmare.

"Pixies exist to help humans by fighting their nightmares, Roxie. So serve this court and help us do that. Or don't, and go back to the human world. Selene was defined by her actions and ended up a coward who caused more problems than she solved. If you take her place under my command, your first task will be to clean up her mess, the so-called Queen of Tears. How will your actions define you, Roxie? As someone who couldn't commit to saving her loved ones because she let doubt and pain hold her back? Or as a dream knight who didn't hesitate to rush forward and save those she loved?"

Part of me wondered if I was being manipulated again, but I put those thoughts aside. The queen had clearly told me I was welcome to return to the human world without so much as another thought of serving her.

But no matter the cost, the fact remained that if I did nothing, my friends would die in Hiawatha's nightmare.

I walked back to where I first appeared in the dream court and stood. The queen followed me, but she grabbed a long two-handed sword from behind the throne on the way back.

"What is your answer, Roxie?"

"I will serve the court," I responded and kneeled.

"You know what to do," the queen said, and I nodded.

I pulled the bracelet from my pocket, and without even looking at the object threw it up in the air, holding my left hand high. The bracelet slid down onto my wrist, and my body began to glow and hum once more. Everything around me turned to silver, and I remembered Selene's words: "And when I found you, saw just how pure your heart was, and how powerful your transformation would be, I knew you had to be the one to take my place."

The ground shook around me as my eyes glowed brighter, and my final set of wings appeared, both sets now growing to their full size. I hovered off the ground a few inches, and my hair lofted around me. The blue bracelet shattered, and water washed over me with a cold chill, changing my clothes into a long and flowing white dress, similar to what my future self had been wearing. Underneath my dress, my shoes changed into long white boots that went half-way to my knees.

I returned to the ground and looked at my queen.

"Take the oath," she said.

And words appeared in my mind, so I spoke them.

"I, Roxie, do hereby swear to serve my queen as a member of the Dream Court. I will uphold all the honor and responsibility my queen calls for and spend my days fighting nightmares to rescue those of the mortal realm."

"Now go, save your city from the nightmare that has swallowed it, and return to this court under the next full moon," the queen said, raising her sword and cutting open a tear in the space to my right.

A portal of white light stabilized, and I saw Dan's shop on the other side. I took a deep breath and said, "Hold on, everyone. I'm coming."

Then I flew through the portal without any hesitation, knowing exactly what I had to do next.

Chapter Sixteen
(Dan)

Another bead of sweat ran down my forehead as I blasted perhaps the 50th dark armor into a nearby building. My wand hand was shaking, and I didn't have much more to give. Looking down at Eely, I saw her shaking as well. We were both about tapped, and it seemed the dark armors could sense that in some way.

Eely let loose her smallest fireball yet, and the dark armor it was aiming for simply cut it in half, sending explosions to its left and right.

"Dan, I've... I've hit it," Eely said, shrinking back down to her small size and shaking even harder.

She was about 20 feet away down the block from the storefront where I stood.

"Eely!" I yelled.

A dark armor approached her and raised his sword.

"Disploda!" I yelled, pointing the wand at the armor.

A small burst of fire knocked it back a few inches. It stared at me but said nothing.

"The wand is out of juice," I muttered.

Last resort, I thought as the armor stepped forward again aiming for Eely.

I reached into my pocket and found the medallion of one nymph who owed me a favor, the bronze medallion with an Irish wolfhound carved on the front. The coin was heavy and warm.

I flipped the coin toward Eely as fast as I could. It began to flash red. Then a shockwave from the coin exploded over Eely and knocked the dark armor back again. The shockwave didn't hurt my fox, thankfully.

When I looked up, I saw a familiar customer with two pointy ears and the longest natural red hair standing over Eely.

"Hey there, kitsune. Told you we'd see each other again. Now what exactly is going on here?" Alannah said, looking around.

"Alannah! City swallowed by nightmare, dark armor bad, protect Eely!" I yelled.

She smiled and yelled back, "Love your brevity."

Then she reached to her side and drew her thunder dragon blade. Sparks flew everywhere, highlighting the green tunic and black leggings she was wearing. A rumble of thunder clapped above as the nymph finished drawing her full-sized sword.

She's clearly gotten better with that thing, I thought as the sparks kept flying, this time in an orderly manner.

The dark armor did not care that his new opponent had a shiny blade, as he raised his own and brought it crashing down on Alannah.

She blocked with her sword, holding the dark armor at bay with one hand.

Holy crap she's powerful, I thought.

Eely looked up at her protector and seemed like she wanted to scoff. But she said nothing.

"Oi, can't imagine how conflicted yeh must feel right now, wee fox. But worry not, I'm paying back my debt by protecting you," Alannah said, slashing the dark armor wide open with her thunder blade.

Behind me, I saw a dark armor had run through the front door and was being held at bay solely by Odessa's barrier. But the witch had grown tired. What was once a powerful barrier protecting the entire store was now a mere bubble protecting her and the mirror.

The dark armor raised a gauntlet and punched the barrier, shattering it like glass. Odessa collapsed to the floor, panting.

"Odessa!" I yelled as Alannah took on another armor threatening Eely.

I ran back into the shop just in time to see the armor raise its sword over an unconscious witch. It brought down its sword at the same time the mirror started to gleam with a searing light. I raised my hands to cover my eyes, and when the light died down, I saw a fully-transformed Roxie holding the gauntlet of the dark armor, stopping him right where he stood.

Roxie had clearly advanced in her pixie transformation.

I hope she found the answers she needed, I thought.

While Roxie held the dark armor's gauntlet with her right hand, her left reached toward the ground.

"No more hurting my friends!" she yelled, and raised her left palm. A giant stone hand reached from the ground and wrapped itself entirely around the dark armor. The grip was so tight and fast, the armor dropped its blade.

When Roxie closed her left hand all the way and growled, the earth hand crushed the dark armor with little resistance, mangling it into scrap metal and rendering it lifeless.

I ran over to Odessa to check on her. The witch was still breathing, but she was certainly exhausted like the rest of us.

Roxie wandered over and gave me a hug, asking if I was okay.

"We're a little tired, but otherwise fine. Glad you showed up when you did," I said, returning the hug. "Looks like you made your choice."

Roxie nodded and looked at Alannah as she came in holding Eely loosely with her right elbow. She tossed the fox over at me, and I caught her gently with both my hands.

"She's not a stuffed animal, you know," I said.

Alannah shrugged.

"Whose this pixie?"

Dan motioned at the two of us.

"Alannah, Roxie. Roxie, Alannah."

The nymph nodded at Roxie, and our pixie girl said, "Thanks for protecting my friends. I'm grateful."

Alannah sneered and said, "Just paying off a debt, lass. Speaking of which, Dan, are we square?"

A rumbling from outside started to knock things from my store shelves. We slowly made our way to the front door in time to see a large serpent rising from under the street. It stood up a straight 30 feet high when it was finished. Its scales were yellow, and its fangs longer than Roxie. The serpent hissed and looked down at all of us, trying to figure out who to devour first.

"I'm thinking we might need a wee bit more protection, Alannah," I said, and she smiled, holding her blade up.

"Now it's a party, eh?" Alannah said, smiling.

"I can help," Roxie said, stepping forward. But I put a hand in front of her.

"No. Alannah is a capable fighter, believe me. She's a nymph huntress, and she's slaughtered the most dangerous mythical beasts. You need to find the Queen of Tears and end this, Roxie. You're the only one who can," I said, looking down at her.

Her silver hair floated around, and she said, "Okay... but I need to find my family first. And where's Kairen?"

"He should be fine. He can manipulate dreams again. The phantom doofus is supposed to be out protecting people from these dark armors," I said.

Roxie nodded, and Alannah said, "I'm going to run forward and strike the beast. When I do, you take off in whatever direction your family resides."

The pixie girl braced herself, and Alannah took a moment to aim, then she rushed forward and jumped up, attracting the serpent's attention. She slashed the snake open about seven feet off the ground with a streak of her lightning blade.

Roxie took the opportunity to run outside and fly off toward her home. The pixie's wings carried her at a dazzling speed through the darkened sky.

"She'll bring us the morning," I said, and dragged Odessa and Eely further into the shop.

* * *

(Roxie)

As I flew over downtown Fayetteville, I saw shattered windows, smashed cars, injured residents, and other acts of extreme ruin. The giant and wicked moon above me highlighted people running in fear from these dark armors. Over on Dickson Street, people barricaded themselves in bars and clubs, trying to avoid the enemy.

Nearby on the biggest college campus in Arkansas, students ran toward any buildings they could see, trying to find shelter. Knights chased them down showing no mercy. In a nearby cemetery, another giant serpent had erupted from the ground, heading toward a large apartment complex looking for its next meal.

An anger stirred in me, but it was not without conflict. Hiawatha had brought forth all this pain, but she was just reacting like anyone else would. She wanted revenge on the descendants of those who she felt had wronged her, the same way I felt with my father. The same way I felt with Mr. Parker.

She didn't know it was all Selene's actions that had caused her pain. And as I struggled with how to deal with her, my heart sank. I didn't want to fight Hiawatha, not after learning what Selene had done to her.

I heard Tessa scream inside our loft. Zipping down from the skies, I smashed through the living room window and pummeled the dark armor holding Jenna by the throat and away from her. Her face was purple, and I saw Mom groaning on the ground, the back of her head bleeding.

"Enough of this!" I yelled..

I ran along the ground and summoned forth a pink laser sword to my right hand. It hummed and pulsed as it cut along the ground behind me. I rolled under the dark armor as it swung its sword at me with one hand. When I came up, I severed the arm that had been holding Jenna. It fell to the ground.

The dark armor brought its sword down upon me, but I cut the blade clean in two. Before My opponent could understand what was happening I sliced the armor into five different pieces.

They hit the ground with a resounding CLANK, still sizzling from my blade. I tossed it behind me, and the weapon vanished in a puff of silver smoke.

I hope copyright laws aren't enforced in dreams, I thought.

Running over to my Mom, I saw that the bleeding was minor. She'd been thrown into the fridge and bumped her head. But since this was a dream, I decided to try something.

Cradling Mom's head on my lap, I summoned a bright light to my left hand. Then I placed it over Mom's head and closed my eyes, breathing in and out slowly. When I felt her stir, I sighed with relief.

The gash on the back of her head was gone, and she slowly opened her eyes.

"Roxie?" she asked.

I nodded and slowly helped her up.

"Is that you, Roxie?" Jenna and Tessa asked in unison.

"It's me, everyone."

And with that, they all ran forward and threw their arms around me, sobbing, Tessa the loudest of the three.

"We thought you were abducted!" Tessa shouted.

"How did you do all that?" Jenna asked.

"Are you okay, Priss?" Mom asked.

"Okay, I don't have a lot of time here because I'm the only one who can stop this nightmare. I'm going to rush through the last month of secrets I've been keeping from y'all and get you up to speed. No questions, okay?"

The three exchanged glances and nodded.

I took a deep breath.

"A month ago, this pixie woman appeared and gave me the ability to travel into dreams. So I started traveling into nightmares each night, and turning them into pleasant dreams for folks across Fayetteville. This magic slowly turned me into a pixie. There's a girl named Hiawatha who calls herself the Queen of Tears, and she's plunged Fayetteville into a nightmare. My friends and I are fighting to end it. Just before she plunged everyone into her nightmare, Dad kidnapped me. I escaped. Now I need to go find Hiawatha and stop this nightmare once and for all."

Mom looked more confused than anyone. Tessa sort of kept up with me, but Jenna rubbed my head and said, "Next time you think about using magic to transform into a mythical creature, I want to know about it beforehand."

"Promise," I said, and turned to go.

Mom put a hand on my shoulder.

"Be careful, Priss. When you get back, and you'd better come back, you're grounded for lying to me about your hair and glowing eyes," she said, pointing a finger in my face.

"Psh, I answer to Queen Andrama now. She's a little bit of a higher power than—" I was interrupted by Mom picking me up.

"I'll show you a higher power," she yelled and tossed me down onto the couch like a sack of potatoes. "Well look at that. Even with all your pixie powers, you still flop down like any old daughter of mine."

I lay there for a moment, waiting for the room to stop spinning. Dark suits of armor were nothing to me, but Mom was still some kind of WWE hotshot who I would never be able to defeat.

Well that was embarrassing, I thought and stood up, smoothing out my dress.

"Like I said... grounded," Mom said.

"Fine, but I can only be grounded for a month, Mom."

"We'll see about that," she said as I took off flying out the living room window.

Rising up into the sky, I saw there was no way I could protect 100,000 people from the dark armors and search for Hiawatha at the same time. I needed footsoldiers of my own.

Flying over Wilson Park, I saw a large field I could use. I put my hands together, and a mound of brown seeds appeared in a little puff of smoke. I smiled and let them fall from the sky into the grass below. Scattered across the park, the seeds took seconds to root and sprout into little rose golems.

They looked like tiny people made of stems with roses for heads. Then they began to grow and grow and grow some more until they were about seven feet in height. I didn't have time to count all of them, but I knew they'd be fierce foes for the dark armors. Cut off a piece, and they'd regrow. They'd be able to defend the people of Fayettville and heal anybody injured.

"Protect the people of this city!" I ordered from the sky above, and they took off running in all directions.

Now to find Hiawatha, I thought.

* * *

(Kairen)

As I cut down the last dark armor in front of me, I kneeled to the ground to catch my breath. How many had I destroyed? 15? 20? And yet they still came.

"The Queen of Tears must be able to make an unlimited supply," I said, looking around the empty food court. Several tables and the main piano over by the coin pool were smashed. The trees growing up toward the skylight above had been cut to ribbons.

At least I'd gotten everyone out of the mall to my knowledge. Saving 100,000 people from nightmare creatures was difficult business.

Looking around, I saw the restaurants all empty, the Japanese place, stir-fry grill, taco joint, Chick-Fil-A and Sbarro were all abandoned. I walked over to Sbarro and realized behind the shattered glass guard meant to separate customers from the employees sat a single slice of Sicilian style pepperoni pizza left on the rectangle dish.

I looked around and made sure all the dark armors were gone, all the customers too. Then I smiled and looked down at the piece of pizza. I picked it up. Excellent. It's still warm.

Just as I was about to take a bite, the enormous glass skylight above me shattered. Frightened, I jumped and dropped my slice to the floor.

I looked at it sitting there upside down on the beige tile floor. Bummer. Then I growled and looked up at the skylight to see Hiawatha standing on a steel beam. She wore simple brown trousers and a white button down shirt. Around her neck she wore a crescent moon necklace on a silver chain.

She hopped down to the floor, and I yelled over at her, "Couldn't let me have one snack, could you?"

"No, my former thief, I could not. I did have a perfect spot figured out for a showdown with Roxie, but then I noticed you poking around, slaying my minions, and making a mess of my nightmare. Look at you, Mr. New Suit," the Queen of Tears said.

"Still not sure who this Roxie is everyone keeps talking about. But I hope to meet her soon. She sounds like a fun gal. But you. You I do know. And I seem to recall we have a score to settle," I said. I picked my blade and approached her.

The Queen of Tears smiled, and her eyes glowed violet.

"You may have gotten just a little bit of power back, but you will still find my abilities far outweigh yours, my former thief," she said. A ball of purple fire took form in her hand.

"Let's put that to the test," I said, picking up a chair and hurling it at her. She threw her fireball at the chair, completely melting it, and I took the opening to zoom in from her left. I slashed upward with my blade, but she leaped back, just barely avoiding the tip of my blade.

"Talk about a close shave," I said, smirking.

"You want to get close, thief? I think you'll regret it." She summoned two more balls of purple fire, one in each hand.

She threw one at me, and I leapt out of the way. The other caught my shoulder, sending me hurtling backward into a support column. I grunted as I slammed into it, burning pain filling a shoulder that had already been stomped on by a few dark armors.

The Queen of Tears didn't give me any chance to catch my breath. As soon as I hit the pole, she lobbed more fireballs at me. I ducked and rolled away.

Gaining my ground again, I raised my left hand, spawning several chains that burst from the ground and ensnared the Queen of Tears at a safe distance away from me.

"You just hold tight, babe. I'm going to end this real quick," I yelled, rushing toward her.

She smirked when I was mere feet away, and "crap," was all I had time to mutter. Her whole body flashed purple for a split second. She burst out of those chains, and the force knocked me back across the other side of the room.

"Your ability to alter dreams is nothing!" the Queen of Tears said, raising her hands and picking up every shard of glass that fell from the skylight.

"You gotta be kidding me," I said, shaking my head. I grabbed a nearby table and threw it in front of me for cover.

She flung every shard of glass she could at me, and one piece was long enough it went right through the table and stopped two inches from my nose.

Dang, Fayetteville. Maybe you need some thicker tables in your mall, I thought.

When she finally ran out of glass to throw, the Queen of Tears appeared in front of the table and smashed her foot into it with all her strength. The table knocked into me, and we both went flying backwards, smashing through the entrance of a cell phone repair shop.

"I'm getting pretty tired of this," I muttered as I rolled out from behind the table.

I glanced around for my sword, but it was nowhere in sight. But I had to make a stand. She couldn't win this. So I staggered out of the cell phone repair shop and came face to face with the Queen of Tears.

"I'm going to finish this, you monster. You took my brother from me and tortured him for weeks. Believe me when I say I'm going to end you."

"What you need to understand is that the only way I let my servants leave is death, thief. And when I kill you once and for all, I'm going to find that brother of yours, lock him in an even smaller cage, and throw him down into the deepest pit I can summon."

Without another word, I raised my right hand to the air and bent a piece of a steel beam from the skylight down until it snapped. Then I drove that pole into the ground just behind the Queen of Tears. It was centimeters away.

She looked behind her and smirked.

"You missed," she said.

"Close enough," I mutter.

The Queen of Tears looked up above her, trying to see what I was concocting. Then, I aimed the biggest bolt of lightning I could muster down at that pole like a lightning rod.

With such a bright flash and then a resounding boom, I shielded my eyes, feeling every hair on my body stand straight up.

When I could finally look again, I saw the food court full of smoke.

"I'll bet she's shedding a few tears after that one," I chuckled, just before a piece of that steel pole flew out of the smoke and impaled me right through my right shoulder, pinning me to a wall.

I screamed as pain seared through my entire body. It felt like my arm and collarbone were on fire. I reached over with my left hand and barely grazed the piece of metal pinning me to the wall. Even the little motion made me scream and want to vomit.

My breathing grew ragged, and I saw the Queen of Tears step out of the smoke. Her outfit was singed in a few places, and her hair might have been a little messy, but she otherwise looked untouched and unbothered.

She held another piece of my makeshift lightning rod in her right hand.

"I warned you that your dream altering abilities were nothing compared to mine, thief. Now I'm done playing with you. You're never going to see your brother or anyone else ever again," she said, raising her right arm.

I'm sorry, Jonas. Your bro gave it his best shot, I thought.

"Goodbye, phantom thief."

Then she hurled the piece of steel at me.

* * *

(Roxie)

I flew down out of the sky and snatched a piece of steel flying toward Kairen's head, stopping it an inch in front of his nose.

"That was cutting it too close," I sighed, staring at a boy who didn't remember me anymore.

His head leaned back toward the wall he was pinned to and let out the biggest sigh of relief I've ever heard in my life.

"Having my life saved is pretty awesome. Having it saved by a cutie like you is top notch," he said, smirking.

I looked down at his shoulder, and my heart began to hurt.

I'd gladly let you call me cutie again if it meant you knew who I was, I thought, remembering Dan's price.

"Who are you?" he asked, adding another dagger to my already-stabbed heart.

I fought back tears and forced a smile to say, "I'm Roxie."

"Oh you're the one everyone keeps talking about. I swear, the way Dan and the Queen of Tears drop your name, you figure I would have met you before," he said.

"You'd figure..." I said, turning away so he didn't see the solitary tear fly down my left cheek. I wiped it away and turned back.

"This is going to hurt, so hang on," I said, pulling the metal out of his shoulder.

He screamed as I did so and then passed out from the pain, his head sunk to the left.

"You did good, Kairen. I'll finish it from here," I said, healing his shoulder and turning to face Hiawatha.

"Well, look at you, Roxie. You went full pixie after all," she said as the last of the smoke blew away.

I took a deep breath. I had to get through to her, no matter what. Kairen had fought her and lost. And although I felt like I'd have a better shot at winning, that wasn't what I wanted to do here.

"Hiawatha, listen to me. I don't want to fight you," I said, putting my hands up.

She laughed and said, "Well that should make killing you fairly easy, pixie."

"I'm serious, Hiawatha. I know your story. I saw how Robert rallied your friends and family to lock you up," I said.

Hiawatha scowled at the mention of the name, "You don't know what you're talking about!"

"I do know! I watched what happened to you, Hiawatha. And I know what really happened that day so many years ago."

"Stop calling me that! I'm the Queen of Tears!" she shouted, trembling the entire mall.

I kept my hands raised and took another step toward her. The snarl across her face had grown even more wild. There was about 20 feet between us.

"I'm not playing games, Hiawatha. And you need to hear this. Robert didn't lie to have you sealed away. He really was scared of you. But the person who possessed him and had him kill Edward and George was the same person who turned me into a pixie. Her name was Selene, and she confessed to me just before she died that she was behind it all," I said.

Confusion swept across Hiawatha's face. I wasn't making any moves to attack her, and I was speaking the truth.

I took another step toward her.

"Selene did this to you because she was scared of your abilities. And I am so so sorry for what she did. I wish I could fix it. I can't, but you can. You can still undo this. We can fix all the damage to this city," I said.

Hiawatha shook her head. Tears started to run down her smooth cheeks.

"No! I know you're lying, pixie. This is just some twisted game to get my guard down. But you're not the one who plays mind games with me, Roxie! I'm the one who plays them with you. Nobody is able to mess people up like I can!"

"Hiawatha please!" I said, taking another step, but she reached behind her and pulled out a long whip. She cracked it forth and struck my left ribs, breaking a few.

I cried out as it felt like a chunk of me had been shattered open. The pure blunt force and speed was unimaginable. And I sank to my knees, whimpering.

"I told you to stop calling me that! My name is the Queen of Tears. It has been for more than 200 years now!" she said, still crying.

With another crack of the whip, she shattered the rest of my left rib cage, and I shouted out in pain.

"Get up, pixie. You're the last piece I need to eliminate before I can finally enjoy this nightmare, tormenting the descendants of those who betrayed me."

I whimpered as pain shot up and down the left side of my body. Putting all my weight on my right leg, I slowly stood.

"They were manipulated into betraying you, Hiawatha. They

loved you, especially Tala. She was heartbroken when they carried you away that day. I saw her face. But the people of this city have done nothing to you. You have to let them go," I said.

She brought the whip down on my left shoulder now, and I sank back down to my knees crying.

"Why aren't you fighting back? What kind of game is this?" she yelled.

"Hiawatha..."

"Queen. Of. Tears! Are you deaf? I'm the one they locked away in the dark for two centuries. I'm the nightmare of this city and the only one who has the right to seek vengeance. They wanted a monster, and they got one, Roxie. Your words won't change that!"

With that, she cracked my left arm, just below the elbow, and I screamed again as the room started to spin.

When some of the pain went away, I was able to stand, "You don't have to do this. The Queen of Tears isn't your name. It's the name that was forced on you. Your name is Hiawatha. You're a 14-year-old girl with a gift for interpreting dreams. You can go back to being her again. Just wake up."

"Shut up. Shut up, already!" she screamed as tears rolled down her cheeks.

She clenched her head with her hands and pulled her nails down so hard they scratched her face. Then she broke my lower left leg with her whip. I'd lost a lot of blood by now, but I knew I could still turn this around.

In between tears, I heard Hiawatha shout, "I don't have a choice. This is what they made me! It's all I have left to be!"

"You're wrong," I choked out.

She turned her attention to me again, and I said, "Only you get to decide who you are, Hiawatha. Don't give others that power over you! You can decide at any moment to stop being the Queen of Tears. And I'll help you each step along the way."

Now she dropped the whip and came over to me. But when she got next to me, Hiawatha kicked me backward to the floor. As I hit the floor, I felt my bones shatter like glass. I let out a yelp.

"I told you to shut up with all of this crap!" she yelled, kicking my arm again.

The room spun as I grimaced from the fire of pain coursing

through me. But I knew I was close. I could tell by looking at her face. She wanted this pain to end more than anybody.

"I... know a girl who was locked deep in a cave. The darkness was her only companion. And as she grew hungry and lonely, she cried for help. But nobody came. Day after day, she continued to hope help would come, but it didn't. So she cast herself into a deep sleep, her only way to survive. And her anger burned for hundreds of years. But the girl doesn't realize the people who hurt her were tricked. It wasn't their fault, just like what she needed to do to survive wasn't her fault."

Hiawatha climbed on top of me now, her weight adding more pain to my left side, and she began to choke me, screaming, "Stop talking! Stop talking! Stop talking, and just die already!"

As I sputtered and gasped for air, I managed to choke out, "It's your dream. Check my memories."

And for a moment, she stopped, and placed her hands on my mind, driven by curiosity, and needing to know if what I said could even possibly be true. I felt her picking through my memories, and when she came to Selene's death, I saw her go limp. She'd discovered the truth as I had. We were both victims of this pixie's cowardly mistakes.

"Tala..." Hiawatha whimpered, covering her face with her hands and sobbing even harder. "I want Tala back."

She sat there continuing to wail about an entire life lost and all the pain she'd endured. And I slowly reached up my hand, fighting all the pain in my body and rested it on her cheek after wiping away her tears.

"I'm sorry for what she did. But you don't have to be alone anymore. And you don't have to be the Queen of Tears anymore. Just wake up, and I'll make sure you're never alone again. I'll bring you out of the cave, I promise."

She put her left hand on mine and asked, "And then what?"

I took as big a breath as possible with my broken ribs and said, "Then you live a normal life. You go to school. You make friends. You eat too much junk food. You dance. You fall in love. You find your passion. And no matter what happens, I'll never leave you alone. I promise."

Hiawatha closed her eyes and placed both her hands on my right hand.

"I want that," she squeaked in between sobs.

"Then let's end this nightmare and wake you up. I'll need your help, though. I want to undo all the damage that's been done to the city and erase everyone's memories of this horrible night," I said. "Except for my friends. Leave their memories intact please."

She nodded. Then we joined hands together. A bright purple and silver glow filled the mall. Slowly our light grew till it consumed the entire city. Every bit of damage, every injury, every terrible thing that'd gone wrong on this night was whisked away, and nobody was any the wiser.

When I opened my eyes, I was standing in a dark cave. I filled the darkness with the silver glow of my body.

There, a young girl about 14 was beginning to stir. She opened her eyes and squinted when she saw my light.

"Roxie?" she asked.

"It's me. Let's get you out of here once and for all," I said.

She stirred for a moment but just before I could help her, Hiawatha began to shudder a bit. Like a terrible nightmare I watched the color of her eyes began to fade as wrinkles etched their way into her skin. Her once dark raven hair faded to a pale gray.

"Hiawatha... what's happening to you?" I asked.

Before she could draw another breath to speak, her wrinkles stretched over her entire face, and her limbs shrank before my very eyes.

"I'm more than 200 years old, Roxie. Now that my magic isn't keeping me together, I guess it's catching up with me," she said.

I put my hand over my mouth as tears came to my eyes.

"No! That's not fair!!"

Hiawatha allowed a small smile to appear on her face and looked down at her rumpled hands. Her nails began to yellow slightly, and her breathing slowed.

"Quick! Go back to sleep. Maybe we can fix this in the dream world! I know we can stop this," I whimpered. I'd watched Selene die, and I didn't want to lose another soul, not after all I'd been through.

She doesn't deserve this. It's a mistake! I thought, trying furiously to figure out a solution.

"Roxie, it's okay. It was only a matter of time. You can't pause time forever and expect not to pay a price," she said, her youthful voice swallowed up in a gravely tone.

I shook my head, unable to say anything else at the moment. I just kept thinking "It's not fair," over and over.

"Hey now. Didn't you promise me to take me out of this cave? I'd like to see the sunshine for however long I've got left," she said.

It took everything I had to pull it together. She'd just woken up, and I doubt she wanted to be greeted by the blubbering mess that was me.

"Let's get you out of here," I said, tears still falling down my cheeks.

She nodded, and I helped her up. She tried to stand on her own, but her legs were just too weak. She nearly collapsed. So I carried her piggyback style out of the cave, through the gate that had long sealed her in, the Ossa Key still stuck in the lock. At last we came to the mouth of the cave, and I saw we were not too far from the shores of Lake Wedington.

The cave entrance had been covered with thick vegetation, and the sun was starting to rise in the east, filling the sky with pink and orange hues. A dragonfly buzzed near my face, and I screamed for a second, nearly dropping Hiawatha.

Her long hair blew in the morning breeze as she inhaled every breath of free air she could, finally out of that cave for the first time in centuries.

"You faced down the Queen of Tears, but dragonflies scare you," she said, chortling.

"Well... it was huge and by my face. Just about anything with that criteria freaks me out," I muttered.

The rapidly aging woman shook her head lightly and took another deep breath before coughing. I flinched.

A ray of light fell upon us rising over a nearby tree. It was morning time. No more dreams, no more nightmares. Just this, this moment and it all was happening so quickly.

Now Hiawatha really smiled as her own milky eyes started to water.

"It's all I wanted... to see the sun again, to breathe free air once more," she said.

Her hair was all gray now, no black left. And it was quickly thinning.

"All these colors... they're so beautiful," Hiawatha said, coughing again.

I set her down in a patch of clovers, and we rested for a minute. As she leaned back against the trunk of a birch tree, I saw Hiawatha close her eyes.

"Hiawatha?" I asked.

She seemed to have shrunk before my very eyes. I watched her cough and shudder some more, the pain of it all shaking her body. Her legs curled up, and I watched as she tried to open her eyes once more. Yet, they remained closed..

"No no no no! This isn't supposed to happen! Hang on! I can fix this, Hiawatha!"

With her eyes still closed, she whispered, "It's okay, Roxie. This is what had to happen, what always had to happen. There's nothing to be done."

"No please! I promised you. We were going to go to school! We were going to dance! I was going to introduce you to Jenna and Tessa. I wanted you to have a normal life," I cried, taking her hands. "That's not enough! It's not enough! I wanted to save you."

She smiled and said, "You did enough. You saved me. I'm not the Queen of Tears, anymore. Now I'll just pass on as Hiawatha."

"Please," I pleaded.

"   You know... after all these years living in dreams, I feared I'd forgotten the differences between those worlds and this one. But it is real, Roxie. The dirt and grass, the air and bugs, the warmth and light, the loss, the pain, and all the love. They're all real, and you brought me back to them. It's better than any dream either of us can conjure. Now, I must let it go one last time. Now, I'd like to see my Tala again. So, t hank you, Roxie, for everything." She exhaled her final breath. Her head hung over, and I caught it. I sat there for the next hour with her in my arms under the tree, crying.

Epilogue
(Dan)

Roxie helped me carry out one last box into the back of that red dusty van her father never came back for. Most of the back was loaded up now. We'd also put in a small mattress, though, so I could sleep back there if I wanted.

"That's the last of it?" she asked.

I nodded and smiled.

Odessa came up behind me, and I turned to give her a hug.

"I'm gonna miss you," I said, trying not to let her see I was fighting back tears.

"I know you will. I'll miss you too, Daniel. But I know you'll stop by from time to time. And remember, you still work for me, even if I'm letting you take Funky Dan's on the road. You still help customers and deal in enchanted items," she said, letting me go.

I nodded.

"Don't worry. I'll watch him," Eely said, hopping up on my shoulder.

Odessa gave her a kiss, and I smiled.

"Thanks for helping me load everything up, Rox. You're gonna pop into my dreams now and again, right? Keep me updated on your adventures as a full-blown pixie?"

She smiled and lightly punched my shoulder.

"You know it, old man. Try not to have too much fun out there."

"I'm sad Kairen couldn't make it by," I said.

"Yeah, well, Alannah told him that if she was seriously going to train him in the art of swords and hunting, he had to leave with her immediately. I don't think he had much of a choice."

I nodded and scratched my beard.

"Oh! I almost forgot. I got you a goodbye gift," she said and pulled something out of her pockets.

"What is this?"

"It's an iPod. You use this little cassette tape cord thing to hook it up to the van's stereo. Then you can find whatever songs you want to play. Eely gave me a list of all your vinyls, and I put all that music on here for you," Roxie said, handing the device and cables to me.

I smiled. The last thing I was worried about had been taken care of. I had my music.

"What do you have planned for the next couple weeks?" I asked.

"Resting, traveling into a few nightmares, playing a couple gigs with my band, and at the next full moon, I report back to the Dream Court for a month."

"Your Mom and friends okay with that?" I asked.

"It took some convincing, but ultimately I told them I didn't have any choice. Jenna and Tessa have been great. They even got me started on paperwork so I can still attend my senior year every other month. We just have to pretend I have some really bad disease. And I'll have to do all my homework in the pixie world. But...it's as good a compromise as I'm gonna get," I said.

I held my arms out, and we hugged one more time. Then Roxie kissed Eely goodbye and scratched her behind the ears.

"Well I guess I'm gonna hit it. You two take care of the city while I'm gone. I'll keep in touch," I said and walked around to the driver's side door. It squeaked as I opened it, and I hopped inside.

"Did you bother learning how to drive in the last week?" Eely asked, hopping down into my lap.

"Yeah, Roxie taught me the basics, more or less."

"You know, she doesn't have a license either," Eely said.

I just shrugged and hooked up that device she gave me. It took a couple minutes, but soon I had Little River Band playing "It's A Long Way There."

Before I put the van into gear, I sighed and looked back at the store. Odessa and Roxie were talking on the sidewalk.

Am I really going to do this? I thought, feeling butterflies in my gut. Knowing me, maybe it was more worms.

I'd waited all these years bitching and moaning about wanting to be free. Now I essentially was. Funky Dan's almost seemed to be looking at me, the curtains drawn over the front door and windows.

The store seemed to wonder why I wasn't gone yet.

This is what you wanted, right? I thought.

I sighed again and looked down at the steering wheel. If I walked outside the van and asked Odessa to let me stay, she would, right? What was I thinking? Surely I'd seen enough of the world galavanting when I was rich, right? What if now that I'm out of the shop and away from Odessa I turn back into old selfish Dan?

I noticed an eggshell paw touch my right hand and looked over to see Eely in my face.

"Hey, it's okay. I'm right here," she said in a reassuring tone. Had she sensed my inner hesitation?

I looked down at the keys and slowly started the engine.

"It'll be okay. That feeling will fade once you get on the road. I promise," Eely said. I smiled and scratched her behind the ears.

"Yeah. I bet it will."

I pulled the van forward, and we were off.

Roxie and Odessa waved at me, and I sighed.

"I'm gonna miss that place," I said.

"Me too," Eely said. "Can we stop and get a snack?"

"We ate sandwiches like... 30 minutes ago," I sputtered.

"Yeah, but I'm hungry again. So pull over at that Shell station.

"No! We need to get on the road!"

"That gas station is still part of the road," Eely argued.

I sighed and laughed, pulling off into the gas station.

"You are the most beautiful fox in the world," I said. "But you can't come inside."

Excerpt from
The Ozarks Druid
Book Two in the Boston Magic Mountain Series

Chapter One

I've heard it said that peace is more than the absence of conflict. And I have to confess, I wouldn't know too much about that, because my life has always been full of conflict. But tonight might just have taken the cake.

Barb's face was reaching peak red as we screamed at each other. This kind of behavior wasn't anything new from us. But the energy we were each building was certainly hitting new levels.

The two of us each felt like the other was dead wrong, and whoever shouted the loudest for the longest was going to win this argument. When it came to fighting with my guardians, I learned early on there's wisdom in the understanding of 'you win some and you lose some.' But I wasn't going to lose tonight. Barb didn't feel like she was going to, either.

She stood behind the blue living room sofa in her white nightgown glaring at me. Barb already had her night cream in, and her short wavy graying hair bobbed with each jab of a finger she pointed in my direction. I was tempted to tune her out because I knew that whatever she was saying was pure crap. But then I heard the words "ever again."

I immediately zoned back in and hit the rewind button on the cassette recorder that was my brain. Sometimes it felt like I had that little tape recorder thing Kevin McCallister had in the second *Home Alone* flick. I mentally pushed the button next to the << arrow, and I heard the whine of plastic parts and tape. Rherherherherhe....

"You can never see Abigail ever again," I heard Barb's voice say.

Of course, in real time, she had moved onto another sentence. But I was still processing what I heard her say.

"Fuck that!" I yelled, and I saw the whites of her eyes grow wider.

I didn't tend to curse too much. It wasn't a religious thing. I just felt like those words existed to exclaim things, excitement or rage. And if I used them too often, I felt like their impact would become cheap. But she had just told me I wasn't allowed to see my girlfriend of two years anymore.

"What did you just say to me?" she all but hissed, walking around the sofa and getting closer.

"You heard me the first time, Barb. I'm not going to let you tell me I can't see her. She's important to me," I said, blowing some of the long red hair out of my face.

The room was about to hit a new temperature, an unmatched level of heat.

Barb's eyes grew still a little more as if I'd just slapped her.

"I have told you repeatedly to call me 'mother.' And I know you know better than to use such profanity in this house, young lady! Not only are you forbidden from seeing that hussie again, you're grounded until the end of your holiday break," Barb said.

I clenched my fists. She'd gone too far. No matter how much I'd come to resent this woman who wanted me to call her 'mother,' not 'mom,' mind you, but mother, I did my best to retain a tiny shred of respect.

Generally, I kept my cursing nonexistent around the house. And I would never physically strike her. But my patience with this woman was thinning faster than a tree trunk between two cartoon beavers.

I'd always joked that there was no way she could be my real mom, but this fight was taking that wishful thinking to a whole new level.

"Okay, 1950s language or not, let's avoid insulting my girlfriend."

"Oh, right. If sinful behavior is going to be discussed, we'd better use hip terminology. What should I call her? BAE? THOT? Maybe we just stick with a classic that's evergreen. Abigail is a whore, and what you two have been doing is an abomination," Barb said, getting her index finger about five inches from my nose.

The temptation to bite it was of the devil. My heart was pounding, and I felt warm enough to actually be sweating, and Barb kept the thermostat on 68 degrees year-round. I clenched my fists tighter and tried to keep some control over my words, but it was getting nigh impossible. Actually, scratch that. It wasn't becoming impossible. That gargantuan task was already past impossible.

"Listen, bitch. You're not going to talk about her like that ever again, you hear me? I care deeply about her. And can we discuss my behavior without using the word 'abomination' just once? I heard enough Levitical law come out of your mouth when I got my tattoo," I said.

Abomination was a favorite in Barb's vocabulary. It described the music I liked, the ink I put on my right shoulder, and now the girl I was sleeping with.

I would never describe Barb as a quick person. She went on a morning walk at 5:00 a.m. several times a week, but it wasn't fast by any stretch of the word.

With that said, I didn't see her right hand move as she slapped me. Barb's hand was a blur as it came up and struck me on the face. It hardly hurt. It had solid contact with my cheek, though. The pain wasn't much to write home about. That same cheek had been broken during a Muay Thai tournament three years ago. Bump a cheek full of screws halfway healed? Now that's some pain, physical pain at least. Of course, nothing quite hurts like the woman who calls herself 'mother' inflicting intentional pain on her child.

That was a different kind of ache, no matter how much I resented her.

In addition to ache, there was a little surprise. Barb hadn't slapped me since I was 13 or 14, and she'd caught me with an unlit cigarette in my mouth.

It did not do anything to calm the rage flowing through my veins. I let out a low growl as I stared straight into her eyes. Barb thought I'd outgrow the behavior, but she was wrong.

She'd let me know on several occasions that she hated my growling. I'd done it for as long as I can remember when my temper got the better of me, and she thought I should have outgrown the behavior by age three or four.

What I knew she hated more was a direct challenge to her authority, and that's exactly what I did as I moved my face closer. We locked eyes. Neither of us flinched. My green eyes locked with her brown ones, and for a moment, I thought lasers would shoot out from one of us.

Neither of us spoke for a solid 20 to 30 or so seconds. My breathing was ragged, and hers was sharp.

I wanted to threaten her to strike/touch me again. I could break her jaw with a back elbow spin, but I wasn't going to do that.

My coach's words echoed in my head, *I'm not just teaching you how to hurt people. I'm training you to know when it's necessary. You're strongest when you exhaust all other options before resorting to violence.*

I could tell myself all day that Barb posed no physical threat to me. The only advantage she had was about four inches of height. I had 13 years of Muay Thai on her. And while rising blood pressure screamed at me, "Do it! Nail her!" I reminded myself I was in control of this situation.

"You listen and you listen well, young lady. These feelings you have are destructive in the worst way. You don't want to hear about Levitical law? How about some doctrine from Paul? Romans 1:24 ring a bell? Talking about homosexual perversion and lusts?"

I tried to bite my tongue as I often did when she got into Bible thumping mode. Was that blood I tasted in my mouth? Was I biting that hard?

"Here's what's going to happen. You're going to give me your phone, you're going to take your Bible, and you're going to stay up the rest of the night writing me an essay on Sodom and Gomorrah. Then, first thing tomorrow morning, we're both making an appointment to speak with Brother Marks to put these sinful thoughts from your mind."

"No, Barb. Here's what's going to happen. I'm going to keep my phone because I pay for my own plan. I'm not going to open a Bible or attend church ever again. And maybe, just maybe, you'll finally read that article I texted you a couple weeks ago about your pastor being arrested after sleeping with a girl a year younger than me."

Maybe it wasn't smart to combine the agnostic fight with the bisexual fight, I thought for a split second before hearing myself laughing internally and yelling, *Nahhhh. Go for broke! The house always wins anyway.*

I didn't think the conversation could get more heated, but right on schedule, Barb was quick to shift gears as a tear I'd classify as crocodile, slid down her right cheek.

"How can you do this to me, Eve?" she asked, hitting me with eyes that were both scornful and sympathy seeking at the same time.

I couldn't place my finger on what exactly it was about my name

I hated. It never felt right. And every time someone called me by it, especially the woman who demanded I call her mother, my right eye twitched. It felt like nails on a chalkboard, only the chalkboard was my soul, if that was possible.

"I've had you in a church pew at least three times a week since the day you were born," she said as I twitched slightly again. "How can you deny the existence of God after all the miracles and love you've seen?"

Laughing at your parent is never respectful. And it had never been more tempting to do in my entire life.

Any love I'd seen in my relatively short life certainly hasn't come from anyone in this room, I thought.

"It's not necessarily that I doubt God's existence, so much as I doubt the accuracy of the book written about our maker from 2,000 years ago translated dozens, if not hundreds of times," I said.

Barb released another tear from her artificial duct and said, "O, my sweet daughter. It's not too late. We can fix this. I'm sure there's a camp we can get you to over the holidays, even if I have to ship you across the country. Your soul is too precious to lose, Eve."

I stomped my foot, which may not have done much for any image of maturity I was attempting to create, but certainly released a little more anger from inside my chest. If I clenched my fists any tighter, I was going to draw blood from inside my palm.

Our old house's heater kicked on and rattled the floor vent behind my left foot.

"No, you Barb. Listen to me. And hear me well. I'm 18 now. I just finished my first semester of college, and you can't ship me off to camps anymore. I'm done with all of it, end of story. You're going to respect my choices. I'm old enough to smoke, old enough to vote, and old enough to make up my own goddamn mind about what I believe in without your input," I said, shoving my finger near her face now.

She was done seeking sympathy. And her brain seemed to have settled on a course of action. Hopefully that course of action was storming off to her room to pray for me or whatever would remove her from my sight. That wasn't what she'd chosen to do, though.

Instead, she walked calmly over to the couch where I'd been sitting and kissing Abi when she came out of her bedroom. The same couch from which she had grabbed Abi by the hair and jerked her up from before throwing her at the front door while screaming.

Barb picked up my purple leather purse and hurled it at me with surprising accuracy, not to mention fury. It hit my shoulder, and the strap slapped my face. Still I caught it. I grabbed it quickly, and thankfully without looking like an idiot fumbling the bag.

"Get out. You're not welcome in this home anymore," Barb hissed, pointing at the front door behind me.

I looked at the wooden white door and scoffed.

"You're joking, right? It's 25 degrees out. Where do you expect me to go at 10:30 on a Sunday night?"

Barb shrugged. There wasn't an ounce of care in her stone expression.

"Maybe find a homeless shelter or one of those warming centers they were discussing on the news. Then you can see what other people who make bad choices look like and the consequences they deal with."

I frowned at her. There was nothing I wanted more than to knock the legs out from that high horse she was standing on.

"You do realize statistically most homeless people are on the street because of mental illness, right?"

"Call it whatever you want, Eve. Free choice, mental illness, some other politically correct term that shifts the blame from where it truly belongs. Just get out," she said, crossing her arms.

"You're going to make the rather large call of throwing me out without even calling John? I think he'd have something to say about this," I said, crossing my own arms and standing my ground.

The wooden floorboards creaked under me as I shifted my weight.

"Your father's itinerary said he'd be playing music until 12:00 a.m. over in Reno tonight. I'm not going to disturb him for your sinful actions. We've discussed your behavior multiple times, and I know he'll agree my course of action is correct. Now get out before I call the police and have them remove you. As you've reminded me, you're 18 now. And I don't have to be legally responsible for sheltering or feeding you anymore. Especially not when you're being a hellion."

I scowled and said, "You know what, Barb? Mother is a title you earn. It isn't the default when you pop a child out of your womb. You want to be called mother? You have to work for it. And throwing a kid out on the streets isn't very Jesus-like because of her sexual orientation and religious beliefs are moving your needle in the opposite direction."

Feeling somewhat satisfied, I pushed whatever feelings of dread I had about where I was going to sleep tonight and turned toward the door. I had my wallet and ID, but my wool coat was upstairs on my bed. I doubted Barb was going to let me go up and grab it.

Just as my hand touched the doorknob, Barb injected a bit of acid in her voice and said, "There she goes, the girl I cradled in my arms. The girl I bought violin lessons for. The girl who had a safe and warm home. Traded it all away for the pleasures of sin. Maybe you can shack up with your whore tonight, Eve. Her mother is already raising one detestable child. What's one more?"

I spun and grabbed a lamp from the long table that sat under our living room's biggest window,. It was covered in white doilies, pictures of the family, and a crucifix. The lamp I grabbed was Barb's favorite, a white porcelain base covered in nesting blue jays. The brown cord jerked out of the power socket with a loud POP and that caused a few blue sparks.

Barb jerked like I was going to smash it over her head, but I had no intention of hurting her, not on the outside at least. I hurled the lamp across the room, to my left, and it smashed into an old oak clock ticking loudly on the wall.

The lamp shattered on impact, but the mounted clock didn't budge. It was made of sterner stuff and didn't even move from where it hung. After the echo of the lamp shattering cleared from my ears, I heard the clock's steady ticking again.

"You want to know where Abi was before she came over here to stick her tongue down my throat, Barb? She was shopping for canned goods and then dropping them off at the little food pantry by the library. What did you do today? You went to church, went out to lunch, and then came home and watched television. Which one of you two do you think was the better person today?"

"That lamp was my mother's, and you will pay for a replacement."

I shrugged.

"Next time I'm at Goodwill I'll see what other tacky lamps they have."

"Get out!" she shrieked in a way that made it sound like her vocal chords were about to burst. I was pretty sure I heard one of the neighbor's dogs barking outside because of it.

"You're a bad parent," I said and stepped outside, trying to keep my tears hidden from her.

I despised the woman. I hated the fact that she'd just thrown me out of the house I grew up in. I loathed the fact that John wasn't here to stick up for me, and then the crushing realization that even if he had been, he probably would have shrugged and said, "Listen to your mother, Eve," like he always did.

I started a growl that worked its way up into a scream and smashed part of the old wooden porch rail with a swift punch on my right. Now two or three of the dogs in the neighborhood were barking.

Looking down at my red knuckles, I sniffled a little bit. And the gusto I got from having the last word with Barb started to fade, leaving the dawning realization I had nowhere to sleep tonight and nowhere to go, and the low was supposed to be 16. On top of all of that, my own family had labeled me an abomination and thrust me to the curb.

Before my brain could start in with questions like "What if I'm not good enough?" and "What if I really am the villain in this fight?" I took the two steps down into the front yard. Then I rubbed my arms covered in gooseflesh and my thin long-sleeve shirt. My shirt was black and had a small X-Files logo on the front. It was the same shade of black as my yoga pants.

God, now I'm homeless AND basic, I thought. *Maybe I can grab a peppermint mocha on the way to nowhere.*

Actually... that sounded pretty good. Stupid irony.

"Cold never bothered me anyway," I mumbled, feeling a thin tree branch snap under my boot.

There were two giant oak trees in our—sorry, my former, front yard. I'd climbed them both several times in my life. Tonight they stood above me, blocking out some of the stars in an otherwise clear sky. A cold and pale moon sat off to the right of my vision.

Telling Barb to piss off was a power play. Unfortunately, as my walk to the bus stop was highlighting more with every step, power plays don't keep you warm at night.

Fayetteville isn't a big city. I mean, it is by Arkansas standards, but 80,000 people isn't much in other parts of the country.

Sure, I could call a ride with the tap of an app, but that would eat into the $332 I had left to my name. Thankfully I'd deposited my check from work on Friday. Part-time florist didn't leave me with tons of cash, but if it came down to it, it would get me a cheap motel room for tonight.

And Sabrina would have breakfast for me tomorrow morning at work. It was a fantastic perk of working at Petal and Stem. My boss always baked breakfast and brought it to me as I opened up the store for the morning. Muffins, pancakes, cinnamon rolls, she made them all, lots of great things. One less meal I'd have to worry about.

Combine that with the fact I'd already had a can of soup before Barb kicked me out, and maybe I was one iota more prepared for life on the street than I gave myself credit for. Two meals in the bag? Things were looking up, at least they were until a possum in the bushes I walked by hissed at me, made me jump, and step into an ankle-deep puddle.

I turned to look at the animal and... I just didn't have any anger left for it. I'd spent all of it on Barb. Now all that was left was spite and self pity, a cocktail I didn't want to finish.

"Have a good night, ma'am," I said and lifted my boot from the puddle. Stylish? Perhaps. Soaked through to the sock? Without a doubt. But hey, you can't get hypothermia from such a small part of the body, right?

My now old home Barb had just kicked me out of sat in central Fayetteville off a road called East Rolling Hills Drive. The DMV always had a heck of a time trying to fit my address in the space on my license. The neighborhood was older, built in the 1940s, which is probably why Barb liked it so much. That was the era she woke up in every day.

I finally came to a stop at a brown metal sign that read, "NWAU Transit Line - Route 4." Fayetteville was a college town and home to Northwest Arkansas University, population, 20,000 students. The campus also operated a free bus line that ran through town. This time of the year when all the students had gone back home to Texas? The busses would be pretty much empty, except for the occasional homeless person trying to stay out of the elements for as long as they could.

Maybe I can ask one of them where to stay tonight, I thought, shivering as the wind picked up.

Checking my phone, I saw the bus would be here in about 10 minutes. I also had a text from Abi. She'd made it home and wanted to know if I was okay.

Crap, what do I tell her? I asked in my head.

She'd come get me in a heartbeat if I told her I'd been thrown out. And her mom, Jen, was the coolest person on the planet. She'd let me crash there for a while.

So naturally, I texted Abi back and told her that I didn't want to talk about it, and I'd see her later. Hugs, kisses, sweet dreams, the works.

I'd kill to have Jen as a mom. She was the technical director for a theater program in town and damn good at it. Jen somehow found a way to make me interested in all these plays I never would have gone to see if she hadn't sat Abi and I down in the front row reserved seats to watch them.

Unfortunately, the arts don't always pay well in Arkansas, and Jen is a single mom. She didn't need another kid under her roof eating her food and using her hot water.

I sighed and waited for what seemed like an eternity for the bus. My nose was running, but thankfully I had a napkin in my purse to use instead of my sleeve.

See, universe? One more iota prepared for being thrown out on my ass... by a woman who claimed to have loved me and raised me from birth.

Thank goodness the bus was here. Hopefully its route would include the following stops: Bittertown, Aloneville, and Hermit Junction. The way I was feeling, any one of those places seemed good enough for me.

I hopped on the long red bus as it pulled up, and yeah, as expected I was the only one riding at this time of the night. That's fine, universe. Not like I needed a kind stranger to offer me a bed or anything.

The bus driver, an older man in his 60s, avoided eye contact with me as I took the third seat back. Well, at least the vehicle was heated.

I rode the bus south into downtown Fayetteville. The bus stopped at the beginning of Dickson Street, which is what the city calls its "entertainment district." It houses lots of great bars and restaurants. It's sort of the lifeblood of the city. The road makes up the northern border of downtown and stretches all the way down to the college campus.

On a Sunday night at 11:00 p.m., it was sparsely populated. It got that way when students went home, and especially two weeks before Christmas.

Stopping outside of Quaker Coffee & Beer, I walked up the steps to a wooden patio with several tables and chairs that hadn't been used in weeks. I stepped inside just as my arms and legs were beginning to grow a bit numb.

Thank the deity I question my belief in for heaters, I thought, rubbing my arms again.

The coffee shop/bar was open for at least another hour, giving me a little time to be indoors before I had to find a new place to be. There was some sort of 80s rock song playing on the speakers, and most of the seats inside were picnic tables on a concrete floor. There were a few tables next to a really long bench seat against one wall.

Above was a second story with some smaller round tables and comfy chairs. That's where I sat after ordering a hot chocolate. It felt warm in my hands. , and I didn't drink it for the first minute. I just left it there in my grasp, feeling its heat sink into my bones. My knuckles were still a little sore from breaking part of the porch rail. My posture got sloppy when I got emotional, something my coach was still onto me for after all these years.

I took my phone charger out of my purse and plugged it in. A battery on 43 percent wasn't going to last me through the night.

Sitting there looking at motel prices and eventually puppy pictures on Reddit, I lost track of time. It was actually 12:05 a.m. when the bartender came upstairs. She had a couple of nose piercings, small silver rings, and her hair was dyed purple.

On her arm was a worn leather Third Eye Blind jacket.

"Hey... we're about to shut it down for the night. If you need this, I'm gonna leave it right here on the table next to you. If you don't, feel free to leave it there, and I'll get it before I leave," she said.

I smiled and mouthed the words "thank you."

It was all I could do to keep from crying at this complete stranger's generosity and kindness.

See, Barb? Another person who was better than you today, I thought.

She took my empty cup and left the coat. I picked it up and slid it on. It was a little big for me, but when I zipped it up, it felt warm.

I walked down the stairs and waved goodbye to her before going outside. The temperature had dropped another few degrees, and I thought I'd wander a bit and see if I could find another place that was still open.

I needed to be a few years older to get into most of the places remaining open on Dickson Street. So I wandered down a side street, maybe made a turn or two. I didn't know where I was going, honestly. But my feet were getting sore as I began to realize my destination was nonexistent.

I passed a closed pizza place called Toppings and came to a small shop with a little pink neon sign that said "Open."

Looking in the window, I couldn't see much. Reddish purple letters on the opposite window said "Odessa's Psychic Shop."

What the hell? I'll get my fortune read or something. Anything to get out of this cold, I thought.

I walked into a shop that was smaller than I was expecting. Red curtains decorated the front windows, though I couldn't see them from the outside. The floor was covered in a thin garnet carpet with a large dark teal rug in the center of a room that was about 20 feet wide and 15 feet long. In the back corner there was a spiral staircase that led to some kind of second story.

Does this fortune teller live in a loft above her business? Because that'd be so cool, I thought.

On the round teal rug, I found two couches facing each other. One was black, and the other was white. They were both made of leather.

Between the couches was a round pine table that was painted with a complex design of black and white swirls. On top of the table were three candles arranged in a triangle. One candle was black. One was white. One was gray. None were lit. The only light came from the neon sign in the window.

A back door stood in the opposite corner of the staircase with black and white beads dangling hanging in front of it.

"Hello?" I called.

The only light came from the neon sign in the window.

"Be right down," a woman's voice said. It was deep and even a little solemn.

Then she walked down the staircase in purple boots and a black qipao dress with white flowers decorating the front. Her eyes seemed to glow a bit in the darkness, and her long silky black hair slowly swished from side to side with each step she took.

In one hand the woman held a long blue kiseru with a tiny butterfly carved into the end. The smoke that wafted out of the end seemed to proceed ahead of her and down into the shop, filling the room with a light tobacco scent, all the best smells of a cigar store, just dialed down several notches so as not to be overburdening.

I looked around at the smoke and wondered if this was part of some cheesy effect for her routine. I barely had $300 to my name and no home now. Was I going to blow money on a fortune reading? Eh. What could go wrong?

She reached the bottom of the stairs and said, "Welcome to my shop."

About the Author

Courtney Lanning is a journalist in Fayetteville at the Arkansas Democrat-Gazette. She's earned a master's degree in multimedia journalism.

When she's not writing, Lanning is probably watching a movie, playing video games, reading or out running.

Her debut novel, *Funky Dan and the Pixie Dream Girl*, is slated for release by the end of June 2021. She can be found on Twitter under @SapphicCourtney or on Facebook under Courtney Lanning - Author

Other Riverdale Avenue Books You Might Enjoy

Crank Palace: A Maze Runner Novel
By James Dashner

Magic University: The Complete Series
By Cecilia Tan

The Macroglint Trilogy by John Patrick Kavanagh
Sixers
Weekend at Prism
Sanctuary Creek

Venomoid
by J.A. Kossler

An Outcast State
by Scott D. Smith